THE SINS OF MY FATHER

INTRODUCING DI GRACE TALLIS

LOUISE BRODERICK

This book is entirely a work of fiction. The names, characters and incidents in it are the work of the author's imagination. Any resemblance to actual persons, living or dead, events or localities is entirely coincidental and have no relation to anyone bearing the same name or names. All incidents are pure invention and not even distantly inspired by any individual known or unknown to the author.

This book was written by a human.

ISBN 978-1-7393049-5-9

This edition published 2024 By Lavender and White Publishing.

Copyright © Louise Broderick /Lavender and White Publishing 2024

The right of Louise Broderick to be identified as the author of this work has been asserted by her in accordance with the Copyright, Designs and Patents Act 1988.

Typesetting, layout and design Lavender and White Publishing.

All rights reserved. No part of the text of this publication may be reproduced or transmitted in any form or by any means, electronically or mechanical, including photocopying, recording, or any information storage or retrieval system without the written permission of the publisher. The book is sold subject to the condition that it shall not, by way of trade or otherwise, be lent, resold, or otherwise circulated without the publisher's prior consent in any form of binding or cover other than that in which it is published without a similar condition, including this condition being imposed on the subsequent purchaser.

A CIP catalogue record for this book is available from the British Library.

www.lavenderandwhite.co.uk

For Kelly, James and India who make me proud every day.

From the author

Please, if you could, would you leave an honest review about this book on my Amazon page. It makes my day when I see someone has taken the time to do that and it really helps with my book sales. There is a link to the page at the end of the book.

Usually writing a book is a lonely job, spending hours alone in a room, with just the four walls and a cat for company.

This book was written while I was doing a MA and feels as if it was written by committee, there was so much input from an amazing network of friends and supporters.

Special thanks must go to Ruari, Stephen and Katie for their guidance and to Morag for steering me in the right direction. A big thank you goes to Tomas for his careful proofreading, and for everyone in my brilliant production team, especially Liz and Les.

Also by Louise Broderick

Trainers
Winners
Just Not You
The Derry Blake Boxset
The Sins Of My Father
Where Is My Daughter?
Why Did He Die?
Plot. Write. Sell.
Writing as Jacqui Broderick
A Pony For Free
The Unwanted Pony
The Cat's Whiskers

Contents

PROLOGUE 1

CHAPTER ONE 8

CHAPTER TWO 15

CHAPTER THREE 22

CHAPTER FOUR 29

CHAPTER FIVE 36

CHAPTER SIX 43

CHAPTER SEVEN 50

CHAPTER EIGHT 58

CHAPTER NINE 65

CHAPTER TEN 72

CHAPTER ELEVEN 79

CHAPTER TWELVE 86

CHAPTER THIRTEEN 93

CHAPTER FOURTEEN 100

CHAPTER FIFTEEN 107

CHAPTER SIXTEEN 115

CHAPTER SEVENTEEN 122

CHAPTER EIGHTEEN 127

CHAPTER NINETEEN 134

CHAPTER TWENTY 141

CHAPTER TWENTY-ONE 149

CHAPTER TWENTY-TWO 157

CHAPTER TWENTY-THREE 164

CHAPTER TWENTY-FOUR 171

CHAPTER TWENTY-FIVE 174

CHAPTER TWENTY-SIX 181

CHAPTER TWENTY-SEVEN 188

CHAPTER TWENTY-EIGHT 195

CHAPTER TWENTY-NINE 202

CHAPTER THIRTY 210

CHAPTER THIRTY-ONE 218

CHAPTER THIRTY-TWO 226

CHAPTER THIRTY-THREE 233

CHAPTER THIRTY-FOUR 241

CHAPTER THIRTY-FIVE 248

CHAPTER THIRTY-SIX 255

CHAPTER THIRTY-SEVEN 261

CHAPTER THIRTY-EIGHT 268

CHAPTER THIRTY-NINE 276

CHAPTER FORTY 284

THE SINS OF MY FATHER
INTRODUCING DI GRACE TALLIS

LOUISE BRODERICK

PROLOGUE

Ungrateful bitch.
    Ungrateful bitch was what Nan called the girl in the cellar. And she was. I knew that now.

I'd hurt myself when I fell into the pile of wood and bricks. My head and my elbow hurt. My knees stung. I knew there'd be blood on them when I looked.

Scrambling from where I'd landed, I watched her run. Ungrateful bitch. I'd only wanted to be her friend.

I'd drawn her a picture.

Nan let me draw when I'd finished the lessons she set for me. I drew a big sun, shining beside a house with a girl playing on a swing. That was me. I couldn't find my green crayon, so I couldn't draw the grass.

The girl had said she liked my pictures. She said she missed the sunshine and her house. I drew the sun, so she could remember. I didn't think she could see it through the tiny window in the cellar where she lived. The window was almost hidden in the bushes at the back of the garden. I'd found it while I was looking for the kitten Dad had given me. Low down, near the grass was a small window. 'Semi-circle,' I'd said, when I saw it, proud I'd remembered the name from my lessons.

The kitten had been nowhere to be found. 'Curiosity killed the cat,' Nan said, smacking my legs when I had told her about the window.

Still I was drawn there when Nan wasn't around.

When I looked down into the room, I could see a girl. She was a different one than had been there before.

Crouched down beside the window I saw my shadow move across the floor of her room. She turned, climbed onto the bed and stood, just below me, her face pale in the light from the window. She'd been crying, her face was all blotchy. One eye was all bruised and swollen. She was older than me. Not as old as Dad. Definitely not as old as Nan. I didn't even see anyone on the telly who was as old as Nan.

'Help me.' Her voice was muffled by the dusty cracked glass.

I crouched beside the glass. The dried clumps of soil dug into my knees. There were bars at the window. She had stretched herself up so she could wrap her fingers around the bars. Her face was close to mine. 'Please.'

'Help me, Mia,' Nan said, when she needed the log baskets filling, or the dishes put away after she had washed them in the sink. What did the girl want? I just stared. Watching her mouth open and close, tears stream from her eyes and snot ooze from her nose.

'Mia.' I heard Nan's voice, sharp, irritated.

I spun away, scrambling to my feet. I was on the swing Dad had made for me by the time she came into the garden. I liked the swing. Dad had tied a rope to a high branch and fastened it around the worn-out tyre he took off his jeep. My legs fitted through the hole in the tyre. Nan had given me an old cushion to put on the tyre so the edges didn't hurt me.

* * * * * * * *

The girl's presence drew me to the window day after day. I found a way to the window, skirting through the bushes at the far side of the garden so Nan wouldn't spot I was making a path. Sometimes I crouched by the window and looked in on her. Sometimes I went into the ruined building, down the steps, along the dark corridor at the bottom and stood beside the cellar door. I knew she was there. I could hear her moving behind the door with the peeling paint. The door was locked. I'd tried to open it. The girl had started banging on it. I ran in case Nan heard her and came to see what was happening. Another time I followed Dad into the cellar, saw him get the key from behind one of the piles of wood.

I only went down there if I knew Dad was out and Nan was busy. I had to be very quiet, so I could hear if she came into the garden.

If I looked through the keyhole, I could see her if the light was on. I could see a bed, and a chain around her wrist, the same kind Dad put around his dog's neck. He said I had to stay away from the dog because it liked to eat little girls. Sometimes the light was on. Sometimes it was dark. Sometimes she was tied up. Sometimes she was free. Mostly she was crying.

* * * * * * * *

She wasn't tied up when I brought her the picture. I could see her shadow pacing up and down in the light which shone under the gap beneath the door. I crouched down and pushed my drawing through. The air coming through the gap smelt of poo and sick and damp. I heard rustling, the sound of the picture being scooped up.

'Thank you.' Her voice sounded like mine when I tried to speak with a mouthful of toast. The shadow moved from the door. I listened, hearing her footsteps padding quietly on the floor beyond the door.

'Did you bring me the orange?' She came back again. I could see her shadow falling along the line of light. I could hear her breathing.

I pulled it out of my pocket. I was pleased I had remembered to bring it.

'Yes.' I bent to the gap beneath the door, but the orange, even though it was the smallest, the one I thought Nan wouldn't miss, was too big to fit. I pushed. Her fingers came beneath the door. They were long and thin and dirty. Her nails were long. If mine got to be that long, Nan would cut them. There were flakes of red paint on them.

'Your nails are dirty,' I said, as her fingers curled around the bottom of the orange. She wriggled her fingers but couldn't grip it.

'I can't get it,' she said. 'Can you open the door and give it to me?'

I took back the orange, turning it over in my fingers. It looked like the sun, only orange not yellow.

'I'd love it, so much.'

'Okay.' I wanted her to have the orange. She was my friend. It would be like giving her the sunshine.

I looked for the key for a long, long, long time. I knew it was there, hidden somewhere in the pile of wood and bricks beside the door.

'Hurry.' Her voice sounded like Nan when she wanted me to collect the chicken eggs, or get up, or eat my food. But hers didn't have the angry sound to it like Nan's did.

I moved some wood. The corner was dark and smelt like the soil when I'd helped Dad dig the big hole. I found the key, pressed into a gap between the bricks. A single, long key. I turned it over in my hand. My breathing sounded like the girl's behind the door.

I put the orange onto the floor. I couldn't use the key with it in my hands. I'd unlock the door. Give her the orange, lock the door and put the key back. Dad wouldn't know. Nan wouldn't know. And the girl would have the orange.

'We can be friends. Yeah?' Her voice came out in short bursts.

'Ok.' I wasn't sure if Dad would let me. He'd say she was his friend.

The key fitted into the lock. It was hard to turn. There was a click as the key moved.

The door burst open, the force of it pushed me down. I fell into the pile of bricks and wood. I glanced up to see her running down the corridor, her legs, the colour of the bread dough Nan made, lit up in the strands of light coming through the broken roof timbers.

The orange lay on the floor beside the open door. She had trodden on it. The skin and inside were squashed into a mush, juice mixed with the dirt from the floor.

I picked myself up, kicking the smashed orange into the shadows and made my way out of the cellar.

Nan stood at the top of the steps. She was still, the wind moving the flowered dress she wore, wrapping the fabric around her legs. Her face had squashed into itself, deep grooves at the side of her mouth, black furrows on her forehead. I came out of the darkness of the cellar, not wanting to look at her.

Like Ursula, the big white pig which lived in the shed when her food was poured into her trough, Nan threw herself forwards, her hands gripping the top of my arms and lifting me skywards.

I had to curl my toes inside my wellington boots to stop them from sliding off.

'What have you done?' Her voice was high, shrieking, a cross between Ursula when she got her food and Dad's the day he had breathed the air from inside the balloon we had found stuck in one of the trees in the orchard. She shook me so hard my teeth rattled against each other. The sky and the trees blurred above me. Then she dropped me and walked away.

I sat outside for a long time. Drawing patterns in the earth with a stick. It began to get dark. I got hungry. I went indoors. The house was holding its breath. I could hear Nan upstairs, the creak of the bed she took to sometimes. I buttered a slice of bread and put it on a plate, taking care to wipe up the crumbs and the knife. While I ate, I got out my crayons to draw a picture. I found my green crayon. It was at the bottom of the zippy case Nan had given me. But there was no one to draw for anymore.

I heard Dad's jeep coming up the long farm drive. The dog on the chain started to bark.

He came in. The kitchen door banged off the wall when he flung it open. He knew what I'd done.

'Where's Nan?' I didn't recognise the fearful tone in Dad's voice. It made me afraid.

I pointed upstairs, pulling my face into the shape which was Dad's and my way of saying she was in a bad mood and to stay away from her.

'Why did you have to let her go, Mia?' Dad asked. His eyes looked sad. His mouth folded in on itself, disappearing into the bristles of his chin. 'She was my friend.'

I didn't answer, I just stood looking at him.

'Put your boots on,' he said, turning away from me. 'We have to go.'

Without waiting for me to say anything he crossed the kitchen and went upstairs. From his padding feet and the way he moved around the rooms I could tell he was trying to be quiet.

I found my boots and put them on. They felt cold and clammy.

Dad brought a bag downstairs with him. 'Hurry, Mia.'

'Someone could have already picked her up.' I didn't think he was talking to me.

We went out into the yard. Far away where the long farm drive met the main road, I could see a white car coming towards the house. He saw it too. 'Shit.'

He dropped the bag and grabbed my hand. His was hot, wet. My fingers slithered in his as he tightened his grip. 'Run, Mia.'

We ran. Through the farmyard, out into the fields. I went as fast as I could, stumbling and tripping over the grass. He was running fast, pulling me so my feet skimmed along the ground. I could hear my calves slapping on the inside of my wellingtons, and our breathing.

We ran into the woods. Our feet rustled through the fallen leaves, yellows, browns. I wanted to stop and kick them up, make them into heaps, but there was no time for that. They flew around us as we ran, the air filled with the smell of damp leaves and soggy ground.

We reached the slope that led up onto the old railway track. Dad's breathing came in short gasps. His hand hurt mine, squashing my bones.

Dad plunged up the slope, pulling me after him our feet skidding and sliding. He couldn't grip my hand anymore our fingers were so slippery. Instead he grabbed my wrist, which burned as he went up the slope, his free hand grabbing at clumps of grass and tree roots to help him up.

At the top we came out of the darkness onto the green grass of the old railway line. I wasn't allowed up here. Just as far as the edge of the woods, Nan said. The air was fresher, cold against my hot cheeks. Dad scrambled to his feet, half falling, a boot kicking at mine as he struggled to stay upright. 'Hurry.'

We ran out onto the railway bridge. And then he stopped. I looked. Ahead of us policemen, bright yellow waistcoats over their black clothes. Dad turned the other way, spinning me around. Out of the woods behind us other men were coming.

'Eddie,' one of them called. His voice echoed in the space between the trees.

Dad let go of my hand. He paced to the edge of the wall, looking down. The bridge was very high. Sometimes we walked underneath it. Huge curved arches made of red brick that soared up into the sky.

Someone was walking towards us. 'Come on, Eddie. Give it up. There's nowhere to go.'

Dad crouched down and put his hands on my cheeks. They were very hot, wet. His face was white, his eyes sad.

'I love you,' he whispered. He pulled me into a hug. I liked his hugs, his arms encircling me, making me feel safe. Then he stood up.

'Don't be stupid, Eddie.' The voice was a challenge, like Nan's when she knew she was going to make me do something I didn't want to.

Dad leant against the bridge. Leaning back on it, looking at the line of men coming towards us. He turned, both hands outstretched on the iron railing.

'Dad?' I said.

He turned to look at me, his eyes fixing on mine. I felt the air move around me as he vaulted the railing. He was good at that. He made me laugh by vaulting over the gates on the farm to show me how clever he was.

For a moment he flew. Through the gaps I saw him land. He looked like the rag doll I'd once left outside on the grass. His arms and legs going in the wrong directions.

A cool dry hand took hold of mine. 'Come on, love. Let's get you somewhere safe.'

CHAPTER ONE

'What do you think?' Mum danced into my bedroom, her arms raised, moving in time to the faint sound of Neil Sedaka's *Oh Carol* which drifted in through the open window. Dad had spent hours putting together a collection of music he thought was suitable for such an auspicious occasion as the Queen's Diamond Jubilee.

I put down the eyeliner pencil I'd been using and watched her come towards me in the mirror. Her heels beat a tattoo against the polished wooden floorboards. Halfway across the room she reached the faded beauty of the Persian rug and twirled around. I watched the red, white and blue stripes of her dress merge into a blur of colour, the delicate fabric flaring upwards, drifting, gossamer-like around her frame.

'Beautiful,' I told her.

'Thank you.' She stopped twirling and came towards me, draping her slender tanned arms around my shoulders and leaning against me. I could feel the warmth of her skin through the fabric of my dress.

In the mirror I saw my nostrils flare, drawing in the warm, flowery smell of her familiar perfume. She put her cheek beside mine, meeting my eyes in the mirror. I looked odd, one eye completed, outlined in black, the perfect upturned flick competed at the edge, the other still bare, naked looking. Her skin was soft against mine. Her eyes were pale, almost luminous, beautiful, sometimes appearing grey, sometimes pale green, sometimes blue. They were gentle, kind eyes. Not like mine.

Our eyes met in the mirror. We looked alike, the same oval shape to our faces, curve to our mouths, even the arch of our eyebrows. People often commented on how similar we were, even though we weren't related, as if our features had merged together by osmosis.

'Will you be long?' She stood upright, swaying gently in time with the music. It was louder now, the smell of cooking food and smoke drifting in through my bedroom window, overpowering the delicate fragrance of the jasmine plant which grew around the window frame.

I shook my head. 'Just this eye to finish.' I picked up the eyeliner pencil and leant forwards to study my reflection in the mirror, glancing back to see her watching me, her face intent, filled with love.

'I'll wait for you.' She began to sway again, humming to the music as she moved towards my window, ducking her head to avoid the slope of the roof so she could lean on the windowsill and look out at the party preparations.

I finished my other eye, the flick of black somehow different from the first one. If Mum hadn't been hovering around waiting, I'd have started again.

'Ready?' She turned to face me, her voice filled with excitement.

I pushed myself up from the dressing table stool, feeling awkward and self-conscious in the simple blue dress I wore. I'd balked at wearing anything too patriotic, no matter how much Dad had gone on about the British theme of the celebration.

'You look stunning,' Mum said, taking my arm. In heels she was taller than me; stray tendrils of her auburn hair touched my cheek as they tried to escape from the careless bun she'd made.

We reached the bottom of the stairs, her heels clicking on the stone flagged hall.

I felt her stride pause, almost imperceptibly, as we passed the hall table with its single overflowing vase of flowers. I knew, even though her head didn't turn, her eyes had moved to look at the picture above the table. A big, colour, blown-up portrait of a young boy.

He was a toddler, dressed in a pair of denim jeans that wrinkled over pudgy legs, and a striped shirt. He sat in grass, surrounded by daisies, his face turned up to the camera, his eyes, that same luminous grey, green, blue as Mum's. Patrick, their son, had died. Meningitis. His illness not detected, put down to a childish chill until it was too late. The boy in the picture watched over us, silently, his presence filling the house with his loss.

Side by side we went out into the bright sunlit garden, blinking at the brightness after the dim coolness of the house.

As we went down the wide bow of the stone steps which led out of the house, beside the tall curve of the pillars beside the front porch, the music changed from some ancient old people's pop music to *Rule Britannia*. Beside me, Mum threw her head back and laughed. One of the clips which had been trying and failing to keep her unruly hair in its updo came out, slid to the ground; more hair cascaded around her face.

Dad came across the garden, handsome in chinos and a striped shirt. I stepped to the side as they embraced, Mum falling laughing into his outstretched arms. 'You look stunning,' I heard him whisper into her hair.

'Thank you.' She bent her willowy body, the gossamer fabric of the dress floating around her as she leant into him, wrapping her arms around his neck.

'So do you.' Dad pulled me into his chest. He smelt of toothpaste, coffee, shaving foam and faintly of the cigar he'd sneaked earlier. He thought Mum didn't know. She did of course.

When he pulled away, he held me at arm's length and looked at me with a proud smile. Dad took my hand and walked in the middle of Mum and me as we crunched across the gravel past the glittering water of the fountain in the centre of the drive and onto the smooth billiard table of the expanse of lawn.

On the patio at the side of the house a vast marquee had been erected, its canvas sides moving slightly in the breeze. The patio doors were open to the kitchen, from where I could hear food being prepared, smell cooking bread. At the end of the marquee a huge barbeque had been set up, a uniformed man deftly turning sausages and burgers. Uniformed men and women were unboxing champagne and wine glasses onto a trestle table. At the far end of the lawn, members of a band were carrying their instruments, unloading them and carrying them across the lawn. Dad had spent hours going through a suitably patriotic playlist for them. I knew I'd prefer the disco which was to start once darkness finally fell.

Guests were beginning to arrive, a trickle of cars and SUVs coming towards the house along the drive which wound beneath a canopy of ancient trees between rhododendrons and neatly mown grass, the pride of Frank, the gardener. Beside the drive, the fields stretched down to the river. There Mum's mares and foals grazed, from which we selected the best for me to compete.

Elegantly striped deckchairs were scattered around the lawn. A few guests were already relaxing in the sun. Dad fetched our drinks, champagne for him and Mum, Buck's Fizz for me. I disliked champagne and preferred it diluted with orange juice.

I watched over the rim of my glass as my friend, Tom, and his parents arrived. He grinned and waved in my direction. His father, the vet who cared for our horses, led the way straight to the bar. I knew, sooner or later, my telephone, wedged in the pocket of my dress, would buzz; Tom would text with some silly message about the occasion and make me laugh and that my boyfriend Josh would scowl.

Mum touched my arm. More of her hair had spilled out of its clasp. She looked giddy with the occasion, flushed with the champagne. 'Mia, I think Tom has a crush on you.' She clamped her lips together as if she couldn't contain her excitement at her insight into my life. I felt myself blush, heat flooding into my cheeks and saw her amusement as she realised she'd been right. Tom, as if he was aware of her eyes on his, turned and waved in our direction.

I met Mum's gaze. 'Stop,' I chided. 'He's going out with Poppy and I'm with Josh. We are just friends.'

* * * * * * * *

We stood together watching the guests arrive, the ladies in pretty dresses, the men in smart chinos and shirts, Union Jack waistcoats in keeping with the occasion.

Mum and Dad graciously greeted everyone; neighbours, and friends they had known through the tragedy of Patrick's death and the renewed joy of adopting me.

Edward Lewis and his prim looking wife, Samantha, friends of my parents, came across the lawn. Edward pulled Mum into a hug then stretched out his hand to greet Dad. Edward's wide mouth spilt into a broad beam of approval. 'Fabulous day. What do you think of the waistcoat?' I saw the amusement in Dad's eyes as he dutifully admired Edward's tightly stretched Union Jack waistcoat.

Oliver Young, an architect who worked for Dad, dressed in chinos and a loud Union Jack blazer came across to us, a much younger woman beside him. He'd been involved with Dad in a project to develop an abandoned warehouse into exclusive apartments and restaurants.

'Happy Jubilee.' After greeting Mum and Dad, Oliver pulled me into a bear hug. Beneath the hideous blazer his shirt front felt damp, his aftershave overpowering. His cheek, tanned beneath his mop of red hair, was slimy with sweat.

'This is Pippa.' Oliver released me and hauled Pippa into our midst. She didn't look much older than me, tall and slender with huge eyes outlined in black. As if the whole concept of the jubilee had passed her by, Pippa wore an alarmingly short black dress and flat ballet pumps. Even with these on she was almost as tall as Oliver. Pippa's face moved slightly into what she probably thought was a smile.

'Hello.' I wondered what on earth she saw in Oliver and realised it presumably had quite a lot to do with his wallet.

'Ah, here's Mark. Oliver held his hand out for the other man to shake. Mark looked utterly uncomfortable in a pale grey linen suit, as if his normal land agent's uniform of a tweed jacket and cords were a skin he had been forced to shed. His only concession to the jubilee was a faded Union Jack bandana tied around his panama hat.

Oliver introduced Pippa to Mark. She took his hand, looking at him as if she expected him to kiss the back of her hand like a gallant knight.

'Where's Oliver been hiding you?' Mark's voice was slippery like a snake as his pale eyes raked over Pippa.

Pippa simpered, delighted at the attention. I felt my lip curl in distaste. I spotted David and Helen Furness, whose farm bordered Mum and Dad's land, making their way over to us, quite clearly our group was the place to be.

'Mia!' Helen pulled me into a hug. She was tall, wiry, her arms strong from the farm work she did. 'Haven't seen you for ages!' Helen always spoke in exclamations.

'I've been busy at uni.' I smiled at her.

'What are you doing?' Pippa asked. Her dark eyebrows rose quizzically.

'I've just finished, but I was doing a degree in Drama.'

'That sounds like a lot of fun!' Helen beamed at me. 'Doesn't it,

David?'

David and Helen bred pedigree Hereford beef cattle. David, as if by the daily interaction with his animals, had become a human version of the cattle he bred. He had a mop of tight grey curls on top of his head and red-rimmed, oddly round eyes which always seemed to have a slightly baleful expression.

'Aye.' David came from somewhere which Dad always described as 'oop North,' his accent strong with long vowels.

Helen beamed at him as if delighted to have dragged a word from her normally dour husband.

'What kind of things did you do?' Helen seemed relieved to have found something we could talk about which wasn't related to cattle or farming.

'I did screenwriting, stage production and acting,' I replied.

'At Bristol?'

I nodded. 'I'm out in the real world now, job hunting for stage roles.'

Helen smiled at me sympathetically. 'What do you do?' She turned to Pippa.

'I work in PR.' Pippa glared at Helen as if daring her to even think she had a frivolous job.

'That's how we met,' Oliver said proudly.

'Lovely. Helen smiled politely. She turned back to me, before continuing, 'Any good roles coming up?'

'I hope so. I could hear the nervous catch in my voice. It was one thing performing at university, but real auditions were tougher. I dreaded the thought of being a failure after all of the money and time my parents had invested in my hopes of becoming an actress.

'Mia's destined for great things.' Dad gave my shoulder a reassuring shake. He disentangled himself from the group, clapping the men on their backs, gently hugging the women, 'Band's going to start soon, grab a deckchair everyone.'

I noticed he smiled politely at Pippa but avoided going anywhere near her. I wondered if Mum had said something scathing to him about the young woman who had been thrust into the midst of the group of middle-aged folk.

'Sit here, darling.' Mum pulled one of the striped deckchairs closer to hers. More of her hair had escaped and clouded around her face. Her cheeks were pink, her eyes bright with what I guessed had more to do with the amount she had drunk rather than the excitement of the occasion.

'Thank you.' I lowered myself into the depths of the chair. I'd seen the playlist Dad had devised and the thought of listening to the likes of *Jerusalem*, *Rule Britannia* and lashings of Cliff Richard did not fill me with delight. I hoped Josh would hurry up and arrive so I'd be able to escape from the old folks' quarter.

'What's this?' Dad sat up in his deckchair, pushing himself upright and putting his glass down on the grass beside him. It wobbled and fell, the amber liquid spilling over the grass.

I followed his line of sight, watching as a police car made its way up the drive, disappearing as the drive curved into the trees and then reappearing as it got closer to the house.

'Have we upset the neighbours with our noise?' he joked, but beneath his words his tone was serious.

Mum beside him had gone quiet, sober now as we watched the police car emerge from the drive and park on the forecourt beside the house. I glanced around the garden. Our guests had noticed too. The hum of noise dropped a notch. I could hear the crackle of the sausages on the barbecue, the clink of ice as one of the waiters refilled a glass.

The car came to a halt and two women got out, one tall with a mane of wavy red hair, dressed in jeans and a leather jacket. The other a policewoman who looked as if her uniform had been issued years before and who had expanded considerably since then, the seams stretching across ample thighs.

As they made their way across the lawn, Dad got to his feet. 'What the hell do they want?'

CHAPTER TWO

'Do you mind if we go inside? The plainclothes officer asked. She looked around the garden, her eyes taking everything in. As her eyes met mine I was struck by what an incredible azure blue they were. Her long auburn hair was pulled back off her face and secured in an unruly-looking plait. Tendrils of hair had escaped and blew around her face. She introduced herself as a detective and her companion as a sergeant. Their names, although she said them, were lost in the swirl of thoughts inside my mind. Her voice was firm, there was no arguing with her. Her accent was familiar somehow, yet not local.

Dad stood silently, glaring at her, his fingers clamped tightly around the glass of champagne he held. His knuckles whitened. I waited for the stem of the glass to snap, but instead he turned away, put the glass down on the grass as gently as if it were a tiny bird, settling it carefully as if to ensure it would not fall. Slowly, he straightened up.

Mum got to her feet; her face, a moment before pink with the champagne and the heat of the day, was grey. Her mouth had clamped into a tight line. I could see lines around her mouth that I'd never seen before; her bright pink lipstick had bled, spidering into her skin.

'What's this about?' Dad had an angry edge to his voice.

'Are you Mia?' The plainclothes woman glanced in my direction. 'Do you mind if we have a few minutes of your time?'

I nodded. Around us the hum of conversation had died away, sounding forced; as if everyone was desperately trying to ignore the fact that two policewomen had just marched into our party.

I thought guiltily of the weed I'd smoked at a party recently. I had some in my bedroom, hidden safely in the gap beneath my dressing table and the skirting board. Surely not that? Something from the past I remembered fragile fragments of? My stomach tightened with tension.

'We are in the middle of a party,' Dad said, his voice filled with tension, the words coming out short and sharp like a machine gun.

Mum took a stride across the distance that separated them and stood beside him, feet firmly planted, her high heels sinking gradually into the ground, so she was in danger of overbalancing. She sensed the movement and pulled herself upright, crossing her arms in front of herself, the champagne glass, empty now, dangling from her fingers.

'We're celebrating the jubilee.' She glared at the two women, as if challenging them to insist on coming inside, breaking up the party.

Beside the plainclothes officer, the plump one shifted from one ugly boot to the other as if the grass were too hot beneath her feet. Around her armpits were the vaguest circles of darker fabric, stained by her sweat. The buttons pulled tightly across her chest, beneath which I could see a glimpse of white, pasty-coloured flesh. She looked uncomfortable, as if Dad and Mum were going to beat her down.

'I'm sorry,' the plainclothes one insisted. 'But this really can't wait.'

Dad glanced around the garden, taking in the band still playing in the background, the clusters of people.

'Just a complaint about the noise levels,' Dad joked, his voice carrying across the garden.

A tinkle of forced laughter drifted towards us.

Dad turned on his heel, taking Mum by the hand. 'Carry on, please. We'll be back out in a moment.'

He began to lead the way across the lawn towards the house, a walk that took him beyond the groups of his friends, past the bar and the food.

The detective moved towards me, holding out a hand to indicate I should move. 'Please.' She was taller than me, slender, her legs taut beneath her jeans. She was muscled, toned, fit.

I set off in Mum and Dad's wake. Tom, beside the bar, turned to watch as we passed, a stain of tomato sauce on the front of his tee-shirt. His eyes met mine and he pulled a face, sympathy and curiosity melded together.

I could feel all eyes on us as we walked towards the house.

It was cool inside, the smell of the flowers crammed into vases more powerful than the vague smell of cooking food. Dad closed the patio doors, shutting out the noise of the party. Here, alone in the room, it was hard to imagine that outside the garden was filled with people.

The plainclothes officer looked around the room, her eyes missing nothing. Taking in the elegant dark wooden floor, the pale-coloured rug that spanned most of the room, the expensive paintings, the elegant furniture, pale silk cushions lined up immaculately just so along the back of the sofa. One wall contained our trophies; my cups, silver and cut glass bowls, won for show jumping, and those Mum won when she was younger, all neatly lined up.

'DI Grace Tallis,' the officer repeated her name, holding out her hand first to Dad and then Mum and finally to me. Her grip was firm, the skin soft but cool. She met my eyes. Hers were blue like the summer sea and as deep and unfathomable.

'And PC Sarah Dean,' the jean-clad detective said, looking in the direction of the plump officer who was staring around herself with open amazement.

'Sit down,' Mum said. The giddy air had gone from her, deflated like a popped balloon. It was hard to imagine that not long ago she had danced across my bedroom floor like a teenager.

She lowered herself into one of the armchairs, crossing her long, tanned calves in front of her like a barrier to keep the police away, her back very straight, stern as if she would take no nonsense. Dad, distancing himself from the whole situation, flung himself down into the armchair furthest away across the room.

The two women sat on the sofa, the PC lowering herself gingerly down as if afraid the movement might split her overstretched trousers.

I perched myself on the edge of Mum's armchair, afraid of what was coming.

The Detective was silent. I could see her eyes roving over me, taking in my dress, my hair.

'Please,' Dad said, his voice impatient. There was a panicked edge to it I had never heard before, as if he were afraid of what was coming. Some crime he had committed. I couldn't imagine Dad ever doing anything worse than speeding. Perhaps he'd not paid a parking fine, but surely the police wouldn't come for that.

'We've come from the Devon and Cornwall force,' the Detective said.

She looked directly at me, her eyes meeting mine as if to judge my reaction. In the course of speaking she had shuffled to the edge of the sofa, leaning forwards, her hands resting between her knees, elbows resting on her thighs. 'I've met you before, Mia,' her voice softened. 'I was a young police constable when your father... I took you from the bridge to the police car. Do you remember?' Her words trailed away to silence.

I shook my head, fighting an urgent need to run from the room and hide beneath my duvet. 'No.' I lied. As I spoke I pictured the cool hand holding mine, being led out of the woods, figures rushing past us towards where my father lay. 'No, I don't remember.' My voice betrayed the panic I felt. I didn't want to see the images. I never wanted to remember them. 'That's okay,' Tallis said, softly. Beside her I heard the PC swallow. I glanced at her, seeing how she was staring fixedly at some distant place on the carpet. It looked like she wanted to disappear beneath it. I was painfully aware of how she avoided looking at me.

'We're here because we've found remains,' DI Tallis paused, as if trying to frame the words, fighting to make them into something we'd understand. 'Near Blackthorn Farm.'

'Remains?' Mum spoke as if she couldn't quite get her head around the word. I watched the tableau unfold, Mum's eyes widening, Dad's face closing in on itself, his eyes becoming watchful. I noticed the way his eyes flickered restlessly over me and then back again to the police officers.

I knew what it meant. Knew why DI Tallis was looking at me. Why PC Dean couldn't. Why Mum couldn't get her head around the word. Dad was staring at his hands as if he had never seen them before and couldn't quite understand what to do with them.

Tallis paused, a pink tongue flickered between her lips, she pushed them together, moistening them as if they were too dry for her to be able to speak. She nodded as if her voice had disappeared. Then she seemed to gather herself up, to proceed with the news she had come to impart.

'We believe they are connected to your father,' she said after a moment.

The words hung in the air, flimsy. I couldn't quite get them to sink into my mind. I could hear the grandfather clock ticking, time slowly trickling past.

Taking another breath, Tallis plunged on, as if deciding it seemed there was no point in being kind and gentle and polite. 'We believe they are more victims of your father.'

Mum's hand slipped over mine. Her fingers were icy cold.

'A man who farmed near Blackthorn Farm, where you grew up, was doing work with an excavator. Draining ditches.' I could see Tallis watching me, as if to judge my reaction.

Out of the corner of my eye I saw Dad push himself upright in the armchair.

'He unearthed the remains of a number of bodies. Buried in barrels.' Tallis was looking at some point above my shoulder as if she couldn't bring herself to look into my eyes.

Mum brought her hand to her mouth to stifle the strangled-sounding gasp she made. 'A number of bodies?'

'When were they found?' Dad finally found his voice. I forced my head to turn, to look at him. His eyes were on me as if he had no idea who I was, as if I were a stranger.

'A few days ago,' Tallis said. 'We've been waiting for confirmation of all the identifications.'

PC Dean, suddenly found her voice. 'There were four bodies.'

'Couldn't this have waited? Did you have to come today?' Dad lifted his hand in a gesture I assumed was meant to encompass the party.

I'd grown up knowing my father had kidnapped young woman and killed them, that my grandmother had been sent to prison for helping him. Mum and Dad had gently told me about my background when they felt I was old enough to understand. It was something we never spoke of now, as if it were something grubby that was best hidden and forgotten about. I wondered fleetingly why the policewomen thought it necessary to tell us about yet more victims.

Tallis spoke, her eyes holding me, forcing me to focus on what she was saying. 'Mia, I'm sorry to have to tell you that one of the bodies is your mother, Glanna Pendrick.'

The breath I took felt icy cold against the back of my throat.

'Mia?' Someone said my name. I forced my head to turn, looking first at Dad, then at Mum, their faces indistinct blurred shapes. Dad made a noise, as if he had tried to frame a question and somehow the words wouldn't form.

'We've informed Glanna's parents.' My mother's parents. My grandparents, people I'd never thought of, except as distant fragile concepts at the barest edges of my imagination.

Glanna, my mother, who for so long had lived on the very edge of my consciousness suddenly had a life of her own. Exploding into my life with her death. I hadn't heard her name spoken for years, never even thought of her, she was a shadowy figure who I believed had gone away. Left me. I'd had no idea of what had happened to her.

In quiet, lonely moments I had imagined her coming to find me. Thought about how I'd react. Wondered if I'd forgive her for leaving me. If she'd be proud of the person I had become. Now I knew. All my life she had been lying dead. In a barrel. I had a sudden vision of her, limbs curled, tucked beneath her, lying beneath the soil while the world went on above her.

I couldn't imagine the farmer, his machinery unearthing the barrels, wondering what they were, looking, finding the rotted flesh. I wondered fleetingly what would have remained, flesh, a skeleton? And now my mother lay somewhere, laid out, poked and prodded, investigated as if she were something to marvel at, to poke and prod and dissect and not a child, a mother, who had lived and died.

'The others…' Mum said, her voice frail and indistinct.

'We aren't sure of them all yet,' Tallis said. 'We are looking through the lists of missing women. We've identified Glanna Pendrick and another young woman. Hopefully soon we'll put names to them.'

Mum got to her feet, pushing herself up from the depths of the armchair as though she had aged twenty years. Without any conscious thought I stood and half stepped, half stumbled into her arms. I buried my face in the warmth of her shoulder, a strand of her hair soft against my cheek. Her arms holding me were the only thing that kept me upright.

My mother was dead. She'd been dead a long time. She hadn't gone away after having me and left me alone. She was never going to come and find me.

'Mia. I'm sorry,' Dad's arms circled the two of us, his head resting on mine. I could see a strand of grey shining in his dark hair.

'Darling. Oh my poor baby.' Mum's hand stroked my hair.

'I always thought she'd left me.' I began to sob, a harsh noise, as if my whole existence was being ripped from me. I pulled away from their arms and stood, my hands damp with tears, sticky with snot covering my face. Through my fingers I could see my parents' faces, white with shock, concern etched in every line.

'I'll get some tissues,' Mum said, turning away, practical as ever.

'Here, sweetheart,' Mum thrust a wad of tissues into my hand. I dabbed at my eyes, wishing I could stop crying, knowing my make-up was ruined, hating being the centre of this maelstrom of emotion.

'Sit down, Mia.' Dad's voice was gentle. There was no trace of the jovial host who had ruled over the party earlier. His hands guided me to the armchair, helping me sit as if I were some delicate piece of china he was afraid would break. I sat. Mum took the sodden wad, replacing it with another fistful of tissue.

'Get Mia some water,' Dad told Mum, before adding, 'Brandy, get some brandy.'

Mum hurried away and was back a moment later, slopping brandy from the decanter into a cut glass snifter.

'Drink this, sweetheart.' Dad perched himself on the arm of my chair, rubbing my back gently.

I grimaced as the fiery liquid hit the back of my throat. Mum, crouching at my feet, caught my eye and shuddered in sympathy. My lips twitched into the semblance of a weak smile.

Dad turned to gaze out of the window where the party went on without us.

Across the other side of the room the two policewomen watched us; PC Dean, her face a blank emotionless professional mask, Tallis, filled with concern, caught my eye and gave me a sympathetic smile. She crossed the room and crouched beside my chair. Mum moved away as if she couldn't bear to be beside the woman whose words had wreaked such havoc on our lives. 'I'm sorry I had to break that news to you.' She took my hand. Her fingers were long, the skin warm against mine. I let my hand lie in hers like a dead thing.

'There was no easy way to tell you,' she said gently.

I didn't want to hear. I wanted to push her away, to run. Run past the party. Run until I could run no more. I didn't want to hear what she had to say. I didn't want her sympathy. I wanted my mother, I wanted her to be real and alive. I didn't want her to be dead, buried in a ditch by my father.

CHAPTER THREE

'Can you excuse me for a few minutes?' I forced myself to my feet. My legs felt unsteady, as if the ground were shifting beneath me. I had the vaguest impression of their faces turning towards me, blurring, dark stars swimming in my field of vision.

'Are you okay, Mia?' Mum's voice far away, indistinct, as if I were underwater.

I opened my mouth to try to speak and only succeeded in gulping air into my lungs.

'I just… er… fresh air...' I blinked, trying to clear my vison trying to stop the room from spinning. Their faces came into focus. I was aware of my mum, the red, white and blue of her dress. Dad, his ridiculous waistcoat, and the two policewomen, their faces watchful.

I turned, looking for a way out, saw the French windows, closed against the noise of the party and the smoke from the barbeque. My vision cleared slightly. Outside I could see more people had arrived and were milling around in the garden, no doubt wondering what was going on. The police turning up at a party. What on earth did they all make of that?

For a moment I had a clear image of them, the gossip beginning, hushed voices discussing what could be happening inside. The undoubted two and two making five, six.

I turned again, this time in the direction of the kitchen, glancing briefly at the faces of my parents and the policewomen. The buzzing in my ears had stopped and my vision had cleared. I could see the concern etched on Mum's face, the two deep lines between her eyes that were always there when something worried her. Her lips, painted so carefully such a short time ago were pale, pressed into a tight line beneath her cheeks.

Dad had that look his face assumed when there was something he needed to solve. I saw it on him on Sunday mornings when he pondered over the killer Sudoku or when something had gone wrong at work and he needed to sort it out. The two policewomen looked merely curious, as if I were a suspect in a line-up.

'We'll give you a few minutes, Mia,' Dad said. He thrust his hands into the pockets of his chinos, smiling in my direction in what I'm sure he thought was a reassuring fashion.

Mum met my eyes. She gave me a tight smile, the corners of her mouth barely moving.

I moved my head, forcing it to nod up and down. 'Thank you.' My voice was different, strangled as if someone had wound a scarf too tightly around my neck.

As I left the room Dad moved to perch on the arm of the chair Mum had sat in when I got up, cupping his hand around her shoulder.

I met Dad's eyes, saw the sympathy there, wished I could hide in their arms and feel safe, like I had when I was a child. I couldn't do that. Not with the police here. Not with the party swelling and growing outside.

I wanted to be alone, to think, to try to make some sense of this new facet of my life. To allow this horrible knowledge to sink in, permeate beneath the gentle, protected life I had become used to.

The hallway from the lounge was in shadow, always the coolest spot when it was hot outside. Strands of light came from the open doors along its length, bathing the blonde wood at either side in a golden glow. Dust danced in the rays. My footsteps echoed on the stone floor, behind me the stunned silence of the lounge. The hum of noise from the party came in through the open windows in the rooms on the garden side of the hall. I forced myself to breathe, inhaling the burning meat smell from the barbeque which had drifted in and mingled with the heady, overpowering smell of the lilies crammed into the cut glass vase on the table below Patrick's picture.

The kitchen was empty of people. Food, dishes filled with salads of all descriptions were arranged on the marble topped island in the centre of the vast room. Heaped bowls of lettuce, yellow rice, colourful roasted vegetables, scattered with feta cheese. Fragrant turmeric roasted cauliflower mingled with wild rice and tiny green peas. Baby new potatoes swam in homemade pesto. Mum had gorged herself on Jamie Oliver's summer salad recipes. I passed a low pottery bowl heaped with tomatoes and layers of mozzarella cheese. Blood red tomatoes, the juice spilling out onto the pale slices of cheese.

I opened the kitchen door, emerging at the back of the house. I glanced towards the side of the house, where the party was now in full swing. In the short time we had been in the lounge more people had arrived. The garden was now a throng of bodies, colour and motion. The noise hit me like a wall, loud laughter, self-assured voices.

I glanced over towards the party as I made my escape towards the stable yard. Josh, my boyfriend, had arrived, achingly handsome in chinos and a dark blazer. I met his eye briefly as I hurried away, wanting to put as much distance as possible between myself and the scene indoors. He raised his eyes quizzically, undoubtedly wondering where I was going. I made some gesture in his direction which I hoped he interpreted as 'having an important job to do and back in a moment.' What could I say to him? How could I explain what I had just learned? My mother was dead and my father had killed her. How could he ever understand that? Josh, with his privileged, protected life.

He raised his glass in my direction in a 'whatever' gesture. I saw his companion, one of my dad's friends, glance around to see what had attracted Josh's attention and then I rounded the wall of the stable yard and was hidden from them.

Reaching the yard, I slowed my stride, forcing air into my lungs. I opened the narrow wooden gate with deliberate slowness and stepped into the silence of the empty stable yard. I closed the gate with equal slowness, glancing back at the house where I had spent the last half of my childhood. Leaning my back against the sun-warmed red brick, I sank slowly to my knees and let out a howl of pain.

I cried, giving rein to the hollowed-out pain that dug into the pit of my stomach. I cried for the mother I had never known until there were no more tears. When I stopped, still sniffling and choking, I looked up to see Solar, Mum's new horse, standing beside the paddock fence watching me solemnly.

Mum was fascinated by astronomy and each of our horses had a suitably starry name. My childhood had been filled with her favourites, Jupiter, Betelgeus, Vega, Antares. And now the latest, Solar, a tall, muscular, handsome grey stallion who was destined to be a dressage horse.

I got to my feet and walked towards him. The cobbles were smooth and rounded beneath the soles of my shoes. The heels slid down into the gaps between the stones. Reaching down, I pulled them off. Solar came over to the fence. He stood quietly beside me, just the wooden rails separating us. Gently I touched the length of his face, letting my hand trail down from his wide forehead to the soft mushroom of his muzzle. The whiskers around his crinkled mouth were long, they would be the first thing Mum would trim off when he started working. Solar let out a long grass-scented sigh and dropped his huge head towards me. I ran my hands around his face, across the flat plane of his cheek and the broad curve of his jaw. His hair was soft beneath my fingers, the skin pliable, warm from the blood that flowed beneath. I lowered my cheek onto his face, letting it rest on the broadest part, right between his eyes. The point where they put the gun when they shoot a horse. My breathing slowed to the steady rhythm of his, each exhalation warm against my rib cage.

From beneath my tightly closed eyes tears prickled and then fell freely, dampening Solar's hair. Once they started the tears wouldn't stop, nor would the gasping noises of sheer anguish that found their way from the very pit of my stomach. My mother, my real mum, was gone. She hadn't left me. She was dead. Gone forever.

'Mia?' A gentle voice brought me back to reality. Some croaking noise fought its way from my throat. Through my tears I could see Tom, my oldest and best friend, standing beside me, his face filled with concern.

I was glad it was Tom who had come to find me, not Josh. Tom I could bear seeing me in crumpled pieces, not Josh. He was fun, life, parties. He'd be too busy trying to be my boyfriend to be able to understand this, the most horrific part of my life ever. He'd never understand. Josh would never want to know that my life wasn't perfect, that the girl he saw wasn't real at all. My whole life with Mum and Dad was a lie. My real father was a psychopathic murderer and my mother a victim he had captured, held prisoner and then killed.

'Sorry.' I composed myself enough to force the word out.

'Here.' Tom handed me a folded pure white handkerchief. What kind of person my age even carries a handkerchief? I blew my nose, wiped my eyes, and for the want of not knowing what to do with the snot-smeared, mascara-blackened fabric handed it back to him. Wordlessly, Tom crumpled it and shoved it in the pocket of his jeans. If he noticed the dampness of the fabric, he never said. He was far too much a gentleman.

'I was worried about you.' Tom is much taller than me, so when he talks, really talks to me, he stoops forwards, looking at me from beneath his eyebrows. It makes deep furrows on his forehead. 'I saw you come out of the house. Knew something was wrong.'

'Did you see my mum and dad?'

Tom nodded. 'I went in the house, they were there.'

'With the police?'

Tom nodded again, his face serious. He glanced towards the house. I followed his eyes, through the strands of wisteria growing on the stable wall to where we could see a patch of garden, figures moving around on the lawn.

'I ought to go back, they're waiting for me.'

'Take your time. Your mum and dad told me what happened. Why the police were here. I said I'd stay with you, take you in when you're ready.'

I nodded, stepping forwards and letting my head rest on his chest. His shirt smelt of clean laundry overlaid with that horrible body spray I'd told him I hated. Poppy, his girlfriend and my best friend, apparently loved it.

Poor Tom was always torn between pleasing her and me, his best friend. Since we'd grown up together and I was the one he knew the best I thought I was the one who should offer him fashion advice. Not her. We even shared a set of old battered photographs of the two of us, toddlers, running naked around an overflowing paddling pool. No one understood him better than me.

'Do you want to go back in yet?' Tom asked, gently.

I shook my head, sniffing back the tears that threatened to spill again. 'Not yet.'

Solar, losing interest in us, moved away, put his head down and began to crop the grass.

I eased myself away from Tom and led the way to the back wall of the stables. I rested my back against the brickwork, feeling the warmth through the fabric of my dress. 'Did you bring any cigarettes with you?'

'Sure,' he shrugged, reaching into the back pocket of his jeans. I didn't remember him actually smoking for a long time, but he always seemed to have a packet whenever I felt the urge to have one.

The pack looked battered, the cigarette I selected curved, undoubtedly to the shape of his buttocks where he'd sat on them. He pulled a lighter from the front pocket of his jeans and lit the cigarette for me, taking it from my hand after I dragged deeply on it and sucking on it himself.

'What did they say to you inside?' I took the cigarette off him and inhaled, drawing the smoke into my lungs and exhaling slowly. There'd be all hell let loose if Mum or Dad ever found us smoking in such close proximity to the stables. Years of having that drilled into me counted for nothing today. After the policewoman had delivered her news, nothing was the same, my whole life had shifted on its axis. I wasn't the person I had been this morning.

'They said...' Tom took the cigarette, drew on it and then threw it to the ground, grinding it out beneath the rubber heel of his running shoes. When he stopped the cigarette had virtually disappeared. He began again, shaking his head as if he couldn't quite believe what he had heard. 'They said your mum's body had been found. Your real mum.'

'My father killed her.' It was hard to say the words, they seemed to come from a part of me I didn't recognise, someone distant and detached.

'Fuck.' Tom never swore. The word sounded harsh, violent coming from his lips.

My fingers smelt of the cigarette as I ran them over my face. My eyes felt swollen, puffy from crying, my cheeks sore, scalded by tears. My long, dark hair so carefully curled and arranged around my shoulders earlier now hung limply. I ran my hands through the strands, feeling the stickiness of the hairspray Mum had used on me. We'd laughed so much, coughing against the clouds of sticky spray, me trying to wave it away, her determined to make me look like a sophisticated young woman and failing appallingly.

'She lied to me.' The words came from my lips so quietly at first, I wasn't sure I had spoken them.

'Who lied?' Tom asked, his voice uncertain, as if he too wasn't sure I had spoken.

'Nan,' I said, remembering her for the first time in years.

I met Tom's eyes.

'Nan lied to me.' My eyes closed, picturing Nan, her arms around me, making me feel safe. 'Nan said my mum had left me.'

Tom shook his head slightly, as if trying to clear his thoughts, see the girl I had been in the one who stood before him.

I slipped my hand into his. 'All the years I hated her for leaving, she was dead.'

CHAPTER FOUR

'We'd better go back.' I patted my eyes with the pads of my fingertips as if by that act I could push back the sore, swollen tissues.

'Are you sure you're ready?' Tom tilted his head to one side to look at me, his kind face filled with concern.

I looked into those oh-so-familiar blue eyes and pulled my cheek muscles into some kind of smile. 'Yes.' There was no way I was ready for what I had to face. How could I ever be ready for that? For finding out my whole life was a lie? To understand finally what my father had done? The women I had known he had killed had been vague shadowy fragments in my imagination. Nan had always told me my mother had left. I'd imagined her returning one day, that she had her reasons for abandoning me. Now I knew the agony of the reality.

Holding onto Tom's arm for balance, I slipped my feet back into my shoes. Teetering slightly, I leant on him as we crossed the stable yard. Usually the stables were filled with our horses and those of the people who boarded theirs with Mum. Today they were empty, all the horses turned out into the fields away from the noise of the party. Tomorrow everything would be cleared away, the horses brought back in and our normal routine would begin again. I glanced around the empty yard, the smartly painted stable doors, overflowing hanging baskets crammed with tumbling purple lobelia and pale pink geraniums and gave a hollow laugh. How could anything be normal again?

Tom opened the narrow gate into the garden and stood back to let me pass, latching it behind us.

'Right.' His chest rose beneath the white fabric of his tee-shirt as he took a deep breath. There was a dark stain on one side where mascara, melting with my tears, had smeared.

We made our way up the stone-slabbed path towards the house. The noise from the party, the hum of conversation, the stupid band bashing out a teeth-clenchingly bad version of *Bohemian Rhapsody* made it impossible to talk. Smoke scented with burnt meat drifted across the garden towards us. I glanced in the direction of the party, picking out familiar figures. On the edge, at the far side of the lawn I could see Josh, his dark hair a mass of curls, his tall rugby player's physique emphasised by his smart blazer and chinos. As I looked, I felt the thrill of excitement I had ever since he had asked me out – sheer delight he belonged to me. He was deep in conversation with one of our neighbours who coached Josh's rugby team. He must have felt my eyes on him for he looked, met my gaze, raised his beer glass in greeting and arranged his face into what I took as an expression of curiosity and understanding and an enquiry about if I needed him. I shook my head, smiled an 'I'll be back in a while see you later, I'm okay' kind of smile.

Poppy waved and smiled. She looked beautiful, delicate, in a short flowery dress that showed off her tanned, toned legs, a dress Dad would say barely covered her arse. She wasn't a bit perturbed by Tom and I being together.

Poppy turned towards us, ungainly, hampered by the massive heels she wore.

Tom winced. 'Poppy looks a...'

'Little worse for wear,' I finished for him.

At the kitchen door I turned. 'I'm okay now. You go back to the party.'

Tom met my eyes. 'You sure?'

I nodded. Not at all sure.

'Do you want me to send Josh in to you?'

I shook my head. 'I'm better on my own.' I didn't want to expose Josh to this, the festering underbelly of my life.

Tom half turned, looking back towards the party. Clusters of people gathered on the lawn, their clothes patriotic, bright reds, blues and whites, glasses held in elegant hands. Of course, they were wondering what was going on in the house, why the police were here. I could imagine the undercurrent of curiosity that must be seeping through the party. To look at them you'd never guess. No one so much as glanced in our direction. That was how I knew they were all dying to know what was going on and yet their veneer of politeness prevented them from asking.

I went indoors, closed the kitchen door, blocking out most of the noise from the party although the thump of *Bohemian Rhapsody* still managed to permeate.

The house felt hushed, as if waiting for the next scene to be played out. I wished I could stay in the kitchen, or just go out to the party, carry on as if nothing had happened, but that wasn't possible. I had to go and accept my fate.

'Hi.' I stood uncertainly in the doorway. My voice sounded harsh; my throat ached from crying. Everyone looked up at me. Mum, Dad, concern etched on their faces. The policewomen, DI Tallis and PC Dean were expressionless. Professional. Coffee cups, Mum's best china, were on the table with a plate of uneaten shortbread. We'd made the shortbread the previous day, intending them to be served with tea later, during the party.

Mum met my eyes and smiled gently. Dad got to his feet and crossed the room to take my arm. I laid my head into his shoulder, closing my eyes like I had when I was a child afraid of something. I had felt safe there. Not now though. There was no escape from my future.

'How are you doing?' he said, putting his arm around my shoulder and squeezing it gently in the way he had to chivvy me into doing something I was daunted by.

Irritation flared through me at the ridiculousness of his words. How did he think I was doing?

'Okay.' It was so hard to speak. My throat felt so dry, my lips and tongue as if they were made of wood. I wondered if anyone had heard me.

'I'll make more coffee.' Mum jumped to her feet, grabbing the coffee pot and hurrying out of the room as if she couldn't bear to stay.

'Do you want to sit down, Mia? DI Tallis said, her eyes seeking mine and locking onto them, giving me no choice but to look at her. Obediently I sat down on the sofa opposite her, my back to the party.

'I'm sorry this news had to come today. Not great timing.' The detective looked past me, over my shoulder. Dad followed her eyes, looking past Mum's prize-winning cups on the windowsill, then outside to the party, regret shadowing his eyes.

I shrugged, politeness making me want to put her at her ease, tell her it didn't matter, it was just a party. But while my mind whirled, trying to find the right response for this kind of situation, I came up with nothing but the helpless shrug.

'This is the worst news you could ever have to hear.'

I nodded in agreement, the pain in my throat seemed to have shifted downwards and wedged itself in my chest.

'I'll just tell you what is going to happen now and then I'll leave you in peace.'

'That's a good idea.' Mum came into the room with a pot of coffee and busied herself pouring it into the cups.

'Yes,' Dad agreed, both unable to get free of the polite social structures which shaped our lives. I glanced at them, both desperately trying to arrange their stricken expressions into something which resembled composure and failing.

'We are going to talk to Elizabeth Hammett… Nancy… She's in…' DI Tallis consulted the sheets she had pulled out of a leather document carrier.

'Peterborough. The women's prison,' PC Dean finished for her.

Mrs Hammett. It took me a moment to realise who they were talking about. Nan. I glanced up, looking first at Mum and then Dad, their expressions frozen. Mum's eyes flickering everywhere but me.

Nan. I remembered her, a vague impression of her bulk, the smell of burnt wood and cooking ingrained in the fabric of her clothes. Vast arms enfolding me, like giant feather pillows. Nan, she had scared me when she was angry, but she had made me feel safe, I had believed she loved me. She had told me my mother had left. That she couldn't take me with her. Nan had known where my mother was. Lying in a muddy field, rotting.

She had lied to me.

'How could I have thought my mother was alive all this time?' I turned to Mum. Her skin was the colour of a wax candle.

'I'm so sorry darling. It's horrible news.' I'd never heard her voice so high, shrill.

The ground, once stable beneath my feet shifted; now nothing was solid. Everything I had known was uncertain. 'What about my father?' I turned to Dad this time, wanting him to be truthful, hoping he'd realise I was strong enough to take anything he said. Was my real dad dead after all? Had I imagined that? Was he too in prison?

Dad leant forwards towards me. 'He's dead. He killed himself. The police took you from the farm afterwards. Do you remember?'

I nodded slowly. I hadn't thought about the farm for years and then it had only existed in vague memories. It was as if I had moved away from it, closed the door on that life and began another. That child had ceased to exist. Now she was knocking on the door, demanding to be let out. The farm. I had an impression of woodsmoke, trees, hills around us, a low stone building. Feeling safe with my father and Nan, even when the foxes were screaming in the night.

The thoughts buzzed around my mind like angry bees, dashing in and then out again as another took its place. I couldn't pin anything down, form any coherent thought.

Instead I focused on DI Tallis, her blue eyes looking at me.

'The case will be reopened. We need to talk to Mrs Hammett. Nan.'

I nodded, as if I had lost the power of speech.

DI Tallis met my eyes. 'Eventually there'll be a funeral for your mother.'

'I want to go.' My throat unblocked, the words pouring from me in a hurried jumble.

'Of course.' She began to gather her papers together and put them into her folder. She glanced longingly at the fresh coffee and then got to her feet. PC Dean struggled up, she'd relaxed, sunk back into the depths of the sofa. There was an undignified scramble as if she had fallen into an icy pond and couldn't get out again fast enough.

And then they were gone, heading out of the front door, leaving us alone in a silence punctuated by the bass beat of *I Got A Feeling* by the Black Eyed Peas.

We stood in the hall, uncertain, strangers suddenly. The life we had lived a few hours ago now fractured. Dad opened his arms and out of habit I stepped into them. Mum moved to complete the circle, our arms around each other. I could feel the soft roll of flesh above her underwear, her breath smelt of coffee, overlaid with the sweetness of the shortbread.

'I don't know what to say, Mia.' Dad's breath moved my hair as he spoke, his voice hushed, close to my ear.

'Your mum...' Mum said.

'Whatever happens next we'll deal with it. The funeral...' Dad spoke as if he were seeing the things we faced spinning past him on a to-do-list.

'Are you going to be alright to come outside?' Mum asked, stepping away slightly, reminding us all of the guests in the garden.

I nodded, disentangling myself from their arms. Somewhere at the back of my mind I had an image of a muddy field, a blue plastic barrel. Nan's face swam into my imagination, her earnest face, telling me she was going to look after me.

I led the way through the coolness of the house and out into the garden. The noise of the party hit us like a wall, the sound of conversation, the blast of music, the clinking of glasses, all brought into sharp focus. Smoke from the barbeque drifted toward me, blanking out for a moment the blur of colour that was the party guests, then it cleared and I stepped forwards into the party.

'Mia.' Josh came to stand beside me. I looked up into his eyes, seeing his serious expression.

'My mum's body's been found,' I said.

He nodded slowly, his expression earnest, silent as if he were seeking the polite, correct response.

'Wow,' was the best he could come up with.

'Yes. I always thought she had just gone away, left me. And she was dead the whole time.' I spoke, watching myself trying to shock him, wanting to knock him out of his brightly lit, perfect world to one where dark shadows lurked. 'Looks as if my father killed her.'

There was a hysterical edge to my voice. I shut my mouth, clamping my lips tightly shut as if afraid of what I'd say if I continued.

'I don't know what to say.' He took my hand and led me to the edge of the garden, sitting down on the stone steps and pulling me down beside him. I looked up at the party. Dad doing the rounds, holding a wine bottle, moving between the groups of people, the perfect host. His laughter a little loud, his voice had a brittle edge to it. His world had been rocked on its axis.

Mum was deep in conversation with Tom, his father and Poppy, glancing occasionally in my direction to give me what she assumed were sympathetic smiles.

I shrugged. What was there to say which would make anything any better.

'My father…' I began, wanting somehow to put the jumbled thoughts into some kind of order, to find the foundations which had once been the cornerstones of my life.

'Mia.' Josh, put one hand on my arm and shook me gently as if trying to wake me. 'That was a long time ago. You belong here now.'

I glanced at him; he was right. This was my life. I'd get through the churned-up mess of my past and move on.

A shadow crossed in front of us. Poppy. She'd taken off her skyscraper heels, looked a little less drunk. There were dark smears of mascara beneath her eyes. 'Tom told me about your Mum.' She glanced back towards Mum as if she couldn't quite understand the distinction between my two mothers.

I closed my eyes, blocking out her pretty face, her flowery dress, her long tanned legs. I couldn't block out her flowery perfume though. I got to my feet. 'I just don't want to talk about it anymore.' I moved past her towards the guests who turned to watch me approach.

CHAPTER FIVE

The last thing I wanted to do was to be at the party, listening to the chatter, watching the groups of people come together and then part again, the constant circle of polite conversation and social convention all played out to the backdrop of Dad's soundtrack of patriotic music.

Mum, and Dad, my adopted parents, had never hidden my past from me, letting me talk about it when I needed to. I grew to understand my real Dad had done bad things, but that he loved me very much. And Nan, I remembered being with her. I had vague memories of crying for them, wanting to go home, being in a foster home. Then Mum and Dad coming to fetch me and taking me back with them to start a new life. Me filling the hole left by their son's death, them fulfilling a need to be loved and cared for in me.

I wanted to lie in the dark, alone with my thoughts. trying to make sense of the jigsaw pieces of my life. I needed to think about my mother and what had happened to her. She had gone, in one hasty sentence, from being someone who I believed had walked away and left me, to someone who hadn't left me by choice, someone who had been taken from me. By my father.

Dad walked ahead of us into the garden, his Union Jack waistcoat moving like a beacon for me to follow. Mum followed, a stride behind, walking lightly on the turf so her heels didn't sink in. I saw Dad glance at the man who was playing the music, his lips moving. A moment later the music stopped. The hum of chatter continued for a moment and then faded.

'And I said to him, will you—' The last person still to talk, Mark the bumptious land agent who had recently moved to the village was hastily nudged by his wife.

Dad paused, like a magician, waiting until the silence was utterly complete, and every eye had turned to him. I stood on the steps leading down to the lawn, slightly separate from the party, Josh stood on the one below me, his hand holding mine lightly. His skin was warm against mine, dry, his grip was strong as if he was afraid I'd run away.

'Sorry to interrupt, everyone.' Dad tucked his thumbs into the pockets of his waistcoat and smiled benevolently at the faces who had turned expectantly to look at him. 'I think by now everyone is aware that we've had a visit from the police.'

For a moment I had a startling vision of some comedy, everyone looking up at him and saying 'no.' But no one did; there was a general murmur of agreement, the guests looked uncomfortable, shuffling feet, glasses were drained. Eyes flickered over me and then slid awkwardly away. I caught Helen's eye. She had been staring at me, her mouth open in a perfect O. I wondered if she were thinking about the farmer, finding my mother's body, thinking of how her husband would have reacted if he had been working his land and found something as horrific.

I dropped my gaze, looking instead at the pale sandstone slab beneath my feet. An ant was making its way slowly past the side of my shoes. I watched it as if it were the most fascinating thing in the world, wishing nothing existed except me and the ant. Josh squeezed my hand, pulling my attention back. I looked up, scanned the faces of people I had known forever, saw the expressions of utter disbelief they were trying to wrestle into something polite. I felt my mouth, without help from me, twist into a wry smile. Of course they had wondered what was going on, no one would have mentioned it, they were too well mannered. They'd have all carried on with the façade that nothing out of the ordinary was happening at all.

'They'd come to tell Mia, our darling adopted daughter, that the body of her mother has been found.' It was the first time I had ever heard Dad call me that; it felt like he wanted to distance himself from me and my aberrant blood.

Everyone nodded as if that were the most normal thing in the world to be told. 'But for now, we know nothing else, so please everyone just get on with enjoying the party, there's plenty of food and drink and the sun is shining for us.' It sounded as if he were announcing there had been a slight hiccough with the barbeque.

Dad turned, flapping his hand in the direction of the DJ. 'Music,' he bellowed, his voice loud with a tense edge to it I'd never heard before.

Josh took my hand and led me across the lawn.

'Josh. Mia. Great to see you.' Our family doctor, Henry Brown, looked first at Josh, then at me. 'Your Dad has done a fabulous job putting on this party.' He knew, of course, what had just happened and had blanked it completely. He looked awkward and uncomfortable in his Union Jack tie and bright blue trousers, so far removed from his usual grey suit. His cheeks were slightly flushed from the amount he had drunk and the sun. The panama hat he'd used to shield his cheeks had now tipped and sat unevenly on his narrow head.

I nodded. 'Thank you.'

Dr Brown didn't mention a word about Dad's speech. It might have never happened. He'd had been the first person I met when I had arrived into the care of Mum and Dad. He had sent me straight to a child psychologist. I had vague memories of her, the smell of talcum powder, orange make-up wedged in the lines of her face, her lipstick bleeding into the lines around her mouth. I'd lain on my tummy on the floor of her office and drawn pictures of trees.

Jane, Henry's wife, was equally hearty. She wore a bright red and white dress, dragged into heavy folds around her bulk with a wide white belt. She'd decorated herself with Union Jack bows, which were stuck into her short curly hair, giving her the odd appearance of an errant Christmas tree.

'I'm sorry to hear about your mum.' Jane had lipstick smeared on one of her front teeth. It was all I could see while she spoke. I focused on that, rather than listen to her lispy voice, being sorry for me, sorry for the death of someone she didn't even know.

I nodded, not sure of what to say. 'Thank you.'

I hated the sympathy I saw in their faces, hated having to make polite conversation while the spectre of me, my dead mother and murdering father hung over me.

There's Oliver,' Josh gave my hand a squeeze. 'Please excuse us.'

'Oh right, yes of course.' Henry and Jane took a step back together in unison. I could see the relief in their faces and knew they were glad to be rid of us.

'I'm sorry about what's happened,' Oliver said earnestly. Beside me Josh shifted slightly, uncomfortable with the drama.

I met Oliver's eyes; they were an odd pale brown colour, flecked with darker shades in the middle.

'Thank you. It's hard to get my head around it.' My arms and hands felt too big; I wasn't sure where to put them.

Tom, having as always, a sixth sense for when he was needed, appeared beside me, Poppy, swaying slightly, clung to his hand.

'I thought you might need this.' Tom thrust a glass of pale-coloured liquid into my hand.

'Thank you.' I closed my fingers around the cool stem of the glass. Bubbles were gently floating upwards in the pale amber liquid. I sipped at the drink. Champagne. Wildly inappropriate considering what had just happened, but I appreciated his kindness. I tipped back the glass, letting the liquid pour down my throat as though I were parched and it was a glass of water.

'Thirsty?' Oliver grinned; his voice had an edge of uncertainty. Was he afraid of what I was going to do?

I managed a polite smile, while the need to escape the gathering grew inside me.

'I'll get you another.' Poppy met my eyes with an expression I recognised as 'let's get legless.' I watched her walk away across the lawn, wondering where she'd abandoned her shoes. No doubt she'd go home without them and they'd be found months later in some obscure place. I was constantly returning items of clothing and shoes she'd abandoned when she had stayed over with me.

'So, your Mum...?' Pippa said, as if the cogs in her brain were working at a slower pace than everyone else's.

'Mia's adopted,' Oliver snapped shortly. Clearly he hadn't been attracted to Pippa for her brain.

That information seemed to slip behind her eyes and sink in slowly. I wondered how she had missed Dad slipping my background into his speech about why the police had come. My adoption was never hidden from anyone, but I'd never heard him blurt it out like that before.

'Ohhhhh,' she breathed, looking at me with naked curiosity.

'Oh fuck!' Tom exclaimed, drawing his arms up around his head as he crouched in a parody of protecting himself. 'This music is The Worst.'

I hadn't been aware, until then, that the music had restarted, but now Tom had spoken I couldn't ignore the awful noise of Aqua's *Barbie Girl*.

'Ouch,' I grinned, reaching to take the second glass of utterly inappropriate champagne Poppy had brought me.

'Can't beat music like this,' Tom deadpanned.

Josh tried and failed to keep in a guffaw of laughter.

'You had a good season,' Oliver turned to Josh, uncomfortable with our near hysteria.

'Yep, brilliant, we won our league last winter.' Neither moved or changed their expression but there was an air of relief that they were now onto safe subjects.

'I miss playing.' Oliver looked at his feet, shuffling his deck shoes. 'Went to Cardiff to see the women's match.' He glanced at Josh and the two of them ahemed as though they were trapping in great guffaws of puerile laughter.

I let out the huge sigh of relief I hadn't known I'd been holding. The attention, at least in this small group, had switched from me onto other, safer subjects. We clung to that, like drowning men hanging onto a life raft in a stormy sea.

The visit from the police, the discovery of my mother's body might never have happened.

I had the sense of being in the eye of the storm; for the moment all was peace, normality had returned. Yet I could feel the clouds growing on the horizon, like the next onslaught wasn't far away.

I sipped at my champagne, seeing myself as if from afar, laughing with my friends, joining in the conversation, smiling. I had the sense the ill-fated passengers on the Titanic would have felt the same way. Carrying on as normal, pretending nothing was wrong, while all the time the ground beneath their feet was tilting and they were about to be plunged to their doom.

'Are you doing okay?' Tom asked, bringing me harshly back to reality. Josh put a proprietary arm around my shoulder.

'Things have been better.'

Tom nodded.

'I'm so sorry about your Mum.' Poppy lurched from Tom to me, enfolding me in a hug. Her body was so slight I could feel every rib. She'd had a dress made especially for the day, white emblazoned with motifs of the Queen's face all over it. One of the shoulder straps had fallen down her arm. Her skin was tanned and she smelt of coconut overlaid with the flowery perfume she loved simply because her favourite pop singer was promoting it.

I remembered and now regretted a heartfelt conversation I had once had with Poppy. I'd rescued her from the tough girls at school and we had slunk behind the chemistry labs for a crafty cigarette. She'd confessed that she hated her dad and I had told her about my mother leaving me. I'd told Poppy how much I hated her for doing that.

'It's just so sad,' Poppy continued, 'she's been dead all this time.'

'Yes, we realise that,' Josh snapped.

'Your father killed her?' Poppy was very close to me. I could smell the champagne on her breath. They all knew I was adopted, that my father had been a killer, but the child that had been led away that day had faded into the background, my past dissipating like a morning mist. I'd become Mia Lewis. I belonged here, with Mum and Dad. My background had seemed to belong to someone else. Until now.

'Poppy, perhaps we should let Mia alone about her mum.' Tom touched Poppy's arm to get her attention.

'Oh, right.' She twisted her face into a quizzical expression. I imagined the thought her ramblings might be upsetting had never occurred to her.

'Great music Dad dad-danced his way into our midst, an embarrassing Mick Jagger on stage impression, as the strains of *Dancing in the Street* drifted across the lawn towards us.

'Yes,' Tom nodded solemnly, 'we were just saying that.'

Poppy tried desperately to contain her giggles and instead made alarming grunts which made Dad glance at her, presumably afraid she was going to be sick.

'You should all eat, the food's ready,' Dad said, putting one arm around Josh's shoulders in a manly gesture of companionship.

'Hungry, Mia?' Dad smiled at me, his eyes focused just slightly over my left shoulder.

I nodded eagerly, hoping he wouldn't know I was lying. 'It smells delicious.'

I couldn't imagine ever being hungry again. I just felt nauseous; there was a tight knot in the pit of my stomach.

'Let's eat.' Tom led the way across the lawn towards the barbeque. The staff, employed for the day from the local bar, had carried out the bowls of salads, while the chef heaped smoking burgers and pieces of chicken onto plates.

Tom was probably relieved to get something into Poppy to soak up the amount she had drunk.

'Find us somewhere to sit,' Josh said, 'I'll grab us some food.'

I made my way to the edge of the garden to one of the tables we had set out the previous day when the occasion had seemed to hold such promise. I busied myself arranging my hair around my face and wiping an imaginary lipstick stain off my glass. Anything to occupy myself rather than sit and look at everyone. I dreaded catching anyone's eye and seeing their interest and concern.

Josh returned with a plate piled with food. He forked his into his mouth with relish while I pushed mine listlessly around my plate. I wanted this over. I wanted these people to be gone. I just wanted to be alone to think.

* * * * * * * *

Finally it was over. The torture had gone on for hours. We acted our roles, Mum, Dad and me, gracious hosts, entertaining companions. In the early hours people started to drift away. My parents' friends, colleagues, neighbours, Tom, Poppy and finally Josh. The house was at last empty and silent. I left Mum and Dad sipping whisky nightcaps and headed up to my room. Sitting on the low stool in front of my dressing table. I took off my make-up, watching the lipstick, eyeshadow and mascara merge into one blur of colour on the cotton pad. Finally, with my face naked, the mask I had hidden behind all day removed, I met my eyes in the mirror and saw the raw pain there. I let the tears slowly drip down my cheeks.

CHAPTER SIX

There was a moment when I woke, when everything felt like a normal after-party morning. I remembered Josh's toe-curlingly gorgeous goodnight kiss. My hangover was slight, just a vague ache over one eye, nothing a couple of painkillers and a mug of coffee wouldn't sort out.

And then I remembered. My mother was dead and my father had killed her. I couldn't think of anything else then but her. Where was she now?

I'd seen enough forensic detective shows to be able to imagine what she looked like. Her body had been shoved into a plastic barrel and buried for decades under tonnes of cold, wet earth. Where was that? I pictured a barren, windswept place, the landscape I had vague memories of.

From downstairs I could hear the muted sound of the radio, the hum of voices. Mum and Dad. What were they talking about I wondered? How could there ever be normal conversation again? Everything had changed. Yesterday I was their adopted daughter, my past neatly sidestepped as if it had been airbrushed out of my life. The visit from the police had changed everything, bringing the past to the surface. Today I was the child of the man who had killed my mother. I wasn't different, but it felt like I was, as if I were tarnished by what had happened years before.

I reached for my phone; there were messages from Josh, Tom and Poppy. Tom's was a kind 'hope you're okay?' Was I? I really didn't know. I was standing, breathing, functioning. But ok? I wasn't sure.

Poppy had sent me a smiley face emoji with the words 'great party.' I wondered if she had been so drunk she had completely missed what had happened.

Josh's was a predictable, 'How's the head? Can't wait to see you. Don't worry about what happened.' Don't worry? What the hell did that mean? What had I got to worry about?

I tapped brief replies.

Outside, when I looked out of my bedroom window, the garden was back to normal. The marquee had been dismantled the previous night after the party and lay in a neatly folded heap, ready to be collected. The deckchairs were stacked beside it, but apart from them the garden looked as it always did, an expanse of neatly mown lawn surrounded by brightly coloured flower borders.

Not wanting to go downstairs, I showered and dressed and put my make-up on with deliberate slowness. My eyes looked puffy, red rimmed. Had I been crying in my sleep, I wondered? I outlined my eyes and put on lip gloss as if I were applying a mask to hide behind.

My dress and shoes lay abandoned in a heap on the floor. I remembered struggling with my zip, wanting to rid myself of the fabric that covered me as if it symbolised everything that had happened during the previous few hours. Once dressed in my more usual jeans and shirt, I picked up the dress and held it to my face. It smelt of the smoke from the barbeque and Poppy's sweet perfume mingled with Josh's shower gel. I laid the dress on the side of my bed; I didn't want to touch it again. Later I'd shove it into a rubbish bag and get rid of it.

Finally, there was nothing to do except go downstairs.

Mum and Dad were in the kitchen and as I came down the stairs their voices, a blurred hum of conversation, became more distinct.

'What is Oliver thinking?' I heard Dad say. 'That girl is young enough to be his daughter.'

'What's Pippa thinking?' I heard Mum say with a snort of laughter. 'Probably about the size of his wallet.' There was the sound of laughter which stopped abruptly as I pushed open the kitchen door.

Mum and Dad were seated at opposite sides of a table littered with plates and mugs. The room smelt vaguely of coffee and toast. The scent of bruised grass drifted in from the open window.

'Morning, darling,' Mum said, her voice sounding forced, too high, brittle. She reached for the coffee pot, lifting her eyebrows quizzically. 'Coffee?'

'How's the head?' Dad's sounded more normal, although his eyes were fixed, not on mine, but at some vague spot just over my shoulder.

'Please. It's fine,' I said, answering them both at the same time.

I sat down, took the mug of coffee Mum handed me, and reached for a slice of the thick toasted bread which was arranged on a plate.

There was an awkward silence, broken only by the sound of my knife scraping butter across the surface of the toast.

'Richard's coming soon to do Solar's injections.' Mum said, talking about Tom's father.

'Rounds on a Sunday?' Dad asked.

Mum shrugged. 'You know what Richard's like. He's a complete workaholic. The fact that Sunday is meant to be the day of rest is irrelevant to him. I wonder if Tom's going to be with him?'

She said 'Tom' with a strange note in her voice. Her assumption Tom had a crush on me drove me nuts. Tom and I were best friends. The best of friends, but that was it. I was dating Josh. Her implication that I should be interested in Tom being with his Dad on his rounds irritated me. For a moment I forgot about the police coming the previous night and fought to keep my temper under control.

'I'm not sure, Mum. I doubt it.' Tom did everything he could to not go out with his father on his rounds. While he'd always longed to be a vet, working with his controlling bully of a father was not what he wanted to do, but it served a purpose, giving him valuable experience before he could set up his own practice. Tom preferred working with small animals to being out on farms and stables, getting pushed around by several tonnes of livestock.

'Oh, that's a shame.' Mum pulled her lips down into a wry expression.

I got to my feet, pushing my plate of uneaten toast to the centre of the table. I couldn't breathe. My whole life had imploded just a few short hours before and here we were making ridiculous small talk as if nothing had happened. Didn't they realise my whole world had just been rocked to its core?

'Mia,' Mum said. I took a stride forwards into her arms. She smelt clean, of expensive soap and shampoo. I began to sob, great heaving animal-like cries of sheer anguish. Behind me Dad's chair legs scraped on the slate floor tiles and then I felt his arms enfold the two of us.

I cried until I could cry no more, for myself, for the life I had here, the person who I had become, who I would never be again, now that everything had changed. I cried for my mother, for hating her for so long, for never knowing her, for her being dead. And I cried for my parents, for the loss of their son and for me as a replacement, now soiled, my tarnished past, buried for so long had now re-surfaced.

'I don't know if this will help,' Mum said when I had finally stopped crying and disentangled myself from them. Her shirt was damp with my tears. 'But Grace, the detective, said if you wanted to see where they found your mum's body you could. If it would help… you…' She said the word mum as if she were speaking a foreign language and couldn't quite get her mouth around the strange word. Her voice faded into nothingness.

I nodded. 'I'd like that.' What a strange thing to want to do. I couldn't imagine anyone seeing where someone had been buried. Yet somehow, I wanted to. It was probably the closest I'd ever get to her.

'I've got her number.' Dad rummaged in the depths of his chinos, unearthed his phone and turned it on. 'Here,' he said a few taps later.

Mum took the telephone from him, wrote the number down on a pad and handed it to me.

'Ring her. Anytime, she said. I'll come with you. Or perhaps you'd prefer Josh?'

I shrugged. It was hard enough to think about going to see the burial site without thinking about the finer details of who would go with me.

'Oh, here's Richard,' Mum said, as a dark Range Rover swept past the kitchen window and crunched to a halt. She hastily shoved her feet into her boots and hurried out.

'I'd better go, golf… late.' Dad began to rummage in his pockets, casting his eyes in desperation around the kitchen.

I reached into the fruit bowl in the middle of the kitchen table and unearthed his car keys.

'Where would I be without you?' he grinned, taking the keys from me and dropping a hasty kiss on the top of my head.

From outside I could hear Mum and Tom's father talking. His voice was loud as he spoke in short bursts, like an aggressive dog barking. Their voices faded into the distance as they headed towards the stables. Dad's car started and drove away leaving me in the silence of the kitchen.

I took a sip of my coffee; the liquid had gone cold. I tipped it down the sink, made a new mug full and threw my uneaten toast into the bin. I pulled my phone out of my pocket. No replies to my texts. I sat, my elbows resting on the table, the phone in my hand, staring blankly at the screen. Did I want to make this call? Did I really want to ask Grace Tallis to take me to the place where my mother's body had lain?

I tapped in her number, listened to the ringing tone. My courage failed; I was about to turn the phone off when it was answered.

'DI Tallis.'

I could hear a horse's hooves, clattering on a road, the wind making a whistling sound in the receiver. She mustn't be working today. I imagined her on a horse, picturing a huge grey horse like Solar; she would be juggling her telephone and the horse's reins as I often did. It was hard to envision her having a life other than being a detective. 'It's Mia... Lewis.'

'Hi, Mia.' Her voice had softened; perhaps she had been expecting someone from work to disturb her day off and was aware of the need to be kinder to me.

'I... er... Mum said...' I struggled to frame the words.

'Mia, would you like to see where your Mum's body was found?' she asked, skirting over my dithering.

'Yes, please.' I wasn't really sure I did. How could I want to see that? And yet it felt as if I'd be somehow close to my mother if I stood where she had lain.

We made arrangements for me to go to Cornwall in a few days' time and ended our conversation.

That done I headed out into the stable yard to tell Mum.

Richard must have done the rounds of looking at the horses in the stables because he was only just getting his equipment out of the back of his Range Rover ready to give Solar his injection. 'The yearlings look tip-top,' Richard was saying as I approached the car.

'Did you...?' Mum asked, turning to me.

'Yes, Wednesday,' I replied, watching Richard look from Mum to me, his expression quizzical at our conversational shorthand.

'How's job hunting going, Mia?' he asked, straightening up from the depths of the boot.

'Good.' I involuntarily took a step away from him.

Tom's father was a ferocious looking man, with weather-reddened cheeks and wild bushy eyebrows. His manner was just as scary, brisk, petulant and used to getting his own way. It was hard to imagine how he could have produced a son as gentle and kind as Tom.

Mum pulled back Solar's stable door and led the way in. The big stallion gave a wary snort. He seemed to grow before our eyes, drawing himself up into a seething cauldron of muscle and power before lowering his head, his huge eyes fixed on Richard.

'Doesn't look like he enjoys visits from the vet,' Richard snorted, a pace behind Mum. Solar shot out a front leg at lightning speed, warning them to leave him alone.

'For a stallion he's usually really gentle,' Mum said. I was aware of a nervous note in her voice.

'You'd better get him caught and held.' Richard's voice was impatient.

He'd been Mum's vet for many years, but even the considerable amount of business she gave him counted for little with him. Everything had to be done how and when he wanted it.

As he took a step backwards to wait for Mum to catch Solar the big horse reared, lifting his front legs away from his straw bed. As his legs came back downwards a front leg lashed out again. A blur of white flashed past Mum's legs.

'Careful,' Richard said, completely unnecessarily. Mum had been around horses long enough to know that one hit from those powerful legs would break hers as easily as if it were a brittle twig. For a moment the two of them, Mum and Solar, stood facing one another. He that dangerous equine combination of anger and nerves, she tentative and afraid.

Without thinking I passed Richard and Mum and grabbed Solar's headcollar, jerking it to get his attention.

'Stop it,' I snapped, the pent-up anger that had been simmering since yesterday's revelations coming to the fore and giving me strength and power I hadn't known I possessed.

Solar shook his head angrily as if I were a fly that was bothering him. My fingers ached with the effort of holding onto the thick leather straps that surrounded his head.

'Be careful. Perhaps we should leave him,' Mum's voice quivered.

'Pass me the lead rope. I held out my free hand to take the lead rope from her hand, which shook as she reached forwards to pass me the length of rope.

Still holding onto Solar's head collar I clipped the lead rope on and threaded it through the straps so it rested on the front of his face, giving me extra control. I could feel the angry heat from his body through my shirt.

The enormous stallion knew I wasn't afraid of him and let out a loud snort, shaking his head, the only way he could demonstrate his anger. A moment later his head lowered and I felt the tension leave his body as he realised there was no point in fighting. Calmly he let Richard push the syringe gently into his neck to give him the vital injection which would protect him from tetanus and flu when he was competing.

The job completed, Richard and Mum left the stable, leaving me to slip the rope from Solar's headcollar. Forgetting his earlier anger, Solar rubbed his huge head over my front, looking to have his cheeks scratched.

'Big baby,' I said, gently stroking his face before leaving the stable to join Mum and Richard.

'Well done, Mia.' Richard clasped my shoulder with a massive hand. 'Tackling that horse was no easy job. There's tough genes running through your veins.'

CHAPTER SEVEN

I hadn't been asleep when my phone rang, but instead was curled beneath the duvet, trying without success to stop the constant stream of thoughts that whirled around in my mind.

'Mia, I'm so sorry, I'm not going to be able to come with you tomorrow. I feel awful letting you down.'

'No problem. I'll be fine on my own,' I replied, wondering if my sarcasm would be lost on Josh. I assumed it would. It would probably never occur to him that I'd needed his company to help me through the ordeal of seeing where my mother's body had been buried since I was a toddler.

'Something's come up at work I can't get out of.'

'It doesn't matter.'

'I hope everything will go okay. Talk tomorrow.' Brief but to the point, that was Josh. He had to get up early to head to the gym or for rugby training before he went to work and so whiling the night away chatting to me had never been part of our relationship. 'I love you,' he added.

I didn't reply. What was there to say? It was too late to ask Tom or Poppy now and I couldn't contemplate having Mum or Dad with me.

Rolling onto my back, I lay with my eyes open, watching the shadows of the trees outside, lit by the full moon, play across my bedroom ceiling. I was used to sleepless nights. Often, before big horse shows, or important days at university, or more recently theatre auditions, I would lie awake, worrying. In my mind I would go over the events of the day to come. Horse shows, running through my lines for a stage show, I could imagine, but this – standing in a field looking at where my mother's body had lain, surrounded by the other dead young women my father had killed, I could not comprehend.

Finally, I must have slept because I woke, bleary-eyed and thick-headed, to find Mum beside me, gently putting a mug of tea on my bedside table.

'How did you sleep?' she asked as I opened my eyes. She'd changed since the police had come. Now I caught her looking at me differently, concern shadowing her eyes, but her expression unfathomable, as if I were a stranger.

'Okay,' I lied, pushing myself upright and taking hold of the mug, cradling its warmth into my chest. 'Josh isn't coming. He's busy at work.'

I heard her sharp intake of breath, her long, exhaled sigh exuding the scent of coffee. 'Oh no.' Her eyes met mine. 'Would you like me to come with you instead?'

Without pausing to consider I shook my head. 'No, really, I'll be okay.' My voice trailed off. I wasn't sure I wanted to be alone, but I couldn't imagine anything worse than Mum being with me. I couldn't comprehend being with her, my Mum, the woman who had nurtured me and loved me for the last fifteen years being part of today, standing beside me looking at the ditch where my birth mother's body had lain.

'Really? I'd like to come. I don't think you should be alone.'

I shook my head. 'Honestly, Mum, no. I'm better on my own.'

She took the mug of tea from me, put it gently on my bedside table and sat on the edge of the bed. Automatically I leant forwards into her arms as she enfolded me. Her hair smelt of hay, she'd already been in the stables for hours.

'If you're sure. I can come if you change your mind.' There was, I thought, the vaguest hint of relief at my decision.

Mum took me to the train station. 'Are you sure you're going to be okay?' she asked as her car bumped over the cobbles outside the station. 'I shouldn't have let you go on your own. I should have insisted…' she wittered, speaking I thought more for her benefit than mine.

'Honestly, I'll be fine. I'll let you know when I'm on the train back.'

Mum had barely stopped the car outside the red-bricked façade of the station before I was out of the car, grabbing my handbag, blowing her a kiss and walking away.

My fingers were trembling so much it was hard to key in the numbers of my online booking confirmation which would print my ticket. I struggled to make sense of the long line of numbers and letters which made up the reference. Behind me, an impatient man sighed and tutted. Finally, the ticket printed, sliding from the slot into fingers that were sticky with sweat.

In the station concourse I bought coffee, a sandwich and a magazine for the journey.

I avoided looking at the newspapers in case there was anything about my mother, or father. For days after the police had dropped the bombshell about my mother being found Dad had been worried the press would be full of lurid stories about the case.

'The detective suggested we steered away from watching the news and taking too much notice of the newspaper coverage,' Dad said, reminding me of Grace Tallis's advice not to look at stay off social media just in case.

The vast station was a hive of activity; the normality of travellers hurrying to platforms, gazing at the announcement boards, arriving and leaving, went on around me.

My train was already in the station. I found my carriage and seat and sank down in it gratefully.

A few minutes later we were off. I sipped my coffee, nibbled on my sandwich, glanced at my magazine as the miles slipped by to the gentle rhythm of the train. Ordinarily I would have enjoyed a day out. I loved to travel. But this was a journey I couldn't imagine making even though my body was physically doing it.

Since leaving Cornwall I'd never been back, but somehow as we got closer the landscape looked familiar; the rolling gorse covered hills, the bleak moors and in the distance glimpses of a startlingly blue sea.

By the time we reached Truro most of the other passengers had got off. As the train pulled slowly into Penzance station, only myself and an excited looking elderly lady remained in the carriage

I gathered my things and let the old lady off before me, smiling despite my nerves as she hurried into the arms of an equally eager looking old man.

Grace Tallis stood at the exit. I'd never imagined what a detective would look like, but tall, slender, dressed in faded jeans and a brown suede flying jacket, Grace wasn't it.

'Hi, Mia,' she held out a hand for me to shake. Her warm fingers gripped mine.

'Did you have a good trip down?' We walked side by side out of the station. Outside, away from the diesel fumes the air had the salt tang of the sea. Seagulls wheeled in the brisk breeze that whipped our hair around our faces.

I could only nod, awed by her presence and the prospect of what the day would bring.

She led the way across the car park to a vast, shiny jeep. Plastic bags of horse feed were laid on the back seat. 'I have a life other than being in the police,' she smiled. 'I nipped out to get feed this morning. Too busy last night.' For a moment she was silent. Brought back, I imagined, to whatever crime she had been dealing with. She started the jeep, turning to me as if to bring herself back to the moment. 'Do you want to eat... or a coffee... or will we just go straight there?'

'I'm okay,' I said, through lips which felt stiff with dryness. 'Just straight there. I guess.'

What else would we do? Take a tour of the Cornish scenery? Go for coffee and cake as if we were old friends? The last thing I wanted was to leave the car park, to journey with Grace to the farm where my mother's body had been found, but I was here now. This was the reason for my journey.

'What about Nan? Will she go to court again now more bodies have been found?' Ever since Grace had broken the news about my mother, I'd struggled to comprehend that Nan had lied to me. She'd let me believe my mother had left me, while she must have known she was dead. I remembered her anger the day I had let the girl free.

Grace shrugged, 'Doesn't look like it. One of my colleagues has been the prison to question her, but she's always denied helping your dad.'

Grace steered out of the car park and accelerated expertly into the line of traffic. The crowded streets of Penzance stretched before us, ice cream shops and cafés, gift shops mingled with high street chain stores. I gazed out of the jeep window, trying to see something which looked familiar from the first eight years of my life, but there was nothing.

As the jeep crawled forwards we passed a newsagent's shop, the front festooned with brightly coloured plastic buckets, spades and inflated rubber lilos. A cabinet on the pavement held all the day's newspapers. Grace must have heard my gasp as I unwittingly read the headline in one of the local papers. 'I Escaped the Clutches of Serial Killer, Eddie Hammett.' Below the headline a blurred photograph of a young woman. The woman I had freed the day my father died.

'Finding the bodies has brought everything back to people's awareness. Here anyway,' Grace said gently. The road cleared and we moved on.

I hadn't ever thought of the young woman I'd freed. She must have been the age I was now. What was her life now? Did she ever think of me, I wondered?

'What's her name?' I asked, the image on the front page of the newspaper had unlocked thoughts and questions I'd pushed to the back of my mind.

'The girl you set free, her name's Susie. Susie Ward.'

The road intersected with another. Grace inched the big vehicle slowly out onto the adjoining road, peering over the steering wheel to see if any cars were coming.

'Do my… Do my mother's… Glanna's parents know about me?' Questions tumbled out of my mouth, the words spilling over one another in a torrent.

'Grandmother. Your grandfather died a couple of years ago. Yes, they do. Once we'd identified Glanna's body. From DNA and dental records.' Her voice faded as she spoke the last sentence, no doubt from consideration of my feelings.

My mother's parents. I imagined the pain they must have gone through. I couldn't picture them, or her. I'd never even seen a picture of my mother. I had no idea if the face looking back at me in the mirror each morning was like hers or my father's.

'And your aunts.'

'Aunts,' I breathed the word, unable to comprehend the vast web of lives connected to me by my blood.

'They didn't want me? They let me be adopted?' I spoke my thoughts out loud.

'I don't know. We had to hand you into the care of social services,' Grace apologised.

I'd never contemplated that perhaps they could have given me a home. Mum and Dad had explained they couldn't afford to have me with them. I'd been so fixated all my life with the pain of my mother abandoning me, I'd never really thought about why her family hadn't wanted me. Now I understood. They must have realised she was dead, had to have known I was Eddie and Glanna's daughter. My father had kidnapped, tortured and raped Susie Ward before I accidently set her free. I'd never told my parents how much I had found out through Googling my father's name, the discussion boards I'd discovered where faceless people hid behind bizarre made-up names and speculated on the fate of the young women who had gone missing in the South West. Why had I believed my mother had gone away, when in my heart I should have guessed the reality? Now I knew.

'Can I see them?' I could hear the desperation in my voice, the longing to be connected to my mother, to them.

'Give them a bit of time,' Grace said, her voice gentle over the sound of the jeep's engine. They didn't want to see me. Why would they? My existence must only serve to remind them of what had happened to their daughter.

'It must be hard to get your head around it all.' Grace braked hard, swinging the jeep into the side of the road as a lorry came around the corner ahead of us.

The road climbed into farm and moorland. Stone walls bordered each side of the road, behind which I could see the rolling hillsides, a patchwork of fields, broken only by the stone walls and outcrops of gorse-covered rocks. Somewhere out there was the farm where I had been brought up, the woods I'd run through with my father after I had set Susie Ward free. Somewhere in the hills was the railway viaduct off which my father had thrown himself rather than be caught by the police.

'What about the other bodies? The ones found with my mum.'

'We've identified Eliza McVay. She was on holiday from Scotland when she went missing.'

'The others? Have they been identified? How many were found?'

'Seven,' Grace said, so quietly I wasn't sure I had heard her correctly. 'We've not got identities for all of them yet.'

'Seven?' I repeated. I knew there'd been two found at the Blackthorn Farm. So many young women. My father's victims.

'Here we are.' Grace's voice had a brittle edge as she steered the jeep off the main road onto a narrow track between thick hedges and tall stone walls.

My heart began to thump hard against my rib cage. The jeep bumped up the track, slewing into potholes and puddles, branches from the hedge scraping against the paintwork.

I pushed open the jeep door and slid out. The wind, blasting off the coast, whipped my hair around my face. I pushed it back with a clammy hand. Ahead of us stretched a huge open field. On the horizon, I could see a blue line where the sea met the sky.

Flapping in the wind, yellow tape billowed from stakes outlining grassy squares.

Seagulls wheeled in the air above us. I could smell farmyard manure, the tang of the sea, hear a tractor working somewhere close by. Head down, I watched my feet carry me where Grace led, our shoes sinking into muddy earth, churned with footprints.

A moment later a chasm appeared in the ground in front of us, the ochre coloured earth raw-looking in contrast with the green grass. In that hole had lain the plastic barrel containing the body of my mother. The bottom of the hole was filled with rusty coloured water. I imagined it seeping into the barrel, lapping against her skin.

'How did she die?' My voice sounded as if it belonged to a stranger.

I glanced at Grace. She was staring down at the hole.

'We're not sure.'

I knew what those words meant. There had been so little remaining of my mother's body they hadn't been able to find out what had happened to her. I pictured a jumble of bones, rotting flesh and fought back the bile that flooded my throat.

'Will you take me back, please?' I focused hard on speaking, enunciating each word precisely. The alternative was to let go of the tight grip I had on my emotions, unleash the anguish, scream at the unbearable pain.

Grace stopped the jeep in the train station car park. 'I'll keep you posted about the funeral. It won't be for a while yet though.'

I nodded, exhausted, physically and mentally. 'I don't even know what my mum looked like.'

Grace reached behind the seats, pulled out a folder, rummaged through the sheaves of paper before handing me one. I glimpsed smiling images of young women as she leafed through before selecting one.

'This is your mum.'

She was smiling in the picture, half turned towards the camera as if the photographer had caught her attention.

I dashed away the tears that began to flow as, for the first time in my life, I looked at my mother's face. My face.

CHAPTER EIGHT

Three weeks later I still hadn't shown Mum the photograph of my mother. As if by keeping the two halves of my life separate, the Mia whose mother had been murdered, and the Mia who had grown up surrounded by love and security would never merge. The child who had been fathered by a man who had kidnapped, raped and murdered young women would not exist. I wanted to be the Mia I had been before the police had blundered into the Queen's Diamond Jubilee party and fractured everything I knew and trusted.

* * * * * * * *

I'd spent the journey back from Cornwall looking at her photograph. I'd locked myself in a rocking toilet cubicle and studied my face in the mirror, comparing it to my mother. In it she looked about my age, full of life and hope, anticipating a life my father had taken away from her. We had the same oval shape to our faces, the same arch to our eyebrows, even the same wide, mischief-filled eyes set above high cheekbones. Our mouths were different, hers small, with rosebud lips. My mouth was wider, my lips fuller and I'd never wear pink lipstick in a million years. Our hair was different too, mine a long, wavy mane, hers shorter, straighter and many shades lighter.

   I'd slid into the passenger seat of Mum's car in the parking area outside Bristol train station. 'How's the day gone?' Clearly she was still worried that I'd been alone, that she should have gone with me.

'It was okay,' I'd told her, not able to frame the words to describe the emotions I had experienced that day. The disconnection I'd felt with reality standing beside Grace in the field overlooking the sea, staring down at the hole in which my mother's body had been found. How could I even try to explain how I had felt looking at the other gaping holes in the ground, the fluttering yellow tape. My father had killed those women. There were still families waiting for news that their missing daughters, sisters, aunts had been found. And families whose long wait was over, a wait that had been replaced by the truth of what had happened to their loved ones. I could never describe the feeling of absolute revulsion at the knowledge of whose blood flowed through my veins.

'We can talk about it when you're ready.' Mum had glanced at me with a gentle, worried expression.

I'd nodded, rummaging in my bag to get out my phone to see what messages had come through while I had been virtually catatonic on the train journey home. I knew I'd never be able to discuss how I felt with her.

Josh's messages had been filled with remorse at not being able to come with me.

I'd tapped back a brief reply, 'It's okay. No probs.' I'd been glad he hadn't gone with me. I couldn't have borne having him there, seeing the reality of the grim details of my past. Perhaps by him not knowing I'd be able to erase those feelings, not be swamped by the knowledge of what my father was, continue to be the Mia I had been before Grace had come into our lives.

Poppy's messages had been filled with junk about a night out. I'd replied, asking where she'd been, wondering if she had even remembered what I had been doing during the day.

Only Tom's messages had sounded as if he had any interest, or concern. 'Hope you're okay. Tough day I'm sure. Chat if you like. Must be hard to get your head around.'

'Hungry?' Mum's words had brought me back to reality. I felt her searching for the words which would return me from the dark place she probably knew I'd gone to in order to reassure me of her love.

Quickly I'd tapped a reply. 'Thanks, I'm okay. Good to know you're there.'

'I am. What's for dinner? Did you ride Solar today?' I'd turned my attention to Mum, wanting to erase the day from my memory.

* * * * * * * *

'Sunnies or wellies?' Poppy looked at me quizzically, dangling a pair of expensive-looking sunglasses on the end of her finger.

'Both I think, according to Tom anyway,' I replied. 'His dad seems to think we're mad going to the Isle of Wight.'

Poppy rolled her eyes. 'He thinks most things we do are mad. I couldn't imagine Tom's dad going to a festival.'

We giggled at the thought of Tom's uptight, bullying father doing something so wild as going to a music festival and camping in a muddy field.

'Both then.' Poppy laid a very new, flower-adorned pair of rubber wellies beside the rucksack she had packed and began throwing in random skirts, shorts and tops from a pile she had heaped on her bed. I shook my head at the sight of the wellies. They didn't look as if they'd ever seen mud. Mine on the other hand, resting beside my rucksack in the utility room at home, were battered, stained by years of mud and horse muck.

'You won't need all that stuff.'

Poppy stopped mid-shoving yet another summery hippy-looking top into the top of the rucksack. 'But…' she began, a frown creasing her forehead.

'Remember Glasto last year. We were in the same stuff for days.'

Poppy let out a long sigh, tipping up the rucksack and tumbling a brightly-coloured chaos of fabric onto her bedroom floor.

'But what to take…' She got to her knees, sifting through the garments.

'I'll leave you to it. Minimal, Poppy. Minimal. Josh and Tom are picking me up at twelve. We're on the quarter to three ferry from Southampton so we haven't time to mess around. We'll collect you then.'

I left her to it and headed home, wanting to check my rucksack before the boys arrived. I tucked a smaller-sized copy of the photograph of my mother into one of the inside pockets. The original I'd put in a drawer, hidden beneath a jumble of tee-shirts and socks. I kept the copy with me, always in the inside pocket of whatever bag I was using. I found myself longing to look at my mother and would curl on my bed, my eyes locked onto hers.

'The forecast is horrible,' Mum said, finding me in the utility room repacking my rucksack for the third time.

'I know.' What difference would that make? Rain and mud were part of the fun of the festival. What were we supposed to do? Stay at home because of a few drops of rain?

Josh's father's Range Rover glided up the drive at precisely twelve. I threw my rucksack into the back which was already laden with camping gear. A rolled-up tent, fold-away stools, cooking equipment, all neatly stacked, amongst boxes of food, cans, and bottles of drink.

Despite my warnings Poppy was still adding things to her rucksack. She hurried out of the house at my side fretting about whether she had enough dry shampoo to last the weekend.

'You'll be having too much fun to care,' I reminded her, miming sinking to my knees with the weight as I took her rucksack to put into the back of the Range Rover.

'I hope so,' she grinned, giving me an excited hug. I breathed in her familiar floral scent. 'You'll smell vile in a couple of days' time,' I told her, slipping out of her arms.

'Ready to party?' Poppy clambered into the back seat, leaning forwards to kiss Tom loudly, before snapping on her seatbelt with a contented sigh.

'Is this blasted rain ever going to stop?' Josh pulled gingerly out onto the main road. 'I can hardly see to drive.' He flipped the windscreen wipers onto a faster speed.

Tom began to adjust the navigation system, keying in our destination. 'Midsummer and we've hardly had any good weather yet.'

'I don't care.' Poppy leant forwards to tousle Tom's hair. 'We're going to see Bruce Springsteen and Elbow.'

'And Tom Petty and Joan Armatrading,' Tom added.

I met Poppy's eyes, shuddering in mock horror as we grinned at each other. His taste in music was appalling.

The rain eased off as we reached the motorway and headed south. Glastonbury the previous year had been our first. Now we felt like old hands. Good camping gear. Minimal food. Who wanted to cook when there were so many food stalls? And plenty of drink. We'd run out at

Glastonbury, although we'd been convinced the lads in the tent beside us had helped themselves. Then we'd been too stoned and drunk to realise. There was no chance of that this year. The drink would stay safely locked in the Range Rover.

* * * * * * * *

It was early evening when we drove onto the Newport camp site. The crossing had been rough, the sea pitching the ferry as if it were a child's toy. Poppy, her pretty face tinged green, curled in the corner of the back seat as Josh drove the short distance from the ferry.

Once we reached our allotted site, Poppy staggered away to find the toilets and didn't reappear until the tents were erected and all the gear unloaded.

'Better?' Tom opened his arms to embrace her.

Poppy nodded her head in agreement from within the folds of Tom's rain jacket.

'Great spot,' Josh said, pulling a can of cheap lager from the stack. He looked around, nodding in satisfaction. We had been lucky. Our tents were pitched at the top of a small rise, close enough to the toilets that we could reach them easily, far enough away that the odour of the inevitable overflow would not bother us. The bins and shower block were equally handy. In the festival field the bands were already doing their sound checks. The roadways and paths across the field were already strips of mud, cars and vans slipping and sliding on the slick surface.

'Let's get wasted,' I challenged, unscrewing a bottle of red wine and taking a long swig of it.

'Let's.' Poppy grinned, pulling the bottle out of my hand and glugging the liquid.

* * * * * * * *

I woke the following morning to the sound of rain on the tent. Beside me in the sleeping bag, Josh slept on, oblivious. Trying not to disturb him I wriggled out of the sleeping bag and into my jeans. The earth felt cold beneath the ground sheet. I unzipped the front of the tent and peered out, the rain dampening my hair immediately. The tents below us, on the lower ground, were already surrounded by a sea of mud. A line of cars and vans were making their way into the site, willing helpers pushing them, people already filthy, their clothes slick with mud.

'Primal Scream today, yeah?' Josh sat up, running a hand through his tousled hair.

'And The Stranglers.' I did the zip back up and wriggled back into the sleeping bag beside him. 'Ughhh, cold and wet out there.'

'Better stay here then.' Josh's fingers found the zip of my jeans and deftly pulled it downwards.

Tom and Poppy were out of their tent by the time Josh and I emerged. Tom had fetched coffee from one of the vans. His jeans were already muddied to the knees.

Poppy was in the front seat of the Range Rover, outlining her eyes with a dark pencil in the passenger mirror.

'Wow,' Tom said, handing us coffee mugs and standing in the shelter of the back of the Range Rover to survey the scene. He pulled a crumpled pack of cigarettes out of his back pocket; when he selected one it was damp and misshapen. He pulled a wry face, rolling his eyes in my direction as he shoved the mangled packet into the plastic bag we were using for rubbish. 'I've never seen rain like it.'

'Looks like we're going to get soaked.' Poppy slammed the car door shut and came to join us, her thin top already wet and translucent, the shape of her breasts and jutting nipples clearly visible.

'Never mind.' I rolled my eyes at Poppy as Josh spoke to her breasts.

We all piled into Tom and Poppy's slightly larger tent and sat amongst their scattered belongings watching the chaos unfold around us. Tractors were towing cars onto the camp site, people slipped and slid in the mud. Cheap tents had collapsed during the night, becoming a jumble of broken poles and soaked fabric which were trampled into the mire.

Poppy and I, giddy with excitement, fetched breakfast, standing in an endless, rain-soaked line to buy bacon sandwiches. 'This is brilliant,' Poppy said, holding out her arms and lifting her face to the rain, letting it soak her clothes and hair. She was less enthusiastic a rain-soaked hour later when, shivering beneath the sleeping bag, her muddy clothes abandoned outside, she changed into a drier pair of shorts and another top.

'It's chaos,' grumbled a man, struggling to keep his balance on the slippery ground beside our tents. 'There's massive queues on the mainland trying to get the ferry. No one can get on the campsite when they get here.'

'A nightmare,' Tom agreed, 'They've had to cancel the cricket at Headingley.'

I smiled as the man gave Tom a blank look as he squelched away across the campsite. Tom was such an old soul.

'Heaven knows how we will ever get off this field.' Tom shook his head in disbelief at the scenes unfolding around us.

'Who cares?' Josh opened the back of the Range Rover and handed cans of lager around. 'We're here now. Make the most of it.'

I touched my can against his. I intended to. The discovery of my mother's body and the trip to her burial site, the horrific knowledge about my origins, I pushed firmly to the back of my mind. This was where I belonged, surrounded by my friends, my wonderful family waiting for me at home. This was who I was.

The appalling weather continued unabated but determined to enjoy ourselves we followed a line of bedraggled festival-goers into the main area and into the relative dryness of the Big Top. The ground was churned to a chaos of mud and rubbish. We kicked bottles out of the way, trampled cans and plastic cups into the mire. The mud dried on our skin and later ran in rivulets of sweat down our bare legs. I clung to Josh's hand as we were jostled by the movement of the crowd. My ears rang with the thump of the music and the ear-splitting shouting and singing of the people who surrounded us. I caught Tom's eye and grinned at him over Poppy's head, her face uncertain by the rowdiness of the dancers. Tom, free of his parents and the seriousness of his job, danced enthusiastically. His voice was loud and tuneless as he yelled the words to The Strangler's *Heroes*.

In the centre of the crowd we formed a tight circle, our arms around each other's shoulders and jumped with wild abandon in time with the music. In the heat of the crush, sweat trickled down my back. Long into the night we danced. I trampled on discarded beer cans as they rolled beneath the rubber soles of my wellingtons and screamed with the sheer joy of being there with my best friends.

CHAPTER NINE

'Fuck,' Josh exploded, standing beside the open Range Rover door. 'Fuck. Fuck. Fuck.'

I stood in the open doorway beside him and surveyed the mess. He smelt rank after three days of shower-less partying in the rain.

'What a fucking mess,' he groaned, his voice thick from the hangover he undoubtedly had now he was coming down from the tablets we'd taken and the oceans of drink we'd downed. 'My dad will kill me.'

The white leather upholstery was streaked with mud. A long pink line of lipstick ran the length of the front passenger seat. The back seat was piled with sodden clothes, abandoned food containers and crushed drink cans. The carpets, once cream, were damp, stained with mud and odd brown stains where we had sat inside out of the rain drinking and laughing.

Poppy squeezed into the gap beside us. 'I'm sorry, I dropped my lipstick,' she said putting a gentle hand on Josh's arm. 'My bad.' Her voice had a whining note like a child pleading for sweets. Josh shrugged her off and began to stalk around the car, muttering about the state of it. I stepped back, watching as he prowled. It did look pretty bad. Mud was splattered all over the once shining black bodywork. Thick red mud was encrusted under the wheel arches.

'We'll get it cleaned before we go home.' Tom was standing at the back of the vehicle, waiting to load the camping equipment.

'Look at the fucking state of this lot.' Josh kicked miserably at the muddy, damp heap of our tents and camping equipment.

'I know my mum's got some carpet cleaner. We'll wipe all this mud off the inside, go through a car wash that will get rid of the mud on the outside,' Tom said, his voice calm, as if he were pacifying a child having a tantrum.

'We'll get coffee while you load up,' I said, gently pulling at Poppy's arm. I hated it when Josh got in a temper. I knew it would be gone as quickly as it had arrived; he didn't simmer with anger, he just exploded and then it was over and done with and forgotten. None of us took him too seriously. Hopefully when we returned with coffee he'd be in a better frame of mind.

As Poppy and I set off towards the catering vans, I glanced back over my shoulder and met Tom's eyes. I pulled an expression of mock horror and caught the look of amusement that flickered across his face at the way Josh was behaving.

We made our way gingerly down the mud-slicked path through the campsite towards the catering vans.

Now the festival was over, everyone was trying to pack up their equipment and get off the camping ground. Tractors were towing vehicles out; a gang of lads were trying to push others. Everyone and everything was covered in mud. Dotted around the campsite, vast skips overflowed with discarded tents, their metal frames and nylon fabric jumbled together with broken seats, inflatable mattresses and sodden sleeping bags.

All around us, people were beginning to make their way out onto the road and towards the ferry back to the mainland and home. Everyone looked exhausted and beyond filthy, their clothes encrusted with mud. What had seemed fun in the heat of the moment, drunk on life, cheap beer and the shared companionship of others was now a layer they couldn't wait to shed.

I longed to be clean again. The shower block near us had stopped working properly on Saturday. The water now tepid and uninviting. There didn't seem to be any point in getting cold and wet in there to get back into chilly, damp, muddy clothes afterwards. My hair was gritty with the red mud which had found its way under my nails and streaked across my face.

'Had a good weekend?' the coffee vendor asked. His expression didn't change at the state of us, he'd been seeing people looking the same all weekend.

We got coffee and made our way slowly up the slope to the Range Rover. The site was already half empty, the tractors working quickly.

When we got back to the car, Josh was in a better mood. 'Thanks,' he said taking the coffee from me. 'We got everything loaded.' He ran a muddy hand through his hair, only succeeding in making it stand up and look more tousled. 'Tom put some cardboard under the camping gear to keep it off the carpets. He found it in one of the skips.'

'Good idea.' I sipped my coffee, smiling at the thought of Tom taking control of the situation and marvelling that he'd managed to find some clean dry cardboard in the war zone that surrounded us.

'Shall we go then?' Poppy hauled open one of the back doors and got in, oblivious to the mud on her wellies.

'Good job I put the remnants of the cardboard on the floor,' Tom said wryly, getting into the passenger seat.

'Well done, four-wheel drive,' Josh said, his voice filled with relief, as the vast vehicle churned its way off the campsite.

The weekend had been amazing, the music fabulous, the company incredible, even the mud and the rain had seemed something to laugh at and bring us closer together. Now it was over though, I longed for the cleanliness of home, for food that wasn't served in a cardboard container and coffee in my favourite blue mug.

'Thank goodness,' Tom breathed, as the Range Rover's enormous tyres hit tarmac and we surged away from the festival. 'Let's hope the queue for the ferry isn't too bad.'

'Or the queue for the car wash when we get to Southampton,' Josh added, his earlier temper dissipated, and his good humour restored.

We grabbed more coffees on the ferry and stood on the outside deck, watching the Isle of Wight slowly retreat into the distance. I'd loved every rain-soaked moment. It had been wonderful to feel like a normal person again.

'Glastonbury next year?' Poppy said, touching her coffee cup against mine in a toast.

'Definitely,' I grinned, slipping my hand into the warmth of Josh's. What could be more fun than being with the three people I loved the most, making plans for our future?

Once on the mainland we found a car wash and followed a line of similarly trashed vehicles into the cleansing machinery. The vehicle emerged shining and as good as new, all trace of the exterior mud washed away.

'We'll stop at my place first,' Tom said, 'Get rid of the camping gear and get the seats and carpets cleaned before you go home.'

'Cool,' Josh said, flicking on the radio and settling back into his seat as he nudged the car into the line of traffic to begin our journey home.

* * * * * * * *

'I'm starving,' Poppy complained an hour later, waking from the doze she'd been in since we left Southampton.

'Me too.' I lifted my head. My neck was stiff from where I'd been resting it against the window, watching the motorway slip by as the powerful Range Rover ate up the miles.

'I'll pull into the next services,' Josh said, turning down the radio and rotating his shoulders to ease the kinks out of his muscles, 'I could do with a break.'

'Two miles,' Tom read off a road sign.

'Burgers, pizza, sandwiches?' Josh said a few moments later as he slowed the car to turn off the motorway into the services.

'Don't mind.' Poppy was wide awake now. 'Definitely need the loo though.'

'I'm going to change,' I told them, reaching in the back for my bag and pulling out my last clean pair of jeans and a rumpled but unmuddy top.

'Me too.' Poppy knelt on her seat to reach into the back and unearthed her bag. In the driver's mirror I saw Josh roll his eyes in mock despair at the mess we were making of his packing.

In the motorway services, Josh found a parking space and deftly eased the big vehicle in between two smaller cars.

'See you back here? Then we'll go for food?' Tom turned to smile at the two of us.

I gave him a thumbs-up sign and followed Poppy across the car park into the toilets.

It felt wonderful to wash my hands and face beneath warm water, even if the paper towels were rough on my skin; at least I was relatively clean.

We settled on pizza, and as we waited for our order to be delivered, we found a corner table and sat down.

A moment later Poppy screamed with delight. She leapt to her feet and hurried across to two girls who were walking across the restaurant. I glanced at Tom and caught his wry smile at her behaviour, a look he swiftly erased as Poppy hurried back to our table with the two girls in tow. From the earliest days of our friendship Poppy had always needed to prove she was as good as everyone else. I had no idea where her feelings of inadequacy came from. There was no need. She was beautiful inside and out, but so naïve, with no understanding of how to be her own person and not want to belong to the tight, ridiculous cliques of malicious girls.

'This is Amber and Velvet.' Poppy pulled the girls into our booth. 'They're at college with me.'

I watched Josh and Tom's eyes flicker over the two tall, slender, extremely glamorous girls. I'm sure Poppy felt as I did, grubby and revolting in the face of their style.

'You've been to the Isle of Wight?' Tom asked.

'Yah,' breathed Amber. She had one of those irritating breathy voices, as if she'd watched too many Marilyn Monroe movies.

'We had a blast,' Velvet drawled. 'Such fun.'

I felt my teeth clench with dislike at the sound of her languid vowels.

'Wasn't the weather awful?' Poppy said, grabbing a knife and fork as the waitress brought our order.

'It looked it,' smiled Amber, raising her finely outlined eyebrows in a gesture of surprise at the huge pizza Poppy was about to tuck into.

Neither girl looked as if they had seen much mud. They were immaculate, their hair glossy and sleek, make-up perfect. Both wore matching pseudo-hippy outfits of tiny shorts, long brown leather boots, clingy Indian tops and brightly decorated waistcoats, definitely channelling their inner Kate Moss.

As if sensing their distaste, Poppy, after wolfing a couple of mouthfuls of her pizza, was picking listlessly at it as if food were the last thing on her mind.

'We were nice and dry,' Amber sighed contentedly. 'Although it did look dreadful when I looked out.'

'My dad got us backstage passes,' Velvet smiled haughtily, showing a line of extremely white, even teeth.

Poppy managed to turn her gasp of jealousy into a cough.

'He's one of the directors of the company which promotes the festival,' Amber informed us with a self-assured smile.

'Lovely,' Poppy breathed, not doing a great job of disguising her jealousy.

'Yah,' Velvet went on, twirling a strand of her glossy dark hair between pale fingers. 'We were partying all weekend with Bruce and Tom Petty.'

'Cool,' I said, forcing myself to speak, determined not to feel belittled in the face of these glamazons even if Tom and Josh were staring at them with open admiration, their pizzas growing cold in front of them.

Amber and Velvet swivelled their heads as if they had just noticed I was there.

'This is my friend, Mia,' Poppy said, quickly, pointing at Tom and Josh, 'my boyfriend, Tom, and Josh, Mia's boyfriend.'

I saw their eyes slide away from me, dismissing my grubby appearance as of no consequence and then glide indolently over Tom and Josh.

'Are you at our college?' Velvet asked, her eyes flickering back to me.

I shook my head.

'Mia's an actress,' Poppy said proudly.

'Yah?' Velvet's eyes held a little more interest. 'What are you in?'

I shrugged, knowing the momentary lift of my status was about to plummet. 'I've just finished a degree in drama at Bristol. I was in a theatre production in Bath. It was my first. I'm auditioning for other roles now.'

Before I could finish speaking Velvet and Amber's attention turned to the boys.

'Where have I seen you before?' Amber asked, touching Josh's arm with pale delicate fingers, topped with long, shining, blood red nails.

'Mia's mum's body has just been found, she was one of those found buried in Cornwall.' Poppy blurted. 'It was in the papers and on television.'

I couldn't believe her utter betrayal of my deepest secret. I felt my cheeks begin to burn as their eyes turned to me.

'The bodies found in a field, buried in barrels?' Velvet said, her voice filled with curiosity.

There was no stopping Poppy now, she had their full attention. 'Mia's father kidnapped her mother, then he killed her after Mia was born.'

Of course, it was more titillating gossip than partying with Bruce Springsteen and Tom Petty. Their eyes turned to me, naked curiosity shining beneath their mascara-laden lashes.

'What?' Amber said, a frown of confusion marring her beautiful face.

'Fuck's sake,' Tom hissed, shaking his head in disbelief at the way Poppy had blurted out my life to two complete strangers in some bizarre demonstration of one-upmanship.

'How could you?' I turned to Poppy, naked rage coursing through my veins. For the whole weekend I had felt normal. I'd been Mia Lewis, the daughter of Carol and Peter, enjoying the chaos of the festival and the company of my friends. Now suddenly, I was exposed in front of two obvious bitches by Poppy in a ridiculous attempt to show them her life was as utterly cool as theirs.

The recent past flooded back over me in a tidal wave of anger and grief. Of course, I wasn't Mia Lewis. I was the daughter of a serial killer. A girl whose mother's body had lain undiscovered for fifteen years, curled in a plastic barrel, submerged in the mud of a windswept field.

'I saw something about that on social media,' Amber said, still looking at me.

Of course. Everyone knew about my past; the media was full of it. So far I'd managed to heed Grace's advice not to look at my social media. I knew why now. I was aware of a whole world of gossip going on. All about my father and the speculation about what he had done.

'Come on, let's go.' Josh pushed his way out of the booth.

Poppy's face was white as I pushed past her, shoving past Amber and Velvet. I was aware of Tom's glance of sympathy as I stalked out of the restaurant in Josh's wake. It felt as if the stench of my past were draped over my shoulders like a cloak.

CHAPTER TEN

'Hope all goes okay today xxx.'

'Thanks,' I quickly replied to Poppy's text message. In the six months that had followed Poppy's shocking announcement to her ridiculous friends in the motorway service restaurant after the Isle of Wight festival I had gradually forgiven her.

'She's such an airhead,' had been Tom's view of what I had seen as Poppy's betrayal. She doesn't mean anything by it, he had told me, trying desperately to plead her case when I hadn't wanted anything more to do with her. She's heartbroken at what she's done, he'd said. I hadn't been convinced, she'd taken my story, my terrible secret and blurted it out to those stupid bitches, just to impress them.

Gradually though, as the months passed, I relented. What else could I do? She was my oldest friend, part of the circle of friends with Tom, Josh and myself.

The pain of her betrayal still stung, though. Even though on the surface we were friends again, still I felt distanced from her, unwilling to share my confidences with her.

'What time is Josh coming?' Dad asked, draining the last of his breakfast coffee.

'Soon,' I said, glancing at my watch.

'I feel terrible we aren't going with you.' Dad got to his feet, crossed the room, stood behind my chair and bent to put his arms around me. I could smell his aftershave and the coffee on his breath.

'Dad, it's okay, I'll be fine with Josh.' I put my hand on his arm where it was wrapped around my shoulders. I could feel the warmth of his skin through the cotton fabric of his striped shirt. He dropped a kiss loudly on the top of my head.

'That bloody horse,' he said straightening up and releasing me. 'Time you handed him over to Mia. She's the only one who can ride the damn creature.' He directed his words across the table to Mum who sat, white-faced, one arm tucked into the makeshift sling one of her livery clients had put it in when she had fallen off Solar the previous evening.

'I'm fine,' she'd said then, picking herself up off the sandy surface of the arena after Solar had managed to dump her during a particularly spectacular bucking display.

'That was a horrible fall,' said Rosie Barker, one of Mum's clients, who had been leaning against the arena fence beside me. Rosie, who worked as a nurse, had fussed around Mum, insisting she should go to hospital, worried that she had broken her arm in the heavy fall.

'Honestly, I'm fine,' Mum had said, holding her arm into her stomach. 'Just banged my funny bone. Please don't fuss.'

This morning though it had been clear that she wasn't fine. She said her arm ached horribly, and she was in quite a lot of pain.

'We should be with you. I've let you down again.' Mum's face was grey with pain.

'Mum, honestly, you need to go to hospital to get your arm looked at.'

Whilst I was glad my parents weren't coming to my mother's funeral, I was also sorry they wouldn't be there to shield me from the pain.

It was hard to imagine I was going to see my mother's remains put back into the ground, this time in a graveyard, in a proper coffin. I couldn't imagine either, that today I would meet, or at least see my grandmother and my aunts.

The occasion was so momentous that my brain felt numb to what was happening.

Hearing Josh's car outside I gently kissed Mum's pale cheek. 'Please text me to let me know what they say at the hospital.'

'Thanks for doing this, Josh,' I said, settling myself into the passenger seat.

'It's ok. You couldn't go on your own.'

I made a noise to show my agreement, my mouth dry now we were on our way. I'd been dreading this day ever since Grace had telephoned to tell me my mother's body had been released and the funeral arranged. It felt strange to mourn someone I had never known, and yet who I had been mourning all my life.

Josh's sports car ate up the miles quickly. We sped onto the M4, then the M5 before stopping at Exeter to get coffee.

'Last services in civilisation. This is where the motorway ends.' Josh handed me a coffee cup. 'We've another three hours to go and all on dual carriageway. It's a nightmare going to Cornwall to surf.'

I nodded, only half listening to him, trying to force the coffee through lips that felt as dry as parchment.

'Didn't you want Tom and Poppy to come?' Josh started the car and reversed expertly out of the parking space.

'No.' I sipped my coffee, unable to frame the words to explain to him why I didn't want them there. Apart from giving Poppy more gossip to blurt out to random strangers, I couldn't imagine the two halves of my life merging.

There'd been no choice but to have Josh with me. My parents were worried about me driving alone to the isolated village where my mother was to be buried, as if the trauma would render me incapable of steering and operating the pedals.

Josh accelerated out of the motorway services and joined the long ribbon of dual carriageway which snaked its way into Cornwall. The route took us across the cold and windswept December wilds of Bodmin Moor. We bypassed Truro and continued west. The rolling hillsides stretched out at every side, broken only by the solitary ruins of the mine ventilation shafts which had once been Cornwall's lifeblood. At Marazion we stopped to buy more coffee from a café overlooking St Michael's Mount.

Penzance was already festooned in Christmas lights, shoppers hurrying along the busy streets. 'Look,' Josh pointed, 'there's one of the gold post boxes. That one must be for Helen Glover, the rower. She got a gold in the Olympics.'

Dragging my attention to Josh I made a noise of agreement.

'Our first gold of the 2012 games. First ever for a woman rower,' Josh continued proudly.

His words blurred into white noise as I fought the nausea that filled my mouth with bile.

We continued along the coast road, winding our way through narrow lanes and tiny villages, the houses colourfully painted in pastel shades.

Finally, Josh bumped the car up onto a grass verge and turned off the engine.

The silence was broken only by the sound of the engine ticking as it cooled and seagulls wheeling in the air above us.

'This is it,' Josh said, taking the key out of the ignition. He fizzed with energy. Movement was the only way for him to deal with the emotion he clearly felt resonating from me.

I stared out of the car windscreen, looking at the huddled tangle of stone-built houses in front of us.

This was the village where my mother had grown up. Ahead of us stretched a narrow lane, bordered by stone walls. At the far end of the lane, beside a wide grassy square, was the church, the clock on its square tower marking the half hour. Thirty minutes until my mother's funeral began.

Which had been her home, I wondered, looking at the village. Which was the house she had left the day my father kidnapped her. Was it one of the houses festooned with climbing ivy, or wisteria, or was it one of the more austere ones, its stone naked, exposed to the wind?

'Mia?'

I glanced up to see Grace leaning into Josh's window.

'Hi.' I forced my lips into a semblance of a smile.

'Can I get in for a minute?' Grace directed her enquiry at Josh.

'Sure,' he nodded, as Grace opened the back door and slid into the seat. She looked different, older, elegant in a dark suit which was a world away from her usual jeans.

'How are you doing?' she asked.

'Okay,' I lied.

'I'll go in with you,' Grace said, her eyes locking on mine.

'Which was my mother's home?' I asked, forcing the words out through the tightness of my throat.

'There.' Grace pointed. 'The one with the wisteria growing up the front.'

With my eyes I followed where she had pointed. That was my mother's home, where she had grown up, where her mother still lived.

'Will Mia's grandmother and aunts meet her?' Josh asked, restlessly turning the car ignition key over in his hand.

I heard Grace's sharp intake of breath, saw her eyes flicker first over me and then down the road towards the church where people were beginning to assemble.

'They asked not,' she said, framing her words carefully. 'They said everything was too raw, the loss of Glanna, wondering for the last twenty years if she was alive and now...' Grace met my eyes and smiled gently. 'Leave them for now. Hopefully when things are easier, they will want to meet you.'

I nodded. The pain of their rejection was unbearable, but there was nothing I could do to force them to meet me.

'Will they know who I am?' I asked. It would be easy for me to tell who they were, of course, they'd be following the coffin, but would they know who I was? 'They know you're coming. They know I'll be with you,' Grace said. 'They'll recognise you anyway. You're very like your mum.'

'Should we go?' Josh was clearly itching to get out of the car and get on with the proceedings.

'Hang on.' Grace put a steady hand on his shoulder to stop him.

'This is for you.' Grace held a delicate silver bracelet out towards me. 'It was your mum's. Her family didn't recognise it. They said you could have it.'

Grace gently dropped the bracelet into my open hand. It coiled there, a thick rope of silver. I could feel the weight of it in my palm. I realised it must have been on her body, buried with her.

Josh ran his tongue around his lips, making a slight smacking noise. I realised I'd been staring at the coil of silver; that both he and Grace were expecting me to do something with it.

'Will you put this on me, please?' The strand of silver was damp from my sweating palms.

'Sure,' Josh whispered back, taking the bracelet in fingers that seemed too big and clumsy to handle it. Grace shifted with impatience, as if she longed to take over the job and do it quickly but felt she should not intervene. He fumbled with the clasp and finally managed to get it fastened

'Thank you.' I touched the bracelet, feeling the pattern of the strands of silver where they were interwoven beneath my fingers. This had been taken off what remained of my mother's wrist by someone in the mortuary. The silver still shone. I wondered if they'd had to clean it before they gave it to me. What had it had looked like spending so long with the putrefying remains? I wondered when it had been put on her. Had my father given it to her, an attempt to force her to love him? Or had it been part of some strange mind game he had played, trying to make her into the willing lover she clearly hadn't been. I turned the metal over and over around my wrist, part of me wanting to tear it off and fling it away, yet treasuring the fragile connection with my mother. I'd no idea what the bracelet meant to her, or him. My one tentative, fragile link to them.

'Come on.' Josh opened his car door, letting in the bitterly cold winter air.

A harsh wind whipped around our bodies, rattling the bare branches of the trees.

'We'll go in, get seats.' Grace steered us past a group of people who stood on the green outside the church. I kept my head down, not wanting to see their curious expressions, to know if they realised who I was.

The church smelt of old stone, damp and dust. Grace directed us to a pew at the back. I wondered had she arranged with my mother's family to keep us out of sight, where we would not upset anyone. The scalding hot pipe which ran beside our pew did little to lift the temperature of the frigid air.

In front of us the seats were crowded, occasionally a curious person turned, as if to see who was coming in and would openly stare at us.

I shivered uncontrollably; my legs trembled so much I could feel them knocking against the wooden pew. Josh took my icy hand in his huge warm one and chafed at it distractedly to restore some warmth to my fingers. On the other side of me, Grace guardedly pulled out her mobile and quickly read through her messages.

As the first notes of music rang out the congregation got to their feet. Grace hastily completed a text before dropping the phone into her bag.

'Are they playing the Titanic theme?' Josh hissed in my ear, his breath warm against my cheek.

'Yes,' I whispered. It must have been a tune that had meaning to my mother's family. Had it been one of her favourites, I wondered? The light in the church changed as the door opened. The congregation turned in one movement, all eyes to the back of the building. I saw Grace glance at me, concern in her eyes as they met mine. A slight smile of reassurance lifted the corners of her lips.

My mother's coffin, shouldered by four men and two women, who I guessed must be my aunts, made its way slowly down the aisle. The coffin was wicker, a single spray of white flowers resting on top of it. There was no sign of the arrangement of red roses I'd sent.

Behind the coffin walked an elderly woman. My grandmother. As they passed, I could see one of the women, the other was hidden behind the coffin. She was tall; her face, ravaged from weeping, stared fixedly forwards. I longed to touch the coffin, to be close to my mother, to feel some connection with the woman who had given birth to me. I didn't move. Instead I remained standing tucked out of sight just as Grace said my grandmother had requested.

As the procession made its way down the aisle, I could see my grandmother's dark eyes flickering from side to side. She was looking, I knew, for me. The hair curling over her collar was grey beneath her wide-brimmed black hat. She was wrapped against the cold in an elegant black coat. Her face was reddened with crying, yet she held herself proudly as she walked behind her daughter's coffin. As she drew level with where we were standing, even though we were positioned away from the aisle, some sense made her turn. She looked directly at me. She met my eye and held my gaze as I looked for the first time into my grandmother's eyes.

CHAPTER ELEVEN

The music stopped abruptly, drawing my attention back to her coffin, now at the end of its journey to the altar. Her mother and sisters must have imagined that she would have one day walked down the aisle, to marry someone she loved. They could never have anticipated before she went missing that this would be the way she would go down the aisle, finally returned to her family after so many years of hoping and wondering.

Beside me, Grace gently squeezed my arm. 'Okay?' she whispered, her breath blowing a stray tendril of my hair.

I nodded. A lie of course.

The congregation shuffled their feet. There were loud sniffs. At the far side of the church someone was crying, a noise of pure anguish. The priest, who I hadn't noticed until he appeared at the head of the coffin, stood silently, head bowed.

After what seemed like an eternity, he raised his head. A ray of sunlight bursting in through a window to one side of him shone on his silver hair. He looked slowly over the congregation, pausing to smile gently at my mother's family before his eyes flickered over the rest of the congregation. He must have known I was there and was seeking me out. I bowed my head, not wanting to meet his gaze and see the curiosity and sympathy I was sure would be there.

'Today,' he began finally, his voice expanding to fill the ancient stone enclosure of the church, 'is a day to rejoice.' I doubted anyone in the church agreed with him, especially my mother's family whose weeping echoed in the dusty space. 'Today we celebrate the life of Glanna.'

There was an expectant silence as the priest fumbled to get his reading glasses out of a pocket and unfold the sheet of paper he held. He began to speak again, his voice toneless, professional. Even to me, an outsider, it was clear he hadn't known my mother, had no knowledge of who he was talking about. The person he described, from the words I presumed my aunts or grandmother had written, was as vague and insubstantial to him as she was to me.

Beside me, Grace twisted an ornate gold ring around her middle finger. I could hear Josh breathing. I focused on the words the priest was saying. I wanted to absorb every detail of my mother's character and life from those who had known and loved her. Maybe, through their descriptions, I would become familiar with the woman who had given birth to me.

I learned of a child who had loved playing on the beach, who had a wild, independent character, who loved easily, laughed a lot. I heard about the student who worked hard, who found her studies easy, especially English. The priest spoke of a woman who loved learning languages and after leaving school was fluent in both French and Spanish. I discovered a person who was kind, gentle, someone who could be relied on in a crisis, and would always have a sense of humour. She loved music; Madonna, Michael Jackson, Queen. Reading was just one of her pastimes, her favourite book *A Year in Provence,* somewhere she had intended to visit one day. His words faded into silence, the awareness of the future which had been denied her hanging in the air.

The priest ended his description of my mother and began her funeral service. One of my mother's sisters, my aunt, spoke, echoing the priest's words, talking about the long years Glanna had been missing and their relief she was now home. Back where she belonged.

Round and round Grace turned her ring. I focused on that, struggling to absorb my aunt's words. The pain she spoke of was so raw.

I was the result of their anguish.

The service ended, with the priest sharing the invitation from Glanna's family to anyone who wanted to join them at the house for tea and sandwiches. I doubted the invitation was meant for me.

My mother's coffin was taken out of the church, wheeled on the trolley it had rested on for the service.

'Your mum is being buried with her father,' Grace said, quietly getting to her feet.

I focused on fastening the buttons on my coat, rather than watching the procession make its way down the aisle. I was aware of the coffin moving over the granite slabs. One of the wheels of the gurney the coffin now rested on squeaked slightly, the noise loud in the silence of the church. From outside came the noise of a car driving past the church and a seagull's harsh cry.

Around us the congregation were beginning to move, stepping out of their pews to follow my mother's family, shuffling slowly as if reluctant to see the coffin being lowered into the ground.

Grace led the way out of the pew. 'Are you okay?' Her voice was gentle.

I moved my head in what I hoped would be interpreted as agreement.

'Will we go to the burial?' Josh whispered. His voice, I felt, filled with the hope I'd want to leave.

I met his eyes. 'Yes.' I didn't want to be there, to watch my mother's remains slide back into the earth once more, but I needed to stay, to be close to her and those who loved her.

I led the way out of the church, joining the slow-moving procession of people out of the timeless air of the church into the bitterly cold December wind.

Outside the clouds had gathered, a dark, angry grey line crouched on the horizon. A vicious wind whipped at our clothes, snatching at our breath. I made my way to where the mourners had gathered around the coffin and positioned myself on the edge of the group, Josh and Grace behind me. I leant into the warmth of Josh's body, feeling his arms enfold me as if he could protect me from the scene before us.

The priest began to speak, his words indistinct, whipped away by the force of the wind. As my mother's coffin was slowly lowered into the ground, I looked up at the people around the grave, their heads bowed, staring at the gaping hole.

I glanced at my family. My grandmother was staring at me. I held her gaze for a fraction of a second before mine darted away, to stare at the churned red earth at my feet. It was long enough for me to feel the full force of her hatred. In that brief moment I could see a glimpse of my mother in the shape of her face, the slant of her eyes. Her eyes, when they'd met mine blazed with contempt.

The funeral was over. My grandmother, sobbing with rage at the loss of her daughter, was led slowly away. There was nothing more for us to do now but leave.

'I'll talk to you soon.' Grace, drew me into the warmth of her body. I stood there, breathing in the faint smell of her shampoo, not wanting to stand alone. She gently untangled herself from me. 'Sorry, but I need to get back to the office.'

I watched her walk away, eating up the ground with her long stride as if she couldn't get away fast enough.

'Home?' Josh said, taking my arm.

I turned as a hand touched my other arm. 'Mia?' My aunt, the one who had spoken about my mother stood beside me. She was taller than me, her hair lighter and straighter, but I recognised the shape of my face in hers. For a woman who I knew was in her forties, she had the clear skin and taut figure of someone much younger.

I nodded, opening my mouth to speak but unable to form any words.

'I'm Morwenna, Glanna's sister. I'm your aunt. Thank you for coming.' Her tone was soft, her accent clearly Cornish. 'This is very hard for all of us.'

I nodded again, longing to touch her, to feel someone who shared my mother's genes. 'Yes.' My throat finally released the single word. Her eyes locked onto mine; green, flecked with hazel, a dark ring circling the pupil. I knew from the photograph that mother's eyes had been the same as hers. Mine were brown, my parents' genes mingling, swirling together, the parts that made me spinning out of the mix to create the combined version of them. I couldn't imagine the courage it must have taken for her to come and talk to me, when she must hate me, despise everything I stood for.

'I'm your mum's older sister.' I felt my fingers tighten their grip on Josh's. Heard his intake of breath as I unknowingly squeezed his fingers too tight.

'You've had a long journey,' Morwenna continued. 'Come back to the house if you want to. It's just up the road, the one with the wisteria. I don't think Mum will be able to talk to you, but if you want to…' She paused, her words fading to nothingness.

'We understand. Completely. It's kind of you to ask us.' Josh spoke when I couldn't. Morwenna moved her head slowly to look at him, unwilling to shift her gaze from me.

'Josh,' Josh disentangled his hand from mine and held his towards Morwenna.

She looked at it uncertainly for a moment before brushing hers against his for the briefest of moments as if he, by association were as tarnished as I.

'We'd love to,' he said.

Morwenna nodded, her eyes flickering over mine. There was a fleeting moment when I thought I should offer her my hand, but she stepped quickly away, and the opportunity was gone.

We followed the line of people, out of the graveyard and up the narrow lane into the village. Had my mother known all these people? I wondered. Beneath the soles of my shoes the lane felt rough, its surface bumpy. Without Josh gently propelling me along towards the stone-built cottage I would have remained on the lane, wanting to soak up the essence of my mother, as if by treading in her footsteps I could feel closer to her.

'Nice house,' Josh said inanely, clearly needing to fill the silence between us. He pushed open the garden gate and stepped onto the stone flagged path. The gate was old, faded, the path hollowed by the generations who had trodden it. I let my fingers linger on the chipped paintwork of the gate, wanting to be where my mother had been, feel the things she had felt.

We walked past flower borders, bare, bar a few determined looking plants, the soil around them neatly turned, ready for spring.

Josh stood to one side to let me enter the cottage. It smelt of coffee, hot food and the heady aroma of flowers overflowing from a vase on a table in the hall. I touched the bannister of the stairs, longing to feel anything with the vaguest association with my mother. The dark wood was smooth and cool beneath my fingers.

'We should go in.' Josh encouraged me gently along the hallway.

The cottage was crowded, the buzz of conversation filling the downstairs rooms.

Morwenna came out of the kitchen. 'Good. You came.' Her voice was brisk. As she came towards us I could smell brandy on her breath. Behind her in the open doorway between the crowds of people, I could see a pine table, pale blue cupboards. My grandmother stood in the kitchen, a crowd surrounding her. Her eyes met mine, icy cold, filled with bitter hatred.

'Come into the lounge.' Morwenna's hand gave my arm the briefest of touches, turning me. Josh and I followed her into a room crowded with people. I was aware of their gaze on me. 'There's tea. Sandwiches.' I looked around the room, seeing for the first time the surroundings in which my mother had spent most of her life.

My eyes swept over a dark wood floor, dark furniture, a bookcase crowded with books. Over the fireplace was a huge photograph of my mother, smiling, her hair swept back, blowing in the wind. She was grinning at the camera, behind her a beach, with a line of grey sea stretching into the distance. She was younger in the picture than I was now. She had been barely nineteen when my father had snatched her. Her whole life should have been ahead of her. I should never have existed.

A woman sitting on a pale coloured sofa, got abruptly to her feet as we came into the room and hurried out. I saw Morwenna's eyes meet hers, saw the anger there, before she was gone. My other aunt. I remembered her from the funeral.

For a moment Morwenna stood beside us, her hands clenching and unclenching as if she was regretting her decision.

'That was one of the last days out we had together,' she said, seeing me look at my mother's picture. 'We were at the beach near Hayle.'

I watched her speak, watched the way her lips moved, the line of her teeth. I knew there were echoes of my mother in her every movement. 'A great day, we were so happy…' Her voice faded to nothing. Her mouth shut with a finality that made me wonder if she would ever discuss her sister again.

I stared at the wooden floor, at the lines between each plank, at the knots and dents. I couldn't speak, couldn't answer her. Everything she spoke about, the memories she had, the future she should have shared with my mother was gone. Because of my father. Because of me.

'Help yourself to food, Josh.' Morwenna gestured towards the laden table at one side of the room. 'You must be hungry. You've had a long journey.' She spoke as if afraid to stop, the words tumbling out of her mouth.

'Sandwich, Mia?' Josh strode across the room. His voice jarred. Morwenna and I were locked together, no one else existed only us. Trapped in our private hell.

'I'm sorry Mum doesn't…' Morwenna said, as Josh walked away.

'Or Kervana. It's too much for them… knowing you…'

I nodded. 'It's ok.' My voice was scarcely more than a whisper. 'I'm so sorry.' I wanted to get to my knees, plead with Morwenna to forgive me for my father's actions and me for existing.

'It's not your fault.' Morwenna's voice cracked. Her eyes closed as if she could blot out everything that was happening.

There was a silence between us while the hum of conversation went on in the room. After a moment she opened her eyes, seeming to force herself away from the hell of loss she was floundering in and to focus on me. 'It's impossible for you to ever be here again. It's too much for us to bear.'

I forced my head to nod in agreement. She was right. I wasn't wanted here.

'Ask me anything about her, while you're here. You must wonder what she was like.' Morwenna said.

I was silent, my mind trying to make sense of the jumble of questions I had. 'What was…' my words faded into silence.

'Do you want to see Glanna's room?' Morwenna's voice cut into my thoughts.

I nodded eagerly, a moment later I was following her up a narrow set of stairs. She pushed open a door and stood back. 'It's just as she left it.'

CHAPTER TWELVE

Below us the hum of noise continued. I could hear snatches of conversation, the clink of glasses, a sudden unexpected peel of laughter cut short as if its owner had been horrified at its inappropriateness.

'I'm sorry about Mum and Kervana. They don't feel able to meet you.'

I nodded, pretending it didn't matter. I met Morwenna's eye. 'Is this okay?' I paused on the edge of my mother's room, longing to go in and yet afraid.

'Go on,' she raised one hand in a gesture to move me forwards.

I stepped slowly into my mother's room.

'It's like she's just gone out for a walk,' Morwenna's voice was barely more than a whisper as if she were afraid to break the spell that seemed to hang over the room.

She pushed the door closed behind us, shutting out the noise from below, before moving past me and bending to straighten the purple duvet on the bed. 'Kervana and I had to share,' Morwenna sat on my mother's bed. 'Glanna had her own room.'

She turned slightly to look out of the window. I followed her eyes, looking at the windswept hillside beyond the neat garden. The grass was dead, brown, the strands whipped by the wind. A single clump of gorse had yellow flowers on it as if it had mistaken the season. Further up the hill stood a solitary tree, bent against the wind. The scene my mother must have looked out on every day.

'Even after she'd gone, Mum kept her room, in case she came back,' Morwenna continued. She got up as if filled with a restless energy which wouldn't let her rest.

'She won't now.' My aunt moved to the window and stood looking out. I stared at the pale-coloured carpet, unable to bear looking at her, hearing the bitterness in her voice and knowing my father had caused that pain.

'We, Kervana and I, moved out years ago.' Morwenna returned to sit on the edge of my mother's bed once more.

Their lives had gone on, they'd grown up, gone on to have existences of their own, while my mother's had stalled the day she went missing. They had become adults, while she would always be a teenager, denied the right of adulthood by her death.

'We live in the village.' I saw her hand lift as she pointed in the vague direction of the huddle of houses. 'Mum turned our room into a sewing room. She started making quilts after Glanna...' Morwenna turned back to me. Silhouetted against the pale wintery light from the window, it was impossible to read her expression. 'But she never changed this one.'

Aware that I hadn't moved since we had entered the room I turned slowly, wanting to absorb the presence of my mother by being in places she had. There was a hushed air in the room as if it waited patiently for its owner's return. The air smelt, not dusty and stale as I had expected, but of the vase of roses on the bedside table. I was painfully aware that while I missed my mother, her family longed for her presence, the things she did, her chatter, her life.

I took an uncertain stride forwards, aware of Morwenna's eyes on me. I wanted to throw myself onto my mother's bed, bury my head into her pillow to see if any trace, her perfume or stray hairs, remained that I could hold close to me. But with Morwenna there, I instead moved to her bookcase. Stretching from floor to ceiling, built into a recess to one side of the fireplace the bookshelves were crowded with paperbacks. Titles and authors I mostly did not recognise. I ran a tentative finger along the spines. My mother had touched these, chosen them, read them, absorbed their detail. They were part of her.

The shelf space in front of the books was dotted with shells, glittery rocks, a heap of bracelets and necklaces.

'What was she like?' I asked, breaking the thickness of the silence.

'My mum?' It was the first time I had called her that to Morwenna. It felt like an act of utter bravery, claiming her as mine.

Behind me I heard Morwenna swallow, the noise harsh in the hushed room. 'She was amazing.'

I turned, Morwenna's words hanging in the air between us. I continued my tentative exploration of the room. On the table beside the bed was a heap of books, a glossy pink stone, a tube of half-used hand cream from the Body Shop. I picked up the hand cream tube. My mother had held this, bought it, used it. Her fingers had been where mine were. I put it down, gingerly, afraid to make any noise in the room.

'Please tell me about her.' I lowered myself onto the bed at the opposite end to Morwenna. The bed was pushed against one wall. A line of stuffed animals and fluffy cushions lined the border between the bed and the wall. I wished Morwenna had left me alone here, I longed to pick up the animals, hold them to my face, be where my mother had been.

Time seemed to have stopped. I was aware of Josh, downstairs, his discomfort at being abandoned amongst my mother's family. I should go back to him, but I could not. I needed to be here, beside my aunt, absorbing every detail I could of my mother and her life.

'I'm the oldest,' Morwenna said. 'Two years older than Kervana and four older than Glanna.'

I listened, letting my eyes rove slowly around the room as she spoke. There was a line of shoes neatly laid out beside a pine wardrobe, purple Doc Martens, towering high heels, summery sandals.

She paused suddenly. 'What do you want me to tell you about?'

'Everything,' I said.

Morwenna took a deep breath and slowly exhaled. 'She was in her second year at Exeter. She was doing a business degree with Spanish.'

My impression from the array of shoes, the swirly prints on the wall and the brightly coloured fabric that poked through the gap in the wardrobe doors had been of someone arty. It was hard to envisage my mother as someone doing a business degree. I'd imagined her as an artist, gentle, ethereal.

'She was just about to move out of here. Into a flat in Exeter with one of her friends.'

Morwenna took a long breath and exhaled in a juddering sigh. 'Mum was dead against it.'

I focused on the jumble of fabrics poking out of the wardrobe, bright colours, blues, purples, something yellow with flowers. I wanted to wrench open the door, burrow in amongst the fabric, bury my face in the clothes my mother had worn.

'She was so funny,' Morwenna continued. In her anguish she'd begun to rub her hands against each other, in a slow, distracted motion, her fingers sweeping over the back of the alternate hand before continuing their journey down her fingertips, onto her palms and back again. 'She could twist Dad around her little finger.' Morwenna gave a small snort of amusement. 'She'd always get her own way. She could get away with murder.'

The word slipped out, was released, hanging in the air between us before Morwenna could stop it. She swallowed loudly, the room filled with the sound of her harsh breathing.

'Hard to imagine she's been gone so long.'

It was the first time since we had come into the room we had spoken of my mother's death.

I daren't speak in case I broke the spell that seemed to have been cast over us. We were alone, yet the presence of my mother hovered very close to us.

'She'd be in her forties now.' Morwenna stopped the compulsive twisting of her fingers and instead rested her hands on her thighs, kneading at the fabric of her skirt. 'So many memories,' she continued, her voice stronger, as if she had closed a door on the presence of my mother's death and instead chosen to focus on happier memories. 'She loved the beach, walking in the woods. She drank cider by the gallon. There was a boyfriend too, Ryan Adams. We used to laugh about that. Ryan Adams. Like Bryan Adams.'

I held my breath, not daring to speak in case I stopped her from sharing her memories. I wanted to soak up every bit of information like a sponge, so that I could hold it close to me, pick over it in the quiet moments when I felt her loss most keenly.

'She'd have loved you,' Morwenna said, softly. She tilted her head to meet my eyes. 'She loved children. Always talked about the big family she wanted.' Morwenna closed her eyes, shaking her head slowly at the memory. 'After the chaos we lived in, three girls fighting, she still wanted a massive family of her own.'

I swallowed hard to move the lump that seemed to constrict my throat. I wanted to howl with the pain but was determined not to. I couldn't waste time crying when I longed to hear all about my mother.

'Do you want to see some photos of her?' Morwenna asked, but then without waiting for a reply she pushed herself off the bed and crossed the room to the wardrobe. As she pulled open the doors, I caught a glimpse of my mother's clothes, the brightly coloured fabric I had glimpsed through the gap. A musty smell overlaid the powerful scent of the roses. Inside the wardrobe were dresses, glittery, floaty, bright coloured fabric. Jeans and trousers hung on jumbled hangers beside skirts of different lengths. Beneath the clothes, the bottom of the wardrobe was piled with neatly stacked sweaters, what looked like a jewellery box was pushed against the back wall. To one side of the clothes were shelves, heaped with yet more books, makeup, perfume, the jumbled chaos of my mother's everyday life.

Morwenna pulled out a stack of photograph albums and returned to the bed, letting them fall onto the quilt between us.

'Here,' she pulled one towards us, opened it and began to flick through it. 'She's a baby here.' Morwenna began to turn the pages; beneath the plastic envelopes I saw a record of my mother's life. 'Such a gorgeous baby.' Morwenna's voice took on a teasing lilt as if by its own vocation, as if she were used to the jokey banter with Glanna.

In the photographs I saw my mother, smiling at the camera, all chubby legs and arms, topped with a happy face and a mass of hair. There were no photographs of me as a baby. No record of me existed until I was nine and was adopted by my parents.

'Starting school,' Morwenna turned the pages. My mother grinned at the camera, her expression filled with confidence outside a stone building I assumed was the local school.

'We're on the beach. Here.' Morwenna, handed me the album. 'You look.'

I flicked through the pages, soaking up my mother's childhood. I didn't remember trips to the beach as a child, trips anywhere. I'd no memory of anything apart from the vaguest impression of the farm where I spent my early years.

How old had I been when my mother had died? Unanswered questions spooled through my mind as I turned the stiff, plastic coated pages of the album. Had we been together for part of my childhood? Had she loved me, found pleasure in caring for me, even though she was held prisoner by my father? Did my presence make up for a life in captivity? Had she been forced to stay because of me? Could she have run and didn't because she didn't want to leave me? Was I the reason she'd died?

'Thank you for letting me see these,' I handed the albums back to Morwenna, not wanting to take my hands off them, wanting to keep the images of my mother with me forever.

'I'm glad you've seen them.' Morwenna stood, crossed the room and pushed the albums back into their place in the wardrobe. There was a finality in her voice that I understood instantly. I wouldn't be welcome to come back here. I'd been allowed into the family for this sliver of time, but that was it. Once today was over they wanted Glanna back. My mother's past would be closed to me forever.

'Shall we…?' Morwenna closed the wardrobe door, carefully tucking in the stray fabric so the doors closed properly.

I stood, aware suddenly that we must have been upstairs for a long time, that the noise levels from downstairs had fallen, the hum of conversation quieter now. I could pick out individual voices, Josh talking to someone.

'What are you doing in here?' The bedroom door burst open and my grandmother stood in the doorway. Her cheeks blazed with colour below eyes red-rimmed from crying.

'I'm just showing Mia Glanna's r…' Morwenna began, coming to stand beside me as if to protect me from the obvious wrath.

'Get out,' she snapped, her voice high, shrill. Behind her, in the rooms downstairs a hush descended.

'We're not doing any harm.' Morwenna's voice was gentle, her words slow as if she were trying to calm a terrified animal.

'I just wanted to see my mum's room.'

My grandmother wheeled in my direction, her eyes locking onto mine. 'I don't want you here,' she spat. Her lips curled over a line of age yellowed teeth. 'You don't belong here.' A droplet of spittle, sprayed in her vehemence, hit my cheek, cold against the warmth of my skin.

'This is my daughter's room,' she spoke coldly now. 'You're no part of her. You belong to whatever bastard sired you.'

'Mum…we agreed she could come.' Morwenna took a stride backwards away from the force of her mother's words. 'Mum, this is Glanna's daughter. Mia is part of Glanna.'

'I want her gone, now!' My grandmother's voice rose again.

'I'm sorry.' My words were little more than a whisper. I took a stride forwards, needing to get out of the room. Slowly my grandmother moved aside to let me pass, drawing herself away from me as if the very touch of me were repulsive.

I made my way downstairs on legs that trembled, while above an argument raged. 'Can we go please?' Josh, hearing the row, was already waiting beside the front door.

I glimpsed the faces in the lounge. Kervana, my other aunt, glared at me coldly. We wrenched open the door and hurried out into the bitter winter afternoon.

Josh pulled slowly out of the parking spot on the grass verge. The tyres crunched on the rough lane. Looking out of the side window as we glided past the church, I could see the dark rectangle where my mother's body had been returned once more to the earth.

CHAPTER THIRTEEN

'She didn't mean it against you.' Tom took a sip of his gingerbread latte and smacked his lips appreciatively. 'Think what she's been through, losing a daughter, not knowing if she was dead or alive for all those years and then finding out she was dead.'

I traced a circle in the spilt liquid of my sweet, sickly Black Forest latte, before slowly raising my head and looking at Tom. He'd listened patiently, yet again to me recounting the day of my meeting with my mother's family and how much my grandmother's rejection had hurt me.

'Think how you'd feel.' He unwound his scarf, finally heating up in the warmth of the café after the bitter cold December sleet outside.

I tipped my chin in an impression of a nod. I couldn't think about how my grandmother felt. I had enough horror of my own to deal with. In the weeks after my mother's funeral I had replayed the confrontation with my grandmother over and over again, each time quailing inwardly at the hatred she'd directed against me.

I'd told my parents that everything had gone well. I'd vaguely mentioned meeting Morwenna. I couldn't bear to share the pain of the funeral, my grandmother's aggression. The Mia who had gone to Cornwall was a different one from their daughter. It was impossible to share those hours with them. I didn't want to feel their sympathy, for them to try to make sense of my grandmother's actions.

I couldn't share the pleasure I had felt looking at the photographs of my mother. I loved them both so much; they'd made me feel safe and secure when my whole world had rocked on its axis. I'd pushed Cornwall to the very back of my mind, put those memories behind a wall of steel I never opened. To want to go back, to delve into my origins seemed an utter betrayal of what they had done for me.

Josh, when I tried to talk to him about it on the way home after the funeral, had brushed away my upset, telling me my grandmother and Kervana would get over it, that we'd go again and they'd be nicer, have adjusted to the idea of having me in their lives. I knew they would not. I'd felt the full force of their hatred.

I'd wondered if I'd ever see Morwenna again or if she would cave in to the pressure of her mother and ostracise me. I'd no idea where she lived, or even what her surname was. She'd pointed out her husband to me and I had a hazy memory of her mentioning sons too. There had been so many people crammed into the cottage I could not separate one face from another.

'Give her time,' Tom continued. 'I bet eventually they'll come around to having you in their lives.'

'Perhaps.' I drank more of my latte, wincing at its milky sweetness.

I couldn't imagine my grandmother ever softening to the idea of me. Every time she looked at me, she would remember my father. Just being near me would remind her of the loss of Glanna, what had happened to her, the last contact they'd had before she had disappeared.

It was hard to imagine that pain. The confusion and worry when someone vanished without a trace, wondering if they had gone away through choice, if they'd had an accident and were lying somewhere, in pain. Or if, like my mother, they had been taken, snatched from their family by someone who would rape and murder them.

'I don't really even know what happened to her.' I met Tom's eyes.

'I know,' he said gently, his expression filled with concern. 'Perhaps it's as well you don't.'

Perhaps he was right. Maybe it was good that I didn't know the truth about what had happened to my mother. What my father had done. It was bad enough to know that he had snatched her and then later, at some stage after I had been born, something had happened and he had killed her. Not only her, but other women.

I couldn't look into Tom's eyes any longer and mine slid away, gazing around the festive café. Tinsel hung from every available place, along with posters advertising special seasonal drinks and food.

'What fucking kind of genes are floating around in me?' I closed my eyes, wanting to block out the images that played in my imagination.

'Stop, Mia.' Tom reached across the table and put his hand over my wrist, as if by holding onto me he could stop the dizzy journey my imagination was taking.

All around us the tables were crowded with exhausted looking shoppers, weighed down with the hats, coats and scarves they wore and hauling heavy shopping bags around. In a few weeks Christmas would be over, and everyone would be complaining about how hard up they were. The festivities seemed pointless. I'd no Christmas spirit at all this year. Normally I'd be busy at home helping Mum and Dad put up the tree and decorations. This year though everything seemed so forced.

Tom drained the dregs from his cup and glanced at his watch. 'I'd better go. Should be meeting Poppy at half past. Christmas shopping. More perfume and a handbag she's seen.'

I watched his gaze flicker over me. I knew he was torn between the two of us. Whilst I knew I'd never feel the same about Poppy since the incident in the motorway restaurant, as she was Tom's girlfriend I had to accept she'd always be a part of my life. I forced myself to focus on Tom and nodded. 'Enjoy!' I tried to make my voice as cheerful as I could. Poor Tom. I hated that I was the cause of him being torn between us. Perhaps one day I'd be able to fully forgive her. But not yet.

Tom grinned, pulling his lips into a wry smile. Poppy was a nightmare to shop with. On many occasions I'd been dragged from shop to shop in pursuit of the perfect lipstick or skirt. It was something I'd learned to avoid if possible. 'I need to go too. Audition.'

'God. Yeah.' Tom pulled an excited face. 'Best of luck.' He pulled me into a huge hug, hampered by the shopping bags we both carried.

I walked out of the café with him and watched him walk away to meet Poppy. I missed her company desperately and clearly, she did mine. I wished I didn't feel the need to keep her at arm's length now. Her texts in the days that followed had been filled with remorse. I longed to make up with her properly, but the pain of her betrayal was too intense. I sighed, my eyes filling with hot tears before brushing them away, forcing myself to focus on my audition, turning and hurrying to the theatre.

* * * * * * * *

'You've read the role?' Guy Firth, the theatrical director asked with a flamboyant raise of his eyebrows. My longing for the part began to increase. I needed a job, but I wanted Dad to meet the director just as much. I loved watching my very heterosexual, masculine dad react to the company of the camp gays the theatre attracted. He tried always to be serious and interested in what they were saying and yet struggled to hide his fascination at their flamboyant gestures and behaviour.
I nodded my head. 'Yes.'

'Read then, darling.' Guy flapped his hands in a gesture which I took to indicate I was to proceed. A huge diamond ring glittered on his little finger, sending shafts of light dancing around the stage.

Someone handed me the script. I didn't need it, I knew the role off by heart; a tough woman, broken hearted by the death of her lover in the war. I began to say the lines, glancing at the script occasionally, although I'd memorised them already. Practicing for the role had occupied much of my time since Josh and I had come back from Cornwall. I found comfort in absorbing the lines, picking up the nuances of the character. It helped me forget the pain of the funeral, my bewilderment at what had happened to my mother, and my regret at having fallen out with Poppy.

Below me in the front seats were Josh, who had met me at the theatre door and the other actors who were auditioning. Guy and the producers faded into insignificance as I performed, becoming Eloise, the heartbroken woman. The emotion of my mother's funeral, kept tightly in check, flooded back to me. The pain I felt that day, which I'd had to keep tightly trapped inside, bubbled to the surface. I felt every bit of Eloise's pain as if it were my own.

'Thank you,' one of the producers got to his feet, waving his hands for me to stop.

There was a jarring sensation as Eloise left me and I returned. In the seats beside Guy and the producers I could see the other actors who were auditioning, watching me. I hadn't been aware of any of them being present while I had been on stage.

'We'll let you know, dear.' Guy's gaze flickered over me for a long moment and then back to the list of actors on the clipboard he held. 'Next!' He bellowed in a surprisingly deep and masculine voice.

I hurried down the steps and into Josh's arms.

'That was fabulous,' he said, pushing me gently away so he could look at my face. 'Very impressive.' Clutching my hand proudly, Josh led me out of the theatre into the now dark streets which were still filled with shoppers, my head buzzing with delight at how well the audition had gone.

* * * * * * * *

My happiness continued into Christmas. Mum, Dad and I spent the day together as we always did. The grooms who worked for Mum always had Christmas Day off so I cleaned out the stables while Mum, her broken wrist now in a support rather than the heavy cast, mixed up feeds and filled hay nets. Afterwards we feasted on a huge breakfast and then settled down to open our presents. Mum, as always, knew exactly what I wanted and I unwrapped mine to find the black leather handbag I'd admired in one of the designer shops months ago.

'You are amazing,' I said, kissing her, smiling at her kindness, the way she had noted the bag I liked and had made a point of going back to get it for me in secret. Dad's card to me contained a lovely wedge of money. I held it to my face, making a pretence of breathing in the new money smell. 'Lovely.' I grinned, knowing exactly which shops I was going to hit in the January sales.

They both loved the presents I got for them, a posh new shirt for Dad and expensive perfume for Mum.

'What did Josh get you?' Mum said, as we tidied up the discarded wrapping paper.

'This,' I said, showing her the necklace.

'Beautiful.' Mum fingered the chain around my neck. 'He's very clever to find one to match your bracelet.'

I nodded, my fingers going instinctively to the slender links of silver that had belonged to my mother. I had never told Mum where it had come from. Josh had given me the necklace the previous evening. We'd gone out for dinner with Tom and Poppy. Josh and Tom had been friends since childhood. I didn't want to be the person who came between them because of my fragile relationship with Poppy. There was no way I was going to be able to avoid her; regardless of my feelings she was part of my circle of friends. I knew I needed to forget what had happened and move on. Tom had given Poppy the perfume she loved and the bag she had chosen. Her present to him was a brightly coloured cashmere jumper, which Josh admired, but which I knew Tom would hate wearing, even though he'd dutifully do just that to avoid hurting her.

I'd bought Josh a very expensive fountain pen. 'To sign contracts,' I told him as he ripped open the wrapping paper and gave an exclamation of delight.

'Babe, you are the best,' he'd grinned, kissing me loudly on the cheek.

I enjoyed the day with my parents. Spending hours lingering over dinner, chatting about the horses and the cruise Mum and Dad intended to take to celebrate their wedding anniversary. The day of my mother's funeral and the heartbreak that followed it seemed to have been pushed into the background. I felt normal again. The shadow of my dead mother and my father's horrendous actions had gradually slipped into the background. I belonged here.

My mother had been buried. I mourned her loss, what had happened to her, her stolen life, the pain that had caused her family. I'd had no part of that. I understood that now. I was just as much of a victim of circumstance as she had been, but that past did not define who I was. With Christmas came the New Year. The time to make a fresh start, aim for new goals. My parents hosted a big lunch for their friends and mine the weekend following New Year's Day. We all sat around the dinner table, the usual crowd, enjoying the food, the conversation loud, laughter filling the air. I sat at one end of the table with Josh, Tom and Poppy.

'This meat is fabulous,' Josh complimented my mum on her cooking.

'Thank you, Josh,' Mum lifted her wine glass in a salute to him. Her cheeks were flushed pink from helping with the cooking and the amount she'd drunk. Because of the injury to her wrist Mum had supervised Dad cooking, making him lift the saucepans, and roasting trays.

Tom met my eyes and rolled his skywards as Oliver's loud braying voice sounded over the buzz of conversation.

'Any plans for 2013 Mia?' asked Pippa. Oliver's young girlfriend had tactfully been seated by Mum, so she was near to us youngsters rather than the older ones of her boyfriend's generation.

'I—'

Before I could finish speaking Mum interrupted. 'Actually, I've a plan for Mia.'

I turned to look at her, aware a silence had fallen around the room.

'If you'd like to, Mia,' Mum said, 'I'd like you to take over the ride on Solar. Compete him for me.'

I put down my knife and fork with a clatter and got to my feet. 'Thank you!' I hugged her, unable to contain my delight. Solar. Mum's incredible horse was going to be mine to compete.

'Phone.' Poppy handed me my phone. Her smile showed her genuine delight at Mum's offer.

'I didn't hear it,' I grinned, disentangling myself from Mum's hug. 'Hello?' I pressed the accept button.

A moment later I ended the call and threw down my phone.

I met Mum's eyes and saw the raw concern there before I opened my mouth and let out a scream of joy. 'I got the part. Guy has just offered me the role.'

CHAPTER FOURTEEN

'Hang on, Josh.' My phone vibrated in the pocket of my jeans as the lift came to a stop.

Josh strode in front of me as the doors opened. He leant against the wall; his body language full of impatience.

'It's Poppy,' I said, pulling the phone out and looking at the screen. 'Just need to…' I scrolled through the message, 'reply to this… girls' night out… Thursday… yes, perfect.' I tapped a reply quickly and pressed send, aware of Josh's excited expression. In the months that followed, since our falling out, Poppy, had done everything she could to win my trust and friendship again. There were constant invitations for lunch and coffee. Still inwardly stinging at her betrayal I wanted to keep her at arm's length, but her eager overtures were hard to suppress and gradually I found myself unable to resist her invitations. I was so busy rehearsing for my stage role I didn't have time to dwell on our argument.

'Sorry,' I said, meeting Josh's eyes. Contrite. He'd told me he had something to show me and now I'd spoilt his moment.

I took his hand and stood on tiptoe to take hold of his tie and draw him towards me so I could kiss his cheek. He smelt delicious; that heady masculine aftershave I loved. I fancied the pants off him in his smart business suit.

'This way.' Josh levered himself upright and set off down the corridor. 'This is the top floor,' he told me as we walked on folds of plastic through which I could see a pale green carpet. I wondered if Josh was moving his offices from the out of the business park to a more central part of the city. 'It's all brand new.'

The corridor stretched the length of the building, warm spring sunlight streaming in through windows at either end. The air was filled with the smell of fresh paint, new carpet and cement.

We passed a couple of doors, brass plates giving their numbers, right to the last door. Josh fished a key out of his jacket pocket.

'Come in.' He pushed open the door. I followed him, blinking at the bright light that streamed in through a window that stretched the length of the vast room.

'Josh,' I breathed, turning slowly to take in the room. 'This is gorgeous.' And it was. We were standing in a fabulous kitchen, ultra-modern stainless-steel units sat above an old-looking wooden floor.

'Isn't it amazing?' Josh went to the enormous fridge and pulled open the door. It was empty bar a solitary bottle of champagne and two glasses. 'This used to be a mill. It stood derelict for years.'

I nodded, realisation slowly sinking in. I knew exactly what the building had been. Dad and Oliver had tried to buy it to do exactly this, convert it into high-end apartments, but hadn't been able to raise the money they'd needed.

'And now, half of this floor is mine.' He deftly turned the champagne bottle in his hand, holding onto the cork until he succeeded in wriggling it out of the top. He poured the liquid into the glasses and handed one to me. 'Come and see the rest of it.'

Clutching our champagne glasses, we walked around the building, our footsteps clattering on the wood floor and echoing around the vast space.

The architects had done a wonderful job of designing the apartments. The space had been turned into huge, airy, light-filled rooms. The kitchen led into a lounge, empty but for two leather sofas which faced each other across a brightly-patterned rug. There were three bedrooms. One Josh had completed, with a wide king-size bed, complete with a white duvet and piles of plump pillows. The others were empty. The master bedroom had an en-suite and there was another bathroom, with an enormous bath in the centre.

'What a view from the bath,' I exclaimed, going to the window and looking out. Below us stretched an incredible vista of Bath, the beautiful pale stone buildings lit up in the late spring sunshine.

'Come and look at this view.' Josh took my hand and led me back into the lounge. We stood at the window which stretched from floor to ceiling. It was quite disconcerting, like standing on the edge of a cliff. I stepped back, not trusting myself to stand pressed up against the glass. 'See,' Josh pointed. 'The Royal Crescent. There's the river.'

'Josh,' I breathed. 'It's utterly beautiful. And all this is yours. I'm so proud of you.'

He deserved this. He'd worked hard building up his company, designing software which he sold to businesses internationally. I would listen intently when he told me about his work, but really had no understanding of what he did, except that the software made manufacturing systems run better.

'Makes all those late nights working seem worth it now.' Josh clinked his glass against mine and drained half of his champagne.

'Here's to you.' I took a big gulp of mine, the icy liquid exploding into bubbles on my tongue.

'And to you.' Josh took my glass out of my hand and wrapped his arms around me. 'My genius, famous actress girlfriend.'

I tilted my chin to look into the blue eyes I loved so much. They were the turquoise blue of a tropical sea. 'I'm not a famous actress yet,' I smiled. 'I don't think one role makes me that.'

'You will be though.' Josh took my hand and led me back into the kitchen. 'Haven't you seen this?' He grabbed a newspaper from the kitchen unit. 'Here.' He unfolded the paper and spread it out.

I scanned the page, my breath loud in my ears as I shook my head in disbelief. 'They liked us,' I said, my voice sounding disjointed like it didn't quite belong to me. I read on, my eyes flickering quickly over the page. 'Newcomer Mia Lewis gives a dazzling performance in her first lead role.' At the top of the article was a photograph of the performers on stage, me in full costume, my face clearly showing all the anguish in my character's life.

I refolded the paper. 'Wow.'

It was hard to take in the praise, to imagine that the reviewer had enjoyed the performance so much.

We'd worked so hard over the early part of the year in rehearsals. I hadn't thought much further into the future than our first week when the show opened in the beautiful Georgian Theatre Royal. Those first performances were actually warm-up events for when the production opened officially in London's West End. Sometimes performances didn't make it beyond their first showing in Bath. But we'd made it. For the next six weeks of our run I was going to be living in a hotel in London, performing on stage there. It was everything I'd ever dreamed of.

'Of course, it was good,' Josh said, tilting my chin with his fingers so I was looking straight into his eyes. 'Everyone said it was brilliant last night.'

I smiled at the memory, walking off stage to the sound of stamping feet and loud applause. Josh and I had eaten dinner afterwards with my parents. Tom and Poppy had come to the restaurant to congratulate me. As I got up to greet them Tom had pulled me into an enormous hug. 'That was brilliant. You were amazing.'

'Wasn't she just,' Josh had got up and stood beside me, slipping a possessive arm around my shoulders.

'Well done,' Poppy had said, her voice high and brittle. At first, I had put it down to the amount she'd drunk, but later I wondered if she resented my success. I'd tried to put that feeling out of my mind. Why would she think that way? I'd love to see her being a success and I hoped she felt the same way about my ambitions.

'Josh.' I glanced at my watch. 'I'd better go. I need to be at the theatre in an hour.'

My stomach began to constrict with the excitement of the evening ahead. The preparations, make-up, getting into my costume and then the performance itself. It was a delicate balance between knowing my lines and being able to switch abruptly if someone fluffed theirs or forgot a cue. It was a heady blend of excitement and sheer terror.

'Just a minute.' Josh grabbed my wrist and pulled me into his body. 'We're a great team, aren't we? You and I.'

I nodded. He paused, closing his thick eyelashes over his gorgeous blue eyes. Of course, we were. I looked at him.

'You the famous actress. Me the high-flying businessman.'

I pulled a wry face at his description of us.

Josh opened his eyes, regarding me solemnly. 'I'd love you to move in here with me. Be a proper couple.'

'Yes, please.' I pulled his mouth down to meet mine. 'But I really need to go!'

* * * * * * * *

The second performance was just as good as the first. The newspaper report had given us a much-needed boost of confidence. The air in the dressing room buzzed with excitement before the performance, everyone terrified of not matching up to the glowing report in the newspaper and on social media. We applied our make-up, got into our costumes. There was nothing else that could be done now, except our performances.

'You were all brilliant,' the director said afterwards. Following our encore, we were sitting in the dressing room. Adrenaline still fizzed and crackled through our veins after the tension of the evening. I was hot and sticky, longing to take off the heavy make-up and the stiff, hot costume, but still we listened, basking in her praise. 'Good job, Mia,' she said, 'You did a great job of rescuing Terry.'

I nodded. One of the other actors had blanked for a moment. I'd heard his momentary pause and had improvised, watching him until he joined back in, literally seconds later, but without my quick thinking the action would have floundered. Regardless of what happened in my life away from the theatre, once I was on stage the world faded into soft focus. Performing I had the feeling of absolute peace. This was where I belonged, bringing characters to life on stage.

Beside me my phone pinged with a message arriving. 'I'll see you at the front door. You were mega-brilliant. Superstar.' Poppy's message said.

I wished I hadn't agreed to go out with her tonight, that I was going to meet Josh to talk about our new life together in his sumptuous apartment. My face cleaned and redone, I had a quick wash in the ladies' loos, got changed, and hurried outside to meet Poppy.

'Top job tonight.' She had hidden herself behind one of the pillars outside the façade of the theatre and jumped out, clapping me on the back as I stood looking for her.

'Thank you!' I brought my hands up to my face and pulled an expression of uncontainable excitement, jumping up and down on the spot. This role was everything I'd hoped for during the four long years I'd been studying drama. A good performance here could set me up for bigger roles, television perhaps, even films.

'Hollywood beckons.' Poppy grinned, slipping her arm into mine and leading me down the steps and towards the elegant streets of the city centre.

'I hope so,' I said, sincerely. That would be truly everything I wanted from my career. To act in films, to be able to make a decent living portraying wonderful characters. I had no desire to be famous, to walk down a street with people hurrying after me to get my autograph. No longing to be mind-blowingly wealthy. I just wanted to act, to absorb myself in the different characters and give them life.

'Where are we going?' I asked, Poppy's heels clicking on the pavement as she walked purposefully beside me.

'Lillie's. Cocktails are half-price tonight,' she replied, giving a little squeal of excitement.

* * * * * * * *

The club was already packed when we arrived. 'Let's find some seats,' I yelled in Poppy's ear. My feet ached from the high heeled shoes I'd had to wear for my performance. I longed to sit down for a while to absorb the atmosphere of the bar and reflect on the show.

'Fine,' Poppy yelled back. Her voice carried a note of irritation at my request. I knew all she wanted to do was to get as drunk as possible and dance the night away.

She led the way across the club, skirting past the dance floor, waving and shrieking a greeting to someone in the crowd. There was an empty booth at the far side of the dance floor. As we slid in, I slipped my shoes off, wriggling my toes in delight.

Here the music was not as loud, we'd be able to chat for a while. I longed to tell Poppy about Josh's apartment and him asking me to move in and to talk about my role and how much I was looking forward to going to London.

'I'll fetch some drinks.' Poppy rooted in her handbag and unearthed her purse. 'Mojito?'

I nodded eagerly, getting my phone out to text Josh while she was gone.

She returned a while later, clutching the drinks, with three identikit blondes in tow.

'I've found Chardonnay, Paris and Kinvara, friends from work,' Poppy said as the girls wriggled into seats opposite me.

'Hi,' I smiled, glancing down at my phone as Josh's reply arrived.

'How do you know Pops?' Chardonnay, Paris or Kinvara asked.

'We were at school together,' I replied, wishing she hadn't brought them over to our table. I'd wanted to share my news with Poppy.

'Oh. You're the actress,' one of them breathed as she leant forwards resting her elbows on the table. 'In the play at the Theatre Royal.'

'That's me.' I smiled, the joy of the tremendous reception we'd had earlier still coursing through my veins.

'Poppy told us about you.' One of the other blondes leant forwards, twirling a strand of her hair between red-tipped fingers.

The other one, who until now had been sitting back in the booth sat upright as if she had just realised who I was.

'Yeah, the one who...' she paused, no doubt seeing Poppy's stricken expression.

'The one who... what?' I said coldly, picking up on their curiosity. 'What?' I repeated as the four of them feigned a sudden interest in their drinks.

'The one whose mum was in all the papers in the winter.' Her expression challenged me. We'd made a point of not looking at the newspapers, as Grace had advised.

'Yeah, the one whose dad buried her after he'd kidnapped her and killed her after you were born.'

I heard the words but wasn't aware of who had spoken. Instead I looked across the booth at Poppy.

'Poppy?' I said, the bitterness of her treachery sending waves of pain through my chest.

Slowly she raised her head. As she met my gaze I saw, etched on her face, raw shock now I knew she had betrayed me again.

CHAPTER FIFTEEN

She cried. Literally. The. Whole. Way. Home. I was the one who had been betrayed, whose whole life had been laid bare and she was the one who was upset.

There was no point in staying in the club, the whole evening was ruined. Aware of the curious gazes of the three blondes I slid out of the booth. 'I'm going home.'

'Mia. Wait for me.' Poppy's voice quivered with unshed tears above the thump of music.

I pushed my way across the dance floor and barged through the line of people who were waiting to come into the club.

'I'm so sorry.' Poppy's heels clattered on the stone slabs of the pavement as I hurried away.

'I didn't mean to tell them,' she sniffled, setting my teeth on edge.

The night air was chilled now the warmth of the day had gone; the silence of the empty city closed around us.

'Why did you tell those fucking bimbos about me?' I brushed away the tears that were spilling down my cheeks.

A middle-aged couple walking towards us tutted at my swearing.

'What?' I roared, directing the full force of my pain at the woman.

'Come on.' Her male companion glared at me, pulling her away.

'They were just curious about you,' Poppy said between sobs. 'I was telling them about you playing the lead in the show and the rest of it just came out.'

'The rest of it just came out? I shook my head, trying and failing to find a tissue in my bag.

Wordlessly Poppy handed me a crumpled one from hers.

'They don't care,' she said. 'Honestly, Mia, they're such bimbos, they aren't interested. All they care about is music and fashion and what's going on in *Big Brother*.'

'Why don't you just take out a bloody advert in the local newspaper, just in case there's someone you've missed telling about me.'

'Stop it.' Poppy turned to face me. Her mascara had run, making dark streaks down her cheeks. A drop of snot trickled from her nose, glistening in the glow from the streetlights. She dashed it away in an angry gesture. 'I made a mistake. Okay?'

I pressed my fingers to my face, determined not to spill the bitter tears of frustration that stung behind my eyes. 'Who are they going to tell? My life story is hardly one they'll want to keep quiet.'

'They won't say anything.' Poppy said, chewing her bottom lip. 'They promised me.'

I felt sober now, the effects of my earlier cocktail gone. Instead a heavy tightness of tension sat in my chest. I wanted to rage, to shout, slap her until the pain she had caused had gone.

'You're so stupid,' I spat, the anger coursing through my veins turning me into someone I didn't recognise. 'I don't want people to know who I am. I don't want to be known as the girl whose father killed her mother. Killed many…' The words stuck in my throat. How could I say what my father did? How many young women he had killed. How many lives he had ruined.

Beside me Poppy blew her nose loudly, before finally saying quietly, 'You are though, aren't you?'

'No.' A wave of exhaustion hit me. I closed the gap between us, leaning in to speak to her. I could smell her perfume, the sweetness of the cocktail on her breath. I was so close to her I could see the individual strands of her false eyelashes. The darkness cast her face into shadow, but even so I could see her sorrowful expression.

'Don't ever tell anyone anything about me. Ever. Ever again.'

'I won't. I promise.' She drew away from me. 'Please can we go home now?'

I flagged down a taxi. We sat in a silence broken only by Poppy's choking sobs, at opposite sides of the back seat, a vast chasm of pain filling the space between us. I caught the taxi driver looking at us in his rear-view mirror, saw the naked curiosity in his eyes. It seemed to take forever to drive out of the city to Poppy's home and then the three further miles to mine. I took the money Poppy had wordlessly handed me as she had got out of the taxi, added my half and handed it to the driver.

As the lights of the taxi drove away I sank to my knees, pushing my fist into my mouth to silence the scream of utter anguish I could not voice.

* * * * * * * *

'How did it go last night?' Dad asked, as I wandered into the kitchen the following morning.

'It went really well,' I told him, deliberately not mentioning the disastrous encounter in the night club. I'd hoped to have come home in the early hours, drunk. Instead I had never felt more sober. I'd lain awake, my heartache at Poppy and her stupid friends making me toss and turn all night. I'd finally slept as the spring dawn arrived, sending streaks of blue light across the sky. I had to forget how thoughtless she was. I had to believe she hadn't meant it maliciously. I couldn't carry that pain into my evening performance, or into riding Solar beforehand. Both deserved better. Solar would pick up any tension in me and wouldn't relax and work properly and on stage I had to give my all.

'I wish we could come and see you every night.' Dad poured me a cup of coffee.

'You'd soon get bored.'

'Maybe, but we are going to come and see you when the show gets to London.'

London. The very thought of the production being there made me smile. The tension between my shoulders dissipated. I was an actress. In a stage production that was going to be on in London. I had to put the pain of what Poppy had done behind me.

'We are so proud of you.' Mum came in, still, like me, in her pyjamas; her arm, recently out of its cast was protected by an elasticated support. She was already working with a physiotherapist to build up the strength in her limb. She leant over me to drop a kiss on the top of my head. 'You've worked so hard to achieve this.'

She snuggled up against Dad, the two of them looking at me, their faces filled with love and pride.

'You're going to have a fantastic career.' Dad's voice was filled with delight.

'I've got something else to tell you.' I sat back in the chair and looked at the two of them. 'Josh has bought one of those beautiful apartments in the old mill block.'

'Lucky bugger.' Dad's face filled with regret at his aborted attempt to buy the building. 'I bet they are gorgeous. I know the architect and designers; they always do a fabulous job. Wish I could afford to use them.'

'Well,' I said, in my best dramatic voice. 'He's asked me to go and live with him.'

'Oh my God!' Mum jumped up and down on the spot. 'Mia, that is so exciting. Of course, you said yes?'

'I did,' I grinned, glad my news had given them so much pleasure. They loved Josh; he was the perfect prospective son-in-law. Smart, wealthy, ambitious, everything they could wish for in a partner for me. 'I'll still be here, though, to ride Solar,' I added quickly. There was no way I was going to give that up. After being on stage, riding Solar was my greatest pleasure. Mum and I had planned an autumn filled with shows now he had learned the basics.

'I'd better go and get dressed.' I pushed my chair back. 'Mum's going to help me work Solar.'

'He's going so well.' Mum took Dad's mug off him and sipped the liquid, wincing at the strength of the coffee. 'Ughh, put a sugar in mine,' she said, handing it back to him. 'Mia and Solar have their first competition in a couple of weeks' time. He really works well for her. You should have seen the course they jumped when we went to Field Farm for a practice round.'

I clamped my lips tightly shut to hold in the grin I could feel building as Dad's eyes glazed over. He might live surrounded by horses, with two horse-obsessed women, but he did not share our interest.

'I'll go and get dressed,' I repeated, getting to my feet. 'I'll head straight outside after and warm Solar up.'

'I'll be out soon.' Mum was already stirring another heaped spoon of sugar into the coffee Dad had poured for her.

I was thrilled at how pleased my parents were at my news. Life was wonderful, I told myself, sternly, determined not to let the awfulness of the previous night ruin everything. There was so much good in my life. Josh, my career, Solar. Success beckoned. Poppy could go to hell. I'd cut her out of my life. Somehow. She'd proved to me she wasn't a friend who could be trusted. Once the short run of the performance was finished, I'd be working in London for the run of the show. Then I'd be back in Bath, living with Josh. I'd stay friends with Tom, but the nights out as a foursome would have to stop. My mind whirled. I couldn't have Poppy in my life any longer.

Car tyres crunched on the gravel outside my bedroom window. One of mum's livery clients, I assumed, used to them driving from the stables to the house to chat to her about their horses.

'No!' I heard Dad shout. The front door slammed.

'Just one...' the sound of a muffled voice reached me, coming from outside.

Curious, I got to my feet and looked out of my bedroom window. My room was at the front of the house and looked out above the front door. There were two cars I didn't recognise parked outside the house. There, on the gravel, stood three men and one woman. A huge camera was slung around one of the men's necks. I knew instantly what they were and why they had come. Reporters. Someone had told them my story. Poppy, in anger at our fallout, or one of her stupid friends.

'Mia!' Dad's voice sounded a strange mix of anger and concern as he shouted up the stairs to me.

I hastily finished applying a slick of lip gloss. 'Coming.' I called and walked out of my bedroom.

At the bottom of the stairs I could see the shapes of the reporters through the glass panels in the front door. They'd retreated away from the door and stood in a group, leaning against one of their cars.

'Dad?' My parents sat at the kitchen table, a wide fold of paper open in front of them.

'Those bastards brought this.' Dad pushed the newspaper towards me. 'It's a mock-up of an article they intend to run. They want our comments.' Beside him Mum's cheeks were grey, her eyes shining with unshed tears.

'Why can't they leave us alone? How did they find you?'

Slowly I lowered myself into the closest chair, my legs trembling beneath me. I knew exactly how. I pulled the open mock-up towards me, my eyes flickering over the headlines and photographs. There were photographs of me on stage. They'd been taken on opening night. I was taking a bow after the performance, holding hands with my fellow performers, flushed, a grin of pure delight splashed across my face. There were others. People in white romper suits, a stretcher between them bearing the covered remains of what must have been one of the bodies. An old house, a jumble of sloping eaves half hidden in trees, and blurred photographs of a young man, beside a line of headshots of young women, one of whom I recognised as my mother. Above the photographs, blazoned across the two pages, the headline, 'Murderer's daughter in top theatre role.' My eyes swept over the article, seeing the bold print announcing my father was suspected of killing eight women during the 1980s, one of whom was my mother.

'Mia!'

There was banging on the front door. 'We want to talk to you. There's great interest in that article. We want to get your words about what it feels like growing up as the daughter of Eddie Hammett.'

I glanced at my parents, stood together beside the kitchen sink, their faces white, shocked, the debris of our relaxing morning piled on the worksurface beside them.

'Bastards,' Dad hissed. His knuckles were white where he gripped the marble worktop. Mum was staring at the kitchen door as if she expected the reporters to burst through it.

'Why the fuck have they come here? How did they fucking know?' Dad never swore. I'd rarely ever seen him even lose his patience which made his words all the more frightening.

I knew why they'd come. I knew exactly how they knew about me.

Dad inhaled slowly. I felt the air move as he walked past me. His hand dropped briefly on my shoulder. Mum levered herself away from the kitchen units and sat down opposite me, her eyes locking on mine.

'It's okay. This will go away,' she said, taking my hand in her icy fingers. 'There's no story.'

In the hall the front door opened.

'Get the fuck out of here!' Dad's voice was loud, angry, filled with tension.

'We are going to publish the story,' a voice said, 'Mia should give us a comment.'

In an anger filled voice, Dad snapped, 'No comment. Leave us alone.' The door slammed. A moment later car tyres crunched on the gravel. The reporters were leaving.

Dad came back into the kitchen and sank down in the chair beside me, his face flushed with temper.

'There's no story for them,' he said, calmly, sliding his hands across the table to cover mine and Mum's entwined hands. 'If you see them again, just say no comment. I'm going to talk to my solicitor, see if there's any way to stop them printing anything.'

I nodded, utterly numb.

'How the hell did they know who you were?' He shook his head.

I stared at the table, our abandoned coffee mugs and breakfast plates. We'd shielded ourselves against the media reports that had come out when the bodies had first been discovered. None of us had watched the television news, no newspapers had been read, I'd avoided trawling through social media and looking at the toxic online crime forums. Of course, everyone at the party and Mum's clients all knew, but no one had mentioned it. None of them would have been disloyal enough to betray my parents, or me. My past had been neatly avoided, politely pushed away. Until now.

* * * * * * * *

Dad was insistent I carry on as normal. Mum and I worked Solar. He was brilliant, we flew over the fences as if he had wings, but there was no joy in the experience. Poppy's betrayal and the visit from the reporters played over and over in my mind.

Later I went in to the theatre to do my performance. Once I had my stage make-up on I finally began to relax, looking forward to losing myself in my role.

'Mia, darling,' the director came to the dressing room. In my mirror I saw the faces of the other performers, watching him, filled with curiosity. 'We need to have a little chat.'

I got up and followed her out of the room, wondering what she needed me to change. Put more emphasis on the emotion in one of the scenes? Stand differently when I delivered some of the lines?

'What?' I'd been so focused on my role I hadn't been listening properly.

'I'm sorry, Mia. Reporters have been calling me all day trying to get a hold of you. They're determined to print this lurid story about your father.'

I felt my mouth drop open. Why couldn't they leave me alone? I'd been a young child when I had lived at Blackthorn Farm. I'd had no idea what my father had done. What did the reporters want me to tell them?

I repeated my Dad's words. 'They'll get fed—'

'Mia.' She held up her hands in a gesture which indicated I should stop talking. 'Please listen to me.'

I closed my mouth, swallowing hard to ease the tension in my throat.

'We can't have this kind of adverse publicity associated with the show. It's going to follow us to London. The audience won't see you as Miranda, your character. they will just see Eddie Hammett's daughter. The child of a mass murderer.'

I shook my head, forcing myself to stand upright, while my whole body trembled.

'No.'

'I'm sorry, Mia, I wish it didn't have to end this way. You are a very talented actress but the show has to come first.'

The reality of her words hit home. 'You're sacking me?'

She twisted her face into a sorrowful grimace. 'I'm sorry. It's for the best. I'm sure there'll be other roles when this has died down.'

My face still painted in the guise of my character, the director led me away from the dressing room. In the corridor my understudy avoided meeting my eyes. One of the stage-hands handed me my bag. He'd collected all my things while the director was sacking me. They led me to the back door of the theatre, the traditional escape route for those wanting to avoid curious crowds, and out into the open air.

'There's already reporters out the front,' she said. 'Best if you go out this way.'

The door closed behind me, shutting me out of the theatre. Somehow, I found the strength to walk away, down the steps, away from the theatre. My career in tatters.

CHAPTER SIXTEEN

'Do you need the script?' One of the director's assistants offered me a pile of papers.

I shook my head. 'No, thanks. I know the role.' She hurried across the stage, leaving me alone in the spotlight. I took a deep breath, calming myself, absorbing the atmosphere of the theatre. The stage beneath me was dusty, patterned with footprints.

'When you're ready. From the opening line,' came a disjointed voice. Below me, in the gloom of the theatre I could see the shapes of three people sitting halfway up the rows of seats.

'Thank you.' I smiled, feeling the familiar peace slide over me. I loved the stage, being in front of an audience, completely absorbed in a character.

Speaking the familiar words from a performance I loved, I began. The pain of being sacked from my last role faded into insignificance. The media had gradually lost interest, there were other dramas for them to write about. On stage I forgot the competitive atmosphere backstage, where others of a similar age waited, desperate for a chance to shine. My life, the trauma I carried on my shoulders during my normal existence faded away. I pushed other, more recent rejections away; I wasn't suitable for every role. Rejections were part of an actress' life. Taking a deep breath I became the character I was auditioning for, our psyches blending. All I had to do was move and speak.

'Thank you.' A voice from the seats interrupted me, bringing me back to reality with a jarring jolt. 'That was great.'

'Can I get your name?' asked the first voice again.

'Mia,' I said. 'Mia Lewis.'

The forms moved, merging together. I couldn't hear what they were saying, but I could imagine. The audition scenario becoming sickeningly familiar.

'Thank you. We'll be in touch,' another voice said.

I thought it held a hint of disappointment.

I glared at the shapes, the pain of rejection settling uncomfortably in my stomach. My mind, still half absorbed in the intricacies of my character, struggled to grasp their curt dismissal. Of course, they didn't want me in their production. It was nothing to do with my suitability for the role. They knew what had happened in my first production, remembered the drama that had accompanied the revelations about my past. No matter how long I waited, or how far I travelled to auditions, still the shame of my past followed me. My hands ached from where my nails had dug into my palms.

'Thank you.' A theatre assistant tugged at my sleeve. 'This way.'

I wanted to shrug her off, slap her smug looking face. I longed to leap down into the seats and rage at the director and producers for the way they had cast me off as if I were a piece of dirt for something I had nothing to do with. It was my father who had killed those women. He who kidnapped them and had held them prisoner. Not me.

My jaw ached with the effort of smiling as I walked off the stage.

'How was it?' One of the people waiting to audition asked as I passed them.

'Great,' I lied, knocking against someone in my rush to get through the crowd. 'Sorry.' Her cry of pain followed me as I kept going, desperate to get away from the theatre. The exit door hit the wall with a metallic bang as I flung it open and rushed out, stumbling down the steps in my haste.

At the bottom of the steps I stopped and leant against the wall of the theatre, trying to calm the thoughts that swirled and fought in my mind. What would my life have been like if it hadn't gone so spectacularly wrong? I'd have finished my first lead role in the theatre. If only Poppy hadn't shared the horrors of my past everything would have been so very different.

There was no relief. I got the train back to Bath, heading for the apartment I was now sharing with Josh. I'd thrown my door key at him before I'd left that morning. I was wound up about the audition, afraid they'd reject me because of what had happened with my last role. He'd told me I was being ridiculous. The key had bounced off his cheek and ended up on the floor. He hadn't given it back to me and I hadn't picked it up. I wished now I had, longing for the bolthole as well as the security of our relationship.

I longed for the peace and quiet of the elegant building, wanting to be alone to lick my wounds. Josh would be working of course. I sent him a short text to tell him I'd done the audition, hoping he would offer to come out and meet me for coffee. As usual there was no reply. He'd message me later when he'd dealt with the priorities of work. His car was outside, beside mine, but that meant nothing. He often left it there and walked to his office. I sat on the wall opposite the building, watching a slender girl pull open the door. For a moment I considered running across the road, shouting at her to hold the door for me, but there was no point. I couldn't get into the apartment even if I got into the building.

There was nowhere to go but to drive to my parents' house. I dreaded seeing the concern on Mum and Dad's faces and hearing the sympathy in their voices. I put off going home for as long as I could, but eventually there was no option.

'Oh darling, that's so disappointing.' Mum pulled me into her arms.

'There'll be other roles.' Dad ruffled my hair as he moved past me and pulled a bottle of wine out of the rack. 'Perhaps you could go back to uni, do a teaching degree. Teach drama?'

He pulled the cork out of the bottle, took glasses out of the cupboard and poured the wine.

'Would that be an idea?' he asked, handing me a glass.

Slowly I brought my eyes up from the table, where I'd been focusing desperately on the flower arrangement. There was nothing I wanted to do more than act. Drama had been the focus of my life, alongside riding, for as long as I could remember. Being an actress was the only thing I had wanted to do, ever since I'd been one of the three wise men in a primary school Nativity play shortly after I'd been adopted. Teaching would be a poor second.

They were both trying to find ways to sympathise, offer me options, when there weren't any. Because of my past. Nothing to do with my talent. Decisions made to not give me roles were strictly down to my suitability for the PR machine.

'I don't want to do that.' I hated seeing the pity in their faces, the confusion at my rejection and their longing to wave a magic wand and make everything ok for me.

'It might be an option if you aren't getting any work.' Dad sat down at the kitchen table, turning his wine glass in his fingers, in full management mode, as if my life were some business problem he needed to sort out.

'You'd be a great teacher, Mia,' Mum said, sitting down beside him and looking up at me. 'It's only a year-long degree, put that with your drama degree and you'd be set to teach.'

'You'd still be in the drama world,' Dad continued. 'Perhaps it would be a way into roles on stage?'

'Yes,' I nodded, forcing the corners of my mouth into the semblance of a smile. They'd obviously already looked into me doing a teaching degree, expecting the rejection when I had been so full of hope. I knew, if I asked, they'd tell me exactly where I could do the degree. Offer to pay for it, suggest where I could stay. 'It's a very good idea, but really it's not what I want to do.'

'So...?' Dad, his voice full of frustration at me rejecting his plan, raised his hands in a questioning gesture. His shoulders headed skywards until his neck disappeared into the collar of his shirt. 'What are you going to do?'

'I don't know.' I closed my eyes as tears began to fall, resting on the precipice of my cheek bones before making the slow journey down my face. I clamped my hand over my mouth in an effort to stop the gulps and gasps of agony that fought to escape.

'I don't know,' I said again, hearing the anguish in my voice. Then there was nothing I could do to stop them; tears flowed freely as I released the pain and anger trapped inside me.

'Sit down, darling.' Mum put her arms around me, guiding me gently towards one of the kitchen chairs. I sat obediently, my legs trembling beneath me now that the floodgates of my torment had been opened.

'I don't know who I am any more,' I wrestled the words past the constricted muscles of my throat. 'Before the party. Before the police came...' I began, trying to explain my confusion. 'I was your daughter. All that...'

How could I put into words the jumbled thoughts about my past, the vague shapes of a life I barely remembered? The girl I had been then, living in a deserted farm where my father kept young women prisoner.

'Everything that happened before I came to you didn't matter.' I took a shuddering breath, glimpsing up at the concern on their faces.

Dad nodded his agreement. He opened his mouth as if he were going to speak and then seemed to change his mind, to let me talk while I could frame the words.

'When the police came I realised I wasn't just your daughter.' I looked up, met Mum's eyes, saw the pain there.

'Now everyone knows about me. My mother and father... People see me differently. See me as part of what my father did.'

'Mia, they don't.' Mum came around to my side of the table, put her arms around me, and pressed the softness of her cheek against mine. I could smell the lavender scent of her shampoo, the faintest hint of mint toothpaste on her breath.

Dad closed the circle, wrapping us both in his arms. He was silent, I knew he understood what I'd said was true.

I gently eased out of their arms so I could continue talking. 'There are so many questions I have, so much I want to know about my background.'

The faintest shadow of a grimace flashed in Mum's face before she smoothed it away.

'Do you really need to know?' Dad pushed his hands into the pockets of his cords. 'Just put that behind you, forget it all. You're still our Mia.'

I glanced at him, wishing I could tell him he couldn't close the door on my past and hope it would go away. The lid had been lifted and nothing could push the foulness back in.

'I want to know who my father was...'

Dad poured himself another glass of wine, flashing the bottle in our direction, raising his eyebrows in enquiry. I pushed mine forwards, longing for the escape of feeling very drunk.

'I want to know who Nan was. My mother. The other women my father killed.' I dragged the glass towards me across the table; some of the liquid slopped out, the puddle expanding, finding a crack in the ancient pine surface and dripping slowly through onto the tiled floor beneath. 'And the girl I rescued. Susie Carne.'

I dipped a finger into the spilt wine and traced a circle on the table, making that my whole focus, aware, without looking that my parents' eyes were on me. The air was filled with their helplessness, their longing to protect me from my past.

'I want to know everything that happened.'

'What will that achieve?' Dad's voice was filled with frustration.

'I don't know, Dad.'

'Forget about the theatre. Stay at home. Ride Solar and the other horses. Have a summer competing.' Mum's voice was equally full of desperation.

'I want to do that,' I said, meeting her eyes and smiling gently. 'But I truly need to find out who I am.' I could feel the secure life I had known here shift beneath my feet, the foundations which had gone to create the person I was beginning to crumble. Nothing would ever be the same again.

'Mia, you're our daughter!' Dad's voice was loud and harsh. 'We love you. We want the best for you.'

My eyes flickered to the pine French dresser at the far side of the kitchen. There, amongst the rosettes Mum and I had won and photographs of our life together, was a solitary frame, larger than the others. Patrick a chubby toddler, grinned, his eyes staring out at us as if he surveyed the scene. Without his death there'd have been no place for me here. My life with them would never have existed.

Mum pushed her hands onto the surface of the kitchen unit behind her, launching herself forwards. She began to pace the kitchen. One of her socks had come down slightly when she had taken off her wellington boots earlier. The tip flapped as she paced.

'Knowing any of this won't make any difference to you.' Mum raised her face to the ceiling, gesturing with her hands in frustration. 'You can't change anything that happened. You don't need to know. Please stop this. Just forget it all, let it stay in the past.'

I shook my head. 'I have to know.' My knuckles whitened as I gripped my hands into fists. 'I have to know why people look at me the way they do. I want to know why my grandmother and my aunts won't have anything to do with me.'

Dad let out a long sigh. 'Your past really doesn't matter. It doesn't make you who you are.'

Mum stopped her pacing, stood opposite me, her fingers gripping the top of one of the kitchen chairs. 'Please forget the past. Put that behind you. We'll do lots with the horses. See if we can qualify Solar for

Olympia. Break-in the new young horses.'

I nodded, longing to slip back into the life I had before the police had shattered it with their news. A life where I'd felt safe, a life with my parents, the horses, our life of competing, where no one looked at me as if they expected me to attack them.

'I'd love that,' I agreed, meeting her eyes. My cheeks stung with the tears I'd shed. My eyes felt raw; I knew if I looked, the skin around them would be swollen.

Mum came to me, rubbed her hand gently on my arm. 'You'll always be my little girl,' she said softly. 'Whatever happened before, whatever your father did, none of that matters. Here is where you belong. With me and your dad.'

I nodded, my throat tightening again.

Training Solar and the young horse would give me something to focus on, rather than worry about my non-existent acting career. Mum and I made a work plan for Solar, shows which would hopefully qualify him for the end of year show at Olympia. The thought of jumping him and competing at the highest level would give me other things to focus on instead of the rejection I had encountered in the theatre world. I'd find solace in the hard work. It was impossible to ride without being completely absorbed.

'I'd better go,' I said. Hours had passed since I'd arrived. Josh would be leaving work soon. He'd sent me a brief text, saying how sorry he was I hadn't been considered for the role and that he was looking forward to seeing me later. The row was over. Forgotten about.

I walked out of the kitchen, picked up my bag and car keys. 'I'll see you soon, thank you for everything,' I said, hugging my parents, before turning and heading out to my car. Patrick's eyes in the portrait in the hall watched me as I went.

CHAPTER SEVENTEEN

'My life is going on, but this noise is going on in my head.' I mimed a circular motion with my finger beside my temple. 'I don't know who I am anymore.'
Josh nodded, his face filled with understanding.

'Who was I? Who were my mother and father? Who were the other girls my father killed?' The floodgates opened and the heartache behind them was released.

Josh pulled me into his arms. I rested my face against the warmth of his shirt front. He smelt of clean laundry and the expensive body wash I loved. We'd made up after our row, when he had returned from work. As I had started to tell him I was sure I wouldn't be considered for the role all of my anguish had poured out.

'Fuck Poppy for being so disloyal.' I could feel the tension in his body as he spoke. 'Why did she have to…'

'I'll never have anything more to do with her.' I sobbed, feeling my tears soaking into his shirt fabric.

'Either of them. Tom or Poppy.' Josh's voice was deep against my ear.

I nodded. I wasn't sure I wanted to cut Tom out of my life. He'd been mortified when I'd messaged him about what Poppy had done. But since that evening, Josh and I hadn't seen either of them. I imagined Josh was secretly relieved. There was no reason for him to be, but I knew he felt threatened by my friendship with Tom.

'Josh, I need to find out who I am. What happened at the farm.' My parents' words faded into insignificance. I couldn't focus on my future until I had made sense of the past.

Josh's chin brushed against the top of my head as he nodded.

The words spilled out now in an uncontrollable torrent. 'I've looked online. There's a few articles there, horrible message boards, but it's all so long ago. I've tried calling Grace, but she won't tell me.'

'If the police can't say, there have to be newspaper reports,' Josh said, his voice vibrating in my ear. 'I bet there are old copies in the newspaper offices. We could go and look.'

'Go to Cornwall?' I pulled away from him so I could look at him and saw the sincerity in his face. 'Me and you?'

'Yeah, I'd love to get away from the office for a few days. I owe myself some time off.'

'Josh.' I shook my head in disbelief. 'You are amazing. Are you sure you want to do that? I could drive myself down.'

Josh shook his head. 'You aren't doing this alone.'

We made plans. We'd drive down to Cornwall mid-week. Go to the newspaper offices to see what articles we could find. Perhaps, if we could find out where it was, go to the farm where I'd been born.

'Josh and I are going to go to Cornwall,' I told my parents the following evening. 'I want to see where I grew up. Find out more about my father.'

'Are you sure?' Dad said. 'I thought we'd agreed you were going to help your mum with the horses.' He put down his knife and fork and looked at me across the table, his face filled with concern. I wished I hadn't agreed to stay for dinner. Josh had a meeting he had to go to, so rather than sit in the apartment alone I'd stayed after Mum and I had worked the horses.

Mum drained the last of her wine, her throat noisy as she swallowed. 'Can't you just put that all behind you?' Her voice was sharp, irritable. 'You don't need to know about your father. He did some terrible things. You weren't anything to do with that. You were just as much of a victim as those…'

'The girls your father…' Dad began.

'The girls he kidnapped, held prisoner, raped presumably, and eventually killed,' I said, my voice sounding cold, detached.

Mum poured herself another glass of wine. She was pale, a muscle twitching just beneath one of her eyes.

Dad made a noise somewhere between a grunt and a groan.

I took a deep breath, fixing both of my parents in my gaze. 'I need to know what happened around me when I was growing up. It's eating me up, not knowing.'

Dad raised his hands in a gesture of helplessness. 'You're right. Going will help you make sense of it all. See that you belong here. With us.'

Beside him, Mum sighed and then nodded.

'I'm glad Josh's going with you,' she said finally, speaking as if she had been struggling to find something to say.

'He'll look after you,' Dad agreed. 'Once you've been there you'll be able to put Cornwall into the past once and for all.'

* * * * * * * *

'This is so beautiful.' Josh slid the car window down, letting in a blast of salty air and sending the rubbish of discarded sandwich packets and coffee mugs swirling across the back seat.

We both stared, speechless, at the scene. Far below us a line of golden sand, broken only by rocky outcrops was bordered by an expanse of pure azure sea. Beside us stretched farmland, a myriad of shades of green, grassland, hedges and trees creating a picture book patchwork below a sky of unbroken blue.

'Amazing isn't it?' I whispered, awed by the beauty of our surroundings. When I'd come here for my mother's funeral, my impressions had been of bitter cold, browns and greys beneath a slate sky. This was completely different. The air felt gentle against my cheeks. I felt a curious sense of belonging. My father's evil deeds and my mother's tragic death could not take away from the beauty of the land.

We found the newspaper offices easily.

'We've come to see the newspaper archive,' Josh told the receptionist. ' We've got an appointment.'

'Of course.' She led the way through the office, long dark hair swishing from side to side as she walked. She led us down into the depths of the building where the archive, shelf after shelf of bound newspapers, was held.

She showed us how to locate the dates of the newspapers from the spine of the boxes and then left us to it.

I sank down onto a creaking wooden chair as Josh began to wander through the archive. Now we were here I was faced with the enormity of the task.

'Here.' Josh staggered from the shelves with a stack of file boxes. 'These date from around the time...' He slid the boxes onto the table in front of me.

They smelt musty, of damp paper, long forgotten. Together we began to sift through the pages, looking for any mention of my father or missing girls.

I read about local burglaries, school sports days, weddings that had happened years before.

'Mia.' Josh's voice was urgent as he slid one of the newspapers across the table towards me.

There in front of me was a report about a missing girl, accompanied by a photograph. My mother smiled out of the pages at me.

'Josh,' I breathed, shaking my head, not wanting to read the report, but unable not to. The words drew my eyes relentlessly into the story.

The hours slid by as we found more stories, more girls missing.

Wordlessly Josh pushed one of the newspapers across the table towards me. 'You?' I looked at the image of the little girl in the centre spread of the newspaper, tangled hair, holding onto the hand of a policeman as if her life depended on it, terrified eyes staring straight down the camera lens. My eyes. The little girl was me.

I'd never seen a photograph of me from before I went to live with Mum and Dad. Nothing of my past existed. Beside the image of me was one of my father, probably taken for a driving licence or something official. He glared at the camera, head slightly bowed, his eyes looking up at the lens, impassive, his expression impossible to read.

A third image showed a tangle of buildings, set amongst trees. The farm where I'd been raised until I'd set the actions in motion which would cause the death of my father. In the foreground policemen were leading away a woman, her head down, arms straining against the hold of the men. Nan.

There was a smaller, blurred photograph of a young woman. Susie Carne, the girl I'd freed.

I pushed the newspaper away for Josh to read. There, outlined in black and white was everything I'd wanted to know. The horror of what had happened at the farm.

'Shit. Mia.' Josh said finally, his face pale in the weird glow from the strip lights that illuminated the room. 'He was some truly fucked up piece of work.'

CHAPTER EIGHTEEN

Josh had booked us a guest house on the edge of Penzance. The area had the air of once being a smart residential area. Old Victorian houses were set back from the quiet tree lined road in neatly laid out gardens.

There was an awkward moment when the owner presumed we were married and asked for our surname as we checked in. We'd spoken at the same moment saying, 'No, we're not married,' with almost comedic timing. We chuckled about the incident as we walked back to the town along the prom to find somewhere for dinner. The early evening seafront was crowded with people strolling, taking the air after work and with holidaymakers making their way back from the beach below us.

We found a restaurant and ate. I couldn't taste anything. My jaw worked mechanically but everything was tasteless, the knowledge I had gained today swirling in my mind. I was aware of talking to Josh but had no idea what we spoke about. Eventually the conversation died out and we sat, watching families struggling to get small over-excited children to sit and eat rather than running riot around the restaurant.

Normally it would have been fun to explore the pubs, find a nightclub, wander back to our accommodation just as the first light of the summer dawn was streaking across the sky, but neither of us felt in the mood for that. Instead we walked slowly back to the guest house.

We let ourselves into one of the parks close to our guest house and sat on a bench as the night drew in around us.

I closed my eyes, trying to block out the images of the young women whose photographs I had seen in the articles. Somewhere, families still mourned the loss of them. Because of my father.

'I can't bear this.' I leant forwards, resting my elbows on my knees and covering my face with my hands. The sobs I'd tried so hard to keep contained wrenched themselves from somewhere deep inside me. 'How can anyone do that to another person…?'

I'd seen the photographs of my father, read the reports about him, but it was hard to contemplate the reality of what he had done. What had made him so evil? My vague memory of him was of someone gentle, quietly spoken. He'd kept young women prisoner. Done whatever he had to them in the darkness of the cellar. Killed them when he became bored of them. I was part of him. The genes that had made him do that were floating around in my body.

'Mia.' Josh got off the bench and crouched in front of me. He took my hands. Mine felt icy against the warmth of his skin. 'You're not your father. Whatever made him like that doesn't mean you are like that. You're good, beautiful, inside and out.'

I touched his hair. The strands were silky beneath my fingers. 'Josh thank you for being here for me. I'd be so lost without you.'

Josh sat down beside me, the length of his thigh inches from mine. I could feel the warmth of his body. 'How could someone do that? Want to kidnap someone your age? Then kill them. Mia, it's hard to imagine what kind of a man he was.'

In the silence that came between us I could hear him breathing. Feel my heart thumping against my rib cage.

* * * * * * * *

'It's up there.' Josh turned off the Sat Nav which had navigated us through narrow lanes, criss-crossing the countryside, always with the sea close by, to a narrow grassy track. I let out a long breath, trying to rid myself of the nauseous sensation which had rested in the pit of my stomach since sometime in the middle of the night.

Something had woken me, a shout from outside, people returning from the pub. Any semblance of sleep had been ripped from me then. I lay awake, tangling the rumpled sheets around legs which were first too hot and then too chilled. A kaleidoscope of images flashed into my mind as I lay in the nether land between wake and sleep. A blurred bulky form I thought was Nan. A tall, willowy man with sad eyes, the shadowy shape of a house, trees. I woke with a jolt from a doze in which I was being pulled through trees by a man, my feet not touching the ground.

'Can we drive up there?' I asked. The track was narrow, almost blocked by briars and leafy twigs.

'I think so.' Josh shoved his car into four-wheel drive and we jolted forwards onto the track.

'That doesn't sound good,' I winced as the tangled undergrowth at the side of the track scraped against the paintwork.

'Give the valet company something to work on,' Josh said wryly, steering to avoid a particularly low branch.

I wanted to stay in the green tunnel of leaves, the sunlight playing on my eyelids forever. The last thing I wanted was to reach the end of the track and see where I'd grown up. The briars ended and the track ran for a short way between stone walls to a rusted metal gate, hanging on its hinges. A chain secured by a rusty padlock fastened the gate to a stone gatepost.

'Who owns this place now?' Josh asked.

I shrugged, 'No idea. My Nan I guess.' The word 'Nan' rolled easily off my tongue even though I had barely spoken it for years. Once released I couldn't get away from the association I had with the place and all that had happened here. I was part of this. The farm was where I had been born. Where my mother had died.

Josh jumped out of the car, waded through the tangled long grass on the track. The padlock opened after one bang from a rock then Josh hauled the gate out of the clinging tendrils of grass and weeds, pushing it back into the hedge on the other side.

'Ready?' he said, getting back into the car.

I made a noise somewhere in between a whimper and a moan. How could I ever be ready for this?

Josh took my sound as agreement and drove on.

Once away from the track the land around us opened out into overgrown fields. At either side stretched grassland, dotted by outcrops of rock, tangles of gorse and clumps of small trees. The track snaked through the grassland, moving steadily upwards to a cluster of trees through which I could see the familiar shape of a tangle of pale stone buildings.

I pushed myself to the edge of my seat, found myself staring through the windscreen, memories flashing through my mind. I opened my mouth, forcing air into my lungs, wishing I had the strength to tell Josh to turn the car around, wishing I'd never agreed to come.

The car bumped on up the drive. I closed my eyes, not wanting to see, fighting to breathe against the tight band of tension that had closed around my chest.

Josh was silent too, as if smothered by the atmosphere of the land and the buildings which drew us relentlessly onwards.

'Do you remember it?' Josh asked.

I opened my eyes as we drove into a weed-entangled courtyard in-between the deserted buildings. Above us, in the treetops, birds were singing. The sky was blue.

'I don't know.' I shook my head, pushing my body back against the seat rest as if to protect myself from the buildings. Unable to sit still, I pushed open the car door, sucking in a lungful of clean, warm air. The courtyard was still, as if it were waiting for me to return.

'Maybe…' Without me being aware of him moving, Josh had got out of the car and come to stand beside me.

I hadn't been conscious of anything but the vaguest memory of the house, but now I was outside it seemed so familiar. 'That was my bedroom.' I pointed towards the far end of the house. Below the eaves of the roof, through a cracked pane of glass, I glimpsed faded pink curtains.

'There was a wood floor, a round rug, I had a single bed, a desk where I drew pictures. I didn't know I remembered that.' My voice was high, with a brittle edge to it.

I closed my eyes to block out an image of my father crossing the courtyard heading towards a tumbledown ruin at the opposite side.

'I want to go in,' I said, setting off across the courtyard.

'Mia, it's probably not safe,' Josh said, following me.

I was beyond caring. I needed to get inside the house to remember what it was like.

'We shouldn't… wait… don't, Mia.' Josh put a restraining hand on my arm. I shrugged him off, shoved at the front door. It opened, with a protesting shriek of rusted hinges and swollen wood scraping across the floor.

Once inside I stopped abruptly, Josh cannoning into me. Everything was covered in a layer of dust, swathes of dust encrusted cobwebs hung from the rafters.

It was like a theatre set, laid out before us. The layout so familiar, as if a curtain had gone back in my mind to reveal it to me. I touched the stair rail. I'd come home. I'd expected the farm to feel horrific, that the fear and despair which must have been contained within its walls would seep out and into my blood. Instead it felt peaceful, silent, as if it had been waiting for me to return.

'I used to draw there.' I pointed to the expanse of pine table which stretched in front of a vast open fireplace. 'I lived here until I was eight.' My voice sounded strangely disconnected, echoing slightly in the dusty space.

'Yeah.' Josh sounded uncertain. I wondered if he wasn't sure how to respond, if he was appalled by what had happened here, or if he could feel the expectant air of the house.

'How do you feel now you've seen it?' Josh turned slowly as if trying to imagine the house as it had been, but without answering I left the house.

'I want to see the cellar.' My voice sounded loud, childlike in the silence of the courtyard. Halfway across the courtyard my footsteps slowed, as if the air I moved through had become heavier, pushing me back.

The cellar was below the ruined house at the opposite side of the courtyard. Seeing it now as an adult I realised the house where I lived had been built after what was now just the crumbling walls of a cottage. It had probably been erected when the old one became too hard to maintain. Once the newer house had been built the old one had been left to slowly sink into decay, crumble in on itself. Only the cellar remained, somewhere my father had made good use of.

'You don't need to go in there,' Josh put his hand on my arm as I stood at the top of the stone steps that led down into the musty-smelling darkness.

'I want to see.' I shook his hand off and plunged down into the damp silence, one hand on the damp, slimy wall to steady myself until my eyes adjusted to the dim light. Ahead of me was the dirty concrete floor, at the end an open door, sagging on broken hinges.

'Wait.' Josh caught up with me, his breath loud in my ear. I could feel each exhalation waft my hair as he moved behind me. Down here it was chilly, the only light filtering in from the broken rafters above us.

The air in the cellar seemed oppressive, as if the fear and hopelessness in the atmosphere had soaked into the walls. Did Josh, I wondered, understand what this place was, what had happened here? What my father had done?

'This is…' I struggled to frame the words. 'I know.' Josh's voice was harsh as if he found it hard to speak.

'How can you want to be with me knowing what my father did?'

'Mia, that wasn't your fault. Your father did those terrible things, not you.'

We reached the end of the corridor. The wooden door had rotted and collapsed in on itself.

'This is where the girl was. Susie Carne. The one I set free.'

'You were very brave.' Josh slid an arm around my shoulder, drawing me into the warmth of his body as we stood in the doorway.

I shook my head, fighting the lump in my throat which made it impossible to speak. I hadn't been brave. I'd been stupid, wanting to talk to the girl in the room, thinking she wanted to be my friend, while all the time she wanted to trick me into letting her out. My stupidity had led to the death of my father, the end of the world I had known until them.

The light in the cellar room was green. The grass had grown up around the low window, filtering the light through the blades giving the impression of an under the sea world.

An image of my mother swam before me, the laughing young woman my aunt had described. My father had imprisoned her in this dank room.

There was a low single bed. A small chest of drawers, the leg of which had collapsed so it sat lopsidedly, resting against the stone wall. In one corner was a shower, a filthy plastic curtain hung dejectedly beside it. There was a bookcase with yellowing books.

The walls were a patchwork of bare stone and crumbling plaster. In places stained wallpaper clung, in others it had fallen revealing yellowing whitewashed plaster. There were marks on the plaster, short scrapes in sets of seven, marking the passing of time. There were too many to count. Had my mother made them? Or one of my father's other captives.

My eyes were drawn relentlessly to the bed, to the rope ties on each corner of the bed frame. Was that how I had been conceived? My mother, captive here, my father tying her down so he could rape her. How many other young women were there whose fate had been the same as hers? Killed by my father, while I played beside the fire in the house across the courtyard. How long had my mother been here before she died? Had she given birth to me in this cellar, loved me for a time until he had killed her? 'I need…' I shoved Josh away and ran, as Susie Carne had, through the open door, along the corridor, pounding up the steps, my feet slithering and sliding on the damp stone, out into the light.

CHAPTER NINETEEN

'Mia!' Josh followed me out of the cellar to where I had stopped, in the middle of the weed-strewn courtyard, surrounded by the ruined buildings of my childhood.

'I can't take all of this in.' I could hear the note of desperation in my voice. I turned slowly, looking at the abandoned stone buildings, the canopy of trees above them. Far above in the clear blue sky a single seagull soared on the breeze.

'It's okay.' He opened his arms to wrap me in a hug. 'How could you?'

I rested my cheek against the hard-planed muscles of his chest. Even after two days' travelling his shirt still smelt of clean laundry. I breathed in the tang of a new aftershave.

'Do you remember being here?'

'Bits.' I nodded. I'd always had vague impressions of my life here. Being here brought long-buried memories flooding to the surface.

I remembered sitting on my father's knee. Being enclosed in his arms, feeling protected. The smell of hay on his shirt. It was hard to relate that gentleness to the person my imagination conjured up for me to look at now, with the adult knowledge I had of my father.

I remembered Nan. Being warm and safe in bed. Her sitting on the bed beside me, gentle hands on my hair, a soft voice singing to me. No matter how hard I tried, though, the words of the song evaded me. They floated just out of my reach, like vague shapes in a mist. Just as strongly I remembered being afraid of her. I had a powerful memory of hiding beneath the table while she raged.

'Oh. Look.' I eased my way out of Josh's hug as the sloping branches of a tree caught my eye. 'It's still here.'

I led the way across the yard, through a wide gap between the buildings into an overgrown orchard. There on a low branch of an old apple tree, a rope swing turned gently in the breeze.

'My father made me this.' I shook my head, surprised at how seeing the tree had brought back the memory. The rope was prickly beneath my fingers, the tyre suspended from it green with moss. 'After all this time it's still here.' I remembered my father throwing the rope up over the branch. He'd tied on the old tyre, helped me into the circle and pushed me. I remembered swinging higher and higher. I had a vivid picture of Nan coming across the orchard with an old sweater to put under me so the rim of the tyre wasn't uncomfortable beneath my legs.

The sweater was long gone, but the tyre remained.

'We ought to head home.' Josh's voice brought me back to reality.

I nodded, sliding an unwilling hand off the tyre, not wanting to end the tentative connection to positive memories of my father.

'That's the tractor shed,' I said, remembering the position of the building as we crossed the courtyard.

'Have we got time? Can I just…?' I asked, but was already hurrying across the yard to the open fronted shed.

Inside it smelt of old oil, musty hay and dust.

'This was my father's tractor.' I paused in the doorway, letting my eyes adjust to the light.

My steps were silent on the dusty floor as I moved into the dimness of the shed.

The tractor was a big, square-fronted Massey Ferguson, its red paint faded and chipped. Rust patchworked the engine cover. The massive tyres, flat and perished, were still stained with mud.

The mudguard was pitted, mud encrusted beneath my fingers as I touched it, remembering my father pulling me up into the cab. Driving over the fields, feeling like a queen being up so high, looking out over the countryside, leaning my body against the warmth of my father.

I closed my eyes, feeling his presence so close to me and rested my head against the coolness of the mudguard. The thoughts that flooded into my mind were unbearable, the gentleness of my father combined with my knowledge of his crimes whirled around me.

There was so much of my father in the shed, tools I remembered him using, cans and containers of unidentifiable farming and machinery liquids.

After all of this time his tools were still in the shed. I moved away from the tractor, trailing my fingers over them, while Josh stood uncertainly in the doorway, his presence more of a distraction than a comfort. There were boxes of nails and screws, the orange rust coating my fingers as I touched them. I crouched to pull his toolbox out from beneath the workbench, some distant memory reminding me of its presence.

I remembered trailing around the farm behind my father as he repaired fences, tinkered with bits of machinery. The tools were heavy in my hands; I sifted through them, slowly. My father had been the last one to touch these. I squeezed my hands around the wooden shafts of the hammers and unidentifiable bits of metal as if I could absorb his presence.

'We should go.' Josh stood beside me.

'Of course.' I stood up, slowly, not wanting to leave. The buildings felt comforting, as if they had been waiting all this time for me to return.

'I'll put this back.' Josh picked up the centre of the toolbox, to move it. As he lifted, the centre section came out and the main toolbox remained on the ground. 'Shit, sorry,' Josh crouched over the toolbox to put the section back in place.

'Josh,' I said, the underneath of the centrepiece catching my eye. There, in a hidden section beneath the toolbox, was a layer of plastic bags. 'Wait.' I lifted out the plastic bags, turning them over in my hands, seeing their insides beneath the faded plastic.

'Oh fuck,' Josh breathed, seeing what was I was holding.

He crouched beside me as I tipped out the bags, their contents spilling out onto the dusty floor. Necklaces, purses, bank cards, and a faded hair slide lay on the floor at our feet.

Scrambling to my feet, I lurched away from my father's trophies, my stomach knotting as I vomited repeatedly.

My head pounding, I stood to lean against the dampness of the shed wall, the stone rough through the fabric of my shirt. My legs trembled violently beneath me as I watched Josh's long fingers sift slowly through the contents of the bags.

'The police mustn't have found these.' His voice, little more than a whisper sounded tremulous. 'We should hand them in.' He began to bundle the necklaces and pathetic looking human debris into the bags.

I couldn't bear the thought of more investigation into my father's crimes. What was the point? It was over. He was dead. The women were dead.

'Leave them.' I shoved myself upright and wrenched the bags out of his hands, dropping them back into the depths of the toolbox.

'Mia, they belong to...' In the gloom of the shed Josh's skin was pale, his eyes wide with revulsion.

'Please.' The metal of the toolbox scraped against the cobbled floor as I pushed it back beneath the workbench. With a final shove it disappeared once more into the darkness. I wanted to keep the good memories I had of him, cling to them with all my might; with them perhaps I could banish the thoughts of the evil man his actions made him. I'd loved him; how could I love someone who was so filled with evil that he could kill, rape, take young women off the street and hold them prisoner?

Young women my age, with their lives in front of them. He'd done that and then been gentle and kind and loving to me. Protected me and made me feel safe, while those women were chained in a cellar just across the yard from my bedroom.

A band of tension tightened around my forehead.

'Please can we go? I put my hand on Josh's arm. He closed his eyes, taking a long juddering breath which he slowly released. When he finally opened them his eyes flickered around the room before slowly focusing on me.

'Yes, come on.' His eyes rested on my hand. I felt rather than saw him make a decision not to shove me away.

As we walked across the yard a movement caught my eye. At the far end of the paddock behind the house, faded yellow police tape fluttered from posts in the ground where some of my father's victims had lain.

* * * * * * * *

'How did the weekend go?' Mum asked as I walked into the kitchen.

My parents were sitting at the newspaper-strewn kitchen table, a bottle of wine between them. She sounded as if I'd been away to a house party with friends, rather than to discover the grim reality of my past.

'Good... good.' I moved to lean against the kitchen work surface, struggling to find words to explain to them what I'd discovered.

'Did you find out what you wanted?' Dad's fingers twirled the stem of his wine glass.

'I think so, it was...' The explanation of what I had unearthed, everything that had happened over the weekend had no place here. How could I tell them about the contents of my father's toolbox, my memories of the house, my knowledge of the dead girls? How could I let that horror into their lives, see the genteel shelter of their existence exposed to the filth that had spawned me?

'It's very beautiful in Cornwall.' I lifted a wine glass out of the cupboard, poured myself a glass. 'The sea is amazing.'

'Yes, isn't it?' Mum took a deep breath, seeming relieved we were on a safe subject. 'We used to go to Padstow when I was a girl. We stayed in a guesthouse on the harbour.'

'Rick Stein's first restaurant was there.' Dad plunged into the safer waters of our conversation with the relief of someone who had been trudging across a desert and found an oasis.

I sipped my wine, my cheeks aching with the effort of smiling, as I looked from one to the other while they battered the inane conversation backwards and forwards. Gradually the conversation dried up. There was an awkward silence broken only by the sound of their wine glasses being lifted from the table.

'You don't need to go there again.' Dad tore his eyes from the table to look at me.

'Let that all go now.' His voice held that preaching tone he had used for lectures about studying hard for my exams. 'That's all in the past. You belong here.'

'Darling...' Mum pushed herself away from the table and wrapped her arms around me. 'You must try to move on. Your grandmother and aunts... I know it hurts you, but they don't feel they can let you into their lives. Eventually you'll be able to accept that. You're not responsible for what happened, for what your father and his mother did.' There was a strand of hay stuck on the front of her fleece. It prickled against my cheek. 'We're your family, we love you so much. We just want you to be happy. Forget the past. Forget all of that.'

That. My early life, my beginning, summed up into one dismissive word. That.

I pulled her closer to me wanting to feel safe, to absorb the love I knew was there.

I nodded, gently sliding out of her arms, digging my fingernails into my palms to stop myself from crying out with the agony of carrying my past. I wanted to shake it off, forget I'd ever had an existence before I lived here, but I couldn't.

'I'll take my bag upstairs.' As soon as we'd returned from Cornwall Josh had remembered a boys' night out he'd been invited on. 'Sorry,' he'd said, deleting the text message he'd just received. 'Boy's night out. I'd forgotten. I guess you'll stay at your parents tonight?' It was a statement rather than a question. I'd nodded, imagining the apartment full of drunken men he'd undoubtedly bring back in the early hours. I didn't mind. I'd rather be at my parents' house than stay in the empty apartment alone with my thoughts.

I went to my room, seeing it with the detachment of a stranger. I couldn't associate the person who had grown up in this luxury, surrounded by peace and security, with my memories of the child I had been at the farm. In the time since the discovery of my mother's body I had lost all sense of who I was. I could never go back to being the person who Mum and Dad had raised. The girl I had been stood beside me, wanting to be given life again. I needed to know more, to understand who I had been. I had to understand who my father was, what had happened to my mother and to the other young women whose lives he had stolen.

No matter how much information Josh and I had gleaned from the newspaper archive I still found myself irresistibly drawn to the Internet. I knew there was nothing I would find there which would make me feel better, but like an addict I found myself needing the pain that looking would cause.

Dumping my bag on the floor I pulled out my laptop and turned it on. No matter how Mum and Dad tried to protect me, to absorb me back into the security of their life, my past danced in the foreground. No matter how much they said I belonged here and I should forget what my father had done I was powerless against the urge to pick at the scab and see what lay beneath. The burden of not knowing was something I could not bear.

With a few clicks on my keyboard I was in my father's vile world and those who speculated about it. I scrolled silently, unable to stop looking at the hate-filled messages. I tapped in Nan's name and watched as reams of posts and articles appeared on my screen. I shook my head to try to rid myself of the pain at my stupidity at not questioning my past before. Tormenting myself I began to sift through the online posts, through the lurid speculation about what Nan had done, if she had helped my father, or if she was so stupid she didn't realise what he was doing.

My head began to ache with the effort of trying to remember. At the farm I had only had vague impressions of my life, distant memories triggered by being there, and seeing things brought others to the forefront. I had to know what had happened, what the reality of my existence had been at the farm. There was only one person who could tell me that. Nan.

CHAPTER TWENTY

'Here, darling.' Mum stood beside me with a steaming mug of hot chocolate. I pushed myself upright in the window seat where I'd been lolling.

'Thank you.' I juggled the mug and my Dan Brown book.

'You always loved this spot.' Mum tucked the rug I'd draped over my legs under my toes. 'Are you feeling warmer now?' The window seat had always been my favourite place. I loved to sit here, with the curtains drawn, shut off from the rest of the room. The deep recessed window looked out over the garden. I was level with one of the flower borders; tall plants and bushes, whipped by the winter storm, lashed against the glass beside me.

I sipped the chocolate, feeling the liquid slide down my throat, its warmth spreading through my body.

'Yes, thank you.'

'Is it ever going to stop raining?' Mum looked out at the rain with a shiver.

'Not according to the forecast,' Dad said, coming into the room with a heap of property brochures in his hand. He threw an armful of logs onto the wood burner and sat in the armchair beside it.

'I don't remember a winter like it,' Mum said, moving to sit with her back to the wall beside the wood burner, soaking up the heat.

'What time's Josh coming?' Dad looked at me over the top of his reading glasses.

'As soon as he's finished work.' I shrugged my shoulders, shaking my head in mock despair. 'You know what he's like.'

'It doesn't matter anyway,' Mum said, moving away from the wood burner and curling in the armchair opposite Dad. 'It's only a casserole. Nothing will spoil.'

'Are you going back into town with him after dinner?' Dad leafed through the brochures, tossing them to the floor beside him as he discarded them.

'Yes.' I turned back to my book, smiling at Dad's inevitable, 'The roads are terrible with this rain. Floods everywhere. Stay here.'

'We'll see.' I met his eyes and saw the concern there. I knew Josh wouldn't want to stay. Apart from being closer to work in the morning, being at his apartment meant we could wander around naked, eat a midnight feast in bed. Far more fun than being here.

'How did you get on today?' Dad threw down the last of the brochures.

'Fantastic.' Mum brought her knees up to her chin and wrapped her arms around her legs. 'They were brilliant.'

I met her eyes and grinned.

'What a rotten day though,' Mum told him. 'I was bundled up in waterproofs and woolly hat and boots and still frozen.'

I shivered at the memory of Mum laying waterproof rugs over Solar's back to try to keep him warm and dry. She'd draped another over my legs, tucking it under my thighs. Still the icy rain had made its way down the collar of my raincoat and found a way down the back of the saddle so that I was sitting in a puddle of cold water. I knew when I got off, I'd look as if I'd peed myself.

'Field Farm?' Dad's voice carried a note of triumph at having remembered which of the various arenas we had attended today.

'That's right.' Mum beamed at him, impressed.

'Bloody cold spot at the best of times.' Dad shuddered. He'd often come with us to competitions, helping Mum with her horses and the two of us with the various ponies I'd ridden.

'The ground was horrible,' I told him. 'Warming up was a nightmare.' The sandy surface of the warm-up area was waterlogged, the surface sodden and spongy. I'd ridden amongst the other competitors, the sand splashing up to coat our horses' legs and girths and our damp, cold leather riding boots.

'How did Solar go?' Dad asked.

'Amazing,' I replied, knowing the single word did little justice to the incredible horse. He'd been tense when Mum and I unloaded him from the lorry, his muscles tight against the cold weather and the excitement of the environment.

I'd worked him in the warm-up area, amongst the chaos of the other horses, the heavy rain battering against us, yet still he had settled. I'd felt his muscles relax, his neck and jaw soften to me, letting me control his immense power.

I'd no word in my vocabulary which could describe the feeling of going into the arena on him. Mum stripping the waterproof rugs off his back and from around my legs. The noise of the rain hammering on the roof high above us. The crowds, standing in the spectators' gallery, shivering, hands cupped around warm drinks. I'd felt him assess where he was before he settled, letting me canter him around the dusty surface, our tension rising as we waited for the start bell. And then our round. Me controlling him with infinitesimal shifts of my weight, turning him left and right as we soared over the fences as if they were utterly irrelevant.

'Amazing,' Mum echoed my words. 'He is going to be one hell of a horse.'

* * * * * * * *

'Glass of wine, Josh?' Dad waved the bottle in Josh's direction.

'Just one,' Josh held his glass across the table to where Dad was brandishing the bottle. 'Small one, I've got to drive.'

'In this bloody weather too,' Mum started again. 'I don't know why you don't stay here tonight.'

'Work tomorrow; traffic is always bad getting into the city. Easier if I'm at the apartment then I can just walk to my office.' Josh was well practiced in fobbing her off.

Under the table, Josh's thigh rubbed seductively up against mine. I knew the weather didn't have much to do with his impatience to get back into the city.

'Excited about your graduation?' Josh asked me as Mum piled plates with her delicious-smelling casserole.

'Of course.' I smiled brightly at him, hoping no one would notice the brittle note in my voice. I was dreading my graduation, the questions about how I'd done since finishing my course. I still had no idea how to explain to anyone about what had happened. My parents had tried to console me, reassuring me that the loss of my first big role was just a blip, something that happened to most people, but most people didn't lose jobs because their father was a murderer. They'd tried to tell me that people would forget my past. Something more interesting would come along. But I wasn't convinced. The horror of my past seemed to wrap around me like a cloak I couldn't shift.

'I'm so sorry I'm not going to be there.' Josh laid his hand over mine. I clenched my fist, the sides of my fork handle dug into my palm.

'I know…' I forced an air of hilarity into my voice, 'fancy going to China to an international conference of software development companies instead of Exeter to see me get a piece of paper.'

A ripple of polite laughter tinkled around the room.

'Your big day too.' Mum's face creased into a frown. 'Josh away and Dad and I leaving you after the grads to visit some old friends.'

She twisted her mouth into a wry smile. 'We'll go for lunch first though, after the ceremony, and then we'll get the train the rest of the way from Exeter to St Ives. It's a shame not to see my godmother while we are so close. She's so old, poor dear, not sure if she'll be around much longer.'

I stopped listening as Mum spoke about her plans for after my graduation. The muscles in my cheeks ached with the effort of holding the smile. My big day, my graduation and no one to share it with. I pictured driving home alone, miserable at being left by them all.

'What?' I said, suddenly aware of Mum speaking again.

'Yes, sorry.' She steepled her fingers and rested her chin on the tips of her fingers. 'Poppy's Mum rang and asked if we could take Poppy with us. Old Mrs Adams, Poppy's gran is really ill. She's only got a few weeks they think. Poppy's Mum said they couldn't leave her.'

I met Mum's eyes; she raised her eyebrows in a gesture of helplessness. 'I couldn't very well say no.'

I stared at the remnants of my meal, my stomach churning. 'It's fine.'

It was anything but fine. I'd barely said a word to Poppy since she had betrayed me. The thought of having to be in her company for a whole day was not something I relished.

I caught Josh's appalled expression and knew it must mirror my own.

As we drove away from my parent's Josh finally exploded, 'Fucking hell. What was your mum thinking of? Saying Poppy could come with you.' It was rare for Josh to ever say anything negative about my parents.

'I know,' I shook my head in despair. 'A whole day with that stupid bitch.'

'I'm so sorry I'm not going to be there,' Josh said, taking my hand. 'This damn conference.'

'It's okay, honestly, I lied, dreading him going away and me having to go to my graduation with Poppy for company.

I can't wait to get you home,' Josh said huskily as we hurried out of the car park towards the apartment. He nibbled gently at my neck. I breathed in the masculine smell of him, glad for the distraction.

* * * * * * * *

A week later, Poppy and I were in the back seat of Dad's Audi as we hurtled down the motorway towards Exeter.

'Your dress looks lovely,' Poppy said. Her voice had a high little-girl note that set my teeth on edge.

'Thanks.' I stared out of the window, watching the scenery slide past. 'Yours too,' I added, aware of the long journey we had to make. Whatever I felt about Poppy and the end of our friendship, there was no point in making myself miserable all day.

'I wonder if Jenny Rowe will be there today?' Poppy asked, clearly making as much of an effort to be civil as I was.

'I hope she's not got that awful bloke with her. What was his name?'

The ice, if not broken was definitely cracked and we managed to make stilted conversation the whole way to Exeter.

'Feels weird to be back here.' Poppy pulled a face as she pushed open the passenger door when Dad finally found a big enough parking spot on one of the side streets. I nodded, my stomach clenched into a tight knot of tension, wondering how I'd cope with the questions about my career from others on my course, if anyone would have discovered my past.

'Thank you so much for the lift.' Poppy hugged Mum. 'I'll go and find everyone from my course. Good luck with the presentation, Mia. I'll meet you after the ceremony.'

As she hurried away, her heels tapping on the concrete path, I breathed a sigh of relief to be rid of her. Things were never going to be the same between us again. We'd been the best of friends, from primary school, right up to attending university. But she had betrayed that friendship and there was no way back.

We made our way into the university grounds and into the vast hall where the presentation of the graduation certificates would take place. I found Mum and Dad seats and then hurried off to get my gown.

'Mia.' Alice, one of my course mates, leapt towards me, enfolding me in a warm hug. 'You're back.'

I hugged her, my face buried in her wild mane of ginger hair.

'Imagine,' I said, drawing back to look into her eyes, 'we made it. Completed the course.'

'I know…' Alice opened her mouth, eyes wide and squealed in delight.

'How's life outside uni?' I asked, looking around the room. Other students were collecting their gowns. Some I recognised and waved to.

'Brilliant, dahling,' Alice, intoned, theatrically. 'I start a walk-on role in Coronation Street next month.'

'Oh. My. God.' I copied her look of amazement. 'That is so cool. You deserve it though, you were so good.'

'Thanks,' Alice shrugged, humbly. 'How about you. Aren't you in that…? Oh…'

My jaw ached with the effort of maintaining my smile.

'I… er… Oh, look there's Bethany.' Alice dropped a hand softly on my arm and was gone. I turned slowly, trailing her progress into a group of girls who had been on our course. I forced my lips into a smile and raised a hand in greeting as they turned to look at me, averting their eyes.

* * * * * * * *

'What a lovely ceremony,' Poppy sighed contentedly as she clipped on her seat belt.

I backed the big car out of its parking spot and pulled out into the line of traffic. If she thought I was going to chat to her like I'd done when we'd been having lunch with Mum and Dad she'd another thing coming.

'Yes. Wasn't it?' I snapped, flatly. 'I just loved being the pariah no one wanted to talk to.'

'What?' Poppy said, as if she were three steps behind me and hadn't realised how angry I was.

'Yes,' I continued, the words snapping from my lips like machine gun fire. 'It was wonderful knowing everyone knew what had happened to my fabulous stage role. And why.'

'Mia.' Poppy's voice was stern, like a schoolteacher admonishing a naughty pupil. 'Please stop this. I didn't expect the girls to tell anyone else. I don't know why I told them. I was so stupid. I've regretted that every single day.'

'Regretted it every single day,' I mocked her in a fake posh, whining, nasal voice.

'I wish I hadn't come with you,' she sobbed, searching through her handbag for a tissue

'So do I,' I snapped, turning on the windscreen wipers as the heavy rain began again.

Her sobs were loud even above the pounding of the rain on the roof. I set the windscreen wipers to their highest speed, peering through the dusk as they swished the worst of the water away.

I pushed my foot onto the accelerator and the powerful car surged forwards. I longed to be home, to curl up alone on the sofa where I could howl away my anguish.

'Please slow down,' Poppy sounded frightened, the headlights of cars coming towards us shattering into myriad fragments on the rain spattered windscreen.

'Shut up!' Her fear irritated me more. A band of tension tight across my back was making it hard to breathe. I had to get her out of the car. I couldn't bear her near me any longer after the hurt she had caused me. I'd protected her while we were growing up and this was how she had repaid me.

We turned off the motorway.

'Nearly home now,' I spat between gritted teeth.

'Good,' Poppy said in an equally nasty tone.

I swung the car around a tight bend, straight into a deep flood.

The impact spun the steering wheel out of my hand, the big car plunging and bucking like a wild horse.

Beside me I heard Poppy's frightened gasp as we hit the submerged grass bank, the car's tyres finding grip and rushing forwards, over the verge. In the light from the headlights I saw the bare branches of a hawthorn hedge as we crashed through it. Water cascaded around us, the weight of the car sending spray soaring skywards.

There was a deathly silence in the car, broken only by Poppy unclipping her seatbelt and the fear in her voice as she said, 'Mia! We're in the fucking river.'

CHAPTER TWENTY-ONE

'Help me! I screamed, kicking wildly against the cold water. I fought for the surface, icy tendrils of weeds clutched at my ankles, wrapped around my thighs. I struggled harder, fighting for my life.

'Mia... Mia. You're safe. It's okay.'

I opened my eyes, focusing slowly on the nurse in a lilac uniform who was bending over me. I moved my legs compulsively, still feeling the weeds clinging to my feet.

Her fingers were cool against my arms as she gently held me, encouraging me to be still.

'You're in hospital. You're safe.' Her accent was Nrthern, with the sing-song tones of the North East.

I struggled to sit up, pushing her hands away, looking at her properly for the first time.

'Welcome back to us,' she smiled. She wasn't much older than me, her eyes a vivid green. Her short hair, slicked back over her ears, was jet black. 'Can you remember what happened?' she asked. Her voice was gentle. Without waiting for my reply, she continued, 'I'm just going to take your temperature.' She eased a plastic device into my ear.

I shook my head. 'How did I...?' I touched the pale blue fabric of the shapeless garment covering me.

The nurse fastened a blood pressure cuff around my arm and inflated it. 'Do you remember the accident? Your car crashed. Went into the river,'

'River?' I repeated, hearing the confusion in my voice.

'You were lucky, someone saw the car, found you on the bank. Much longer and you'd have...'

I shook my head, feeling my eyes widen with confusion. I looked around the room, seeking something familiar in the airy hospital ward. I was in a small room with just one other, unoccupied bed. Through the window I could see a scrap of grey sky. A lone seagull flew past, elegant on outstretched wings.

'Your Mum and Dad are here.' She released the pressure on the cuff. There was a ripping sound as the Velcro sides parted. 'I'll let them in to see you.'

I lay back on the pillows, my mind racing.

'Mia. Darling.' Mum hurried into the room, Dad at her side. 'Thank God you're safe.' She leant over me, burying her face in my shoulder. When she drew away the pale blue fabric was dotted with her tears.

'I don't understand.' My eyes fixed on hers. I tightened my lips in an attempt to stop the tears from falling.

Dad came to the other side of the bed. He sat down and took my hand. 'We've been so frightened. Thought we were going to lose you.'

'What happened?' I asked, my eyes darting between their concerned, love-filled faces.

'The car went off the road into the river. You were driving home.'

I shook my head in disbelief, shaking Dad's hand away so I could wipe away the tears that were falling freely down my cheeks.

'How?'

Mum sat down heavily on the opposite side of the bed, her shoulders slumped as if she were exhausted. 'Can you remember anything?'

I met her eyes, knowing my face had dropped into an expression of utter confusion and panic. 'I don't know.'

'After grads,' Dad said, 'you were driving home. The ambulance men thought you'd hit a flood and gone off the road into the river.'

'You've been here for a couple of days,' Mum said gently. 'We got a phone call from the police while we were in Exeter.'

'Exeter?' I could hear the panic in my voice. 'Why were you in Exeter?'

'Darling, we went to your grads. Then Dad and I went on to Exeter to see my godmother. You and Poppy drove home.'

'Poppy?' I pushed myself upright, panic making my breath short.

'Where's Poppy?'

Dad pulled me into his arms. I buried my head against his shirt front, breathing in the clean smell of the fabric. 'Darling, I'm so sorry. Poppy died.' His voice was little more than a whisper.

'Poppy's dead?' My voice sounded robotic with the realisation of what had happened.

'Thank God you're okay.' Dad stroked my hair, his hand moving over the shape of my head with a gentle touch.

I drew away, falling back against the pillows. My breath sounded ragged as I covered my face with my hands, wanting to block out the dreadful knowledge.

Mum pulled me into a hug, completed by Dad's arms encircling both of us. I let them support the weight of my body, the knowledge of Poppy's death making it impossible for me to move.

'Where's Josh?' My voice was filled with panic.

'He's away. On business.' Dad's eyes met mine.

I nodded my head slowly. Remembering. 'Hong Kong.'

'That's right.' Dad looked relieved.

'He was really upset.' Mum said. 'We let him know what happened. He's been messaging Dad to see how you are.'

'See,' Dad pulled his phone out of his pocket, found the messages and handed them to me to read. 'Tell Mia I can't wait to see her. Tell Mia I love her. Tell Mia I'll do a video call when she's home.'

'Tom's here,' Mum said gently, drawing herself out of our circle. 'Do you want to see him?'

Without waiting for my reply she moved away from me.

My face still buried in Dad's shoulder I felt rather than heard the door open, letting in a wave of cooler air. There was a sudden clamour of noise; I breathed in the hospital smell of disinfectant.

'Tom,' Dad's voice was gentle.

He gently untangled himself from me and stood up. 'We'll leave you for a while. Bring some coffee back.'

Mum and Dad left the room, closing the door quietly behind them, leaving us in an oppressive silence.

Slowly I lifted my eyes to look at him. Tom's face was grey, with dark smudges beneath each eye. There were lines at the side of his mouth I'd never noticed before.

Without a word he came towards my bed and sat down beside me. I tumbled forwards into his arms, feeling his grip tighten. I buried my face into his hair. I'd missed him so much. 'I can't believe it,' I mumbled into his hair. It was hard to speak, my throat felt as if I was being strangled. 'Poppy. How can she be gone?'

'Mia,' his voice cracked. He began to sob, his tears wetting my neck. 'I should have taken her. I shouldn't have gone to work.' I stroked his hair, feeling his body heave as he sobbed. 'How can she be dead?' His head shook against my shoulder as if he couldn't believe what he was saying.

'It was my fault,' I whispered.

I could feel his head move against my face as he protested. 'No. It was an accident. I know she'd hurt you, but you were friends. You'd have made up.'

'We had made up,' I lied. How could I tell him about our final moments together? That we'd had a horrible screaming row in the moments before the car left the road.

'I'm glad you were with her,' Tom said gently.

The young nurse who had been beside me when I opened my eyes came back into the room. 'Can Mia be left alone?' Dad snapped, walking in just behind her, Mum at his heels.

'It's okay, Dad.' It felt an immense effort to even take the steaming cup of coffee from him. I lay back on my pillows, the effort of dealing with everyone exhausting.

The nurse glanced at Dad as if assessing how much of a nuisance he was going to be while she went about her work.

'Mia,' she said, her tone brisk, as if there were a million things she needed to do. 'The police are here. They want to have a quick chat with you. Are you up to talking to them?'

'Of course she isn't!' Dad spat.

'Peter,' Mum admonished him.

'I'll see them.' I nodded weakly.

Two plainclothes officers came in. One a tall, willowy woman, her hair drawn back severely from her face. As she crossed the room, I envisioned Poppy whispering in my ear about her awful dress sense and how a lick of make-up would make a world of difference to her appearance. Beside her was an older man, short with a gentle round of a belly pushing through the open sides of his suit jacket.

'Mia.' The man's smile didn't reach his eyes.

The nurse dragged two chairs from the side of the room and positioned them beside my bed so they could sit and talk to me.

'I'm going to go,' Tom said, folding me into a hug. I closed my eyes wanting to stay there, safe and protected.

'I'm sorry about your friend,' the female officer said as Tom closed the door behind him.

I glanced at the two of them and to Mum and Dad, hovering protectively behind their chairs.

'Thanks.' I stared at my hands. There was a livid bruise on the back of my right hand I hadn't noticed before.

'Do you mind if we ask about the accident?' The man spoke, his voice toneless as if he were reading off a script.

I forced my head to shake. 'No.'

'What happened, Mia?' The woman leaned forwards to appraise me from beneath dark eyebrows that were in desperate need of plucking.

I shook my head again, gulping as I struggled to stop the tears from falling. 'I don't know.' My voice was little more than a whisper.

'Can you remember anything?' It was his turn to coax.

I looked at them, saw the naked interest in their eyes. My throat constricted, making it impossible to talk.

'Driving.' I closed my eyes, covered my face with one hand. 'Just driving and then…'

I pulled the bedclothes around, huddling into a hunched ball, drawing my legs up to meet my chin, moving frenziedly as if I could fight off the memory of the water closing around us.

'We were in the water.' My voice sounded loud, harsh in the silence of the room. 'I couldn't get out… She was screaming… Poppy. She was screaming.'

'That's enough.' Dad's voice was filled with anger as he hurried around to the side of my bed, pulling me into his arms.

'Please leave her alone.' Mum's hand touched my hair, stroking me gently as if I were a nervous horse she could soothe by her touch.

'Okay,' the man said, holding his hands up in an attempt to protect himself from Dad's wrath.

'Obviously the crash investigators will be looking at the car,' I heard the woman say. 'Checking it for mechanical problems.'

'We understand that,' Dad growled. 'The car was only a year or so old. There was nothing wrong with it. Mia hit the flood and went off the road. Nothing more than a tragic accident.'

'Of course.' I glanced up to see the woman officer nodding solemnly, her face twisted into a gentle smile as she caught my eye. 'Terrible thing to happen. I'm so sorry about your friend.' She touched a hand to the top of my arm, probably the only part of me she could find that wasn't enfolded in a hug from my parents.

* * * * * * * *

The hospital released me a day later. I ached with tiredness, my body bruised and scraped. Dad got me a new phone to replace the one I'd lost in the accident. Josh called, his conversation filled with concern. Dad brought my laptop in so we could Skype. 'I'll be home in a couple of days,' Josh said, sitting on the balcony of his hotel, the skyline of Hong Kong in the background. 'I'm so sorry about Poppy. Tom must be devastated.'

I'd nodded. 'I've made him come round here. I don't want him to be alone. We've been out walking. He seems glad of the distraction.'

'I bet he is.' The kindness of his words could not disguise the jealous note in his voice, clear even over the vast distance that separated us.

I sighed, ignoring the jibe. Tom was my oldest friend. Josh was my boyfriend. I didn't want him to feel threatened by the relationship I had with Tom. I'd hated mine and Poppy's row coming between us. I'd missed his friendship.

I was over the moon when Josh was home. Being back in his arms was wonderful. He'd taken me back to his apartment, kissed every one of my multicoloured bruises.

I'd been glad to get away from home. Mum and Dad had flapped around me as if I were some delicate piece of china they were afraid would break. I knew they meant well, but I needed time to be alone with my thoughts, to let the enormity of what had happened settle in my conscious.

In his bed that night, I finally began to cry. Josh took me in his arms, cradling me, rocking me gently as I sobbed. I began to talk about the time I'd spent with Poppy, our lives together, beginning at school, things she'd said, while he stroked my hair.

'Everyone blames me,' I sniffed, looking up to meet his concerned expression.

'They don't,' he said firmly. 'It was an accident. Simply a tragic accident.'

'If only I'd taken the other road,' I sighed. 'None of this would have happened.'

'You'll feel better after the funeral,' he told me, even though I'd no idea what he was basing his statement on. Josh breezed through life; trauma and tragedy seemed to give his gilded existence a wide berth. I nodded. Perhaps I would. I snuggled into the warmth of his body, soaking up the heat generated by his torso and the length of his legs, where they rested against the backs of mine.

When I woke it was still dark. Josh was gone, his side of the bed cool, the duvet tucked around me. I sat up, aware of the low rumble of his voice. 'Josh?' I pushed the duvet away and stood, shivering in the night air.

My feet soundless on the thick carpet, I crossed the bedroom and opened the door. I could hear Josh's voice more clearly now, although just the sound, not individual words. He'd closed the door to the room he used as an office when he worked from home. He worked so hard, these late-night calls to clients abroad must be a nightmare to deal with, coming as they did at all hours. Gently I opened the door, his eyes met mine as I leant on the doorframe.

'I'm going to have to go,' he said, raising a finger to indicate he would be just a moment.

'Really?' I heard disappointment in a voice that sounded distinctly female.

'Sorry, yes. Hopefully that issue is solved now.' Josh's voice was coolly professional.

He ended the call and came towards me. 'I'm sorry, did my call wake you? Just a client with a software issue.'

'Sounded like you were talking to a woman.' I hated the neediness I could hear in my voice.

'Yes,' he sighed, impatiently. 'She's a client. Mia, please don't start this shit. You're friends with Tom. I understand that. I have friends and colleagues that are female too.'

He folded me into his arms. I rested my head on his tee-shirt, letting my hands slip beneath the elastic of his boxer shorts to glide over the tightness of his buttocks.

'Okay,' I whispered. 'Are you coming back to bed?'

He seized my wrists and pulled them upwards away from his body. 'I'm shattered, Mia. I need to sleep.'

CHAPTER TWENTY-TWO

Poppy's funeral was held one dark December day. Josh and I travelled in Dad's car with Mum. They'd had to replace the crashed one with one, which, weeks after they'd got it, still had that unique new car smell.

'I can't believe we're at Poppy's funeral,' Mum said. She looked beautiful in a tight-fitting black coat and a dramatic wide-brimmed hat. 'Such a tragedy. So young. Her whole life ahead of her.'

Josh helped me out of the car. He looked breathtakingly handsome in a dark suit, his dark hair freshly trimmed for the day. 'Are you doing ok?' He asked me, his voice full of concern. I pulled the corners of my mouth into the semblance of a smile, smoothing down the front of the black dress and matching coat I'd bought especially.

'Tom.' Dad held his hand out for Tom to shake, before drawing him into a hug. Mum put her arms around the two of them, resting her cheek on Tom's shoulder, I could see her whispering words of reassurance in his ear.

Tom looked terrible. His immaculate black suit hung on his frame. He'd lost a lot of weight, his eyes sunken in, his pale cheeks red-rimmed.

'I'm so sorry.' Josh clasped Tom to his chest as Dad released him.

When it was my turn, I pulled Tom into my arms. He swallowed, the noise loud against my ear. As he drew away, he met my eyes, shook his head slightly as if words were impossible and walked slowly towards the crematorium. I glanced at Josh who was staring fixedly at the ground.

'Another funeral,' I whispered, slipping my hand into Josh's, our shoes crunching on the gravel path. 'I can't believe it.'

As we took our seats, I glanced at the congregation, seeing the hunched form of Poppy's mum in the front pew, Tom's arm around her. Poppy's other friends and work colleagues were together in a group. I saw one of the blonde bitches who had so effectively wrecked my career glare at me. I stared back until finally she dropped her gaze.

I spent the whole service with my face buried in a handkerchief, unable to stop crying once Poppy's flower-heaped coffin made its way down the aisle and onto the stand from where it would eventually go to be cremated.

The service was conducted to the accompaniment of the sound of heartrending sobbing. I joined in, crying uncontrollably as Tom spoke of Poppy, telling the congregation some of the words I had given him as well as his own thoughts. I knew I couldn't have stood in front of everyone and spoken about her. We walked out of the crematorium to the sound of Celine Dion's *My Heart Will Go On* as Poppy's body made its way into the fire.

I forced myself to walk slowly out of the building, fighting the urge to run into the fresh air out of the oppressive atmosphere.

'Hang on, I have to send a text.' Josh pulled his mouth into a grimace of embarrassment as he disentangled his hand from mine.

I watched him walk away, shaking my head in disbelief. Even at Poppy's funeral he still put work first.

'Mia.' Someone touched my arm. I turned to look into the red-rimmed eyes of Poppy's mother. Her mouth twisted as she spat a stream of hatred at me. 'I'll never forgive you,' she hissed.

I caught a glimpse of Tom's shocked face as she continued her outburst. 'You killed Poppy. She said you were evil. I can't prove it, but I know she was right.'

'Ruth,' Tom put his hand on her arm. 'It was an accident. Mia would never hurt Poppy.'

Behind Poppy's mother I could see the mourners, some with white shocked faces, others staring at me, their expressions openly hostile.

'Please, we need to go.' Tom was pulling at Ruth. She was glaring at me, her mouth a thin tight line as she readied herself for her next onslaught.

He succeeded in moving her away from me, towards the floral

tributes which were lined up beneath an archway.

For a moment, I stood alone. Mum and Dad were engrossed in conversation with someone I didn't recognise. I stared at the ground, not wanting to meet anyone's eyes.

'Thanks for abandoning me.' I took Josh's offered hand as he returned to me, tucking his phone back into his pocket. 'I really appreciated your support.'

'You didn't need me.' Josh turned to face me, releasing my hand, before snapping churlishly, 'Tom seemed to be perfectly capable of looking out for you.'

* * * * * * * *

'I don't know what to wear,' Mum poured herself a second mug of coffee. 'What do you wear for an inquest?'

I met Dad's gaze and saw his impatient eye-roll. 'If you don't hurry up and decide,' he said, 'we'll miss it altogether and it won't matter what you're wearing.'

He got up from the breakfast table and began to clear the plates away, stacking them into the dishwasher. 'Something formal, but not too severe. And don't forget Poppy's mum is meant to be the centre of attention, not you.'

'I'll do that,' I said, easing myself in between Dad and the dishwasher. I hated being treated like a valued guest when I stayed over. Josh had gone to a conveniently vital two-day meeting with clients, so I'd spent the previous night back in my old room.

'Navy suit?' Mum asked.

'That's perfect,' I interjected, feeling Dad's growing impatience with her.

Mum's indecision showed just how nervous she was about the whole occasion of Poppy's inquest.

'I hope Ruth doesn't have another go at Mia,' Mum sighed, gently covering my hand with hers.

'She's in terrible pain over the loss of Poppy,' Dad said gently. 'She's just venting and Mia's the only one she can blame.'

He pulled me towards him. I let my cheek rest on his shirt front, breathing in the coffee on his breath and the cigarette he'd had outside the front door earlier. In the weeks that followed Poppy's death he'd gradually taken up smoking again, going from the occasional hidden cigarette to openly devouring a pack a day.

'Please, Carol, get ready. Mia's fine. I'll look after her.'

'I'll be two minutes.' Mum hurried away. 'Shit,' she said as some of the dark liquid slopped from her mug onto the floor.

'Go!' Dad sighed, impatiently. 'I'll sort it out.'

He grabbed the dishcloth, hunkered down so he could wipe the spill, and then tossed it into the sink.

'I'll be glad when this is over,' he said, pulling out the chair opposite me and sitting down. We were both ready. Dressed for the occasion. He in a dark suit, with a white shirt and colourful tie, me in a smart navy and white-spotted dress. I'd bought the dress on a shopping trip to London with Poppy. It had been our last big trip together before the devastation of our falling out.

'Me too,' I agreed. The police had said the coroner would just go over the night Poppy had died. I'd have to say what had happened.

'Obviously just a tragic accident,' Dad had said when the police had told us the date of the inquest. 'But still horrible for you to have to recall it all.'

What could they ask me that I hadn't already told them? 'I remember driving home, hitting the wall of water and then after that… nothing,' I'd told them.

'Finally,' Dad said, as Mum came into the kitchen. 'You look perfect.'

Dad found a parking spot close to the courthouse and we trooped across the road together. Ahead of us, I spotted Tom with his father. I didn't recognise the charcoal grey suit he wore, bought I assumed for the occasion. He walked beside his father, his head bowed, shoulders hunched as if he carried an unbearable load. Dad took my hand, mine feeling small and insignificant against his.

The inside of the building smelt of disinfectant, overlaid with sweat, dust and an overwhelming sadness. The inquest was held in the courthouse alongside the normal day to day affairs of criminal proceedings and divorces.

The foyer of the building, high-ceilinged and airy was populated by smart-suited solicitors, clutching bundles of files. There was a seating area to one side where a group of scruffily-clad lads slouched. They looked up as we entered the building, my heels tapping on the tiled floor. Realising we clearly weren't part of any court proceedings that concerned them they turned away. A court clerk led us through the building out of the public area to a waiting area, lined with ancient, battered wooden benches. 'Wait here,' she said, gesturing to the benches. 'You'll be called when they are ready for you.'

Obediently we sat. Dad, Mum and I on one side of the waiting area, Tom and his parents on the other. Tom's father, dressed in his usual uniform of tweed jacket and pale cords, looked impatient, tapping a brogue-clad foot on the tiled floor as if he couldn't wait to get out of the building. Tom met my eyes briefly, his mouth twitching slightly into a shadow of a smile before his eyes slid away from mine down to the floor.

The foyer doors swung open once more and the court clerk led Poppy's mum into the waiting area. She was surrounded by some women I vaguely remembered seeing at Poppy's funeral.

'Who are they?' Mum whispered in my ear.

I shrugged, conscious of Poppy's mum's eyes on me. 'Just friends of her mum I think.' I couldn't remember Poppy having any other relatives apart from her mum. As far as I knew her father had left before she was born.

The clerk returned, the rubber soles of her shoes squeaking on the tiled floor. 'When you're ready…' She pushed open the door into the courtroom.

I moved to get up, but Dad's hand on my arm stopped me. I waited, to let Poppy's mother and her coven walk in before us. I felt the air change as they passed, the whisper of hatred that seemed to emit from their every pore.

'Ok?' Dad said as they moved through the swinging doors into the courtroom. As if by one accord we rose, followed by Tom and his father. I stood uncertainly, feeling the blood pound in my head. My legs trembled beneath my dress. I took an unsteady stride forwards, glad my parents were beside me.

The courtroom was smaller than I had expected, a few rows of seats in the centre and the same on each side. At the far end was a raised platform with what I assumed was the coroner's desk. There was a small area to the side of the coroner, separated from the rest of the court by a wooden partition that divided them from us. Here sat the media. Without knowing who any of them were I instinctively sensed their role, felt their curiosity as they stared blatantly at us.

Silently the court clerk showed us, with a wave of her hand, where we should sit.

Poppy's mum and her friends sat in the centre of the courtroom, slightly in front and to the side of us. Tom and his father sat opposite us. Tom, his eyes fixed on the floor, looked pale, his face drawn and anxious.

The court clerk gestured for us to stand. As one we rose, staring at the top of the room as the coroner came in. I didn't know what I had expected, but the coroner wasn't it. Middle-aged, she looked as if she had stepped out of the pages of a fashion magazine; she wore an elegant suit and had neatly cut ash-blonde hair.

After pausing for a fraction of a second to look at us, she sat, a professional smile just creasing the corners of her eyes. 'Today is not about blame, or what caused the accident. We are here simply to determine the cause of Poppy's death,' the coroner intoned, once the proceedings had begun.

Mum gripped my hand. Her fingers entwined in mine were cool, the tips painted blood red. On my other side, Dad's arm slid around my shoulders, pulling me in towards the warmth of his body.

I glanced at Poppy's mum. Her eyes were fixed on the coroner as if no one else existed. Despite the warmth of the day she wore a dark overcoat, a dark grey dress just visible beneath. She'd tied a red scarf around her neck; it clashed with the livid pink of her tear-stained cheeks. There were harsh, ugly lines around the sides of her mouth. She'd aged in the months since Poppy's death, become bent and old. I thought about how Poppy would have hated seeing her looking so old and how the same fate would never happen to Poppy. Death had meant that Poppy would stay forever young in our minds. She'd never grow old and ugly like her mother.

As if she felt my eyes on her, Poppy's mother's head jerked upright, her eyes darting in my direction before fixing on mine. I twitched my mouth into a faint smile of sympathy, unable to tear my gaze away from the hatred I could see there.

A dark-suited court clerk directed me to the stand when it was my turn to speak. My hand trembled as I took the Bible and intoned the oath. My voice sounded faint, insubstantial as I spoke, answering the coroner's gentle questioning. I fixed my eyes on a point just above her right shoulder as I recounted, in a halting voice, what I remembered from the night of the accident.

'Thank you, Mia.' The coroner dismissed me from the stand, her expression sympathetic as she met my eyes. I moved away from the stand stiffly, a tight band of tension locking my shoulders.

The pathologist took the stand and swore the oath.

I huddled into Dad's body, shivering despite the warmth of the day. Mum's hand covered mine, her skin soft, comforting. I watched, listening as the pathologist spoke, hearing him talk of the bruising which covered Poppy's face and body. I couldn't shake the image of Poppy's corpse, laid out for him to examine. How could he see her as a medical challenge rather than see her beautiful young body?

'And that, you consider is in keeping with a car crash?' The coroner asked.

'I do ma'am.' The pathologist nodded.

'And the cause of death?'

'Drowning.'

My single cry, visceral and harsh pierced the silence of the room.

I leant forwards in my seat, unable to look at Tom, or Poppy's family, my body trying instinctively to curl into a ball as if to protect myself from the pain of that terrible knowledge.

Poppy's mum's primeval cry of despair followed mine. It echoed around the room, remaining on the air long after the harsh notes were silenced

'In keeping with a car crash and subsequent submersion in water?'

The clinical words had no resemblance to what must have been Poppy's actual death, her panic, struggling to get out of the car, the terror of knowing she was trapped, dying in the bitter, icy darkness.

The coroner took off her glasses, shuffled her papers into order and pronounced her decision. 'Death by misadventure.'

CHAPTER TWENTY-THREE

They were too polite to stare openly, but as I rode Solar into the ring, I could feel their eyes on me. Months had passed since the inquest into Poppy's death yet still I knew they watched me curiously from over the rims of beer glasses, from behind the curtains in the living accommodation of horse lorries and through elegant, mirrored sunglasses from the benches around the arena. I wondered, in the quiet moments while getting Solar ready, sliding the bridle over his elegant head, fastening the girth around his belly, what they thought. Beneath their expressionless gazes was I Mia, the daughter of a murderer, or Mia the girl whose best friend had died in a car crash?

'Number twenty-seven. Mia Lewis with Solar,' the loudspeaker system boomed out over the ring. Anyone who hadn't been looking before was now. I eased the pressure on Solar's reins, shifting my weight slightly in the saddle. Solar, understanding, bounded forwards into his powerful canter. The world around me faded, became simply a blur of colour. Nothing mattered any longer except this magnificent horse and me. All I had to do was to guide him around the course, control his power and enthusiasm.

The bell rang, indicating we could start. I sat down in the saddle, feeling the tension in his back begin to ease as he settled, focusing on what he had to do.

The fences, enormous when I had walked the course earlier with Mum, seemed smaller now, yet I knew they weren't. I'd stood in-between one of the spread fences and with my arms outstretched could barely touch the shoulder-height front and back poles. All I had to do was to control his exuberance and ensure we kept to the line Mum and I had planned to ensure he met each fence at precisely the correct place.

We turned towards the first jump. Solar's ears twitched, his attention flickering between me and the imposing obstacle. They pricked forwards as he locked onto the fence. I felt a surge of power as he took off, soaring over the poles.

His power made the course seem simple. As we jumped, I was vaguely aware of the arenas beside us; pink faced little girls, pigtails flying, galloped diminutive ponies in one of the showing classes. Bull-faced farmers in white coats walked cows around the perimeter of another.

'That's a clear round for Mia and Solar,' came the excited tones of the announcer as I rode out of the ring. 'The first one today.' Whatever he thought about me, there was no escaping the fact that Solar was an incredible horse.

I slid from the saddle and walked towards Mum who was hurrying towards us, her face flushed with delight. 'Brilliant!' She was hugging me and patting Solar's sweat-stained neck all at the same time.

'He's amazing,' I said, letting her tuck her arm into mine as we led Solar back to the horse lorries.

'So are you.' Mum drew me closer to her. 'That was a tough course.'

'Where's Josh?' Mum asked as we reached the lorry. She began to pick up the equipment we had discarded earlier in our haste to get Solar ready, tidying his brushes into their container.

'Not far away.' I busied myself unbuckling Solar's girth. 'He'll turn up soon.' My voice sounded too high, betraying the irritation I felt. Josh had met us at the show, the biggest in the area, and had promptly left to get coffee in one of the catering tents with some friends.

'He's not that into horses.' I turned to face Mum with a careless shrug, and sighing, breathed in the scent of crushed grass and sweating horse.

'There's so much for him to see here other than horses.' Mum gave me a sympathetic eye-roll and turned to look across the showground. The lorry park crammed with vehicles was on a slight rise. Below us, stretching out to every side was the show, arenas filled with horses, ponies, and farm animals of every description. Spreading out around the arenas, marquees were filled with food vendors and artisan makers of beautiful clothes and jewellery. Further away were lines of tractors and assorted agricultural equipment where the farmers wandered, meeting friends and lusting over the latest pieces of farm equipment.

I couldn't imagine Josh finding much to look at in the agricultural area, or that he'd be watching the farm animals' parade. He was far more likely to be socialising with the group of friends he'd told me he was meeting, sitting in the food area, consuming quantities of champagne and Pimm's. I was surprised he'd wanted to come at all. He had no love of the countryside, despite spending his childhood there. His love was the city, and his work. There seemed little point in him being here, he clearly wasn't interested in being with me.

'I'll text him in a while. Meet up somewhere.' I slipped Solar's bridle off, pushing his huge head away as he tried to scratch himself on me.

'Good idea.' With a deftness born of practice, Mum took Solar's bridle and handed me a leather head collar to slip over his nose.

'We've a good few hours to wait until the jump off, if there are any more clear rounds.' Mum's watch had slid around on her wrist. She turned the face to check the time. 'I might head off, see if there's anything nice in the designers' marquee. Do you want to come?'

I shook my head. 'I'll go and find Josh.' I led Solar up the lorry ramp into the cool interior. As I tied Solar's lead rope I saw Mum walk away and sighed, resting my face against the hard muscle of Solar's neck. I breathed in his warm horse smell and the scent of fresh hay on his breath. Last year we'd eaten lunch together, found a spot beside the jumping arena to watch the other competitors as we drank coffee and nibbled on sandwiches. Now there seemed to be a wall between us all. Nothing had been the same since my mother's body had been found and since Poppy had died. Both of my parents and Josh had been horrified about what Poppy's mother had said to me at her funeral. They'd told me to take no notice of her, that she was distraught, didn't know what she was saying, but still, I carried her accusation deep inside me. They tried to hide the changes, but I could feel the vague shift in their reactions to me. Josh and I grew further apart. I'd tried at first to stop the cracks when they appeared, but now the distance between us seemed like a vast chasm I had no idea how to bridge it. Time was a great healer, I told myself, we'd grow closer again. In time.

'Hey.' I broke out of my thoughts as Tom came up the lorry ramp towards me. He'd changed in the months since Poppy had died. Thinner, his face pale, his eyes shadowed by a pain even our friendship could not cure.

'Hi.' I walked into his open arms, hugged him to me, breathing in the doggy smell of his shirt. 'How is it going?'

Tom drew away, shuddering dramatically. 'Terrible,' he grinned, and there was a flash of the old Tom, full of life and humour. 'I've been measuring ponies all morning, fighting with aggressive mums over the height of their little darlings' ponies. I've just come from judging the 'Dog I'd Most Like to Take Home' competition. Ughh, what a nightmare. I don't know which was worse, the snapping terriers or the labradoodle trying to shag my leg.'

'How did you end up having to do that?' I asked, standing on the edge of the ramp and looking out at the showground. 'I thought your dad liked doing the show stuff.'

Tom pulled a wry face. 'Dad's a rule unto himself. He's currently wandering around the tractor section chasing up clients who owe him money.'

I smiled sympathetically, imagining the poor farmers coming to face with Richard's wrath.

He sat on the edge of the ramp. 'I'm sick of him, Mia,' he sighed, rubbing at a stain on the front of his pale chinos. 'He's such a bully. Go here, go there. Why didn't you do this…?'

He brought his shoulders up around his ears, puffing out his cheeks. 'I miss Poppy.'

I took his hand, feeling the warmth of his fingers in mine. 'So do I.'

'She made all this shit with Dad seem irrelevant.' Tom gripped my fingers. 'Now she's gone I've nothing to look forward to, no one to talk to at the end of the day, moan about how rotten my dad is.'

'I know.' I put my arm around him and pulled his head onto my shoulder. 'Nothing's the same without her.'

We sat quietly together, in the sunshine, watching the activity of the show unfold around us in a companionable silence, both lost in our thoughts of Poppy.

'How did Solar go in the jumping?' Tom asked. 'I wanted to come and watch but I got stuck with the pony measuring.'

'We got a clear round,' I told him, watching the smile of delight spread across his face. I wished Josh had been with me, sharing my joy, rather than socialising with his friends.

'That's really brilliant. Let me know how you get on,' Tom said, getting to his feet. 'Better go, I'm supposed to be judging the 'Best Pet Rabbit' competition in…' He glanced at his watch. 'Shit. Now.'

There were four of us in the jump-off. Solar, as if he knew the pressure was on, jumped like a stag, letting me turn him with the lightest shifts of my weight. We finished three seconds faster than any of the other competitors.

'You won!' Mum yelled, unable to contain her delight.

'Well done,' Stevie Shipman, one of the other competitors said, riding his horse into second place alongside me. 'You rode really well. About time you had some good luck.'

'Thank you,' I agreed, wondering if he was referring to the car crash that had killed Poppy, or my father's penchant for killing.

'Do your lap of honour,' the ring steward said, fastening a red rosette to Solar's browband. As if he knew he'd won, Solar took off at a gallop around the ring as soon as I eased his reins. We hurtled past the collecting ring. I glimpsed Mum, leaning on the fence, her face split into a huge grin. Past the spectators' area we galloped, the wind loud in my ears as Solar stretched to hurtle down the long side of the arena.

At the far end of the arena, ready to leave the ring, I slowed Solar, sitting in my saddle and gently putting the lightest pressure on his mouth. As he slowed, I saw the crowds around the Pimm's tent turn to look at me. There was Josh, surrounded by his friends. He saw me look and raised his glass in greeting as we cantered past.

'I'll go and find Josh,' I said, as we untacked Solar back at the lorry.

'Good idea,' Mum said, taking the saddle from me and shutting it in the tack locker.

'We'll leave in what… say an hour.' She consulted her watch. 'Give you time for a drink with Josh and me to go and see if the nice lady in the designer tent will reduce the price of the rather nice cashmere sweater I've got my eye on.'

I walked beside her through the lorry park until we reached the edge of the showground.

'See you back at the lorry,' she said. 'You did so well today. Dad will be thrilled.' She pulled me into a hug.

I found Josh still outside the Pimm's tent. I manoeuvred my way through the crowds to his side. 'Hi.' I laid a gentle arm on the sleeve of his navy linen blazer.

'Oh, Mia. Hi.' He turned, some of the contents of his glass spilling out over his pale, wine-coloured jeans. He was wearing a burgundy-and-white striped shirt I didn't recognise. He dropped a kiss on my cheek. His breath smelt of coffee and Pimm's.

I glanced at his friends, all dressed in dark linen jackets, expensive cotton shirts and chinos. There were girls too, all in tiny short tweed skirts and tight striped shirts ridiculously paired, for the height of summer, with long brown leather boots.

Beside their elegance I felt dirty and scruffy in my stained jodhpurs and riding shirt, my leather boots swapped for deck shoes.

'You know everyone,' Josh said, handing me the remains of his Pimm's. I looked, seeing the familiar faces. Slightly apart from the others, dressed in a short red dress and sandals was the girl I had seen come out of Josh's apartment building. Feeling my eyes on her, she turned to face me, returning my gaze with a smile.

'Fancy an ice cream?' Josh was already moving away from the group, leaving me no choice but to follow him. 'You did great today,' he said as we stood in line for artisan, organic goat milk ice cream.

'Solar did it all. He was brilliant. I'm not sure if I should take him in the Grand Prix later.' I didn't want to stop talking, for that horrible and now familiar silence to descend between us.

Josh handed me an ice cream. I ran out of words. He lowered his head and put it to one side, looking at me from beneath the thick fringe of his eyelashes. We stood now on opposite sides of a vast chasm, which had gradually been opening for the last year. Filled with misunderstanding and mistrust, there was no bond between us any more.

'That girl…?' I met his eyes.

'Alice.' He knew exactly who I was talking about.

I watched a chunk of my ice cream slide past the cornet and splatter on my shoe.

'I saw her come out of your apartment.'

I saw the guilt in his eyes as the colour flared in his cheeks.

'We've been out a couple of times.' Josh met my eyes, the guilt replaced by a challenging gaze.

'While I was busy coming to terms with the fact that my mother was murdered.'

He looked down at his deck shoes. I focused on his bowed head, the curling strands of hair. How long had it been since I had touched it? Nothing had been the same since I found out about my mother. The discovery of her body had driven a wedge through my whole life, splitting everything that was familiar, driving an abyss through it.

'Mia,' he said finally. I glanced up to see the girl, Alice, watching us, her expression like an obedient spaniel. She was slightly taller than me, her mouth smaller, but she was similar to me. A taller, cleaner, newer, untarnished version of me.

Around us people moved, going about their business, skirting around the private hell we had entered. 'I'm sorry. This... us... just doesn't work anymore. I'm sorry, but I want to call it a day.'

'Josh?' Tears pricked at the back of my eyes. 'I know things have been difficult, Poppy... Cornwall...' It was impossible to expand on all that the word Cornwall encompassed.

Josh glanced towards Alice. I followed his eyes to see her smile sympathetically at him.

'I'm sorry Mia.'

I dropped my ice cream and grabbed the front of his shirt, pulling the fabric towards me as if I could physically prevent him from leaving. My nails were grubby, broken, bitten to the quick in places.

'Please don't do this.'

'You'll be fine Mia,' Josh's eyes were filled with distaste as they raked over me. 'You and Tom.'

That familiar argument. 'Tom needs me. He's just lost his girlfriend in case you'd forgotten.' My voice sounded unnaturally loud. I was aware people had turned to look at us, that Alice had taken an uncertain stride closer.

'How could I possibly forget?' Josh closed his hand around my wrist and wrenched my fingers away. 'I'll drop your stuff round to your mum and dad's.'

'Fuck you!' I spat. In his eyes I knew I was tarnished, dirty, a failure. Not the person he wanted to be with.

I walked away, my wrist burning, knowing Alice's eyes were on me.

CHAPTER TWENTY-FOUR

Tom walked beside me through the woods, our footsteps padding on the dead leaves and crunching the dead twigs.

'Beautiful here, isn't it?' he said softly as if he were afraid to break the silence between us.

'Yes.' I breathed in the peaty earth, the air cool on the back of my throat.

'Here it is,' Tom said as we came to a clearing in the woods. The trees bordered an area of long, flower-filled grass. The light filtering through the canopy of leaves above us cast flickering shadows over the grass. To one side of the glade was a wooden bench.

'It's a lovely tribute to Poppy,' Tom said, leading the way to the bench. He gently touched the brass plaque on the backrest which gave Poppy's name and the dates she had been born and died. 'She loved it here.'

I rested my elbows on my knees, watching the shadows move over the grass, aware of a whole life Tom and Poppy had lived that I hadn't been part of.

'I'm so lost without her,' Tom sighed, his whole body moving with the effort of pulling the breath into his lungs.

'It was lovely of her mum to organise the bench.' I looked away from the sheltered glade into the dimness of the trees, half afraid I'd see Poppy's mother coming to visit the bench as we had. The thought of coming face to face with her again was not something I could handle.

'How are you?' Tom asked gently. 'Without Josh?'

'Oh, you know…' I brought my heels up to the bench seat and folded my legs so I could rest my chin on my knees. Above us a bird, began to sing, its trill expanding over the woodland. I watched a single leaf, falling floating down before coming to rest in the grassy glade.

'It's hard…' I struggled to speak, my throat tight. Even though over the last few months I'd felt Josh draw away, was conscious of him wanting to spend less time with me and I'd rarely stayed at his apartment, still, him telling me it was over and knowing he had replaced me so quickly and easily hurt like hell.

'I blocked him on all my social media,' I said, closing my eyes to shut out the memory of scrolling through my newsfeeds. Seeing our whole relationship spool past, us in each other's company before we began dating. Later came photographs of us after our first date, standing self-consciously, our hyper-awareness of one another painfully obvious.

There were photographs of when we were very much a couple, holding hands, laughing together. Closer to our breakup the images told the story of our distance. There we were, in each other's company, together but clearly already moving apart.

'Good idea.' Tom pulled the sleeve of his rugby shirt down, breathed on Poppy's name plaque and rubbed at it with the fabric.

I was aware of the choice I had been able to make. It hurt me less to cut Josh out of my life, forget him, not look at the photographs. Tom did not have that release. To him Poppy was always going to be perfect, irreplaceable, their relationship unspoilt by reality.

I didn't tell him about the night I had blocked Josh and deleted the images of him. The pain of that night was too terrible. I'd pinched a bottle of Dad's red wine and taken it to my room, alternatively crying and drinking as my life with him was deleted.

The next morning I'd woken with a vile hangover to find Mum leaning over me with the plastic bowl she'd given me as a child when I'd had tummy bugs. 'Stay in bed,' she'd said, her voice gentle and full of understanding. 'I'll get you some painkillers.'

I was grateful to have her there, looking after me.

'I wish I could forget Poppy,' Tom's voice was harsh. He screwed his mouth up and closed his eyes with the effort of not crying. The tears won. I gently put my hand on his arm as a howl of sheer anguish burst from him.

'You will,' I said, softly. 'In time you will.' I twisted my mother's silver bracelet slowly around my wrist, waiting until he stopped crying. He wouldn't forget, I knew that, but time would help him cope with her loss. I'd mourned my mother when her body had been found, the pain had been immeasurable. But I'd survived. I'd endured rejection from my grandmother and my aunts. I'd coped with Josh's rejection of me and I'd survived Poppy's betrayal.

'Josh is an idiot to let you go.' Tom's voice was thick from crying. He sniffed loudly, wiping his face on the sleeve of his shirt, staining it with his tears.

I shook my head. 'He's well shut of me. There's no good in me.'

'Don't say that.'

'Tom,' I said gently, 'Look at me. My father was a nutjob who kidnapped women and killed them. I killed Poppy. Poppy's mum was right. There's evil in me.' The words floated from me and rested in the air surrounding us.

'You didn't mean to kill Poppy. That was just a terrible accident.'

I rested my head on his shoulder and released a juddering sigh. 'Everybody thinks I did. I can see it in their faces.'

I felt Tom shake his head. 'No.'

'They think I'm like my father. That I'm full of the same evil he was.'

Tom pushed me upright, turning my face so he could look at me. 'Don't even think that. You set the girl free. The one your father had…' Tom was silent for a moment, before continuing, 'You helped her. Quite clearly you aren't evil. You aren't your father. Focus on the good you did.'

I pulled the corners of my mouth down, shaking my head slowly. 'There's so much I don't know about my past. Who I am.'

Tom got to his feet and held out his hand to pull me upright. 'Perhaps it's time you found out.'

CHAPTER TWENTY-FIVE

'You need to stop looking at these.' Mum came into my room with a cup of tea and found me staring, like a rabbit caught in headlights, at my laptop, scrolling through the vile messages. The force of hatred in the messages was like a tsunami. People who had read about my father were speculating about what had happened at the farm. Talking about how evil he was, how I must have known what was happening there. And how evil I was, because I carried his genes. There were others, weird people who wanted to be friends with me, know what my life was like. There were links to forums where people discussed my father's crimes, chatted about why he had kidnapped and killed. What had driven him to rape.

'Please, darling.' Mum sat on the edge of my bed, her hands cupped around the mug of tea. 'It doesn't do any good to see those. All it's doing is hurting you.'

I knew that, but I still signed into them, occasionally, in secret, drawn by some grim fascination, some inner self-hatred which made me want to read them.

I nodded. She was right. While she watched over me, I deleted the accounts.

* * * * * * * *

'Oh, come on.' I slid my hand under Tom's arm. 'Tell me what to get you for Christmas.'

We dodged and weaved our way along a crowded Oxford Street, side-stepping and hurrying past dawdling, shopping-laden crowds. Above us the sky was inky blue, the encroaching darkness broken only by the sparkling Christmas lights festooned above us.

During the summer months the pain of our respective losses had brought us closer together. Our friendship gave us the support we both needed. I'd been thrilled when Tom had announced he was coming to London to watch me compete Solar at Olympia, one of the biggest shows of the season.

'I don't know,' Tom shrugged. 'I don't know what to get you either.'

There was a crowd of people waiting to get through the doors into the department store.

'It's hard,' I said, pausing while we shuffled slowly forwards into the warmth of the shop. 'What do you buy a boy who is a boy friend, not a boyfriend?'

I tugged off my scarf as we walked through the cosmetics section. At either side of us, beautifully made-up girls offered us free samples.

'There is something you could get me,' Tom said, stopping abruptly.

'What?' I asked, arranging my face into a questioning look, half-joking, expecting him to come up with some mad suggestion.

'A kettle,' Tom smiled.

'Kettle?' I quizzed, wondering how I'd missed the joke.

Behind us someone tutted at us for blocking the way.

'Yes. I need one. Seriously,' Tom said, smiling at my expression. 'I'm leaving home. Getting my own place.'

'Tom!' I said in delight. Remembering the last time I'd heard about anyone getting their own place, Josh's face came suddenly into focus; I blinked it away and returned my attention to Tom.

'I think it's time,' Tom's eyes fixed on mine.

I nodded.

''Mia I'm so sick of living at home. Having my Dad always on my case.'

Tom took my arm and led me through the crowded shop. 'I'm twenty-five, it's time I had my own place anyway.'

As we reached the end of the beauty department a gorgeous young woman manning a perfume counter came towards us. 'Would you like to try this?'

She held a spray towards me, taking my arm before I could protest and spraying me with a perfume I recognised immediately as the one Poppy always wore. Tom's nostrils flared as he breathed in the familiar scent.

We walked on in silence, Poppy's presence drifting between us.

'In another few years I want to set up my own practice,' Tom said as we stood on the escalator to the electrical department.

'You should,' I told him, glad the silence had been broken and the spectre of Poppy had faded into the background once more. 'Will you set up something locally, or move away?'

It would be brilliant to have Tom in practice nearby. I knew everyone would be delighted. Mum certainly would rather use him than his dour father. 'Loads of people would love it if you were on your own.' I hopped off the escalator in his wake.

'I couldn't stay local,' Tom said as we walked through the quieter aisles of the electrical department. 'It wouldn't be fair on my dad.'

'So you'd move away, then.'

'Yep. Not for a few years though.'

Tom reached the shelves of kettles.

'Far away?'

'Probably. I really like the Lake District.' He picked up a shiny kettle, examining it intensely before putting it back and selecting another. 'I've done some research and apparently there's a shortage of small animal veterinary practices.'

'That's a great idea.' I tried to put an excited note into my voice to show I was pleased about Tom's plans and knew I'd failed. My voice sounded dull and flat. I couldn't bear the thought of him leaving.

'How about you pick one and I'll meet you in the café,' Tom suggested.

I nodded, turning away so he wouldn't see my expression.

The shine had gone off the day. I'd be utterly alone. Even though he was talking about something in the distant future, the realisation of how much I relied on him and enjoyed his easy company hurt terribly. I grabbed a pale cream kettle, took it to the check out, paid, and went to the café to find Tom.

'Got you a great present. You'll never guess what it is.' I forced a smile onto my face, shaking the bag at him.

'Hope you wanted this.' Tom pushed a latte across the table towards me. The barista had designed a heart in the froth on the top of the liquid.

'How are we doing for time?' he asked. 'We need to be back at Olympia by six, or your mum will be flapping.'

'Solar's class doesn't even start until nine.' I rolled my eyes in his direction, shrugging my phone out of my back pocket.

'It's only five,' I put the phone onto the table so he could see.

'Drink up, we had better go.' Tom drained his coffee and stood up. 'There's a taxi rank not far away.'

The London streets were packed with cars and people. It seemed to take forever for us to reach the indoor showground at Olympia.

Away from the Christmas bustle of the shopping area, the stables hummed with quiet efficiency. I breathed in the familiar smell of horse, wood shavings and bedding, trying to calm myself. Tom's plans were in the future, he wasn't going to leave immediately.

'There you are.' Mum emerged from Solar's stable with an armful of his brushes. 'Had a good time?'

'Lovely,' I replied, 'I'd better go and get changed.'

Tom dropped a gentle kiss on my cheek. 'I'll see you after. Best of luck.'

I left him talking to Mum while I went to the lorry park and got changed. After a week of sleeping in it the living accommodation was still neat and tidy, a testament to Mum's obsessive cleaning up after me. Everything was always put away after we ate, the dishes washed in the tiny sink, my clothes neatly hung on hangers beneath plastic covers. Dad, unable to bear the miniature living of the lorry accommodation, was driving down after work for the final competition of the show.

In the morning we'd pack everything up and head home. No one would leave tonight with the promise of the big after-show party. Tom had driven down the previous evening and had slept on a camp bed in the horse section of the lorry. Mum occupied the bed above the driver's seats and I slept on the fold-out sections of the seating.

With Mum's attention to detail, everything I needed - my jodhpurs, shirt, tie, jacket and boots - were just where I could find them.

Once changed, I went back to the stables. Mum had tacked Solar up. She led him out into the corridor between the stables and held him while I mounted. Despite the long show he still felt excited and full of life as I rode away to the crowded warm-up area.

Horses cantered sedately around the edge of the sandy ring, their riders silent, tired after the long week, everyone focused on this, the biggest class of the competition. I began to warm Solar up, gently walking him around, letting him settle to the noise and bustle of the ring. Feeling him relax beneath me, I pushed him gently into a trot and then into his beautiful rocking horse canter. Mum adjusted the practice fence and we soared over.

I loved the shows. Everyone was focused on their own horses. Here I competed on an equal footing. No one would judge me for my past, no matter what they might think.

'Seventy-four,' the ring steward shouted out our number. I turned Solar and rode him out of the practice ring. We stood beside the huge curtains at the entry to the arena. When they swished back Solar barely flicked an ear to signal he had noticed. At first, he had been spooked by the movement, but after a week at the show he was used to everything now. We rode into the ring. Spectators crowded around the arena, their seats arranged in tiers high into the roof of the building.

Silence fell. The hush was so intense I could hear the jingle of Solar's bit, his hooves thudding on the sandy surface. Far above us in the spectators' gallery someone coughed.

My parents were up there somewhere, and Tom.

I gathered up my reins and pushed Solar into a canter, circling around the arena, past the vast, brightly coloured fences we would soon jump.

The bell rang, signalling it was time to begin. The edges of my world blurred until only Solar and I existed. I could feel the saddle beneath my legs, the stirrups beneath the soles of my boots. His mane, as we cantered, fluttered gently up and down with his rocking rhythm. I felt him take a deep breath which matched my own as we turned and faced the first jump.

'That's a tough one,' I remembered Mum saying as we walked the course. The awesome array of brightly coloured poles faced the collecting ring, where the other horses were. A scared horse would want to find the safety of his companions. The fence had been designed to distract the horse and intimidate the rider. We soared over it, Solar flicking his heels as we glided over the jump to land safely on the other side. I felt him pull slightly towards the collecting ring as we circled away, but his body adjusted as I squeezed my legs around him, turning him into the second fence.

We soared over each of the fences, the commentator's words a vague blur in my ears. 'And that's our first clear round,' I heard him say as we crossed the finishing line. I bent over Solar's neck, hugging him, patting the hard muscle in sheer delight. He had tried his hardest for me.

There were just five of us in the jump-off, competitors who had completed the first round safely without knocking a fence over. Mum fussed around Solar and I while we waited to go into the second round to jump off against the clock. I focused on my breathing, ignoring everything except the fences and the horse beneath me.

Our jump-off round was foot perfect. Solar flew around the course, keen to do his job, but listening to me, letting me control his immense power. We won by two seconds.

Above us the spectators were already beginning to make their way out of the arena and the course builders starting to collect up the show jumps as I rode in with the other competitors to collect our prizes. I eased my reins, letting Solar stretch out as we began our gallop around the ring under the spotlight.

Dad, beaming with delight, came to the stables with Tom as Mum and I were putting Solar's equipment away and bedding him down for the night.

'Brilliant round.' Dad hugged me to him, his voice filled with pride.

'Well done you.' Tom pulled me into his arms as Dad released me.

Once I'd showered and changed we made our way to the hotel where the after-show party was being held. Dad got us drinks and found us a quiet corner. We made our way through the crowds who raised glasses in my direction and offered smiles of delight at my win.

'Here's to you.' Dad raised his glass in my direction.

'To Solar and Mum,' I grinned back, 'They did all the work.'

'I love doing it!' Mum beamed, her eyes, fixed on mine, were filled with love.

'Tom's told me he's moving out of home,' I told my parents, pulling Tom towards me.

'Fabulous news,' Dad said. He never made any secret of his dislike for Tom's arrogant father.

We drifted away from my parents. Mum and Dad were going to spend the night in a hotel; Dad refused to stay in the lorry, no matter how comfortable it was.

'You were brilliant tonight. You rode so well. You deserved to win.'

Tom's mouth was close to my ear above the noise of the music.

'I'm glad you're going to move out of your dad's house too – and go on your own eventually,' I told him, trying to be pleased for him. Although the pain of losing him was intense, I consoled myself with the fact that it wouldn't be for a few years.

'That won't be for ages yet though,' Tom said, pulling me towards the dance floor.

We began to dance, our bodies swaying in time with the music, jostling and bumping into the others on the crowded dance floor.

Mum and Dad had disappeared back to their hotel by the time Tom and I emerged, sweating and exhausted from the dance floor. We wandered slowly back to Olympia and let ourselves into the lorry. Around us the lorry park was filled with the sound of parties going on in the vehicles.

As we went into the living accommodation of the lorry, Tom turned to open the door into the horse area. 'Bedtime for me,' he said, pushing the door open. 'I'll see you in the morning. Sleep well.'

'Good night, Tom.' I met his eyes.

He stood in the doorway, the cold air from the back of the lorry filling the living accommodation.

'Can I stay?' His voice was husky, barely more than a whisper in the dim light.

As I met his eyes he stepped forwards and wrapped his arms around me.

I nodded, resting against his shirt front. 'Yes please.'

CHAPTER TWENTY-SIX

'A kettle. Just what I wanted.' Tom held up his unwrapped Christmas present as if it were a trophy he'd been awarded.
Mum beamed at Tom.
'Lovely,' Dad nodded sagely. 'Wise move buying property.'
We'd had an early start, Tom and me. His dad had given him Christmas Day off with the proviso he did the early morning calls. Our day had started with the two of us out on one of the local farms, dealing with a cow who was struggling to give birth. I'd watched, awestruck as Tom had worked his magic and delivered a large healthy calf.

The farmer's wife had insisted we ate the massive fried breakfast she cooked for us before we came home. Fortunately, that had been the only emergency call. Tom had dispensed a syringe of antibiotic to one dour farmer who didn't seem to have any concept of the festive season and then he was free for the rest of the day, his father and a locum taking the next shifts.

If Mum was smug about Tom and I getting together she never mentioned it. We'd been best friends forever, so being in a relationship had seemed odd and awkward at first. We were both afraid of spoiling the easy friendship we'd enjoyed but even though it was early days it did seem as easy as being friends. Tom was gorgeous, always great company, reliable and kind. There was none of the dangerous passion I had experienced with Josh, but the ease of our relationship was a blissful relief.

'What have you got, Mia?' Mum asked as I opened my present from Tom.

'Oh, they're beautiful,' she said as I showed her the silver earrings I'd picked out in London. The eye-catching studs looked like links interspersed with tiny silver balls. They were similar to the bracelet Grace had given me that had been found with my mother. I still wore the necklace Josh had given me but had not told Tom where I had acquired either.

Mum recognised the similarity immediately. Her smile stretched tightly across her face.

'It's lovely, darling,' she said, her fingers brushing briefly over the coolness of the metal.

'This is from me and Dad,' she said, turning away abruptly to seize a large parcel from the heap beneath the tree.

We opened our presents, cashmere sweaters for my parents. My present from my parents was a beautiful new pair of riding boots.

Tom was easy company. He'd been part of our lives for so long it did not feel strange to have him around. I set the big table for lunch, listening to him chatting easily with Mum and Dad as he helped them prepare the food. After lunch, Tom and I did the stables, going through the daily routine of refilling water buckets and giving the horses their feed and hay, while Mum and Dad curled up on the sofa to watch a favourite film.

'I'm glad to get you alone,' Tom said, trapping me in the corner of the feed room. 'I don't think anyone will miss us for a while.'

Ages later we walked back across the yard, hand in hand. My parents hadn't missed us; they were both snoozing peacefully, Mum sprawled across Dad's legs, his head lolling back on the armrest of the sofa, the film still playing. They stirred as Tom rescued the fire, throwing logs onto the dying embers to coax it back into life.

'Well, I think I'm going to go up to bed,' Mum yawned sleepily sometime later, looking pointedly at Dad. We'd spent the rest of the evening watching yet another old film, playing chess and helping Dad with the 2000-piece jigsaw which would occupy much of his relaxing time until Easter, by which time the garden would be in full bloom and he'd be out there tending to it.

Tom and I sat in the lounge, watching the embers of the fire die down.

'Bedtime?' I stood up, holding out my hand to pull Tom to his feet.

'Yes please,' Tom pulled me into his arms.

I listened o the gentle crackle of the embers of the fire and the sound of our breathing. I wanted to be in his arms, to feel his skin against mine, to feel him inside me. We hadn't spoken of the future, of his plans to eventually move away, to work in another surgery, away from his father. That all seemed far away; for the moment there was just the two of us and that was all that mattered.

* * * * * * *

'This is perfect,' I said, turning a slow circle in the middle of the lounge of Tom's new home.

'Thank you. I think you're perfect too.'

Hand in hand we walked through the house. It was newly built, on the opposite end of the village from the older houses where my parents and Tom's father lived.

'Will you help me pick out stuff for the house?' Tom asked, as we stood upstairs in one of the three bedrooms.

'Of course.'

'Better get your seal of approval on anything I buy, since I like to hope you're going to be spending a lot of time here.'

I grinned, slipping my arms around his waist and kissing him gently. I liked that he didn't automatically assume I'd be moving in with him.

My jumping career with Solar was going from strength to strength. Every day I rode the magnificent horse I loved him more. Mum and I had mapped out a season of shows where we would jump. I couldn't wait. Life seemed to have done a circle, from the shit I'd gone through in the last year to finally having a bright future.

'You can cook me dinner when I come back from a show,' I teased.

'And you can have my breakfast ready when I come back from early morning calls,' Tom teased back, poking me in the ribs with a finger.

* * * * * * *

My heart sank as I saw Grace's number come up on my telephone.

I'd moved on, pushed all of what had happened in Cornwall to the back of my mind. It hummed there, in the background, like the noise of a fridge in a silent kitchen. My everyday life continued as I built my plans and hopes for the future, with Solar and Tom.

'Hello.' I answered the phone eventually, after staring at the screen for a long time wondering if I dared ignore it.

'Mia.' Grace's voice was familiar. She sounded as if she were talking to me from outside, the wind noise loud in the phone. 'I got a call a few days ago from Susie Carne.'

I could hear my breathing, feel the knot of tension twist in my stomach. The life I had tried to ignore, push to the back of my mind, forced its way up to the front again. Whatever I did, it was always there, rearing its ugly head, something I could never escape no matter how hard I tried.

'Yes.' My voice was little more than a whisper.

'She'd like to meet you,' Grace said. 'If you'd be willing to.'

'Yes.' It seemed the only word I could say; my mind buzzed with thoughts and images, leaving me unable to frame a logical thought. Susie Carne. The young woman I had freed. She had been my age then, kidnapped by my father, held prisoner in the cellar Josh and I had stood in last year. I'd set her free. By accident. I'd wanted her company, to give her the orange she'd asked me for. She had run as soon as I opened the door.

My fingers automatically went to the tiny scar on my wrist where I'd cut myself as I fell when she flung open the door.

'Could you come to Cornwall to meet her?' Grace's voice was distant against the buzzing in my head, like angry bees.

'Yes,' I repeated, listening as Grace made arrangements and promised to find a time and place that suited Susie. There was no talk of anything suiting me. Susie was the victim here. Her life almost taken by my father. What, I wondered, ending the call, would have happened if I hadn't opened the door that day? Would my father have killed her? Would she have been one of the rotting corpses the police eventually found? Would I still be on the farm? Would there have been other women if I hadn't put a stop to what my father was doing, even unwittingly? I ended the conversation wishing I'd asked about the other bodies that had been found with my mother's and what had happened to Nan since the police investigation had been reopened.

* * * * * * * *

Tom offered to take time off work to drive down with me.

'No way are you going on your own,' he said, when I told him of Grace's call. 'We'll go together, make a weekend of it.'

I couldn't imagine combining something as horrific as meeting Susie with a pleasurable trip where we'd sit watching the sunset and admiring the scenery, but I was equally glad of his offer.

I couldn't imagine meeting Susie on my own, even with Grace beside me.

Tom's Dad was furious at him taking time off work, unleashing a torrent of abuse neither of us expected.

'You need to focus on your job, Tom,' Richard had snapped as we stood together in the surgery after asking him for the weekend off. 'It's ridiculous, driving to Cornwall just for a few days.'

'Dad, Mia needs me with her.' Tom's voice was cold, with a tough edge to it. His fingers gripped mine as he drew himself up to his full height in the face of his father's wrath.

'Mia needs me.' His father mocked, glancing at me with disdain. 'She doesn't need you. Your responsibility is to the practice. To the clients and animals you are here to look after, not to Mia.'

'I don't need you to come, Tom. I'm okay on my own, honestly, Grace will be there.' I ventured, aware of how tremulous my voice sounded.

'See, she's just said she doesn't need you.'

'Mia does need me.' Tom's voice was filled with anger.

'I don't want to cause a problem,' I said, forcing my eyes to stay fixed on Tom's father.

'A vet has a duty to his patients. You can't take time off when you feel like it.' A muscle twitched beneath one of Richard's eyes.

'What the fuck?' Tom's voice was incredulous. 'Dad, you owe me some time off.'

Richard glared at me. His grey eyes flickered over me as if I was something he couldn't quite identify. 'Tom's got a responsibility to the surgery. The last thing he needs is you wheedling your way into his life, manipulating him into ruining his career.'

'Dad. Stop it. Don't you talk to Mia like that. I'm taking the weekend off, whether you like it or not.'

Tom stalked out of the surgery, leaving me to glare coldly at his father before I hurried out behind him.

He was shaking with anger. 'Bastard. The sooner I'm out of here the better.'

My parents, while not as vile in their condemnation of our plans, were equally unimpressed by our decision.

'Oh, Mia,' My Dad's tone was wounded, like I was a child, when disappointment hurt more than his anger. 'You don't need to keep bringing this up, let the past go.'

'I can't, Dad,' I told him, 'I owe it to Susie to see her.'

'I don't see why.' Mum's voice was brittle as she faced me across the kitchen. 'You helped Susie. You don't owe her anything now.'

'What can this possibly achieve?' Dad asked, pouring himself a glass of wine. He raised it in a gesture to offer Mum a glass. She shook her head, waving her hand in a distracted gesture. 'I don't see why she needs to meet you.'

'I want to see her, see if I can make sense of what's in my head.'

I longed to meet Susie. She was the only person who had any link with my father and Nan who I could talk to. She was the one person who could give me some answers to what had happened at the farm, what my father had been like.

There were so many newspaper reports and online articles that I knew the hard facts. My father had kidnapped young, vulnerable women and held them prisoner. Because of my existence there was the assumption that he had raped and it was known that he had killed his prisoners. But I wanted to hear Susie tell me her story. I wanted to know what had happened to her while she was held in the cellar. I needed to find out how my father had kidnapped her; was he charming, persuading her into his car or had he just grabbed her off the street? There was so much missing information that I longed to discover.

Dad shook his head. 'Mia, it would do you more good if you forgot Cornwall. Put it out of your mind. Focused on who you are now. Not who you were then.'

'I can't,' I told them. 'I just can't.'

I needed to sit in the same room as her. I wanted to hear her recount the story of what had happened to her before the day I had set her free. The day that my good deed had resulted in the death of my father. I wanted to discover what her life had been like after I had released her. Was she, like me, tormented by the memories of what had happened?

My memories were such vague, shadowy impressions I had no idea whether they were real or not.

* * * * * * * *

We arranged to meet Susie in an interview suite in the police station, somewhere quiet and private and neutral.

I was glad Tom had come with me, grateful for his support, and that he was there to hold my hand. We drove down to Cornwall, leaving his house early one morning, just missing the rush hour traffic as we passed Exeter and headed west. While the roads were clear, there were thick snowdrifts blanketing the hillsides as we drove across Bodmin Moor. The sky above us was leaden with the promise of further snow. Penzance was almost deserted as we drove through the town to find a parking spot.

Grace smiled gently as we were shown into her office. 'Thank you both so much for coming down. I know this will be such a help to Susie. Perhaps give her some closure.'

It was hard to imagine what her life must have been like since she'd been my father's prisoner. What he had done haunted me every day. My memories were hazy. Hers were clear. She had been held in that dark cellar by my father. She knew what he was capable of. What would it be like to live with that every day?

'Have any of the other bodies been identified? What's happening with Nan? Has she been questioned about them?'

Grace's eyes met mine. 'There's been some progress, we've identified four more of the bodies so far. Your gran is adamant she knew nothing about the girls.'

I saw her eyes flicker away from mine, her expression filled with a doubt she quickly erased and replaced with a more neutral one.

Susie was already in the suite when Grace opened the door.

She looked older than I had expected, her face puffy from crying, dark hair tangled around her face.

'Oh my God,' she said, bringing a hand to her mouth to stifle a cry. 'You look so like your father.'

CHAPTER TWENTY-SEVEN

As I approached her, Susie pushed her chair back, the legs scraping loudly on the lino floor, and half stood, her hands, the knuckles white, gripping the edge of the table. I had wondered if I'd recognise her. I had a vague recollection of a slender, pretty girl. She was far from that. Her body was bloated; beneath the cheap looking sweater she wore I could see a roll of fat oozing over the waistband of her skirt.

'Susie,' Grace's voice was gentle as if she were calming a frightened animal. 'This is Mia. You wanted to see her.'

Susie's eyes were wide in her tear-stained face. They fastened on mine. I could hear her breathing, loud and ragged over the hum of noise from the rooms beyond ours.

'Mia's come all the way from Bath,' Grace put a calming hand on Susie's arm, as if to physically drag her back from whatever private hell she had been sucked into. 'With Tom, her boyfriend.'

Susie brought a hand up to touch her hair, smoothing it around her neck in a distracted gesture. Her eyes were an incredible shade of blue, the pupils rimmed with black.

'Would it be better if you sit down, Susie?' Grace laid a hand on her back, her voice calm, gentle.

Susie took a long juddering breath and slowly sank back into her chair.

Tom's fingers entwined in mine were clammy. I led him forwards to the table, releasing him so we could sit down.

I folded my hands on my lap, then brought them to the seat, where I tucked them under my thighs, as if they had become appendages I was not used to owning and had no idea what to do with them.

Across from us, Grace took a seat beside Susie. Her leather jacket creaked against the chair back as she sat down. Her long mane of red hair was tied back into a ponytail, as it was when she was working. Her skin, in the harsh light of the interview room, was pale, the freckles on her nose standing out.

Susie's mouth twitched, clamped shut tightly and then opened again as she exhaled a long breath. Her teeth were uneven, one of the front ones chipped. Her skin was slick with sweat.

'You've got his eyes,' she said finally, the words seeming to come from the depths of her soul. 'Black, evil eyes.'

Beside me, Tom let out a long breath, exhaling as if he had been keeping hold of it for too long. I fought the instinct to close my eyes, to shut them away from her, knowing the pain it must cause her by seeing my father's eyes looking out from my face.

'I can't help my eyes,' I said, hearing the tension and hurt in my voice. I had set her free. I'd rescued her and all she was doing was lashing out at me.

'Mia helped you.' Grace's voice was firm as if she sensed my hurt. 'You wanted to see her, remember, to thank her.'

Susie pulled a crumpled tattered tissue from the sleeve of her shirt and dabbed ineffectively at her eyes, sniffed loudly, and then blew her nose before looking around for somewhere to dump the ruined tissue. Grace got to her feet, found a bin and put it by Susie's side.

'Thanks.' Her voice was little more than a whisper.

'I did want to thank you,' Susie said, looking at me. Her eyes flickered over mine before she looked away, staring at her ragged nails clutching the edge of the table. 'I hadn't realised how it would bring everything back.'

I nodded. 'I understand.' Seeing her brought memories back to me, memories I had pushed to the back of my mind, had not dared look at.

Tom was very still; I could hear him breathing.

'I wonder what would have happened if you hadn't done what you did.' Susie's many chins quivered.

I turned my bracelet around on my wrist, fingered the tiny scar from the cut.

'You were very brave.' She finally met my eyes. Her hand, when she lifted it to fiddle with her hair, trembled.

Tom took my hand. I met Grace's eyes, knowing she knew the truth. I hadn't been brave. I hadn't been trying to set her free, just opening the door to talk to her.

'Why did you want to meet Mia?' Tom said, his voice cutting into the brittle atmosphere.

Susie shrugged. 'I just thought it would help me. Put it all behind me, if I met her and said thank you for letting me out.' She shifted in her chair as if the tension in her body was locking her muscles.

'How did it feel to you knowing I was there?' Susie asked, twisting her hands together compulsively, the sound of the skin like sandpaper on wood. 'Trapped in that cellar, alone, frightened.'

I opened my mouth, trying to form the words. I shook my head. 'I didn't know.'

'Didn't know?' Susie spat suddenly, her voice loud and harsh, 'You came every day to look in on me, gloating while you were outside, looking at me, chained up to the bed, waiting for him to come back and...'

I shook my head again, my mind filled with buzzing like angry bees. I wished I hadn't come. What did I expect from her; that she'd be grateful to me, nice to me, make me think that I was a good person, that I had no connection to my father and all that had happened on the farm? 'I didn't understand what was happening.' I finally found my voice.

'How could you not know what was happening? How could you think that was normal? For someone to be imprisoned underground while you were wandering around outside?

She'd got to her feet, enraged, leaning over the table towards me. Instinctively I drew myself away from her, afraid of the anger that coursed through her.

Grace put a controlling hand on Susie's arm. 'Susie, Mia was only eight, she didn't understand what was going on.'

Susie span around, directing her anger at Grace. 'How couldn't she know? Was she fucking stupid or something? How could she think that was normal? What kind of animal is she?'

I shook my head, my eyes seeking the understanding I saw in Grace's gentle eyes. 'I didn't understand,' I repeated, 'I didn't know why she was there.'

'Susie.' Grace got to her feet, towering over Susie's plump form. 'Sit down, please don't be aggressive towards Mia, she's come here in good faith. To try to help you.'

For a long moment Susie stood, glaring at me, turning her head to glare at Grace, before finally she sank back down into the chair. The legs squeaked in protest on the lino floor.

'Just don't seem right to me,' Susie said, sullenly. There was a burr in her voice I'd come to recognise as Cornish. I wondered if my father had spoken with the same accent, if, had things been different, I would have sounded the same.

'Will you tell me what happened to you?' I asked, suddenly finding my voice. If we were doing soul searching, I wanted to know all of the details that I'd wondered about. 'How did my father take you prisoner?'

She seemed to deflate as she calmed down slightly. 'I was at college.' She fixed her gaze at the table, picking at a piece of loose skin beside one of her ragged nails. 'I'd been to a party. I was walking home. It was late at night.'

I could hear myself breathing, feel Tom's fingers gripping mine, feel Grace's eyes on me.

'He was parked up at the side of the road.' Susie's voice was brittle with bitterness. 'Said someone had run over a cat and he was trying to find it. He was worried it was injured.'

Susie shook her head as if she couldn't believe her own stupidity.

'So fucking naïve,' she sighed. 'He seemed so kind, so worried about the bloody cat...' 'Don't do this if it hurts too much,' Grace said gently.

Susie made a noise that sounded like a cross between a snort and a grunt.

'We went looking in the undergrowth. The next thing I remembered was being in the back of his van. The bastard had hit me over the head, knocked me out. Such a fucking cliché, looking for an injured cat.'

Was that how my father had taken my mother? I wondered. How had he tricked her into the van? Had he forced her, knocked her out? Did she trust him initially, think he was kind and gentle?

I was still thinking about my mother when Susie continued. 'I remember him pulling me from the back of the van. He was holding my hair.'

As I glanced at Susie, she twisted her head, wincing as if remembering how my father had held her.

'He had a hand over my mouth.'

I could see the fear in her face as she remembered what had happened; though so long ago, it was only yesterday to her. I imagined how that would feel, the fear, the anger at being taken prisoner, not knowing what would happen. How on earth would you survive that? The terror of the unknown.

'We went down some steps. It was dark. Before I could see a house, lights on. I fought him, I wanted to get away, to scream, get someone to help me. He was shaking me, hurting me.'

I watched Susie take a gulp of air. She ran her hands through her hair, with fingers that quivered. Beside her Grace was watching, her face a mixture of fascination and sympathy.

'I thought he was going to kill me.' She was silent, the emotions flickering over her face. 'He raped me. I was screaming, but he didn't stop.'

She buried her face in her hands, gulping and sobbing. 'And then he just left me.'

I had a sudden, vivid memory of Nan pulling me back from my bedroom window, me kneeling there, hearing screaming during the night. 'It's the foxes,' she'd told me.

I'd stopped getting up to look out of the window, knowing it was just the foxes making that noise.

'That was your father.' Susie spat, her lips curled upwards like a dog snarling. Across the table, Grace shuffled a stack of papers. In the silence I heard her swallow.

'How long were you kept for?' Tom asked, his voice breaking across the tension.

Susie glanced at him, her face filled with hatred as the memories surged inside her; for a moment she looked as if she had forgotten he was there and then closed her eyes as if to focus her thoughts.

'Weeks,' she whispered, pulling at her clothes in a distracted gesture. 'Seven weeks he had me there. Seven weeks he raped me. Seven weeks she looked in through that window at me.'

'And then Mia let you out,' Grace said quickly, she seemed determined not to let Susie give in to the anger she was focusing on me. 'Mia rescued you.'

Susie nodded slowly, her head bobbing up and down like one of those plastic dogs on the back windows of cars. 'She opened the door. I ran.' Susie gave a snort of derision.

'What happened to you afterwards?' I asked.

'After...?' Susie's voice was harsh, distant, as if she were still in the cellar with my father, fearing for her life, when freedom was some distant dream she couldn't contemplate.

'How have you been since Mia set you free?' Tom asked his words felt deliberately chosen to remind her of my role.

'Free?' She frowned, her lips moving around the word as if it were some strange unknown concept. 'I'm not free.'

Susie looked up, her eyes locking onto mine. 'Every day I'm afraid. I don't have relationships, with anyone. I can't trust anyone. I could never look at a man. Have any kind of relationship. I sleep with the light on. Lock every door and window, check those constantly. I rarely sleep. I doze, listening to every noise.'

Susie pushed herself upright, leaning over the table towards me to jab a finger into my chest.

'You let me out of that cellar, but in here,' she jabbed aggressively at her head as if she hated herself, 'in here I'm still there, waiting for him to come back. Oh, I know he's dead.' Susie pushed herself away from me, shoved her chair back so hard it slid across the room. 'But inside my head he's as alive now as the day he took me prisoner.'

She glared at the three of us, half turned to leave and then crossed the room to stand in front of Tom. 'How can you be with her?' she spat, spittle flying from her mouth. 'Look at her. Butter wouldn't melt in her mouth. But she's part of him. She's got his genes. She's as evil as he was.'

I shook my head, trying to rid myself of her words. I heard the door crash shut as Susie left. The room filled with silence. Across the table, Grace took a long breath and exhaled slowly. Tom's chair creaked as he came to crouch beside me, his arms around my waist.

I rested my face on the top of his head, feeling the warmth. I took a slow breath. I could smell the shampoo he had used that morning, before we left home, before Susie Carne had brought a wrecking ball into our lives.

I wished we hadn't come. I'd imagined her thanking me for freeing her, for being grateful to the new chance she had at life. Instead she'd accused me of being like my father. I possessed his genes and in her eyes I was as evil as he was.

'Mia, you mustn't take any notice of her.' Grace came to stand beside me, perched her bottom on the table and looked at me. I met her eyes, saw the sympathy there. 'I would have never thought she was going to do that.' Grace said, her cheeks flushed and angry. 'She gave me the impression she wanted to thank you.'

'She's right though, isn't she?' I said, the words tumbling from my mouth in a torrent I couldn't stop. 'I do have my father's genes. Why didn't I understand what was going on in the cellar?'

'How could you understand?' Tom had got to his feet and stood beside Grace, the two of them looking down, their faces filled with concern. 'You were eight. You'd never left the farm. You'd no experience of life.'

I shook my head, 'But I knew they were there, shut away, her, other women. It just never seemed anything to concern me. They were just there.'

The women had just been in the cellar, part of everyday life. I'd watched them from the tiny window. But it had never occurred to me that they shouldn't be there, that the father I loved was doing wrong. I'd loved him. He was kind to me. How could he harm someone?

CHAPTER TWENTY-EIGHT

'Mia, you mustn't take what Susie said to heart.' Tom held me to him. His scarf, wound around his neck against the bitter wind, was soft against my cheek.

We stood beside the seafront, on the promenade. A thick sea mist rolled in off the coast. Droplets of mist coated Tom's hair and glittered on his eyelashes.

'How can I not take that to heart?' I pulled away from him, staring into his eyes, seeing the kindness and concern.

'You're not bad. You're not your father.' Tom's fingers dug into my arms. He shook me gently.

'She's right though,' I said, pulling out of his grasp and moved away to lean on the railing and stare at the beach twenty feet below. The sea surged below us, the air filled with the noise of the pebbles crushing against each other as the churning waves pulled them back and forth.

I breathed in the salty air, wiping away the mixture of tears and sea mist.

'I knew there were women in the cellar,' I said, staring down at the pebbles, focusing on the pale colours, grey, beige, white. 'But I'd no more have let them out than I would one of the dogs or the cows or the sheep.'

'You were afraid to.' Tom came to stand beside me, his arm touching mine. He put his foot up onto the rail. The tip of his shoe was stained with mud from where we had walked across the park after we'd left the police station.

'No,' I shook my head, 'I wasn't.' I had a clear image of my father, laughing with me, throwing me into the air, kind, gentle. I wasn't afraid of him. I felt nothing from him but love. It had never occurred to me to let the girls out, that they could have been afraid of my father. Hurt by him.

'But you didn't do that because you are bad...' Tom's voice had a desperate edge to it as if he was struggling to find some way of justifying my actions. I knew he couldn't bear the thought of picturing me being part of what had happened at the farm.

The beach below looked very tempting. With one quick movement I could be over the rail, fall headfirst to the pebbles, end the torment that swirled inside me. Perhaps sensing that urge in me, Tom took my arm and drew me away from the rail.

'Come on, we should go home.'

Wordlessly I nodded, longing for the peace of home, to be with people who loved me, where I could feel safe. I wanted to be where no one called me evil. Except I knew that place didn't exist anymore. There was nowhere I could escape my past.

Tom sped out of Penzance, as if by fleeing we could leave the past behind us. I longed to be away from my past, from Susie, from Grace, from my relatives, everyone who knew the truth about me. As we drove, I found myself looking back, wanting to absorb the rocky shoreline, the rolling hills of my birth. I was filled with regret at leaving this place. This was where I came from, where my heart belonged. Leaving felt like I was heading once more into exile.

* * * * * * * *

Tom dropped me off at my parents' house before heading back to his own. I'd promised them I'd call in to tell them what had happened in Cornwall. I wondered if Tom was glad to be away from me. If perhaps he needed to put his own thoughts into some kind of order.

'Please don't worry about things,' he'd said gently. 'Forget about Cornwall, about Susie, it doesn't matter. It's not who you are.'

The house was empty. Dad's car wasn't outside. I could hear voices from the stable yard. After dumping my bag in the hall I went in their direction.

Mum was in the sand arena, riding Solar. The two of them the picture of focus and attention. I saw her gently lift one heel back and Solar leapt forwards into the beautiful rocking horse canter. His ears pricked as he cantered around the arena. Mum's face was a picture of concentration. I knew what that canter felt like, the power, the endless feeling of energy effortlessly controlled by your weight and seat.

'Hello.' I crossed the yard and stood beside the arena rail.

'Oh, darling, you're back.' Mum slowed Solar, turning him across the arena to me. She looked flushed with pleasure, her eyes flickering with guilt at being caught riding what had become my horse.

'How is he going?'

'Oh, he's incredible,' she said, breathlessly. 'Perhaps I could take him to some dressage competitions in the summer.'

'That's a great idea.' I reached over the rail to stroke Solar's nose. 'Be good for him to do that as well as jump with me.'

Mum leant down to rub his powerful neck. I knew she regretted giving me the ride on Solar, but without my confidence he would never have been as good as he was. He'd have walked all over Mum and have become unmanageable.

'Tell me how Cornwall went.' Mum slid from Solar and pulled the reins over his head; she had to stand on tiptoe to slide them over his ears.

I slipped through the rails and stepped into her arms. Solar nudged at the two of us with his head. 'It was horrible,' I whispered, closing my eyes and resting my head on Mum's shirt front. She smelt of horse, the flowery scent of her perfume deep in the fabric. Her jodhpurs were stained and there were strands of hay stuck on her shirt.

'Come on, let's put Solar away and we'll talk in the house.' She gently levered herself out of my grasp. I followed her across the sandy surface, our feet sinking into the soft depths, making walking hard. I helped untack Solar, easing the bridle off his elegant head as she pulled off his saddle.

We worked in a unison born of long practice. I threw his rug up onto his muscular back and fastened the belly straps while she did the front fastenings.

'Tea?' Mum asked as we closed Solar's stable door. 'Thanks, Vicky,' Mum said, as one of the grooms came to take the saddle from her.

We walked silently, side by side up the stone flagged path to the house. Mum made tea while I sat at the kitchen table, shrugging off my jacket in the AGA warmed kitchen.

'Tell me.' Mum pushed a mug of steaming tea in front of me. The chair legs squeaked on the kitchen floor as she pulled it back and sat down.

'She's so full of hate,' I said, trying to frame the words to describe my encounter with Susie. 'I'd expected her to be grateful to me.' I shook my head. 'How naïve could I be? She's so damaged by it all.'

Mum sipped her tea, shaking her head as she tried to find something to say to make the situation better. I hated myself for putting her through this. Our lives had been so calm and quiet and filled with love until Grace had wreaked havoc with the news of my mother's body being found. Mum had not been equipped to deal with this, the fallout from a life she could never imagine.

'She told me I was evil. I had my father's eyes. I was part of him…' I sighed, closing my eyes in an attempt to block out the thoughts that swirled in my mind.

'Darling, you're not.' Mum grasped my hand over the table. Hers felt cool against my hot skin. 'You're lovely, you're kind, gentle. You're not your father. You know that.'

I shook my head. How could she say I was kind and gentle? My father's blood ran in my veins. It must follow that I was as capable as vileness as he was. I pictured Poppy's mother, at the funeral, her face close to mine, telling me she knew I was evil.

'Please just stay here,' she said, grasping my hand firmly as if she could hold me. 'You need to forget Cornwall. Don't go back there again. We love you. You're loved here. Focus on riding Solar, your new life with Tom, there's so much good in the future for you.'

I nodded, forcing my head upward to meet her eyes. There was an indented line across her forehead from the pressure of her riding hat.

'You're not part of what went on at that farm.' She slid her hand away from mine and cupped her tea mug. 'Remember that, Mia. You belong here. You're loved so very much.'

I forced a jagged breath into my lungs, wishing I could go somewhere where I could scream away the agony that raged inside me. Instead I pushed it down, forced myself to forget Cornwall, forget the hatred I had felt from Susie, the knowledge of my history and the evil that rampaged in my blood.

'I love you, Mum.' I shoved my chair back and pushed myself into her arms, breathing in the horse scent, feeling safe in the circle of her arms.

'Love you too,' she whispered, her breath warm against my hair.

* * * * * * * *

'Don't forget, Vicky has tomorrow off, but Alison is coming in instead,' Mum said, a week later, dashing from one side of the kitchen to the other. 'Where the hell are my reading glasses?'

'Come on,' Dad sighed impatiently, standing in the kitchen doorway. 'It's going to be a tough journey, there's snow forecast.'

'Ugghhhh,' Mum groaned, 'I'm sorry I feel so angry about having to go to Scotland. My poor friend, Annie. I know she's devastated about her husband being ill, but I wish I hadn't agreed to go and be with her.'

Dad, in the doorway, rolled his eyes, and his voice when he spoke had more than a hint of wryness. 'You said you wanted to go. 'I need to be with Annie' were your very words.'

'Yes, yes,' Mum snapped, finally locating her glasses on the kitchen windowsill. 'That was on the spur of the moment, I didn't really think about how hard it always is to leave the yard at a moment's notice. Everything to be arranged...'

'Mum,' I said gently, taking her arms and steering her towards Dad. 'I'm going to stay here, with Tom, I'm perfectly capable of looking after things. We'll be on the yard if there are any problems. You need to be with your friend.'

She stopped then, all of the impatience and fluster leaving her like a balloon deflating. 'You're right, I'm being a total idiot.' She picked up her handbag, shoved her glasses in the top and smiled wryly at Dad. 'Right, let's go.'

She was halfway down the path towards the car, before she turned back to where Tom and I stood in the doorway. 'Don't forget, the farrier is coming on Wednesday.'

'Yes, Mum,' I smiled, blowing her a kiss, 'It's written in the diary. Have a good trip. Goodbye.'

I grinned, waving and then, pulling Tom inside, banged the front door shut, leaning on it and puffing out my cheeks. 'I didn't think they'd ever go!'

* * * * * * * *

'What's that?' Tom sat up in bed, snapping on the light.

'What?' I blinked against the light.

'That.' Tom's hand touched my arm. 'Listen.'

I sat up, blearily, glancing at my watch. 'It's three o'clock,' my voice was thick with sleep.

'What the fuck is that?' I asked, instantly awake as I heard the noise that had woken Tom. From one side of the wall, in-between the wall that separated my bedroom from my parents' came the distinctive sound of scratching.

'Jesus,' Tom's expression was appalled. His hair stuck up at odd angles. 'There's a bloody mouse or…'

The noise came again, loud, determined scratching.

'Something bigger.'

'Ughh, no,' I shuddered, hating the thought of something verminous so close to me, afraid of it bursting through the stone wall into my room.

'We had a rat in the surgery wall a while ago, the bloody thing had burrowed into the tiniest gap.'

Tom leapt out of bed and banged hard on the wall with his fist. The noise stopped momentarily and then began again, more determinedly.

'There's some poison in the stables,' I told him. Mum was terrified of rats and kept a constant supply of bait locked in the medicine cabinet in case she ever found any vermin droppings. Our clowder of five huge cats seemed to keep the vermin population down as I rarely saw any in the stables, despite the amount of food and hay available for them.

We ended up sleeping curled up at opposite ends of the sofa, the quilt dragged from upstairs to drape over us.

Before he left for work the following morning, Tom bravely investigated the rooms. 'I can't see where a rat has got in, but you don't want it running about in the gap between the walls.'

'Ughh, no.' I shuddered.

'If I can get behind this panel,' Tom said, emerging slowly from the depths of Mum's wardrobe where he'd been on his hands and knees looking for a way into the wall. 'Then I can put some poison down. Hopefully that will get rid of our furry friend.'

'It's no friend of mine,' I shuddered, pulling a face.

'Can you clear out some space in the wardrobe? Tom asked looking wryly at the depths of the crammed wardrobe. 'I'll take out that panel when I get back later.'

* * * * * * * *

The work in the stables completed and all the horses ridden, I came back into the house, showered and then set to work clearing out the bulk of the clothes in Mum's wardrobe. I worked gingerly, aware that the creature had no way of getting into the house, and yet still afraid of coming face-to-face with it.

'Mum!' I sighed, hauling armfuls of summer dresses out of the groaning, bent rails of her wardrobe. There were clothes here I remembered her wearing years ago. I felt a jagged dart of tension as I lifted out the dress she'd worn the day of the Jubilee party.

I heaped the clothes onto her bed and then set to work lifting out the boxes of shoes that were piled on the floor of the wardrobe. High heels, flats and sandals, were carefully wrapped in tissue and placed neatly in the boxes.

There was a final box, lodged right at the back, which felt different from the rest. As I eased it out it felt heavier than the others. Nosily I flipped off the lid. I sat down on the edge of the bed; the dresses slid onto the floor as my fingers were drawn relentlessly to the letters inside the box. They were all unopened. And addressed to me.

CHAPTER TWENTY-NINE

My legs gave way and I sank to the edge of the bed. Slowly I sifted through the envelopes. They were in date order, the last from a few years previously. They were all written on cheap paper, with a prison postmark. They were all from Nan. She'd been writing to me for years and my parents had chosen to keep the letters from me.

I slid slowly to the floor. The dresses, heaped on the bed cascaded around me, a pile of brightly-coloured fabric like discarded flower petals. They smelt of stale perfume, musty from being stuck in the wardrobe for so long.

A wave of nausea hit me. I scrambled to my feet and dashed into the en-suite, retching up yellow bile, my stomach aching from the effort. When the retching stopped, I made my way back to the chaos of the bedroom, the discarded dresses pooled on the floor beside the boxes of shoes and the innocuous-looking one that was stacked full of letters addressed to me. I sat on the edge of the bed, my feet slipping on the dress fabric. I kicked them away until I had cleared a space around me.

Slowly I lifted out the envelopes, shifting through them. There were twenty, maybe more. I lost count. The letters had been addressed to Mia Hammett, care of the Social Services. Hammett, my father's surname. I'd never seen myself addressed by that name before.

I turned the letters over; the writing was spidery, unformed, childlike.

The earliest dated from shortly after I was eighteen. I'd never had a birth certificate. Was the date on the letter my proper birthday?

In the silence of the room I could hear my breathing, feel the thud of my heart against my rib cage.

I had a sudden memory of a woman looking out of the window of a police car. She had wild dark hair, a hand was pressed up against the glass, reaching towards me. Nan, being taken away by the police.

I remembered sitting in another car, a policewoman beside me, who I knew now to be Grace Tallis, arm around my shoulders as I sat in silence. Then a room, adults, other children. Bunkbeds, crammed into a room. Their faces, staring openly at me, while I curled beneath the blankets. I had an impression of a routine of school, the chaos of being around other children. I had no problem remembering how much I hated it, the noise, the constant presence of people. I had longed for, cried and screamed for my father and Nan. I could picture a room, people sitting on plastic chairs, looking at me as if I were a curiosity. I'd learned to talk politely, to smile, and they left me alone. Another memory was of a woman, smelling of fried food and cigarette smoke, who brought me in a car to Mum and Dad where my life began again. I stopped being Mia Hammett and became Mia Lewis.

When Tom returned, a few hours later, I was still sitting on the bed. The world had gone on around me while I sat, my fingers growing cold and stiff around the pile of envelopes.

'Right let's get this panel out.' I imagined it hadn't occurred to Tom that I had been sitting on the bed since he left.

He hauled a clanking bag of tools onto the floor beside me and disappeared into the depths of the wardrobe. 'Mia, will you pass me the cross screwdriver.' His voice was muffled.

Slowly, as if I'd been underwater for a long time, I forced myself to focus on him. Pushing myself off the bed, I unzipped the heavy canvas bag and found the tool Tom wanted and handed it to him.

'That's a hammer.' His voice had an edge of male exasperation. 'Screwdriver. It's a long metal thing with a wooden handle.'

I forced myself to focus, pushed the swirl of emotions to the back of my mind, and found the required tool.

'Thanks. Right, just get this off. Mr Bunting at Kingdom Farm says to nail the poison to something otherwise the buggers take it away. I looked outside; I think they've burrowed in through the broken grate. Probably found their way into the loft somehow and the cavity between the walls. This will sort them out.' He chatted away while I leant against the wall, unable to move, afraid if I tried my legs would give way beneath me.

'There,' he said after much banging and swearing. 'Got some poison nailed to the beam and I've put the panel back. The screws aren't tight so we can get in there again and check.'

He scrambled out of the wardrobe, his rubber-soled shoes squeaking on the wooden floor. He held the screwdriver towards me and then seeing my expression said, 'Mia, what on earth is it?' He threw the tool in the general direction of its bag. It clattered and bounced across the floor before coming to a stop.

'What's happened?' He pulled me into his arms. I could feel the thud of his heart through his ribcage.

'Look,' I said, my voice filled with disbelief at what I had found. 'I found these in the wardrobe. Mum and Dad, they've been hiding them from me.

I handed the pile of envelopes to Tom and watched the expression on his face change from concern, to incredulity, to anger.

'These are all for you?'

'They were sent to me via the social services.'

'And you didn't know these had come for you?'

Tom sank down on the bed, his shoes resting amongst the fabric of Mum's dresses.

I shook my head, standing above him, watching him sift through the envelopes.

'But surely they are meant for you?' The words dripped slowly from Tom as if he couldn't quite get his head around what my parents had done. There were beads of sweat on his forehead. I sat on the bed beside him, watching his long pale hands turn the envelopes over. There was a smear of something unidentifiable, green, beneath the soft dark smattering of hairs on his forearm.

I took the pile from Tom. 'There's so many. They've kept them from me for years.'

'You haven't read them yet?'

I shook my head. I'd been so upset at their betrayal and so filled with anger. Part of me wished I'd never found them, that I could just shove them back out of sight in the shoebox in the back of the wardrobe and forget them. But now I knew of their existence, my life was changed forever. I was also too afraid of what I'd find there.

'Why haven't they destroyed them if they wanted to keep them from you?' Tom's voice was incredulous.

Outside the leaves on the trees danced in the breeze, the spring sunlight casting shadows over the room.

'Maybe they thought they would give them to me…someday.' I shook my head, trying to make sense of the new shift in my life. 'I've no idea.'

'Are you going to read them?' Tom asked gently again.

I nodded. There was nothing I wanted more. I wanted to remember, to find out what Nan had written to me.

The bed creaked as Tom pushed himself off it. 'Look, Mia, I'm going to leave you. I need to get back to work. You'd be better to read these on your own. Call me later.'

He crouched in front of me, stretching his arms along the length of my thighs. His hands were warm through the fabric of my jeans.

'Ok,' I stared at the envelopes, aware of him getting up, walking away, the familiar creak of the stairs, the slam of the front door.

As the sound of his engine died away, I stood, put the envelopes onto Mum's dressing table and began the long process of putting her clothes back into the wardrobe, untangling the hangers where they had got stuck together, arranging the fabric so it hung properly. The task complete, I stacked the shoeboxes into the bottom of the wardrobe. It was dark in there and smelt of old perfume and wood. I wished I could crawl into the darkness and hide.

Unable to bear being in Mum and Dad's room, I went to mine. Shivering despite the warmth of the day, I propped my pillows behind my back and wrapped my duvet around my knees.

The earliest of the envelopes was the one I opened first. I worked carefully, making a hole at the top of the envelope and sliding a nail file along the crease, not wanting to tear the thin paper, treating it as if it were some treasured artefact.

The paper inside was starkly white, lined, cheap-looking. I eased it out, straightened it and began to read.

Nan's handwriting, as on the envelope, was spidery, indistinct, as if she didn't want to put pressure onto the paper. Her writing had the childish rounded letters I remembered making at school.

The handwriting didn't matter.

I read of my childhood, time spent with Nan, her sadness at losing me. I remembered her as I read. Her comforting bulk, being curled in her lap, my head pressed against the soft plumpness of her breasts beneath the billowing shirts she always wore. I read of her hope of regaining our relationship now I was eighteen, the hope I'd understand what had happened at the farm, how my father must have been ill to do what he had done.

As the years slipped by in the letters, I read of her impatience at my lack of a reply, her insecurity and finally her insistence she would to keep writing, that she hoped one day I'd get in touch. I read of her despair at being in prison for a crime she hadn't committed. Above all I read of her love for me.

* * * * * * * *

In the days that followed I had done my work in the stable yard, ridden Solar and the other horses, before retreating to the house where, lost in the letters and my agony at my parents' actions I could hear the sound of the stableyard ebb and flow, chatter, the clatter of horses' hooves on the concrete yard, the silence when everyone had gone.

Tom had arrived every evening after work. I'd gone through the motions of making us dinner, chatting about the horses and what had happened on the yard, listened to him recount his own day. He'd asked me about the letters, but unable to frame the pain and confusion that was trapped inside me, I'd told him they weren't that interesting.

Days later I was again reading the letters when I heard Mum and Dad's car returning. All afternoon I'd lain curled on my bed, alternately absorbing Nan's words and crying from the pain of my parents' betrayal. As they got closer to home Mum had sent me a text. 'Getting a takeaway. Hope you'll stay. Chinese or Indian?'

The sound of the message arriving had disturbed me. I looked at the phone blankly, struggling to return to any kind of reality.

'Don't mind,' I'd tapped hastily and pressed the send button.

The front door banged open. 'Mia!' Mum's voice sounded tired. 'We got Chinese. Come down and I'll dish it up.'

On automatic pilot, I pushed the duvet off my legs, eased myself stiffly off my bed and went out of my room. It was dark on the landing, the only light coming from the hall and kitchen, a shaft of light illuminating the stairs.

'Oh, there you are.' Dad held three big plates in his hands. 'Had a good day?'

'No, not really.' I crossed the kitchen, the letters in my hand. I saw their shocked faces as they realised what I was holding. 'I found these.'

I held up the letters, seeing first Mum's face then Dad's pale. Dad's mouth opened as if he was going to speak, and then closed as if he couldn't form the words. Mum, beside him, sank heavily into a kitchen chair.

'There was a rat in the wall space. We took the back off the wardrobe to put some poison down.' It was very important suddenly they didn't think I'd been poking around in their possessions while they were out. 'I found these when I lifted out the shoeboxes.'

'Oh, darling.' Mum's voice sounded strangled.

'We were going to give them to you.' Dad put the plates on the table with a clatter. The kitchen was filled with the nauseating smell of Chinese, the sweet and sour tang making my stomach churn.

'When, exactly?' My jaw ached from the pain of clenching my teeth together to stop myself from crying.

I moved to the opposite end of the kitchen and leant against the work surface as if I wanted to keep my distance from their treachery.

Mum shook her head, her expression desperate. 'I wanted the time to be right.'

'They were meant for me. You had no right to keep them from me.'

'We thought there'd be a good time.' Dad sat down beside Mum, took her hand as if he wanted to protect her from my anger.

Mum looked up; tears were falling freely now. I wanted to go to her, to comfort her and tell her it didn't matter, but the chasm of pain was too wide. 'We were going to when you were older and then, when your mother's body was found....'

'Everything we did was meant to protect you.' Dad's voice was quiet, firm.

I shook my head. I wished I'd gone back to Tom's before they'd arrived, so I could have avoided this confrontation until I'd got my swirling thoughts into some kind of order. 'Everything you've done was to protect yourselves. To keep me in your perfect family.' The words tumbled out in an agonising howl.

'Mia, it wasn't like that,' Mum said. I watched her get up, cross the room and come towards me. Her arms went around my body, drawing me into her. I smelt her familiar perfume, the same scent that lingered, stale, on the dresses in the wardrobe. Slowly she released me and stepped back, tilting my chin with her fingers so she could look into my eyes. 'Everything we did was meant for the best.'

'You kept me away from my family,' I sobbed. 'Nan is my only relative who wants me. My mother's family have made it clear they don't.'

'Stop this!' Dad pushed himself away from the table, backed to the opposite side of the kitchen where he leant against the sink. 'Okay, we shouldn't have kept the letters from you. We didn't do that to hurt you.'

I unfurled a ream of kitchen roll and wiped my eyes. 'I'm not sure how you worked that one out. How could it not hurt me? Being kept from my family. Being forced to be part of yours.' Anger and the bitter pain made me say the cruel words.

'Please, Mia.' Mum took a step away from me, holding her hands up in a gesture of surrender. 'Can't you see, you don't belong with your father's family. Nan Hammett is in prison for her part in killing those young women. For helping to bury them, leaving their families not knowing what had happened to them.' Her face contorted with distaste. 'You're part of us. Part of this family. You aren't anything to do with what went on at the farm. You're better off here, with us and Tom. Surely you can see that.'

I shook my head. 'Nan needed me,' I said, sullenly, staring at the tiled floor. A drip of grease from the bag containing the takeaway marred the pristine surface. 'She loves me. You just treat me like I'm some possession.'

'Oh, come on Mia,' Dad's voice was terse, filled with exasperation. 'Please, sweetheart. We just wanted to protect you.'

Beside him Mum wrenched out a chair and sat down heavily, covering her face with her hands. 'She's right, Peter,' Mum pressed her forefingers into the corners of her eyes, trying and failing to stop the tears that flowed. 'I did want to keep the letters from you, Mia.' Mum raised her hands imploringly. 'Your childhood was so horrendous. Your father…' Her voice faltered. Dad put a comforting hand on her shoulder. 'I didn't want you to be touched by that again. I wanted to keep you safe.'

'Oh Mum,' I crossed the room and crouched beside her chair, letting her pull me into her arms.

'I'm so sorry,' she said softly, her breath warm against my tear drenched face.

I nodded. 'I'm sorry too. I shouldn't ever have doubted you.'

Beside us, Dad gently put two glasses of wine on the table. 'I don't know about you two but I'm starving.'

Wiping my eyes I gently disentangled myself from Mum's arms. All I could see shining in their faces, as I got to my feet, was their love for me.

CHAPTER THIRTY

The air smelt stale; sweat, old farts, disinfectant and food, all trapped, swirling, with an overriding sense of despair and fear. I shuffled slowly in a line of people along a long pale green, institution-coloured, painted corridor. Whoever had looked at a paint sample of that and decided it was a perfect colour? The soles of my shoes stuck on the sticky floor.

The prison that held Nan was a huge, imposing, modern building, like a sprawling block of flats except for the barred windows.

I shuffled my way slowly along with an elderly man carrying a vast laundry bag, a hard-looking middle-aged woman with two small children in tow, a smart lady in a business suit. We all stared fixedly at our feet, no one daring to lift their heads to make eye contact with anyone in the queue.

'Next.' Two vast prison officers opened the door to a searching area. It was my turn. I stepped forwards. Two yellow footprints were painted on the floor.

'Bag there,' growled one.

I put my bag on the table, where he began to rummage through it.

I moved forwards putting my feet onto the yellow footprints, while the burly woman began to pat me down. Her hands were cool against me, cursory. It was clear from their attitude there was no room here for jokes, no pleasant conversation.

'Anything in here that shouldn't be?' asked the one who was going through my bag.

I itched to make a joke about drugs or alcohol and resisted the temptation; they didn't look as if they had any sense of humour. In my bag there was a bottle of water. The gorilla pulled that out, examining the top to see if it had been opened and refilled with alcohol. Satisfied, the bottle was shoved back and the bag handed to me. I left the search area feeling as if I needed a shower.

The line of people ahead of me shuffled into a vast echoing room. Small wooden tables with hard-looking plastic chairs positioned at either side were arranged in neat rows around the bright room. High above, sunlight streamed in from barred windows. The noise of children rushing to bag tables echoed around the building. At one end vending machines already had queues of people buying coffee and snacks.

Around the room, standing in twos and threes, prison guards stood chatting to one another, their body language tense; it was obvious they were pretending to be relaxed. Watchful for anything that could go wrong.

I found a table and sat down, facing, as did everyone else, in the direction of a metal door where two women guards stood. One had bright yellow bleached hair and an armful of tattoos. Neither looked, despite their slenderness, like anyone you'd pick an argument with.

There had been another row when I told my parents of my intention to visit Nan. I needed to find out about my past. Nan was the only person who knew my mother and father. I was determined to visit her. I'd got in touch with Grace Tallis to find out what prison she was in. Dad had been particularly vile in his condemnation of my decision.

'She's a convicted criminal,' he said, his voice the one he used when he was watching something unsuitable on television, or when he read about dole spongers in the newspaper, patronising, appalled, like there was a bad smell under his nose.

'She's the only person who can tell me about my parents. Can't you see how I need to know about my mother?'

Mum shook her head. There were harsh lines I'd never noticed before at the side of her mouth as she spoke. 'Mia. Please darling, you don't need to know. Just let it go. This is your home. We're your family.'

Dad let out a long heartfelt sigh. 'We can't stop you, Mia, but really, is Nan Hammett someone you want in your life?'

The Nan I knew had made me feel safe, loved. But I remembered being afraid of her too. I needed to know what had happened to my mother. To find out why Nan had lied to me about my mother going away.

'Well you can go on your own if you are determined to go,' Dad snapped, angry in defeat.

'Peter...' Mum's voice was soft, as if trying to cajole him into changing his mind. He shook off the hand she'd laid on his arm.

'No, Mia if you're determined to go, I'm sorry, but we can't be part of it.'

Tom had been mortified that he couldn't come with me. 'We are just snowed under with work,' he'd told me. 'I just can't get away. Why don't you wait? Go another time when I can come?'

'I can't wait,' I'd replied. The need to face Nan, discover the truth about my mother was too strong. I had to see her.

As I drove, my mind was filled with jumbled memories and images. What did I remember? Was my memory skewed? I had no way of knowing. I knew I needed to see Nan, to make sense of the thoughts that churned in my mind. Without seeing her the feelings would go on forever, without any answers.

I hoped I'd hate her, be afraid of her, see her for the evil woman she had been painted as by the media. I wanted to understand she was a woman who knew her son held women prisoner and who could help him dispose of their bodies. I wanted to feel revulsion. To flee back to my parents and my life with Tom and never have to see her again.

Grace, when pressed, had told me Nan only had a few months left of her sentence for aiding and abetting a murderer, for helping conceal his crimes. Once free I'd no idea where she would go. Back to the farm, perhaps, or away? The only way I had of finding the answers to my questions was to ask them while she was still in the prison. Once she'd been let out she could disappear and then I'd never know. The thoughts would stay in my mind, swirling like a washing machine on a spin cycle forever.

I wondered, now, waiting for the metal door to open and disgorge the prisoners, if I would recognise her. How would I know who she was? Would she remember what I looked like?

A loud bell rang. The noise jarred my taut nerves and made me jump. Women dressed in grey sweatshirts and jogging pants began to emerge from the doorway. They were all ages, young, old, some beautiful, some ugly with rage and life, some frail, others fierce.

The women began to disperse around the room. The noise level grew as hugs were exchanged, greetings, squeals of delight from children. One woman peeled off from the group and came towards me. Tall, muscular, her hair a mass of dark curls. I looked at her expectantly, feeling her eyes rake over me as she moved between the tables. I opened my mouth to say something as she got closer to me and then passed. I heard a mumbled greeting as she went to the table beside me.

I glanced back to the stream of women crossing the room and saw Nan. I recognised her from the newspaper articles, not from any memory I had of her. She was taller than I had expected, powerful looking, with a mop of dark hair.

She came straight towards me, her eyes fixed on mine. I didn't recognise her, but her mouth and eyes were the same as mine. Wide and full.

'My love. My little Mia.' She opened her arms. Without hesitation I stepped into them, clasping her in mine as if I never wanted to let her go. 'I can't believe you're here. Thank you for coming.' Her breath was soft against my ear, her voice had the gentle West Country burr.

'Nan.' It was the only word I could manage.

We stood together while the business of the visiting room when on around us, until a harsh 'Hammett' came from one of the guards and Nan gently eased herself out of my arms.

She pulled out a chair and sat down. As I did the same, she leant forwards to grasp my hands.

My brain felt as if it had disconnected from my mouth. I couldn't speak, just stared at her. She was pale, with indoor skin, her eyes shadowed by dark smudges. Apart from lines that drooped at either side of her mouth and creases at either side of her eyes, her face was unlined. She looked remarkably good for a woman who I knew must be in her sixties.

'Nan.' The word came out as a whisper.

Her fingers stroked mine. Her nails were long, painted with a pale nail varnish.

'I wondered if you'd ever come and see me.' There was a tinge of bitterness in her voice.

'I didn't know you wanted to see me.' I closed my eyes to shut out the loneliness I could see in hers. 'I'd only just found your letters.

Mum and Dad...' I paused, seeing anger flit across her eyes. 'They hid the letters. Thought there'd be a suitable time to give them to me.'

'Fuckers,' Nan abruptly released my hands her chair creaked as she leaned back. She folded her arms across her breasts. 'They fucking kept the letters from you,' Nan shook her head in disbelief. 'I've been writing to you for years, as soon as I knew you'd turned eighteen.'

'That first letter, was it on my birthday?' I asked. I'd never known when my true birth date was. My birth certificate had given me an assumed birth date.

She nodded.

I was a week younger than I'd been brought up to assume.

'Tell me about your life. I knew you'd been adopted.' she leant forwards. Her hand slid back across the table towards mine. I pushed mine forwards, feeling my skin slide into hers. Her hand was warm, papery, dry.

I told her about my home, about Mum and Dad, Tom, Solar, my life.

'I missed you,' she said.

As she spoke I had a sudden vision of the newspaper headlines, the lurid details of how she had helped my father.

How could I feel any love for this woman, if she had done what she'd been accused of? If she had helped my father keep women prisoner. My mother.

'The police found my mother's body.' I watched her face, looking for some tell-tale sign of guilt. A dark shadow passed over her eyes and then she fixed her gaze on mine once more.

'I know,' she sighed, 'They came here and questioned me. Poor girl.'

'What happened to her?' I could hear the change in my voice, the high note in it.

'She was a lovely girl,' Nan ignored my question her fingers moving from my hand to touch the bracelet on my wrist.

'This was hers,' I said, drawing my hand away. 'The police found it on her body.'

'Your father gave it to her.' Nan's face crumpled as I looked at her, her mouth folding in on itself as she tried and then failed to keep in an agonised sob. She pulled a tissue from her sleeve.

'But then he killed her!' My voice was loud, filled with pain and confusion. I saw one of the guards glance in our direction.

Nan shook her head, dabbing at her eyes with the tissue. High spots of colour stained her cheeks. 'I thought he loved her. How could he kill her?'

I leant forwards, seeing the confusion etched in the lines on her face; she looked as if she had aged twenty years. 'What was she like? My mother?'

Nan covered her mouth with her hand. The skin looked yellow beneath the artificial lights.

As if she hadn't heard my question she continued, her voice little more than a whisper. 'How could I have reared a child who could kill?' Her dark eyes locked on mine. I traced the dots of age spots on the back of her hand with one of my fingers. Her skin was warm, clammy.

Nan shook her head again, pushing her lips forwards and blowing out a long breath.

I studied her face, looking for some sign of guilt, but what I saw there was pure torment, disbelief and confusion at what my father had done.

'My mother?' I repeated, gently.

'She was beautiful. And strong,' Nan touched a hand to her chest, 'in here. She wasn't afraid of him.'

She released an anguished sob. 'How could my son have that wickedness inside him?'

Nan tangled her fingers together beneath her chin in a compulsive movement. 'So many lives ruined.'

My heart was crashing against my rib cage. Somehow during the time I'd been in the prison I'd forgotten how to breathe. How could she feel sorry for the women my father had killed when she had been there? Living on the farm. Why hadn't she stopped him?

'They found more bodies with my mother, other women that he'd killed. I remember the one in the cellar, the one I set free. You were so angry at me.'

'Not angry, Mia,' her voice softened again. She abandoned the sodden ball of tissue onto the table. 'I was afraid of what Eddie would do. To you. To me.' She let out a long sigh that seemed to come from the depths of her feet. 'I lived in such dread of him. Being in here is tough, but it's nothing like the fear of what he could do.'

It was my turn to shake my head. How could I believe what she was saying when the police had told me something completely different? She had to have known. 'The police said...' I began, my voice faltering.

'The police said…' Nan hissed, shaking her head in disbelief. 'How can you believe anything they say? I knew what Eddie was doing. That he was killing them and tort…' Her voice faded to nothing as if she could not bring herself to say the words. 'I had to protect you. Keep him away from you.'

'But…' The ground beneath my feet shifted, became unsteady.

Nan shook her head again, 'I didn't help him. How could I help him to do that? To young women. He was evil. I was terrified of him.' She put a hand to her mouth and closed her eyes like she wanted to block out her thoughts. Her lashes were thick and long against the papery skin of her cheeks. 'Some woman detective came when they found the other bodies. I told her I knew nothing about them. My own flesh and blood. How could he do that?' Her eyes, when they focused back on mine were filled with tears. 'I've been held here for years; they assumed I was part of kidnapping those poor girls. That I helped him kill them, bury them. They convicted me in court of helping him. I didn't do anything. It breaks my heart that anyone would think I was capable of doing that.'

As Nan met my eyes, I studied her tear ravaged face. I couldn't imagine her kill or be involved in anything my father had done. Even though part of me knew what had happened at Blackthorn Farm, another part of me struggled to grasp the reality of it all. But beyond all of that I wanted desperately to believe her. I was not certain about anything anymore. Mum and Dad had lied to me about the letters from Nan. A court had convicted Nan of crimes she promised me she hadn't committed. She was not evil. She was one of my father's victims, just as the women he'd murdered had been.

'I've been in here all of these years.' Nan was looking at me as if she couldn't believe I was real. 'I loved you so much. All I wanted to do was to protect you. I should have been the one to bring you up, but they didn't believe me.' Nan put a hand to her throat, squeezing the flesh as if she wanted to choke the life out of herself. 'I was guilty,' her voice was little more than a whisper. 'I knew what he was doing, but I had to choose between protecting you, or trying to help them. Eddie, your dad, he did love you, but there was a sickness inside of him.'

'I don't remember any of it,' I said, hearing the note of desperation in my voice.

'You were a child,' she said. 'Mia. I did wrong, but I would have laid down my life for you. Your life was more important than the women he had in the cellar.'

I put a hand to my forehead in a vain attempt to ease the band of tension that felt as if it were tightening more with every moment. I couldn't remember anything of what she spoke of. I remembered feeling love for, but in equal measure fear of her.

'Can you understand what I did? Nan's voice sounded indistinct as if she were exhausted. 'Can you forgive me? Her grip, though was firm, as she took my hand, like she wanted to force her words into my consciousness.

I nodded. Speech seemed beyond me.

Nan smiled, her eyes clouding with tears. The taut line of her shoulders eased. 'Your dad could be the sweetest, most loving man you could ever imagine. He was so happy when you were born.'

I nodded. 'I remember him pushing me on the swing.' I smiled at the memory. 'I went to the farm with my boyfriend.'

Her face brightened. 'I've had to accept being in here. That they, the police, the jury, assumed I was part of it all. They were wrong. They wouldn't believe me. I deserved to be punished for not having the strength to stand up to him, for being afraid of him. My own son.' Nan puffed out her cheeks; the skin looked raw from crying. 'I will get out of here, though, and then I'm going home.' Nan smiled, the tension seemed to ease from her face. 'Then we can start over. Get to know one another properly.'

CHAPTER THIRTY-ONE

I drove away as fast as I could; perhaps through speed I could silence the demons that battered against me. The engine of my car screamed in protest as I thrust my foot on the accelerator so hard it touched the floor. I kept it there, overtaking lorries, the car lurching from lane to lane, overtaking everything that got in my way. I wanted to put distance between me and the prison. I wanted to be home.

Seeing Nan had opened up so many questions. I remembered kindness and love at the farm, but also I had an impression of being afraid. My father had killed those women. I knew that. Nan had spoken of being afraid of him, of what he did, of needing to protect the two of us, even if that meant sacrificing the lives of the young women. It was impossible for me to fully grasp what our lives had been like, the fear she must have lived with every day.

I wanted to hate my father and yet all I remembered was a kind, gentle man. In my mind it was impossible for me to merge the two halves of his personality.

At the prison I'd seen the pain in Nan's face; she lived with the guilt of knowing she had known the monster he was, but her need to protect me had been greater than her need to escape. I couldn't imagine the torment she'd lived with at the farm and clearly still did.

I wanted an escape from the thoughts that flooded into my mind; why hadn't she run, taken me with her? Was she brave, staying to protect me, or had she just buried her head in the sand and ignored what was going on?

The wind from one huge articulated lorry sent my car slewing across the road. For a long, sickening moment I was sure it would touch the metal guard rail, wrestling with the steering wheel to keep it in the right lane.

That steadied me. I drove into the next service station and sat, my hands tight on the steering wheel until my breathing returned to normal, my heart pounding against my rib cage.

I bought coffee, cupping my icy hands around the warmth of the cup, sipping a brew so hot it burned my mouth.

I called Tom, wanting the reassurance of his voice. When he answered, I could hear the wind battering into the mouthpiece and imagined him standing in a windswept field. 'Just delivered twin lambs. I've no idea what time I'll get home. Do you want to go to your Mum and Dad's and I'll ring or message you when I'm back?' His voice was loud as he shouted into the storm. 'How did it go?' Even though a vast distance separated us I could hear the concern in his tone.

'Okay, weird, but okay.'

'What was she like? Did you remember her?'

'She was nice.' The word seemed so trite. 'I did remember her.'

'Good.' I could imagine Tom struggling to find the right words to say.

'Tom, she told me she knew what my father was doing, that she was afraid of him. She told me how she carries the guilt of not standing up to what my father was doing because she wanted to protect me.'

'Yeah. Right.' Tom's laugh faded to an awkward silence as he realised I'd believed what she'd said.

I didn't know what to think anymore. I didn't want to have to decide who to believe. I wished I could run away, not look back. I wished that my mother's body had lain hidden forever. That I still had my lovely life with Mum and Dad, my theatre career, Josh. Poppy. I wished I'd never found Nan's letters.

Nan's words rang in my ears. 'I've missed you. I want us to spend time together when I get out, put all of those years behind us.'

She'd hugged me as visiting time ended, cupping the back of my head with a warm hand. I remembered those hugs, the total envelopment of my body in hers. The security I'd felt, the total feeling of belonging.

A guard had separated us, the strident ringing of a bell signalling the end of visiting time, insistent in the background.

'Just a few more months and I'll be out of here,' Nan had said, her breath warm against my cheek. 'Write to me, I want to know all about your life now.'

I'd left, promising I would.

* * * * * * * *

The house and yard were deserted when I arrived at Mum and Dad's. Their cars were gone and there was no one in the stable yard. I wandered into the yard and let myself into Solar's stable. The big horse chewed placidly on his hay net, cocking one ear in my direction as I automatically straightened his rug.

'Hi, big guy,' I said, putting my arms around his neck and letting my head fall into his mane, breathing in the wonderful horse smell of him.

I stood, letting him support me, wishing I could stay there forever, hidden from the world, safe with the horse who didn't give a damn about who I was or what my background was.

'There you are,' Mum let herself into the stable and came to stand beside me. 'How did it go?' She was dressed in a smart pair of jeans and a tweed jacket.

'I've been out, saw your car in the drive. You weren't in the house, so I guessed you had to be here.' She smiled gently at me, her eyes locking onto mine. I saw only kindness and love there.

I puffed out my cheeks, shaking my head in confusion. My lip still hurt from the scalding heat of the coffee I'd drunk.

'I met her. Nan.'

Mum's mouth gave an involuntary twitch of distaste which she tried to disguise by pretending to check for lipstick stuck in the corner of her mouth.

'The prison is horrible.' I stared at my feet, at the deep golden straw bed surrounding Solar before finally wrenching my head upwards to meet Mum's eyes.

'I can imagine.' Her mouth gave another twitch of distaste. She couldn't imagine. That world, prison, the women in there, desperate, stealing to feed their children, committing dole fraud, fighting for their place in society, having to sell their bodies to provide for their families. Nothing in Mum's golden life would ever have come close to anything that would be remotely like prison.

'What was Nan like?' she continued, cautiously. I could see her not wanting to insult Nan, yet not wanting to encourage me to see her. Nan, I realised with a jolt was Mum's rival for my love.

'I didn't think I'd remember her. What she looked like.'

Mum nodded, stroking Solar's neck.

'But I did, when she came to me. I did remember her. She was like I thought I remembered. Kind, nice, thoughtful, ashamed she couldn't have stopped my father.'

Mum's eyes flickered over my face. 'Kind?'

'None of what was said in the newspapers was true. She wasn't part of what my father did.'

'What do you mean?' Mum's voice was incredulous.

'She told me. She didn't have any part of what my father did. She knew what he was doing, but she lived in fear of him. She should never have been in prison.'

'Mia! The court found her guilty of helping him.' There was a pause before she spat the final word as if there were something unpleasant in her mouth.

I shook my head violently. 'She didn't. She told me she didn't. Whatever my father did she didn't help him.'

'For God's sake, Mia, you can't believe that.' Mum took my arm, shaking it.

'I do, Nan told me. Why would she lie?'

'Because that's the kind of person she is. Don't be a fool.'

'I'm not being a fool. She is so ashamed of staying at the farm, not being able to stop him.'

I saw in her eyes her desperate need to keep me. Mum was afraid of losing me, to the woman who had more claim to me than she did. I knew then why she had lied to me, why she'd hidden the letters.

I wanted to forget Nan. I longed to be able to ignore the feeling of confusion I had about Nan and my past. But she was my family. She loved me, knew me in a way my parents never could. 'You're just trying to turn me against her.' I could hear the anger in my voice, hated myself for it and yet still the words poured from my mouth. Nan had done everything she could to protect me, to make sure nothing my father did touched my life. 'You want to get her out of my life to keep me all to yourself, so you can complete your perfect life. You even kept the letters from me so you could try and cut her out. Well you can't.'

Solar, frightened by the loud voices, retreated to the back of his stable and stood looking at us warily.

'It's alright, boy,' Mum said, softly, crossing the stable to smooth his neck with a gentle hand.

I wished the row would stop and that everything could go back to how it was before. We stood facing one another over a distance which seemed impossible to bridge.

'Let's leave him in peace.' Mum walked past me, pushed open the stable door and stepped out into the darkness of the yard. Outside, the overhead lights cast dark shadows over the yard. The wind whipped at the trees and bushes. Our heads bowed against the storm. We crossed the yard into the sanctuary of the house.

'I don't know what to say to you anymore.' Mum's voice had a bitter edge. 'Since this happened you've become a different person. I don't know who you are now.'

'Oh, it was alright before!' I was surprised at the coldness of my voice. 'When no one knew about my sordid past. When was part of your perfect little circle. The rescued girl who'd been given a decent home and a good education, cleaned up and made to fit in with your posh friends and perfect home.' The words spewed from my mouth in a raging torrent and then hung in the air between us.

Mum blinked slowly. There was a flake of mascara on one of her eyelashes. She looked at me as if I'd punched her in the stomach. I wished I could unsay the words – that I'd never spoken. They'd been so cruel. I'd meant to hurt, and that was what I'd done.

Mum's mouth clamped into a tight line. She put her head on one side and looked at me, the hurt shining in her eyes. 'I'm sorry you feel like that.' Her voice was distant, icy cold. I could feel her moving away from me, the love and support I'd known for so long broken and tarnished by my cruel words.

She shot a small, tight smile in my direction. 'Dad will be home soon, I'll get dinner started.' She walked away across the kitchen; her shoulders stiff, back rigid.

Dad was home when I got out of the shower.

'Mum's having an early night,' he said. His voice had a cold edge to it. 'She's not feeling too well.' From the way he spoke, and the disappointment I could see in his eyes, I knew she had told him what had happened.

I swallowed hard, remembering the feeling of being in trouble from being a child, hating his disappointment in me.

He poured two glasses of wine, pushed one across the kitchen table towards me. 'Mum's made stir-fry.'

'Lovely.'

'Are you sure that's okay for you?'

'Yes, fine.'

'Or would you prefer some pasta? A pizza perhaps?' There was a sarcastic edge to his voice I recognised from when Mum and he had argued.

'I upset Mum,' I gulped at my wine, feeling my throat protest as it hit the back of my palate.

'Yes, I know.' Dad got some plates and tipped the contents of the wok onto them. His movement betrayed the anger I knew was fizzing inside him.

'I'm sorry. I didn't mean to.'

'You'd better tell Mum that.' He scraped viciously at the sides of the pan. 'When she gets up.'

'I will,' I promised, feeling unshed tears beginning to well in my eyes. I hated myself for how cruel I'd been.

Dad, his back to me, nodded in agreement. 'How was your trip to Peterborough?'

He spoke as if I'd been on a shopping expedition. I knew Mum would have already told him everything I'd said to her. I sighed, exhausted from my travels and from the emotional roller-coaster.

'Yes, good. I met Nan.'

Dad flung the knife down with a clatter. 'Mia, all she said to you…!'

He stopped, leaning against the work surface. He took a long swig of his wine as if he couldn't frame the words before plunging onwards. 'It's all bullshit!'

He spat out the last word with such vehemence I drew away from him.

'But…' My voice was little more than a whisper.

'There isn't a but,' Dad continued. 'She's lying to you. Your father kidnapped those women. He raped them and then he killed them. After that he buried them. And she helped him.'

'She didn't help him. Why would she lie to me?'

I got to my feet, fighting the feeling of being trapped and subjected to the full force of his anger. My voice sounded pitiful to me, whining.

'Because she's a manipulative bitch.' Dad's voice had risen in tone and decibels.

'I don't know what to believe anymore.' I turned away, shaking with the effort of controlling the emotions that coursed through me. 'You and Mum lied to me. Nan told me she was protecting me. How do I know who to trust?'

I took a couple of stumbling steps across the floor, still holding my wine glass. I was conscious of the liquid slopping out, splashing onto the floor tiles.

'Mia.' Dad came up behind me, his hands gently grasping my shoulders and turning me around to face him. I slid into the warmth of his body, breathing in the familiar smell of his aftershave and the more vague one of cigar smoke. 'Darling, I know how tough this is. We'll get through it. This will pass. You'll see Nan for what she is. Realise where your home is, with me and Mum. Put everything behind you. You've a wonderful life with Tom to look forward too. A great horse to compete.'

I heard my breath, drawing into my lungs, cold as it passed my lips. 'Yes,' I nodded, easing out of his arms. Of course. I would go back to being their perfect daughter, the shine would return. Eventually my past would be forgotten. Clearly, he expected me to forget Nan, put aside my past, the life I had before.

'Go and say sorry to Mum. Then come back and we'll all have dinner.' Dad scooped up the plates and put them into the AGA.

I went upstairs, apologised to Mum. We cried together, sharing a scrap of tissue to wipe our eyes on and then laughing at our silliness.

'I feel a lot better now,' Mum said, resting her head against the pillow. 'I don't want to fall out with you.'

I nodded. 'Me neither.' I kissed the top of her head. 'I love you.'

Later, after we'd all eaten, I drove to Tom's. His text message to say he had finally finished work arrived mid-way through dinner. He was slumped in the armchair in front of the television, dozing, half a sandwich curling on a plate in front of him.

I let myself in with the key he'd given me and crouched beside him, gently easing the plate out of his hand as he took in a deep peaceful breath.

'Hi, babe,' he said sleepily, waking as the movement disturbed him. 'How are you feeling?'

'Okay,' I said, not wanting to tell him about the row with Mum, or my confusion about who was lying to me. I especially didn't want to relate what my parents had said during dinner, about forgetting Nan and my previous life. Unsaid, but hanging like a dark cloud over us, was the impression that they didn't want that horror in their lives. I knew it didn't fit in with their image of a perfect life with me.

'I'll tell you about it another time.' I kissed the top of his head. 'How did the rest of your day go?'

'Rotten,' he sighed. 'I've been on the road all day, doing calvings, the twin lambs and a horse with a broken leg that had to be put down. I had to stitch up a huge wound on a very angry sheep. Then a packed surgery to deal with, the world and their grandmother wanting their dogs de-fleaing and their nails clipped.'

He got slowly to his feet. 'I tell you what, Mia,' he said, drawing me into his arms. 'I'm so sick of working for my dad. I wish I could just walk away and forget everything.'

'Me too.' I agreed, my voice muffled against his chest. If only we could.

CHAPTER THIRTY-TWO

Things gradually settled down at home after the row over me going to see Nan. Tom was so busy with work that he and his father seemed to manage to rub along together.

The long winter was finally replaced by warmer spring days. I divided my time between Tom's house and my parents' home. Mum and I slowly regained the easy relationship we'd had. I knew how much she and Dad cared for me, how they wanted to protect me. Siding with Nan against them seemed cruel and thoughtless.

Solar, with me riding him every day, got better and better. We had become the perfect team. I loved riding him. I could feel him listening to my instructions, and I in turn trusted his strength and intelligence to power us around bigger and bigger courses. Mum took great delight in finding more shows for us to go to and planned a busy timetable of events during the summer.

Nan, though, remained in my thoughts. Whatever anyone said, I knew she was telling the truth. She couldn't have been any part of what my father had done. I'd written to her a couple of times and had letters back filled with love and her memories of me. She talked of us playing on the beach, in the hay, and of the Christmases we'd spent together. I wished I could remember those times. As I read, I pictured us on a beach, the sun warm on our faces. She spoke of my father. His love for me. And of my mother. She wrote of me being born. My mother's joy at my birth. Through the letters, I built a picture of our lives together. It was easier to imagine happy times than visualise the anxiety Nan must have lived with. The knowledge I had of my father's crimes became something I found hard to associate with the man the media spoke about.

I'd given Nan the address to Tom's house and had not mentioned our correspondence to Mum and Dad. It seemed easier not to. I wondered if they assumed I'd forgotten about my relationship with her, decided to put it behind me.

* * * * * * * *

Tom sank onto the sofa beside me, looking grey with tiredness; there were dark rings under his eyes and hollows beneath his cheeks where he had lost weight.

'Ughh. I've had a rotten day.' He downed his glass of wine and poured another for both of us, holding the bottle up to the light to check how much was in it as he emptied it. 'My Dad is such an asshole.'

'Tell me,' I pulled my feet up onto the sofa and rested my cheek on his shoulder. His shirt smelt faintly of dogs and antiseptic overlaid with the delicious new aftershave he'd started wearing.

'He had booked me on way too many calls. I had to leave three of them, go back to do the evening surgery and then go back out to finish the visits.'

I rested my hand on his thigh, feeling it bounce with tension as he tapped his foot up and down on the carpet.

'Life could be so great. I've this house. You. And no time to enjoy any of it.'

'Things will get better, surely,' I sighed. Tom's father had to give him less work. He kept promising to hire another vet to help out.

'I wish.' Tom ran his hand through his hair in a distracted gesture. 'I'd love to go on my own. It's what I want, but how the fuck will I ever be able to afford to buy or even rent any premises? He's got me exactly where he wants me.'

* * * * * * * *

'What is it about my barbeques that attract this woman?' Dad threw the implements into the side of the barbeque as we watched a now familiar car come slowly into the drive and stop in front of the house.

'Oh God, what is it now?' Mum's expression was filled with concern as she looked across the lawn to where Grace was walking across the grass towards us, her face a perfect mask of neutrality.

Tom reached for my hand, my fingers icy against the warmth of his.

'I'm so sorry. I'm interrupting you. Again.' The scene of the family barbeque clearly hadn't gone unnoticed by her.

'What can we do for you?' Dad picked up his implements and turned the steaks. The meat sizzled and spat on the bars above the hot coals. Above us the sun blazed in a blue sky unbroken by a single cloud.

'I wanted to have a quick chat with Mia, if that's okay?' Grace smiled at me. Her wild auburn hair was held back in a clasp from which stray strands had already escaped and were blowing around her face in the breeze. 'Do you want to go inside?'

I shook my head, dragging my eyes upwards to meet hers. 'It's okay, we can talk here.'

Tom pulled another chair out of the heap on the patio and gestured for Grace to sit down.

He stood uncertainly for a moment, as if he felt uncomfortable in the group, before sitting down and flicking through the messages on his telephone as if he was utterly engrossed in them.

'Can I get you anything, tea, coffee, drink?' Mum's voice was stiff with politeness.

'Something to eat?' Dad asked.

Grace shook her head as she lowered herself into the chair. Her jeans were faded. Over them she wore a striped blue shirt and looked nothing like the police officer she was.

From the stable yard I could hear buckets being rattled. A horse whinnied. Mum glanced in the direction of the noise, her expression distracted for a moment.

'I don't want to telephone, I wanted to talk to you in person,' Grace said, leaning towards me. She steepled her long fingers, resting her pale chin on them, 'Mrs Hammett is due to come out of prison. She's been given a release date.'

For a moment I stared at her blankly realising then who Mrs Hammett was. Nan. She'd written to let me know she had almost served her sentence. I made a small noise of what I hoped sounded like surprise.

Beside Grace, Mum thrust out her lips in an expression of anger. Nan forcing her way into their genteel world, causing havoc as always.

I nodded, feeling Mum and Dad's eyes on me, watching my reaction. 'Thanks for letting us know.' My voice sounded strained, desperately neutral.

'She's going to go back to Cornwall, back Blackthorn Farm,' Grace continued. She sat back, pushing a stand of hair out of her eyes. She was bare-legged beneath her jeans. Her ankles were tanned, hairless.

'Well, thank you. Good to know.' Dad's voice was dismissive. He pulled plates out of the shelves beneath the barbeque, rattling them pointedly.

'I'll let you get on.' Grace took the hint, getting to her feet, easing herself up out of the chair. For a moment she stood uncertainly, as if there were things she wanted to say to me but, sensing my parent's curtain of protection, changed her mind.

Grace stuck her hand out in my direction. I took it, her grip was firm, the skin smooth and soft. 'Call me if you have any questions.' Her eyes when they met mine, were filled with concern.

Dad began to put the cutlery on the table, not giving Grace any chance to shake his hand. She hovered for a moment before walking away across the lawn, raising a hand in farewell.

'Bloody cheek,' Dad snapped as she drove away. 'Why couldn't she just ring? Instead of coming around here nosing around.'

* * * * * * * *

Nan's letter, when it came a few days later, as I had known it would, was filled with delight at soon being let out of prison and looking forward to going home to the farm. I couldn't imagine what it must be like to have been in prison for so many years and to finally see the end coming. How wonderful it would be to be free, not to have anyone telling you when to eat or sleep. I couldn't imagine the task it would be to get the farm into anything resembling home, though; it had been in a terrible mess when Josh and I had been there, the yard overgrown, the rooms filthy. I wondered if she would be afraid of the publicity surrounding her release; if she'd worry about people who believed her to be guilty coming to take revenge on her. People who didn't understand she was innocent of any crime.

I wrote back, promising I'd get the farm ready for her. That I'd be there to collect her when she was released.

Her reply, a few days later was filled with excitement. 'You are the kindest girl. I'm so proud of you. I can't wait to see you again.'

I kept the letter at Tom's and tried to put Nan's release date out of my mind, worrying about how I would do all I had promised without incurring the anger of my parents.

When I'd mentioned going to Cornwall to see Nan when she was released, I'd been subject to the full force of my dad's wrath. 'Mia, please don't,' he'd said, pulling me towards him and holding me at arm's length so he could look at me. He tilted my chin, so I had no choice but to look into his eyes and see the concern there. 'Can't you see what she's doing? She's trying to brainwash you into believing the lies she's telling you. She's not the person she's making out she is. Really, Mia, you need to stay away from her.'

I'd nodded, forcing myself to hold his gaze, to move my head in agreement. I hated him for it. Nan loved me. I could feel that love in her letters, in the brief meeting we'd had in the prison. She was part of me, she'd cared for me when I was a little girl. I knew she was telling the truth and that she had been put in prison wrongly. She was a good person who had been trapped in a terrible situation. I owed it to her to take care of her, to look after her, to be with her now she was out of prison. She couldn't look after the farm on her own.

After that I didn't mention her again. Somehow, I'd find a way to make the farm right before she was released, and to be there to collect her.

'I don't know what's going on with my parents,' I'd cried on Tom's shoulder. I'd woken up in the middle of the night, curled around him, my cheeks wet with tears. Woken by the nightmare I'd been having about being pulled by Nan as I was torn away from her, screaming at her to not let go of me.

'They just don't want me to see her. She's my grandmother,' I'd sniffed, blowing my nose on the tissue Tom fetched from the bathroom. 'How can they keep me from her? Why do they keep telling me she's bad?'

Tom sighed, shaking his head in despair. 'I hate to see you so upset.' He pulled me to him, rocking me like a child.

'Fucking parents,' he sighed. 'My dad's a bloody psycho. I wish I could get away from him. Bloody Cornwall wouldn't be far enough.'

I'd pulled away from him, so I could look properly at him. His skin looked grey in the harsh glare of the bedroom light. His hair was tousled from sleep, his eyes heavy with tiredness. 'Maybe Cornwall would be the answer to our problems.'

'What?' he yawned.

'We could move down there. I could take Solar, compete, get some horses to train. You could open a surgery there. We'd be together. Away from here. With Nan. We could look after her.'

'What about your parents? I can't see them being too happy about that.'

'They'd get used to it.' I could hear the uncertainty in my voice.

Tom nodded, his expression becoming more and more serious as my words sank in.

'You mean it, don't you?'

I nodded, excited now. 'Yes, of course. I'd love to be there. Get to know Nan properly, perhaps my mum's family. We could start a new life.'

Tom lay back on the pillows, his lips moving as he pondered, working out how much it would cost him to set up on his own. 'I've enough saved to buy some basic equipment, if there was no rent. Maybe I could find another surgery to take me on to do locum work.'

The first streaks of light were shining behind the curtains by the time we had finished plotting our future. One that involved us moving to Cornwall and making a life for ourselves there.

'You want to do what?' Dad's voice was incredulous, when I finally plucked up the courage to broach the subject with him. He tilted his head, looking at me sideways as if he couldn't quite believe what he was looking at. 'Let me get this straight. You want to move to Cornwall to live at your father's farm, with Tom and your grandmother.' He said 'grandmother' as if he'd chewed on a steak and found a piece of unpleasant gristle in the meat.

'She needs me.' I faced him across the lounge.

'Needs you?' he repeated, his lips moving over the words as if he were speaking a foreign language.

I nodded, squaring my shoulders against the force of his wrath. I hated these arguments, hated the way he made me feel stupid.

'Darling,' Mum said with a despairing tone. 'Please, see sense.' She put a pale hand over her mouth as if she were going to vomit.

'Please,' I said, close to tears, 'I need to be there. I can compete Solar, get some horses to train. It would be a great chance for Tom to set up on his own.'

'And Nan?' Dad hissed sarcastically, 'What's she going to be doing? Kidnapping more women?'

'Stop it,' I snapped. 'She didn't do that.'

'For fuck's sake.' Dad turned away, his back taut as he stared out of the window. The gardener was driving around the lawn on the ride-on lawnmower, the noise of the engine retreating and becoming louder as he circled.

'Mia.' Mum's voice was quiet, almost drowned by the sound of the lawnmower. 'There's no way I will let you take Solar.'

'But I ride him. He goes well for me,' I said. 'He's mine.'

'Is he fuck yours!' Dad spun around, standing in the window.

I tried to face him but the sunlight was too strong, forcing me to blink.

'He belongs to your mum. We'll sell him if you aren't going to be here to ride him.'

'You can't do that!' I said desperately, feeling him winning the argument, feeling my love for the big horse overpowering my need to be with my grandmother.

'I can,' Dad spat. 'You think you're going to just take him. No fucking way.'

There was no way I could fight against the force of his fury. 'I'm sorry.' I held up my hands in a gesture of surrender. 'Please forget I ever mentioned it. It was a stupid idea.'

CHAPTER THIRTY-THREE

'Oh, darling. What a treat,' Mum said, as I eased Solar to a halt beside her. 'A break in the Lake District.'

'Yes,' I loosened Solar's reins and he put down his head, rubbing himself against Mum to ease an itch. 'I'm really looking forward to it. It will stop me thinking about Nan being released.'

I watched a flicker of revulsion flash across her face before she replaced it with a more neutral expression.

'I'm so sorry.' I stifled a sob. 'I've been such an idiot about all of this. I've hurt you both so much.'

Mum reached up to lay a hand on my knee. 'Darling, it doesn't matter, of course you wanted to help Nan. You're so kind and loving. Of course, you care about her. But I'm so glad you've realised having a relationship with her would be a mistake.'

I nodded, seeing the love in her eyes.

It would be good to get away for a few days, out of the oppressive atmosphere of the house. I'd backed down, of course. Dad had won that battle. In the weeks that followed I promised them I wouldn't leave. I couldn't bear to leave my beautiful horse. Dad had made it clear there was no way I was going to take Solar with me if I left.

We slid into an uneasy truce. All of us consciously seeking words that wouldn't lead us into another row. There were, it seemed, constant reminders of the unease between us, things on the television and in the newspapers, articles about missing people, murders.

Mum and I had the joint interest of working Solar, the stables, but

Dad and I had struggled to find anything to say to one another bar the politest of conversations. I felt his disappointment in me. I knew he compared me to the son they'd lost, Patrick, imagined the perfect relationship they would have had. All he had now was me, damaged beyond repair, with my dark history and even darker genes.

'Who are you staying with?' Mum asked as I kicked my feet free of the stirrups and slid to the ground.

'Oh, friends of Tom's,' I replied, searching my pockets for a treat to give Solar. 'One of them is getting married. Tom's going to the stag night. Me to the hen night.'

Mum pulled the reins over Solar's head and we fell into step towards the stables.

'With girls you don't know?'

'Yes. I guess a hen night is a hen night. Perhaps it doesn't matter.'

As we reached the stable yard I glanced at my watch. 'Do you mind if I nip and get changed? Tom will be here any minute. We're taking my car; his desperately needs a new tyre. Is it okay for him to leave his in the drive?'

'Of course,' Mum said, opening her arms for me to step into her hug. 'I'll miss you.'

Solar, impatient for his saddle to be taken off, nudged at the two of us, pushing us apart.

* * * * * * * *

Tom and I drove away, like a couple eloping, through the village lanes, out onto the main road where instead of heading north we drove around the traffic island onto the motorway and headed south. To Cornwall.

'Thanks for coming with me,' I said, as Tom eased my car into fifth gear and we began to cruise along the motorway. I was glad he had offered to drive.

'I'd hardly let you go on your own,' Tom said, covering my hand with his. His fingers were icy cold. His knuckles on the steering wheel were white with tension.

'I don't think anyone saw us,' I grinned, trying to make a joke of us sneaking away to Cornwall to get the farm ready for Nan to come out of prison.

'No,' Tom said, tensely glancing in the rear-view mirror as if he expected to see one of our parents behind us on the motorway.

We shared the driving, hurtling down the motorway, past Exeter where we stopped in the motorway services for coffee and then onto the smaller dual carriageway to Penzance. There we left any semblance of negotiable roads and headed into the wilds of the west coast, through narrow lanes that wound between high stone walls and hedge covered banks until we reached Blackthorn Farm. The air, when I let down the window, was filled with the smell of gorse and the salty tang of the sea.

'Here we are,' I directed Tom off the narrow lane up the drive to the farm.

Beneath us the grass in the centre of the drive rattled against the underneath of my car.

There was an expectant silence in the yard, as we finally drove in. The old buildings seemed to be watching us, waiting. I took a deep breath, drawing in the silence, trying to picture the farm for the first time through Tom's eyes.

It was hard to imagine the horror that had happened here. My father's sins.

To one side of the yard, set back in the trees was the ruined old house. To the other side the farmhouse stood. Nan and I had been in there, while my father's victims awaited their fate.

I tore my eyes away from the ruined building, the bare rafters, bleached by the weather, like arms reaching up to beg for mercy. I planned to tell Nan she should have it pulled down. Beside me, Tom turned a slow circle. I saw a shadow of tension flicker across his face as he looked at the ruined house and realised what it was.

'Shall we make a start?' There was an edgy note in Tom's voice I did not recognise.

'Yes, let's.' It felt wrong to be here. Wrong to be intruding on the silence of the farm and to have deceived my parents.

I pushed the thoughts away. It would be wonderful to have Nan here. To be able to come and visit her, get to know her properly.

My home with Tom was only a few hours away; it would be easy to come and visit. My parents wouldn't even know. I would hate lying to them, but they'd given me no choice. I owed it to Nan not to abandon her.

The farmhouse door opened slowly with a protesting screech. 'Good job you brought oil,' Tom winced at the noise.

Over the last few days we'd put together a list of things we thought we would need: lots of cleaning cloths and liquids, oil for things like hinges and locks, tea, coffee, a new kettle.

'The electricity is back on,' I said, flicking on the light switch as we walked into the house. I stopped as abruptly, the memories of being at the house hitting me as if I'd slammed into a brick wall. When I'd been here before with Josh everything had seemed so unreal. I took a deep breath, smelling dust and dirt, but underlying that, the familiar smell of woodsmoke, the wooden beams of the house, still lingered in the air.

'I'll unload the car.' Tom hurried out as if he couldn't bear to be inside.

I turned slowly, taking in the long wooden table, the windows, dark now with their layer of dust and dirt. There were wooden chairs, left at the far side of the room beside the old range. I remembered warming my bottom against the enamelled doors.

Tom returned with the box of cleaning products. He shut the front door; there were still coats hanging behind it. A battered-looking green wax jacket, faded in the creases of the elbows, frayed at the cuffs. And beside it, a small yellow waterproof coat. Mine.

At the far side of the kitchen, the fridge, with the electricity now on, hummed quietly, the only sound in the kitchen apart from our breathing.

I forced another breath into my lungs, seeing my father, Nan and I in the kitchen as if they were present and I were watching them.

'Okay?' Tom said gently, standing beside me. 'Does it feel weird to be here again?'

I forced my head to move, rocking it gently on my neck, the only movement I could make. 'Yes.' When I'd been here before it had been like looking at a museum exhibition. I'd been somehow disconnected from it.

'What about you?' I asked, my hand seeking the reassurance of his.

'It feels…' Tom's voice faded into silence as he struggled and then failed to find the words. 'Very strange,' he continued after a moment. 'It's hard to imagine you here as a child.'

His fingers sought mine and squeezed them gently.

'I'll bring more of the boxes in,' Tom said, disentangling his fingers from mine.

I nodded, 'I'm going to look around.'

Breaking myself out of my reverie, I walked slowly up the wooden stairs towards the second storey. I hauled on the stair rail, afraid that if I let go, my legs would crumple beneath me and I would fall. Step by step I went upwards.

At the top of the stairs a wooden hallway, bright and airy, led to the bedrooms. One at the far end of the corridor drew me in. Below me, downstairs I could hear Tom hauling in the boxes, chuntering about doing everything on his own, in a half-serious, half-joking voice.

Mia, said the wooden painted sign on the door. It was painted on a wooden board in bright red, the letters curling, beautiful script. I had a sudden image of my father painting it for me, the tip of his tongue poking through his lips.

Using the tip of one finger, as if I dare not touch the wood, I pushed the door open to reveal my old bedroom. It was like entering a time warp; the crumpled bed still remained, dust-covered, cobwebs festooned the ceiling. This was the bed I had got out of the last day I had been here, when Dad was alive. Slowly I walked into the room, seeing all my old possessions, the bookshelf above my bed, still with my books. The pillow still had the dent where my head had been, the sheets and quilt still crumpled into the shapes and folds I'd pushed them into with my legs as I scrambled out of bed.

My heart thundering against my rib cage, I walked to the window. I'd knelt here afraid of the noise of the foxes. Screaming.

The low window seat was still littered with books, crayons, a collection of plastic farm animals. I sank to my knees, looking out of the window, across the yard to the ruined house where my father had kept his prisoners.

As if I were watching a film, I pictured him walking across the yard as I'd seen him so many times, not understanding then what he was doing. Nan below me, in the kitchen, aware of what he was doing, but afraid to challenge him. I shook my head, blinking to try to rid myself of the vision. I wanted to remember my father as the kind man who had loved me, to shake off thoughts of what he was like behind that gentleness.

Crossing the room, I opened my wardrobe, seeing the stacks of my jeans, little dresses, sweaters, even my underwear and pyjamas. It was hard to imagine how I'd literally been led away the day my father died, to begin a new life. Everything I owned had been abandoned.

'Mia.' Tom's voice in the doorway behind me made me jump.

'Sorry.' I turned to him, forcing myself back to the present. 'It's just very weird being here, seeing everything again.'

'Of course it is.' Tom crossed the floor, peered out of the window and turned, slowly taking in the room.

'This was my room,' I told him.

Tom followed my steps and crouched beside me. Restlessly, he began picking up the farm animals, his fingers turning over the plastic creatures that had been such a big part of my childhood. I fought the urge to take them off him, wanting to preserve every bit of the room as it was.

'We need to make a start.' he put a plastic sheep down gently on the windowsill, glancing as he did at the ruined building at the far side of the yard, his eyes slowly swivelling to meet mine.

'I just want to…' I turned, moving back into the corridor, my boot heels clattering on the wooden surface. I pushed open a second bedroom door and walked into my father's room.

His bed was neatly made, the dark-coloured cover tucked beneath a pile of pillows.

I pulled open the wardrobe. His clothes hung there, arranged tidily on hangers: trousers, shirts, an array of jeans, sweaters stacked in the cubby holes beside. Beneath, on the wardrobe floor, his shoes and boots. I leant into the wardrobe, pulling one of the shirts towards me, wanting to breathe in my father's scent, but all that remained was a musty, damp smell in the fabric. There was nothing of him here.

The room was bland, the small window looking out at the same side of the house as mine, over the ruined building. Had he lain in bed at night looking out of the window, knowing the girls lay chained there?

I backed out of my father's room and crossed the hall. 'This is Nan's room,' I said, remembering as I opened the door, nights when I couldn't sleep, coming into her, curling beneath the duvet in the warm circle made by her body.

How would it feel for her, I wondered, to return here, back into the room she had left so many years ago?

It was exactly as she had left it, her clothes still heaped on a wicker chair in the corner. Even an abandoned plastic basket of dry laundry lay at the foot of the bed. On the dresser a tinder-dry, brown bunch of flowers was festooned with cobwebs and dust.

'We really need to start.' Tom repeated as he shook my arm gently.

I followed him downstairs. He'd cleared the table and arranged our cleaning stuff on it.

We set to work, flinging open the windows, freeing the stale, damp air and letting in the clean, warm sunlight. We brushed the floors and cleaned the surfaces, scrubbing with the cloths and liquids we had brought. We stripped the beds and threw load after load of sheets and duvets into the washing machine, which after so many years clicked obediently into life as if it had only been used a few days previously.

'What do you want to do with your old stuff?' Tom asked, seeing me again in the doorway of my old bedroom.

'Leave it,' I said, stacking the toys into the plastic box they were stored in and putting them into the wardrobe.

'There's no point in keeping your old clothes,' Tom said, his fingers moving over the rows of little dresses. 'Shall we get rid of them. Donate them to a charity shop?'

I shook my head. 'I don't want to. Not now. Maybe another time.' Dumping them would feel like I was destroying the past. I wanted to go through them slowly, alone, let the memories flood in, the tears flow. I felt the same about my father's possessions. Perhaps in them I would get a better idea of him, grow to know and understand him.

'You'll know when you feel ready,' Tom said, closing the wardrobe doors.

We worked all weekend, curling at night into the now clean duvet in Nan's room. My bed was too small, and it seemed somehow wrong to use my father's room.

Tom cleaned and finally managed to coax the range into life, so we could cook dinner.

Later, when we were watching a DVD Tom had brought on his laptop, a text message came from Mum, asking if we were having a good time.

Guiltily I tapped out a reply to say we were.

The next morning, we set to work again. We scrubbed, polished, cast out the dirt and cobwebs until finally the house looked like something liveable. We drove to Penzance and shopped to fill the fridge.

Finally, there was nothing left to do except make the long drive to Peterborough to collect Nan.

CHAPTER THIRTY-FOUR

My teeth ached with gritting them against Tom's incessant tapping of his foot and fingers in time to the music on the car radio. As much as I loved him, I was so on edge my nerves jangled. I hated going against my parents' wishes. What we were doing would hurt them so much. As we drove across the country, I consoled myself with the fact that they would never know.

'What time is she due to come out?' Tom asked, his hand resting gently on my leg.

'Three.' My voice sounded calmer than I felt.

'Okay?' He turned to face me.

'Not really, I'm so nervous. This all just seems so weird.'

Tom stared over the steering wheel, his eyes focused on the road ahead. 'It is weird. It's totally different from anything we've ever experienced. Picking up someone from prison. Having your granny in prison.'

The radio began another song. Tom began to hum along to it, his way of dealing with his nerves. It was the situation, not him, that was irritating me so much. I was glad he was with me, but I was way out of my comfort zone. I hated deceiving my parents. They'd been so kind to me, always. I was deliberately betraying them, lying, telling them I was in the Lake District with Tom when I was actually going to a woman's prison to collect my grandmother. A woman who had served a sentence for perverting the course of justice, helping a murderer, regardless of how much she denied it. They'd warned me to stay away from her, not because they were ashamed of my connection with her, but because they felt she was not going to be good for me. I was not to think of myself, they told me, repeatedly, as the girl I had once been. I was Mia Lewis, a person they loved very much and who they had been lucky enough to have as part of their family. And here I was openly betraying them in the cruellest way possible.

I longed to see Nan. To get to know her, to have her safely back in Cornwall where she belonged. She'd served her sentence; whatever she'd done wrong, it was because she loved me. I wanted her to be back safely at Blackthorn Farm. But just as much, I wanted to get back to my parents and rebuild the bridges I had so thoughtlessly torn down.

It seemed to take forever to get from Cornwall to Peterborough, but finally Tom pulled into the side of the road and turned off the car engine.

'Are we in the right place?' My fingers wound compulsively together. 'Do you think we should check?'

'This is the road your letter said.' Tom smiled gently at me.

We looked out of the car window at the austere towering metal fence with its topping of razor wire. Two high gates marked the entrance to the prison, but there were no friendly faces around who we could ask. A couple of other cars were parked on the side of the road opposite us, but otherwise the area was deserted, filled with an air of desolation. The wind hummed through the wire fence. Beside us an abandoned crisp packet was stuck in one of the gaps; it flapped in a desultory fashion.

Opposite us, a pedestrian gate in the fence opened and a young woman came out, glanced at us, then up and down the road before hurrying away, a black holdall slung over her shoulder. One of the car doors opened in the vehicle opposite ours. An ordinary-looking man got out, pulling the sides of his coat around himself, and looked briefly in our direction before striding over to meet the woman. They hugged briefly before hurrying back to the car and driving away.

'Is it definitely today?' I asked, a bundle of nerves.

'Calm down. She'll be here,' Tom said gently, putting a hand on my arm.

As he spoke the small gate opened and three women emerged. A young hard-faced blonde emerged then walked away, her feet tapping rapidly on the pavement as if she couldn't get away fast enough. An ordinary-looking plump middle-aged lady in a baggy top and jogging bottoms hurried to the other car that was waiting.

'That's her,' I said, seeing the remaining woman looking up and down the street. She looked older than I had remembered, thinner, frail and uncertain.

I shoved open the car door, scrambled from the seat and hurried across the road. A car steered around me, the occupants looking fixedly forwards as if they wanted to rid themselves of any association with the prison.

'There you are,' Nan said as I walked into her outstretched arms. 'Mia. My little Mia,' she whispered into my hair. Her hand stroked the top of my head. I felt the tension leave my body as I snuggled close to her. She was here, with me. Free.

'You're out. Free.' I rambled, my mouth spewing nonsense in my excitement at having her beside me.

'I am.' She released me, holding me at arm's length as she took in a deep breath. 'Fresh air, feels good.' She held her face upwards to the sunshine, pausing as if to soak in the luxuriousness of the simple pleasure.

'My boyfriend Tom's come with me to help with the driving. We should be back in Cornwall in no time.'

'Let's go then.' Nan hooked her arm through mine and we hurried across the road to the car.

Tom had gotten out of the driver's seat and stood leaning against the car, looking at us.

'You've got good taste,' Nan hissed conspiratorially in my ear, giving my arm a gentle tug before smiling at him.

'Tom.' He held out his hand in greeting as we reached him.

'Elizabeth,' Nan held out her hand and grasped his, 'but I'm only called that when I'm in trouble,' she joked. 'Please just call me Nancy or Nan.'

I took Nan's bag, put it into the boot of the car and then opened the front seat for her to get in. 'You sure? I'm happy in the back.'

'No, I want you to see everything.'

Without further argument Nan eased herself into the front seat beside Tom. I got in the back and we set off, easing the car through the back streets until we hit the motorway.

As we travelled, Nan craned her neck to look out of the window, peering up at the sky, gazing at the buildings as we passed them.

'Are the roads always this busy?' she asked, as we hit yet another set of roadworks.

'Yep,' Tom grinned.

We stopped at the next services to get coffee, delighting Nan with takeaway coffees and delicious slices of pizza. 'Haven't eaten this well in…' Nan paused. 'Well for years.' Her tone was light, as if everything she said was a huge joke.

At Exeter I took over the driving.

'Home!' She punched the air as we passed the Cornwall sign, marking the beginning of the county. 'It's good to be home.'

'Jamaica Inn.' Nan leant forwards beside me to peer out of the windscreen, her face filled with excitement like a small child at Christmas. She opened the car window, taking deep breaths of the cold moorland air that rushed in.

The light was beginning to fade as we reached Penzance and headed along the lanes. Nan had been chattering, telling us light stories about her friends and time in prison. I sensed there was a darker side to what had happened in there, but that, she had sealed away; it was past now. She was free.

As we neared the farm she became quiet, looking intently from side to side, saying the names of the villages we passed and then the farms as if reciting much-loved poems.

'Here we are.' I turned the car off the lane onto the farm track. Glancing in my mirror I saw Tom, asleep, his head lolling on the headrest, his mouth slightly open.

Nan was silent now, peering through the window, her nose almost against the windscreen, her breath rapid as if she could barely contain her excitement. We reached the yard and I parked the car, turning off the engine.

Tom behind me woke, stretching, rubbing at his eyes with balled fists.

The car engine ticked quietly as it cooled. Nan was silent, looking up at the house, tears filling her eyes and slowly making their way down her cheeks.

'It's good to be home.' She pushed open the door, breathing in the cool sea tang of the air. 'Thank you, Mia.'

Without another word she got out of the car and walked slowly across the yard, looking up at the house, turning slowly to take everything in as if she were waking from a dream.

Leaving Tom, I grabbed the car keys, hauled Nan's bag out of the car boot and walked after her.

As we reached the house, Nan put out a hand, touching the pale stone as if to absorb its gentle presence. Beside me I saw her intake and exhalation of breath, her shoulders slowly relaxing as the tension left her body.

'Welcome home.'

The front door with its newly-oiled hinges opened easily and Nan stepped forwards.

'Ohhhh.' She turned slowly. 'Flowers,' she breathed, walking forwards to touch her fingers to the delicate petals.

'I think Nan's pleased to be home.' Tom came to stand behind me, drawing me into his body and gently kissing my neck. 'You did a great job of getting this ready for her.'

I leant back into the warmth of his body. 'I couldn't have done it without you.'

I filled the kettle with water and put it on to boil as Tom moved around the kitchen, unwrapping the pre-packed meal we had ready to go into the oven. Above us Nan's footsteps slowly trod the rooms upstairs.

We heard the water flow as she ran a bath.

Dinner was ready when she came slowly down the stairs, wearing the new dress I'd bought for her. The clothes in the wardrobe were not only sour with damp, but old-fashioned now. I'd left them in the wardrobe but suggested the first thing we did was buy her some new clothes.

We ate, sitting at the kitchen table where I had eaten for the early part of my life.

'That's where you always sat.' Nan smiled at me approvingly when I sat in the chair facing the kitchen window. Funny, I had picked it automatically even though I had no memory of it.

After dinner we sat outside in the overgrown garden, lowering ourselves onto the wooden bench against the wall.

'Ah, Mia, you don't know how good it is to be here with you. And you too, Tom,' she added hastily.

'We need to go soon though, the day after tomorrow.'

Nan shook her head. 'You belong here, girl, don't stay away too long.'

I smiled. 'I won't.' I caught Tom's eye; it would be easier said than done. I wanted to be here with all my heart, but my life was back with my parents.

'We'll get everything sorted before we go. Find you a car, get some new clothes.'

'Thank you, Tom.' Nan's voice was filled with gratitude. 'You're a wonderful man. Mia is lucky to have you in her life.'

The following morning we helped Nan find a car from the local garage. If the man running it remembered her he gave no sign. I wondered what it would be like for her, living in a community who were bound to remember my father and his crimes.

It was wonderful to spend time with her, but there was no time to ask her the millions of questions I had. Those would have to wait until later, when we had time together and could get to know one another properly. Now we just had to do the job of getting her settled at the farm and get home ourselves.

We left the following morning, driving as fast as we dared back up the motorway in the direction we had come. I dropped Tom off at his house and drove home.

'Oh you're back.' Mum's face was wreathed in smiles as I walked into the kitchen.

'How was the Lake District?' she asked, wiping a blur of flour off her nose from the pastry she was making.

'Yes, good. Lovely,' I said, unwilling to lie further, to invent a whole set of people and events that had never happened.

* * * * * * * *

She was crying a few days later when I walked into the kitchen. The half-eaten apple pie she had been making the day of my return stood desolately in the centre of the kitchen table alongside a cooling mug of coffee.

'What's the matter, Mum?' I threw down my riding hat on the wooden rocking chair in the corner of the kitchen and crossed the room to drape my arms around her.

'Get off me!' she snapped, twisting and jerking beneath my arms, her fingers clawing at my hands to get them away from hers.

I stumbled back in shock. 'What is it?'

She got up slowly, moving stiffly as she stumbled away from the kitchen table to the opposite side of the room. Her eyes when they met mine were cold, filled with anger and hatred. She turned, snatching a paper from the kitchen table and thrust it across the distance between us.

I uncurled the crumpled paper, straightening it so I could read it, but even as I smoothed the rumpled sheet I knew what it was. A speeding ticket addressed to her. My car had originally been hers. I'd been given it when she bought a new one. We'd never bothered to change over the log book. In black and white was a photograph of me driving, with the time of day and the speed I was doing. I hadn't even seen the camera. I knew from the time and date it had been the morning Tom and I had taken Nan into Penzance when we had shopped for new clothes for her.

I lifted my head, my cheeks burning.

Mum's eyes were full of hurt and anger as they locked onto mine. 'You lying little bitch.'

'Oh Mum,' I reached out my arms towards her.

'Leave me alone!' she snapped, shoving me away, 'I don't want anything to do with you.'

'I'm so sorry,' I pulled out one of the kitchen chairs and sank into it, my legs quivering beneath me. 'I've felt so bad about lying to you. I didn't know what to do. You and Dad were so against me going. I thought I owed it to Nan to be there for her.'

'I don't know who you are anymore.' Mum turned to look out of the window, the line of her shoulders rigid.

'Mum,' I sobbed, going to stand beside her, 'I'm so lost. I'm torn between wanting to help her and still be your daughter.'

'Can't you see,' she said gently, 'we just want what's best for you.'

I nodded and slid with relief into her arms.

CHAPTER THIRTY-FIVE

How could I expect them to understand how much I needed to be with Nan? I knew they thought they were protecting me from the past, but I wanted to know what had happened, to come to terms with what my father had done.

It was so hard to imagine him singing me to sleep at night and then crossing the yard to his victims. There had been a side to him I had not seen, one that Nan had protected me from, even if it meant knowing what he was doing. She had been forced to sacrifice them in order to protect us. How could she have survived that?

Me being with Nan in Cornwall, lying to them, involving Tom, hurt them very badly. The atmosphere was toxic for weeks.

The row afterwards had been horrendous. Mum had shouted and raged at me firstly for going to be with Nan, who she described as a manipulative deviant, but more than that, for my lies and betrayal of her trust. Once she had finished shouting at me, Dad who assumed a look of quiet disappointment, gave me a lecture on the perils of being deceitful.

Once the harsh words were over, Mum and Dad forgave my errors with a sigh and then there was the conscious turning of the page, giving me a fresh start.

Of course, there'd been a lecture about not going to Cornwall again. Not to see Nan. 'She did such terrible things, Mia,' Dad had said. 'Really, you need to stay away from her.'

Mum had echoed his words, 'You belong here, with us. This is your life.'

I'd heard their voices yet still I didn't believe them. The Nan I knew was kind, gentle. She'd done what she had out of love for me.

My parents hadn't been able to lecture Tom, but their disappointment had been clear when he next visited.

'I don't think either of you really understand what an evil person Nan Hammett is,' Dad had said, leaning against the fireplace.

'I'm sorry, sir,' Tom had muttered, his cheeks stained with red.

As if to highlight his words, the fire, blazing logs, spat, sparks showering out behind Dad. He jumped forwards, brushing at the back of his legs. Tom got up to stamp on a small smouldering ember which had already begun to smoke on the woollen hearth rug.

'Thanks, Tom,' Dad had said. 'Ready for dinner?' That had been the end of the lecture. Tom was mortified at our deceit and couldn't face seeing my parents. There was no way, he'd told me, he would go behind their backs again.

It was assumed we'd behave as appropriate adults, that we would do as they said and not go to Cornwall again.

I telephoned Nan regularly, heard her stories about the farm. She seemed happy and was loving being home. During each conversation she asked me when I would visit again and I grew to dread her asking, having to make yet another excuse. But talking on the telephone wasn't the same as being there. I hated being apart from Nan.

* * * * * * * *

'Good night, Dad.' I leant over the back of the armchair and kissed the top of his head.

'Good night, darling.' His voice sounded bleary. 'Thank you for staying tonight. Mum and I will be gone early.'

He'd been dozing on and off for hours, after giving me unnecessary instructions as to what needed doing in the stables while they were away for the weekend celebrating their wedding anniversary. One hand clutched a cut glass whiskey tumbler, the other resting with a half-smoked cigar balanced on an ashtray on the arm of his chair. As I watched, the dark liquid slopped dangerously close to the lip, until he woke briefly, rescuing the glass and settled it in the hollow between his thighs.

'Sleep well.' I stood for a while beside him, watching his eyelids flicker.

He nodded, forcing his eyelids open to look at me, a gentle half-smile creasing the corners of his eyes.

'You too.' He took a drag of the cigar puffing out a cloud of fragrant smoke. 'I'll be up in a minute.'

I stood for a moment, watching as he took another drag of his cigar, the smoke pluming. I wondered if he had any idea how much I loved him. And Mum. How much I loved my home. My life with the two of them. How much I regretted lying to them about fetching Nan out of prison. And the hurt that had caused.

Leaving the lounge door slightly ajar, I walked up the stairs past Patrick's portrait, 'Goodnight, Patrick,' I said to the smiling cherub Mum and Dad had adored. In their eyes he would always be perfect. It was hard for a real person to live up to that.

The light was on in Mum and Dad's bedroom. I tapped gently on the door. Mum was sitting up in bed reading, propped up against a mountain of pillows, her glasses balanced on the end of her nose.

'I just wanted to say goodnight.' I padded softly across the room and sat on the edge of the bed. I loved this room, it was so Mum, all coordinated with a soft, pale cream carpet that picked out the pastel shades of pinks and creams in the curtains and in the thick quilted bed throw draped across the end of the bed.

'Good night, darling.' Mum put her book down spine open on the bedside table and pulled off her glasses, folding them carefully and balancing them on the table between her hand cream and tumbler of water.

'Sleep well.' I wrapped my arms around her. She wore a silky blue-and-white flowered nightdress. Her arms in the soft light of the bedside lamp were tanned, toned from the hard work she did outside with the garden and the horses. I could feel the sharp bones of her shoulder and collarbone as we hugged.

'I love you,' I told her, easing myself out of her embrace. As I got to the door I paused, looking back. She stretched out an arm, flicked off the light and slid down beneath the covers, smiling at me. Her eyes shone with love.

* * * * * * * *

Her terrified screams were unlike anything I could have ever imagined.

Heart pounding, I hurried to my bedroom door, opened it and looked out. The corridor was unusually bright. We always kept a small lamp on. It stood on a small, antique hexagonal table at the top of the stairs to shine a gentle pale light throughout the night. As I opened my door, I could see, shining from downstairs, a bright, flickering glow that made dark shadows over the paintwork and pictures on the stairs.

Thick, black smoke curled, long fingers drifting over the ceiling. I coughed as the noxious smoke hit my lungs. At the far end of the corridor I could see Mum, gazing down the stairs.

'The house is on fire.' I could never have imagined the terror I heard in her voice.

From the direction of the stairs I could hear glass breaking, hear an incredible angry roar.

Before I could move a wall of flame exploded up the stairs, a malevolent kaleidoscope of colours, blue, green, yellow, red, tinged with the streaks of black smoke.

I reeled back into my room against the intense heat, seeing Mum do the same.

As the thick black smoke curled under my bedroom door I grabbed an armful of discarded clothes from my chair and pushed them into the gap in a vain attempt to stop it coming into my room. Behind the door the roar was incredible, filling my ears. Above it I could hear Mum yelling at me to get out and then screaming in terror.

My bedside light went out, plunging my room into a darkness broken only by the flickering orange light.

Fumbling on the floor, choking at the noxious smoke, I found my jeans, dragged them on, flung my feet into my deck shoes, pulled on a sweater, backwards. I grabbed my phone and rushed to my bedroom window.

As I looked out, flames exploded from the downstairs window and began to catch on the Virginia creeper growing up the wall. Slipping my phone in my pocket, I scrambled out of the window. There was no choice but to climb down, to risk the flames and the fire downstairs. Otherwise I would die here, in the smoke and flames.

The heat was intense, I could feel it biting at my flesh; I had to force myself to move and ignore the pain. Choking, spluttering, my eyes watering so much I could barely focus, I slid first one leg out and then the other, turning as I slid off the window ledge, easing myself downwards, towards the flames.

Behind me there was an explosion. I heard my bedroom door crash from its hinges.

I longed to breathe properly but the air around me was filled with thick black choking fumes. Red sparks flew up into the dark night sky, painting the outstretched limbs of the trees with bright oranges and reds. Trying not to inhale the smoke, I scrambled down the thick tendrils, my fingers aching with the effort of holding onto the vine, my feet fumbling. Instinct told me to pull myself upwards out of the way of the flames, yet I knew I must go to the ground. Halfway down I launched myself backwards, using all of my strength flailing in the air to turn. I landed with a teeth-jolting crash on the lawn. My knees buckled and I rolled, tumbling away, over the lawn, covered in glowing embers from the fire.

The biting-hot cinders seared through my clothes, creating scalding tendrils of pain. I rolled, over and over, away from the fire, away from the heat to the cooler edge of the lawn. Black curling pieces of debris littered the lawn like confetti.

Hauling myself to my feet I dialled the emergency services. The lounge, where I'd last seen Dad, was an inferno. Mum's bedroom window was open, she was leaning out, her face terrified in the dreadful orange glow from the fire.

'Dad!' I screamed, running towards the house. The unbearable heat stopped me. The fire was consuming our beautiful home. I could see the flames, curling maliciously over what was left of the lounge. The noise was incredible, breaking glass and above it the terrible roar of the flames.

'Emergency, which service please?'

'Fire!' I tried to make my voice heard above the noise. 'Mum!' I screamed as the connection changed and began to dial again.

She glanced down at me, swaying, her hands clawing at the side of the window as if to support herself.

'Jump, Mum. You've got to jump!' I screamed. I saw her gaze flicker over me as she swayed, she began to move her arms compulsively as if to try to grip the edge of the frame to climb out.

The fire service connected. Above the roar of the fire I begged and pleaded with them to come as quickly as they could, giving them the address. 'Hurry, please hurry,' I cried, severing the connection as I stared back up at Mum. She was now slumped in the window. She wasn't moving anymore, her eyes staring at me. 'Mum, please. Get out,' I pleaded.

The heat forced me to move away from the house, to the edge of the lawn where I waited, shivering despite the intense heat.

I could never have imagined anything more terrifying. I shouted for my parents until my throat ached, vomiting against the noxious air I had inhaled, knowing they were undoubtedly both dead. No one could have survived that ferocious heat.

In the distance I heard the fire engines coming. I half-walked, half-stumbled around the perimeter of the house, watching the flames consume it, seeing the dreadful yellow light illuminate the rooms as they destroyed everything.

As I reached the side of the house, I realised the powerful wind was blowing the long orange tongues, sending them skywards, drifting towards the stables. Glowing embers were raining down on the slate roof.

I began to run, stumbling in my haste; I shoved my way through the flower borders, my feet sinking into the earth. Choking, with lungs still full of smoke I ran on, hearing the fire engines coming up the drive.

The first flames were licking at the roof of one of the stable blocks as I reached the yard. I hauled open the heavy sliding door and ran inside; already the eaves were alight, the horses moving restively in the stables below. I grabbed a handful of headcollars, the barn lit by the fearsome light of the fire.

Solar was my first priority. I pulled a headcollar on over his nose and led him out. He followed me obediently, skittering as we got out into the yard where he could smell the toxic smoke and hear the noise. I led him into the field. Instead of running away as I had expected, he stood, his gaze focused on the red sky behind the stables where the house was being consumed by the inferno.

I let the rest of the horses out. The smoke, by the time I'd released the last one, billowed into the air. The roof was now fully alight, timbers crashing to the floor as they burned. I latched the gate, hearing the horses wheel away, galloping across the field into the darkness beyond the firelight.

Like a sleepwalker I made my way back towards what was left of the house, looking at the shadowy figures, lit by the fearsome glow, wanting to see Mum and Dad standing arm-in-arm reassuring each other. Dad would take control. He'd know what to do. Two fire engines stood in the yard, powerful jets of water shooting skywards over the burning building.

One of the firemen, came towards me. I stumbled, half fell into his arms. 'Did my mum and dad get out?' I whispered.

CHAPTER THIRTY-SIX

Twelve Months Later

Solar began to jog as his hooves touched the hard, golden sand of the beach.

'Wait,' I said softly, easing the reins a little. He tossed his head up and down with impatience, trying to stretch, to pull the bit out of my hands to give himself the freedom he longed for.

I let him go. He bounded forwards with one enormous leap launching into a stretched-out gallop. The beach extended into the distance before us, a golden expanse of deserted sand. We galloped along the shore, the waves occasionally breaking over his flying hooves. He jumped them, leaping into the air as the foam cascaded over his legs. The wind was loud in my ears, the air fresh, salty and clean.

To one side of us stretched the beach, tall cliffs bordering it, to the other side the sea, azure blue beneath an endless sky. Above us, seagulls wheeled, floating on the thermals as they looked for unsuspecting fish, their shadows flitting across the waves, making dark patches for Solar to spook at.

As we reached the end of the beach, I eased the reins, sitting down in my saddle so Solar ceased his heady flight. The rush of noise from the wind stopped. Beside us the waves pushed gently onto the beach, the rhythm soothing.

There was so much sky in Cornwall. Here at the shore, it seemed to stretch to infinity. Sometimes I rode on the moors where myriad shades of green, broken only by granite outcrops and grazing animals, were topped by a wider sky than I had ever imagined. It made me realise how small we were, our lives a tiny insignificant speck.

I let go of the reins, holding them only by the buckle as we turned towards home. I rode slowly back to the farm, the sun warm on my face. Bees buzzed busily on the sweet-smelling honeysuckle growing in the hedgerow beside us.

Solar was more relaxed than I had ever known him, his shod hooves tapping out a rhythm on the tarmac surface. Even though it was still early, the air was warm. Soon the tourists would be arriving, parking on the lane and flooding down to the beach their arms full of blankets, picnic baskets and flasks.

'Hello,' I called, riding Solar into the yard and bringing him to a halt.

Nan, looked up, gently easing her bent back, tending the vegetable plot Tom and I had hacked out of the wilderness for her in the months we'd been here. 'Hello, my love.'

I smiled, sliding off Solar and leading him into the stable. It felt good to be home.

'Had a good ride?' Nan came across garden she was slowly creating.

'We'll have potatoes, cabbage, broccoli, all kinds of veg before winter,' she'd told us, watching as Tom and I had dragged out ribbons of brambles, bindweed and grass. Prison had made her muscles soft. In the beginning she had tired easily but daily she grew stronger. Now, her muscle tone was visible beneath the shirt she wore.

'Fabulous,' I told her, patting Solar's muscular neck. 'The beach is wonderful. He loves it down there. I'd say it will be busy later.'

'In the winter, once all the Emmetts have gone, we'll have the place to ourselves again.' Her lips curled easily around the word Emmett, the Cornish slang for tourist or anyone not from Cornwall.

I nodded in agreement. Tom came home most evenings complaining about how the tourists' cars and the strings of caravans and mobile homes hampered him while he was driving from farm to farm on his calls.

He'd easily settled into Cornish life. The local vet had been glad to have an extra pair of hands and there was plenty of work for him.

The decision for Tom to finally stop working for his dad had been an easy one. After Mum and Dad had died there had been no reason for me to stay. Cornwall was where I wanted to be. With Nan.

I couldn't have stayed at my parents' house. There was nothing left of it. Or of the life we'd shared there. People asked if I'd rebuild the house, repair the stables and continue Mum's business, but I couldn't bear to stay, to be where they had died such terrible, unnecessary deaths.

The house had been left to me as well as my parents' considerable life insurance policies. As soon as I could I put the property on the market. New owners would have to demolish the ruin and re-build.

'I can't stay,' I'd told Tom. Everything reminded me of my parents; the village, friends they'd had forever. Everyone was so kind to me, but being in the same environment, knowing what had happened was something I could not cope with.

Much to Tom's father's annoyance we'd left as soon as we could, doing our best to ignore his icy, 'You'll regret this, Tom.'

'I doubt that,' Tom had said, taking my hand in a show of unity.

Later he'd pulled me into his arms, his shoulders free of the tension they'd become accustomed to carrying.

We'd piled the horsebox with our possessions and the few bits I'd salvaged from the ruins of my parent's home. With Solar and two of the other horses we'd headed south.

Tom had easily found a job. While he worked, I helped Nan. Since Nan tired easily, it was a good excuse to sit in the warmth of the farmyard, soaking up the sunlight and trying to tease information about Eddie and Glanna out of her.

During our talks I discovered the quiet, gentle child my father had been. When I probed more, trying to understand what had made him kill, what our lives had been like, she pleaded with me not to ask. The only thing she would tell me was about her shame at not being able to help the women, that she hadn't the strength to stand up to him, 'I was numb to it all,' she'd told me. 'I'm so ashamed. Those poor girls.'

'I can't Mia,' she'd sobbed when I'd steered one of our conversations gingerly around to my father's crimes. 'Please don't ask me. I can't think about it. I just want to forget.'

I stopped probing. She'd cried so much I'd never broached the subject again and just hoped that one day she'd feel strong enough to tell me more.

'We survived it,' Nan had said, taking my hand. 'Let's forget the past and look forward to the future.'

His saddle removed, I led Solar across the yard. The long grass that had grown up through the cobbles had been killed by the gallons of weed killer Tom had put out. My daily sweeping kept them at bay.

I let Solar loose in the field. He trotted away, head low to the ground, pawing and circling before he finally dropped to his knees with a loud grunt and began to roll. Two of the other horses I'd brought from Mum and Dad's trotted across the field to join him. Tom had gelded Solar soon after we arrived in Cornwall. He was easier to manage than when he'd been a stallion. The remainder of the horses had been sold after the fire or had been taken by their owners to different livery yards.

The farmhouse was cool after the warmth of the sun. Shafts of light filtered in through the windows, dust floated gently above the long wooden kitchen table. I breathed in the fragrance of the flowers in the vase on the windowsill. Having flowers in the house was a habit of Mum's I'd kept.

From the cupboard I pulled two mugs, a plain one for Nan, the other a finely curved china one for me. Mum's favourite mug, which had remarkably survived the fire. Cupping my hands around the mug, I held it to my chest as if I could absorb some remnant of her on the china.

I'd found it in the ruins of the house when the firemen had done their work, deciding eventually the fire had probably been started by a smouldering cigar – Dad's as he dozed in the armchair.

He'd died in the fire. Mum, the firemen had found barely alive, in her bedroom, draped half in and half out of the window.

It took her three days to die. I'd sat beside her bed, holding her hand, one of the few parts of her that had been untouched by the flames. I watched her eyes, flickering around the room and passing over me from beneath the swathes of bandages. I was clutching her fingers when she took her last shuddering breath

.'Here you are.' I handed Nan her mug of coffee, cupping my hands around mine.

'Thanks.' She brought the rim of the mug to her face, sniffing appreciatively. 'Delicious.'

We moved to sit on the bench beside the fledgling vegetable bed. 'It's going to be a huge job,' I said, nodding in the direction of the earth, where I could just see the barest, tiny pale green shoots of life beginning to poke through the soil.

'Will you help me do something?' she said, sipping her coffee.

'Of course, I will.'

'I need to scatter your father's ashes.' Her voice was so quiet I wondered for a moment if I'd heard what she'd said.

'His ashes?' I'd never thought about what had happened to him after he had committed suicide.

'He was cremated when I was inside. I wasn't even allowed out for his funeral. Only the funeral directors were there.'

I glanced at Nan and saw the pain etched in the lines of her face. 'Whatever he did he's still my son. I loved him. Once.' She covered her mouth with a hand, but still a heart-rendering sob escaped. 'His ashes are with my solicitor.' Her tears were flowing freely now. 'I can't just leave them there. I have to deal with them.'

Oh, Nan.' I pulled her into my arms as she cried, her tears soaking through the fabric of my shirt. Where had his ashes been for all the years she'd been in prison? I pictured them left in a cupboard, unwanted, unloved, forgotten. A band of tension tightened around the top of my chest at her pain. 'We'll scatter them wherever you like. Have our own funeral service. Just you and I.' I didn't know what I felt about him. I wanted to love him, but what he had done was so horrific I struggled to even comprehend who he was.

Another funeral. It seemed I was always at funerals. The memory of my parents' funeral was still agony to even think about. Their remains had been cremated. I couldn't imagine what had been found of my Dad. I understood from the gentle words of the police that he had been badly burned. Their ashes had been buried in their family plot alongside their son Patrick, where they belonged. I organised a fabulous headstone for them. 'Much-loved parents of Patrick and Mia.' I knew they'd have loved it.

I drove Nan into the town a few days later and parked outside while she went in to collect my father's ashes. She came out clutching a tall cylinder, decorated with pictures of a yellow sunset over a golden beach.

She laid it on the back seat where it rocked gently as we drove back to the farm. It seemed right that just the two of us would scatter his ashes.

'He loved the hill field,' she told me as I pulled the cylinder out of the car. It was surprisingly heavy in my hands.

With the sun bright on our backs, we walked slowly up the hill behind the house. I carried the ashes, leaving Nan free to walk beside me, her breath coming out in ragged gasps.

It was hard to imagine what I carried was the remains of my father, his body, burned and crushed to dust. What part of him compelled him to torture and kill? Was that in the container, mixed in with the ashes?

'Here,' Nan said as we reached the top of the hill. Her cheeks were scarlet with the exertion, her breathing short and laboured. At the top of the hill was huge granite slab, the likes of which littered the land around the farm. Nan lowered herself onto the sun-warmed surface.

'Haven't been up here in a long time,' she said quietly, looking into the distance. Below us, stretching for what seemed forever, was a patchwork of fields, myriad shades of green, broken only by lines of hedges, tangles of thickets, and groups of animals grazing. Above, the sky, blue with white puffs of clouds, stretched to what seemed like infinity.

'Ready?' Nan said tentatively, her eyes flickering over mine.

Gingerly I opened the cylinder. Inside, the contents reached almost to the top, grey dust topped with gritty black and white flecks.

I dipped my hand into my father. Feeling the powdery substance slide through my fingers. My father, everything he had been, his thoughts and deeds, were now dust. As I drew my hand out it was white, covered in the fine ash. Small puffs blew on the air as my hand emerged.

'You first,' I said, tilting the open end of the container towards Nan. 'You scatter some.' She shook her head, vehemently, her lip curling with distaste. Then gingerly she dipped her hand into the container, withdrew a fistful of the fine powdery ashes. 'Those poor girls. Their families.' She closed her hand around my father's remains. 'Eddie. Eddie. Why?' Her voice cracked with emotion. Slowly she extended her hand, took a ragged breath and threw the ashes high into the air.

A cloud of fine grey dust floated on the air, moving in the breeze, carried like a bird soaring until it dispersed.

As she turned away I scooped my hand into the container and drew out a handful. The ash was heavy in my hand. I threw my arm high into the air, unclasping my fingers. Nan and I stood together watching the ashes blow, billowing away until they became nothing, returning my father to the soil.

CHAPTER THIRTY-SEVEN

'Will you come with me to visit my mum's grave?' Since we'd lived at the farm I'd returned to the graveyard where she was buried. Each time I'd gone I'd felt close to her and found being beside her gravestone comforting. Since being in Cornwall I'd felt her presence around me, as if she stood beside me. Each time I'd entered the churchyard I'd looked longingly up the road towards the village, daring myself to go and find Morwenna. Each time, my courage had failed. I couldn't face another tirade of abuse from my grandmother if our paths crossed. After scattering my father's ashes, I felt a strong need to sit beside my mother's grave. To know her physical remains were close to me.

'Course, when do you want to go?' Tom replied sleepily. Even dropping off to sleep he couldn't disguise the martyred note in his voice.

'When you get chance.' I propped myself on one elbow to look at him.

'Okay.' His eyelids flickered and then closed as he dropped off to sleep.

'Thank you. I appreciate that.' I rolled onto my back and watched the shadows cast by the trees, flickering across the ceiling. We'd moved into my old room, replaced my single bed with a new one, redecorated in shades more suitable for adults.

Tom's breathing changed, becoming slow as he slumbered. He was always exhausted. If he wasn't at work he was busy on the farm. I missed the time we had spent together before we'd come to Cornwall. The easy relationship we'd had seemed to have faded into the distance to be replaced by one which was somehow strained. Something I could not put my finger on had come between us.

A few days later, Tom finished work early and drove us to where my mother had been buried.

With Tom beside me we walked through the graveyard, past new headstones, older ones with words indistinct, to my mother's.

The headstone had been put up since her burial. 'Glanna Pendrick,' it announced. 'Much-loved daughter and sister. Tragically taken from us.'

No line about my loss. That Glanna had been a mother. Reading her epitaph always made my eyes sting with unshed tears of hurt and anger. I hated my grandmother and aunt for cutting me out so completely, as if I had never existed.

I put the flowers I'd brought on the grave and laid a hand on her headstone. The slab was warm, soaking up the heat from the sunlight. I wished I'd known my mother, felt the love she had for me, but nothing could replace the emptiness of her loss.

Tom wandered around the graveyard as I knelt beside the grave.

'I don't want you coming here.' An angry voice startled me. I looked up, blinking in the early evening sunlight, straight into the face of my Grandmother. As I scrambled to my feet I saw she was flanked by Morwenna and my other aunt, Kervana.

My grandmother's face was set in fury as she glared at me.

Shocked at the hatred that flowed from her, I took a step backwards. 'She's my mother. I've every right to be here.'

'Mia!' Morwenna raised her hands in an imploring gesture, her voice loud and angry. 'After everything that happened. What Eddie and Nan Hammett did. The lives they ruined. Now you're living with her. How could you do that?'

I shook my head. 'Nan was a victim too. She was afraid of my father.'

'Afraid of him?' Kervana's voice rose hysterically. 'Is that what that bitch told you?'

'We should go.' Tom's hand touched my arm.

I shook him off, faced the fury of my mother's family.

'Mia. Please.' Tom's voice cut into my conscious.

'I'll go now.' I fought to keep my emotions at bay, to stem the tide of the tears I knew would soon flow. 'But I'll be back.'

'You're not welcome here. We don't want you.' My grandmother's face twisted into a cruel sneer.

I let myself be led through the graveyard by Tom. Our footsteps crunched on the gravel as we reached the path. 'How can they be like that?' Blinded by tears I fumbled my way into the passenger seat of Tom's car. 'They are so wrong about Nan. My father was evil beyond belief, but she was trapped there, living in terror.'

Tom moved the curtain of hair I'd let fall around my face. 'Mia,' he said gently. 'Are you sure she's telling you the truth?'

'What?' I jerked my head towards him. In my mind I'd questioned Nan's account of our lives. How could she have been afraid of him? Why hadn't she walked away, taken me with her. Gone to the police? But what I saw in her eyes when I asked her had convinced me she was telling the truth. She had been terrified of him.

Tom put his hands on the steering wheel and stared through the windscreen. 'Just be careful what you believe, that's all I'm saying.'

My mouth dropped open in disbelief as I stared at him, unable to process his betrayal. 'How can you even say that?'

'Mia.' Tom started the car. 'Nan might not be the person she wants you to think she is.'

* * * * * * * *

The awkwardness between us remained, the distant politeness becoming part of our relationship, the easy friendship we'd once enjoyed had faded into the far distance.

'There's a problem at work,' Tom said one evening as he helped me to rehang one of the field gates. 'Your bill is still outstanding, Solar's injections, castrating the colt. Kathy at the office asked me to remind you.'

'There's nothing outstanding.' I turned to look at him Something akin to a scowl flashed across his face; his eyes flickered first to the blue haze of the horizon, then back to me.

He ran a hand, tanned by the Cornish sun, through his hair in a distracted gesture. 'I'm sorry, Mia, but there is.'

I shook my head, feeling the first prickles of irritation beginning to start deep in my belly. 'Nan paid the bill. I gave her the money. She went into the office with it. Kathy must have made a mistake, forgotten to record the payment or something.'

Tom shook his head, his voice was short, impatient, 'There isn't a mistake. The money hasn't been paid.'

'You need to check.'

'No,' Tom snapped. 'You need to check.'

'What are you saying? That Nan hasn't paid the money she said she had? That she's a liar? Or am I lying?'

'Woah.' Tom flung his arms up in a gesture of surrender. 'Mia, I'm just saying can you check please? It's a bit embarrassing for me to be constantly asked about it at work.'

'Well, I'm sorry I'm causing you embarrassment,' I retorted, hurt making me mock his tone.

'Cheers, Mia.' Tom's cheeks flamed red.

'Look, I'll ask,' I said, turning back to him. Obviously, Kathy the practice secretary had made a mistake. I wouldn't put it past her to make up that the bill hadn't been paid. I'd seen the hatred that had flashed behind her eyes when I went into the surgery to meet Tom for lunch once. She'd disguised it quick enough, but I knew it was there.

'The money hadn't been paid.' Tom met my eyes. There was a golden haze of bristle on his chin. He closed his eyes slowly, the long eyelashes I loved flickering slowly over the tanned skin of his cheekbones. 'I paid it. I told Kathy there'd been an oversight at home.'

I tossed him a suspicious look. 'She's messing with you.'

Tom shook his head. He shoved his hands into the pockets of his jeans, shuffled his feet as if he didn't quite know where to put them.

Somewhere not far away a tractor started up; the smell of manure drifted on the breeze towards us, the engine sound rising and falling as the tractor went up and down the slopes of the field.

'Kathy's been at the surgery for fifteen years. There's never been anything wrong with the accounts, no suspicion of her doing anything wrong. She hasn't made a mistake.'

'Oh, I see.' I raised my eyebrows. Tom stared fixedly at the sunburnt grass at his feet.

'So, Nan's clearly in the wrong because she's been in prison. Anything that ever goes wrong is bound to be her fault.'

'I didn't say that,' Tom said, sullenly. 'What I said was perhaps she made a mistake.'

I shook my head, letting out my breath in snort. 'You did,' I snapped. 'You might not have said it in words but that was what you thought.'

'Stop it, Mia.' Tom's voice was high with emotion.

I couldn't stop, the rage fired in my blood. 'Of course,' my voice was thick with sarcasm, 'because she's been in prison, she's going to be guilty of everything.'

Tom flung his hands skywards in a gesture of disbelief, 'Can you bloody hear yourself?'

'Yes,' I retorted, 'And I can hear you too. I know what you think.'

'No, you don't.' He snapped back, his mouth twisting into a childish grimace.

I walked away. 'Everything she does is going to be looked at and thought to be wrong.' I threw my words back over my shoulder.'

'Mia, you need to really look at what is going on here.' Tom fell into step beside me.

'What do you mean?'

'Nan. She's pushing all your buttons, manipulating you into believing what she wants. Doing what she wants. You have to see that.'

'Stop it.' I stared at him, unable to believe his betrayal of Nan.

Tom rolled his eyes. 'Mia you're too intelligent to believe all Nan is telling you. Seriously, you can't believe she wasn't part of what was happening.'

'She didn't. She told me.'

'For fuck's sake, can you hear yourself.' Tom twisted his face into a grimace of disbelief. He walked away, long strides eating up the ground, his hands thrust deeply into his pockets.

I watched him go.

A few more strides and he turned back. 'I love you.' His voice held an imploring note. 'I want to protect you. From yourself.'

'I don't need anyone to protect me.'

'Clearly,' he said, his voice barely audible over the noise of the tractor. 'We should never have come here. If your parents hadn't died in the fire we'd have still been there. You'd have got over this obsession with Nan and your father, accepted they were part of the deaths of those women.'

'Nan wasn't.'

'Oh come on.' Tom shook his head. 'You know what happened. Your father picked her up off the road, he shoved her into the back of his van and he brought her here and held her prisoner in that cellar.' He pointed to the buildings as if to drive his point home. 'And then he raped her. Got her pregnant with you. At some stage after you were born he killed her. Her hyoid bone had been shattered. That's strangulation. He dumped her body in a plastic barrel. and buried her in a field. And he did the same to other women.'

'I know what he did.' My stomach churned with revulsion at Tom's words. It was the first time he had ever spoken about what my father did. There had always been an unspoken understanding between us that his crimes were skirted over, shoved into the background almost as if they didn't exist. 'But Nan wasn't part of it.'

Now he was furious at the trust I put in Nan and hitting back at me in the cruellest way possible.

'Oh for God's sake, Mia!' Tom flung his eyes skywards as if he couldn't believe my words. 'How can you believe that shit?'

'I do because she told me. Why would she lie? Why have any relationship with me if I was the daughter of someone her son killed?

'She's sick and you're deluded.'

I shook my head. We walked on, still rowing.

'Nan is feeding you any line she thinks you want to hear.' Tom stopped suddenly to light a cigarette, turning his back to the wind. He didn't offer me one.

'Why would she?'

'I don't know, I assume she has some agenda.'

'All I remember of her when I was young is her being kind and gentle. Loving me.'

'You were terrified of her when you let Susie Carne out of the cellar.'

'No.' I shook my head. 'She was afraid of what my father would do to me.'

My memories were jumbled. All she had done was try to protect the two of us from my father. She hadn't had anything to do with his crimes. I believed what she told me.

We rounded the corner of the ruined house. Nan stood in the yard.

She must have heard every word.

'Get that bill sorted out. I'm going back to work.' Tom snapped, stalking across the yard to his car and driving away.

'What's the problem?' Nan said as Tom drove away. It must have been obvious to her that we had rowed.

'Oh, just the vet said the bill hadn't been paid.' I pulled a face to show my embarrassment at having to tell her.

'Not been paid?' she repeated, a frown creasing her forehead.

'Yes, the receptionist, Kathy, said it hadn't been paid.'

'Lying bitch,' Nan exhaled a sharp breath.

'Exactly,' I said. 'I know it's been paid. And Tom doesn't believe me.' Nan's mouth drooped into a sorrowful line.

'He's paid the bill again. So they aren't going to send nasty letters here, chasing the money,' I told her, seeing her eyebrows join as she frowned, looking at me askance.

'Oh.' She walked slowly away across the yard. As she reached the wooden bench beside the house I could see from her fumbling hands as she groped for where the seat was that she was blinded by tears.

I put my hands on her arms, guiding her so she could sit down. She rested her elbows on her knees, cupped her hands around her face. 'He's bound to believe her. She's not been to prison.'

'Nan,' I said, gently, rubbing my hand over her back.

Nan found a tissue and began to cry, huge juddering sobs that seemed to come from the depths of her stomach.

'He doesn't believe that.' I said softly. 'He knows there's just a mistake. It will all get sorted out, you'll see.'

'I'll go down there and have it out with that prissy bitch.' Nan turned to look at me, her cheeks wet with tears. 'Crafty cow has had that money and assumed no one will believe my word against hers.'

'No, Nan.' I rubbed her arm with my hand, feeling the softness of her flesh beneath the fabric.

'I'll deal with it.'

I went inside to make tea, hoping that would make her feel better. I couldn't let her have that kind of responsibility again, she was so vulnerable to people's dishonesty. They would always assume she was in the wrong. Her time in prison would work against her for a long time. At least with me beside her she was safe. I could look after her, protect her. Just as she had done me.

'You're a good girl, Mia.' Nan took the mug from me, cupping her hands around the warm china. 'Your dad would be so proud of you.'

CHAPTER THIRTY-EIGHT

I hated the tension between myself and Tom. I wanted, more than anything else for us to be happy together. No matter how hard I tried I could feel him withdrawing from me, physically and emotionally.

'Why did you have to do that?' Tom's eyes locked onto mine. He pinched the top of his nose with a thumb and forefinger in a stress-relieving gesture I'd come to recognise.

'I'm not going to let anyone accuse Nan of being a thief.' I let out a slow breath.

Tom closed his eyes, shaking his head slowly.

'Say it.' I challenged him. 'Murderer. Accomplice maybe, but never a thief.' My voice had a sarcastic edge to it.

'I didn't say that.' Tom pushed his chair away from the kitchen table, crossed the room, and poured himself a glass of water which he downed in one. 'Mia, I asked you not to go into the office. I said I'd sorted out the money. I paid the bill. There was nothing for you to do.'

'I wasn't going to let Kathy think Nan had stolen the money. That's what you think she did, isn't it?'

'Oh for fuck's sake.' Tom rarely swore, so the expletive seemed all the more vile coming from him. 'I just didn't want you going into the office and making a scene. And that was exactly what you did.'

'I'm sorry. I shouldn't have done that.' I picked up the dinner plates and carried them across to the sink. From the other room came the faint sound of the television. Nan, sensing the uneasy atmosphere between Tom and me had left the kitchen as soon as we had eaten. 'I didn't mean to cause trouble.'

I'd expected Nan and I to go through the bill with Kathy, for her to find the mistake she'd made, for us to laugh about it. I hadn't expected the icy reception we'd gotten from her.

Penzance had been crowded with holiday-makers; the pavements filled with people. Still though, I could see the people who recognised Nan and who crossed the street or ducked into shops to avoid coming into contact with her. Their cruelty was something I found hard to bear. My father had done terrible things, but she hadn't. She was only guilty of having been his mother, of loving him. She hadn't had any part of his crimes, no matter what the locals whispered to one another. We avoided them as much as we could, lived quietly together, rarely venturing out other than to do a weekly food shop in the big supermarket an hour away. It made the contact with locals more difficult to witness.

'Kathy was horrible to Nan.' I filled the sink with hot water and plunged my hands into the suds.

'What did you expect?' Tom moved around the kitchen, clearing the table.

'Not that.' The sleeve of my shirt dropped slightly, soaking up water from the sink.

I shook my head, wanting to rid myself of the image of Kathy's appalled expression as we'd gone into the office.

'Yes. Can I help you?' Her voice had been icy, the words rapping out like machine gun fire. Tom had spoken fondly of her, so the reality of her hatred took me by surprise.

'There's a problem with my bill,' I'd said, as we crossed the surgery waiting room to stand beside the reception desk.

'That's right.' Her voice had a soft Cornish burr which was at odds with the harsh lines around her mouth.

'Could you have forgotten to credit the payment?' I'd asked politely, meeting her eyes and seeing the animosity there.

'I've a record of Nan coming in and telling me she'd forgotten her purse and she'd come back.'

Nan had made a snort of exasperation. 'Lying bitch,' she'd said, vehemently. 'You know full well I paid that bill.'

Kathy had put her hands onto the desk, her long fingers splayed. She'd looked down at her computer keyboard, released a long sigh and finally looked at the two of us.

'That's what happened.' Kathy had shaken her head as if she couldn't believe our audacity in questioning her.

'This isn't right.' Nan's voice quivered with unshed tears. She'd leant over the desk with a speed that surprised me. Kathy had pushed herself back in her chair. 'I'm an easy target for anyone, aren't I? The one that's been in prison. I know what you all whisper. I'm the one who no one will believe.'

'I'm the one whose friend still cries every night for her daughter who your son murdered and dumped in a field.' Kathy had scrambled to her feet, facing Nan.

'I'm nothing to do with that.' Nan's voice had gotten louder. 'I'm sorry for what my son did. I wish there was some way I could beg everyone for forgiveness for being his mother.'

Behind us I'd been aware of people in the waiting room shuffling awkwardly, their curious stares at the scene we'd created.

'You're a liar.' A droplet of Kathy's spittle had splattered on Nan's forehead.

'My son was wicked.' Nan was crying now, tears flowing freely down her cheeks. 'But I promise you I didn't take part in what he did. I was as frightened of him as any of those girls.' With that she'd turned and stumbled from the surgery.

I'd followed her, feeling everyone's eyes on us as we left.

I'd led Nan to the park across the road and sat with her as she sobbed.

'She was absolutely heartbroken,' I told Tom, stacking the final plate onto the draining board.

As Tom was silent, I continued. 'How do you think she feels, knowing people think the worst of her?'

The water gurgled into the drain as the sink emptied.

'It must be hard,' he said coldly. 'Perhaps this was a mistake. Coming back. Us being here.'

'This is her home. She loves it here. She's not going to be driven out of it by the opinions of some small-minded people.'

'Hardly that.' Tom switched on the kettle and began to make coffee. 'There are so many people affected by…' I could see him struggle to find the words. After a moment he began again. 'By what your father did.'

'You regret coming here?' I wrapped my arms around my body, shivering despite the warmth of the evening.

'Of course not.' Tom's eyes did not quite meet mine. I knew he was lying.

* * * * * * * *

The bed creaked slightly as I moved. Easing my legs into the cool night air I slid out of bed.

Wrapping my dressing gown around me I slipped Tom's phone into my hand and left the bedroom. As I pushed open the door I glanced back. Tom lay curled on his side, sleeping peacefully. It was easy, while he slumbered, to forget the awkwardness that had come between us. The friendship we'd once enjoyed had been replaced by a distance I did not know how to bridge.

As I passed Nan's room, I paused, listening for any sound which would indicate she was awake, but heard only deep rhythmic breathing, punctuated once by a gentle snore.

I reached the top of the stairs. Avoiding the top creaking step, I headed downstairs, Tom's phone tucked safely in my dressing gown pocket.

The kitchen was silent, bar the ticking of the clock over the larder door. Through the open curtains the full moon shone, bathing the tangle of farm buildings in a silver glow. Tucking my legs underneath me, I huddled into a corner of the sofa.

Tom's password was the last four digits of Poppy's phone number. He still hadn't changed it.

I tapped the screen to open his messages, scrolling through texts from work, a client asking about tablets for her dog's worms, someone else asking for advice on a lame horse. Those completed, I tapped into his emails, curious about why he'd taken to leaving the room when he answered his phone and why he seemed to constantly be checking for new messages and emails. There was a new one from his father. Unopened.

I flicked through the previous emails, my breath shortening with tension.

The last one Tom had written to his father spoke of the mistake he'd made coming to Cornwall, how sorry he was for the hurt he'd caused.

There were others, talking about how he realised now his father had been doing his best, training him for the hard life of a vet. How he regretted being angry at his father, when he understood now how hard he had been trying.

My jaw clenching with unshed tears, I clicked onto the one from his father. '*Tom*, it said, *don't worry. We all make mistakes. please just come home. I'm longing to heal the rift between us. We can talk when you are here. But just come back as soon as possible. I love you. Dad.*'

Mistake. I was the mistake Tom had talked about. My heart thumped uncomfortably against my rib cage. He regretted having come with me to Cornwall. That was obvious. He'd been so keen to get away from his father, but now, it was clear he realised he was not the ogre he had thought.

Life with me and Nan, the difficulty of living with someone who had come out of prison and a girl who was the daughter of a murderer was too much for him. I wondered when he was going to say something about wanting to go home. Was he planning to tell me, or was he intending to just steal away one night, head out to work one morning and just not return? In the moonlight I could see my knuckles, glowing white with the tension of holding the phone. I wanted to throw it across the room, see it crash against the wall, disintegrate into tiny fragments.

Tears pricked at the back of my eyes and began their slow journey down my cheeks. I pressed delete.

With the email gone he'd never know his father had replied. He'd assume his father didn't want him back. The sense of his betrayal made me feel sick.

I clicked off the phone and went slowly back up to bed. Tom's shape still curled in the bed as I'd left him, the sound of his regular breathing filling the darkness. Gently I put his phone back where I had found it and slid back into bed beside him. He murmured in his sleep as I pressed my body against his, seeking the warmth of his skin against mine. I loved this, having him beside me. I couldn't bear to lose him.

* * * * * * * *

We tried to make a habit of eating breakfast together. Me before I started work on the horses, Tom before he left for the surgery. Nan, after the long years of early morning starts now enjoyed lying in, often waking late in the morning.

'Busy day?' I asked, watching Tom surreptitiously scrolling through his phone screen, a frown creasing his forehead.

'Who knows,' he said, looking up at me for the first time since he'd sat down. 'I never know what there's going to be until I get there, you know that.' His voice was short, sharp, filled with irritation.

I flashed him a quick smile, forcing the muscles of my cheeks to tilt my lips upwards. 'Of course.'

'You?' he said, visibly trying to soften his voice and demeanour.

'Solar to ride. There's a class that will suit him at the Royal Cornwall show.' I took a sip of my coffee. Tears prickled at the back of my eyes. Shows weren't the same without mum there. I missed her encouragement, the sight of her standing beside the ring, watching proudly as I competed. 'I thought I might back Sparrow, the youngster. He's about ready to be ridden. I've done lots of long lining with him' The words tumbled from my mouth, my inane chatter better than the heavy silence that often lingered between us.

'Be careful,' Tom warned. Looking at me properly for the first time that morning.

'I will.' I tilted my head to look at him. 'Are you okay?'

He nodded, his eyes drawn relentlessly towards his phone. 'Just expecting an email.'

'Anything important?'

'I thought it was. But looks like I was wrong.'

'Perhaps it will come later.'

'Maybe.'

I poured more coffee. Outside the birds sang, their notes drifting in with the cool, fresh summer air through the window.

I reached across the table and took his hand, longing to feel his skin against mine. 'I'm sorry we've had a bit of a rough patch.' My heart swelled with love for him. He was so kind, gentle. I adored him. I wanted him to be here with me, for us all to get on, for us to have a perfect world together, safe and secure, here, where no one could ever hurt us.

Tom sighed, nodding his head, slightly. 'You've a busy day,' he said gently.

'I was thinking,' I said as his eyes locked onto mine. 'When the money comes through from Mum and Dad's life insurance, I'd like to use some of it towards setting you up with a surgery. Perhaps we could find somewhere to rent in the village. Open a pets' surgery. Small animals. What you always wanted.'

'That would be brilliant,' he said, his eyes clouding as he considered my offer. I could hear the vaguest note of insincerity. He was a rubbish liar.

'I could help look for premises if you like,' I said, ignoring the signs, wanting to push onwards with my plans, not let him go. He couldn't go. I couldn't bear his rejection.

'It would have been Poppy's birthday today.' Tom ignored my words.

'I know.' Her spectre danced between us. She'd have been twenty-four. I pictured her clearly, her blonde hair swinging, her silly laugh, irreverent sense of humour. She'd been perfect for Tom. I had not seen it at the time, how right they were. His gentleness combined with her lightness and laughter. The madness of a life with me was hard for him to deal with, I knew.

I was silent, wondering what we would have been doing if things had not turned out the way they had. I'd have been living my dream of being on the stage, perhaps now in my first television roles. Mum and Dad might still been alive.

The hurricane that had swept into our lives with the discovery of my mother's body had made Dad drink more. Before that he'd have never sat downstairs drinking alone. He'd have never smoked in the house either.

I'd probably still have been with Josh, sharing his apartment. Perhaps we'd have been engaged now, looking forward to a future together.

I had a clear image of the four of us, tipsy, swaying up the street together, Poppy and I doubled over giggling at something inane, the men, clinging to our arms, laughing at us laughing. It had been a golden time, so perfect. It had all been ruined by me, by my father's crimes, by the wickedness that surrounded me and coursed through my veins.

'I miss Poppy,' I said quietly, taking Tom into my arms. The image of her was something I could never compete with. How can you match a dead person? In his eyes, I knew, she would always be perfect.

'Me too,' he said, his words cutting through me like a knife. I didn't mind him missing her, I understood he would. Somehow the tone of his voice made me realise I was second best, it was her he would love, always and forever.

'I wish she hadn't died,' I said softly, stroking his hair, pulling his head towards me, as if I could ward off the presence of the girl he loved so much.

If only she hadn't told those stupid girls.

'She was so afraid.' I said softly, remembering the night she had died. 'Terrified.'

'What?' Tom's voice was as soft as mine, as if he were afraid of breaking the spell between us.

'In the water,' I said, remembering, picturing her face, the darkness of the cold water surrounding us.

'How do you know?' Tom asked. 'I thought you couldn't find her.'

CHAPTER THIRTY-NINE

Tom's voice was incredulous. 'How could you possibly know she was frightened?'
He stood up abruptly, his eyes, cold and hard, bored into me.
I blew out a breath, trying to cool my fiery cheeks, swallowing before I continued, a nonchalant tone in my voice.

'I don't know, of course.' I tilted my head to look up at him, squinting into the evening sunlight that poured into the window behind him. 'I assume she was.'

I closed my eyes, seeing the water, swirling around us, bubbles breaking the darkness. They were beautiful. I remembered the sound of rushing water, gurgles from the car and in the still-working headlights Poppy's face as her hand released its grasp of my arm and she slid away into the darkness. A moment later the electrics stopped working and obscured everything.

'I was,' I continued sullenly, hating him for his concern for Poppy.

'You managed to get out though.'

'I was lucky,' I stood up, hating his suspicious tone. 'You sound like you're accusing me of something.'

'Course not. Why would I?'

I tried and failed to get him to meet my eyes. 'I just seem to be surrounded by death. Poppy, my parents.' I let go of the tears I'd been holding in. 'Why does everyone around me die?'

'I'm not dead,' Tom's voice softened. 'Don't cry. I shouldn't have even mentioned Poppy. Of course we can look for some premises.

That's a fabulous idea.'

I took a step forward into the circle made by his arms and stood against the warmth of his shirt front, breathing in the smell of the laundry I'd done for him.

* * * * * * * *

My hand was curled around Tom's phone when the bedside light snapped on, flooding the room with light. I faced him, blinking as Tom sat up in bed, his hair tousled his face creased from the pillow.

There was a long, cold, silent moment where I felt as if I were in a comedy sketch and should say something trite like 'Got me.' Instead I put the phone down quietly on the chest of drawers and met his eyes.

'I've changed the pass code,' he sighed, his voice disappointed, like a headmaster dealing with a naughty pupil.

He pushed his pillow behind his back. His shoulders were muscular from the work he was doing, his body maturing. His forearms were tanned, but the rest of his skin was white where he rolled up his shirt sleeves. Patches of red flamed on his shoulders where he'd taken his shirt off at the weekend to help me do something in the garden. It had been so hot, we were stripped off, him to just shorts, me to shorts and a lightweight tank top. The memory of that day seemed far away now, retreating out of reach beyond my grasping fingers.

'Sorry,' I clamped my mouth shut into a tight line, turning it downwards into a clown face.

He sighed, tilting his head downwards as if there was something of great interest on the floor beside the bed. His hair moved as he shook his head.

'Mia, I'm not stupid. I knew my Dad would reply to me.'

I was silent, waiting, listening to the sound of Nan's quiet snoring coming from down the corridor.

'You aren't as clever as you thought you were. Deleting the email, but forgetting to empty the deleted mail box.'

'I'm sorry,' I repeated, taking a stride towards the bed. His folded arms and angry expression stopped me.

'I have no idea who you are any more. Since Nan…. You've changed.' Tom drew his legs up to meet his chest, pulling the duvet around them as if to close himself in a cocoon.

I saw him, like Poppy, drifting away from me.

'I was frightened that you wanted to leave me,' my voice quivered. I hated my tone, hated how needy I sounded.

'I hate it here,' he said quietly. 'I made a mistake coming with you. I want to go home. I belong there, with my Dad.'

'But you hate your Dad.'

He put his head on one side as if considering my words. 'I did, but I can see now how I was just fighting against him. He does know best; we could work together now, as men, rather than father and son.'

'As men?' I fought the urge to mock him, throw back his words in his face. He'd hated his father for so long, hated his bullying, the way he'd forced him to work long hours, put Tom down.

'It would be different now.' He said. 'I've been looking for a way to tell you.'

I moved to the window, opened the curtains and stared out at the darkness. The first streaks of dawn were beginning to break, dark swathes of grey smeared across the red and golden sky. I could just make out the shapes of the buildings, the ruined building which had housed my father's captives, the trees behind, gently swaying in the breeze.

'You'll be fine here. You've Nan. A whole future together.'

'Please don't go. I want a future with you. Without you I'm so alone.' I heard the needy note in my voice, like I was a small child, pleading not to be left alone.

'You and I,' Tom said, 'We weren't meant to be together. We were meant to be friends.'

I shook my head. 'You just want rid of me because of who I am. Just like everyone else does.'

Tom got out of bed. I heard the bed creak as he moved. 'No, it's not that at all.'

He shook his head, pushing back the duvet with a violence that made me step back away from him. 'Come back with me. This place. All that has gone on here. It's evil. You don't belong here.'

'Of course I do. Nan is my family. She loves me. She cared for me, protected me when I was little.'

'Are you sure about that?' Tom's voice had a flat, exhausted edge. He sat on the edge of the bed.

I longed to put the argument behind us, to stroke the hard planes of his body, to make all of the angst between us go away.

'Yes of course I am. Nan is the one person who is always there for me.'

'Mia, you're deluded. She's been in prison for most of your life.' Tom got up, padded across the room to stand at the far side of the window. The gap between us had never seemed so wide. 'How well do you know Nan? Really?'

'Of course I know her,' I hissed. 'She cared for me when I was a child, she's loved me always, even when Mum and Dad tried to keep her away, she didn't stop loving me.'

'Are you sure about that?' Tom looked out of the window, shivering as he stared at the ruins at the far side of the yard. Tom glanced at his watch, 'Fuck it. I'll never get back to sleep now.'

'Let's go back to bed,' I took a stride forwards, put my arms around him and drew him into the warmth of my body. 'Let's forget this. Make a fresh start.'

Tom looked away,

I cupped his face with my hands, pulling his unwilling head around to face me. I smiled gently, 'I love you so much.'

He shook his head. 'I can't stay with you.'

'But the surgery. You could have your own surgery here. With me. I said you could have the money.'

'No, Mia. I'm sorry. But I'm leaving. I'm going home.'

'Please don't go. Stay here. We can work it out between us, be happy again. We'll set up a business of your own. You know that's what you've always wanted. You hated working for your dad.'

Tom shook his head. 'I was wrong. I thought that was the way he was treating me. Now I see he was just teaching me the ropes, not letting me be a spoilt rich boy who waltzed in and inherited the business. He wanted me to earn my place. To deserve it.'

'Go back to your dad and he'll bully you again. You'll be the underdog, doing what he tells you.' I could hear the bitterness in my voice.

I felt the uncertainty in Tom, felt him waver.

Stretching my arm down I found his hand, twisted my fingers into his cold, stiff, unyielding flesh. I knew he couldn't resist me. I felt him soften, his posture slump as he allowed me to lead him back to bed.

He was gone when I woke in the morning. The room was filled with light, already warm from the heat of the sun.

I leapt out of bed, afraid he had left, gone back to his dad. When I looked out his car wasn't in the yard. I crossed the room, hauled open the wardrobe. His clothes were still there. I closed the doors, telling myself I was being silly, that he'd just gone to work. He wouldn't go and not tell me.

Nan was in the kitchen when I went downstairs.

'What time did Tom go to work?' I forced a note of nonchalance into my voice.

'He was gone when I got up.' She took a sip of tea, carried on buttering her toast.

'Okay.'

Nan threw her knife into the sink. It clattered loudly against the enamel surface. 'Are there problems between you?' She turned to face me, her back to the window so I couldn't see her expression.

'Is it that obvious?' I twisted my mother's bracelet around my wrist.

'Come here.' Nan opened her arms and I stepped gratefully into her embrace. I stood, enveloped in her hug as she ran a gentle hand over my hair. 'He's not happy here. That's obvious.' I looked up to see her expression of distaste. 'He hates me. He's made that pretty clear.'

'He...' I began to deny her accusation.

Nan pushed me gently away, holding me at arm's length. 'Of course, he hates me. Everyone does. I've gotten used to that.'

'Don't,' I said, seeing her eyes fill with tears. 'Please don't cry.'

'You know,' Nan stumbled away from me, grabbing one of the chairs to support herself. She wrenched it out and sat down heavily, 'Mia, I'm tired of the hatred.'

Nan's shoulders sagged as if she were exhausted.

I draped my arms around her, resting my cheek on the back of her head. Her tears spilled onto my shirt sleeves, the dampness spreading in ever expanding circles.

'There'd be no reason to go on without you,' Nan put a hand on my forearm. Her tears splattered slowly onto her fingers. 'The thought that I'd see you again kept me going in prison. The beatings, shit smeared in my cell...'

'Oh Nan.' It was hard to imagine what she had lived through inside.

'Tom hates me like the inmates did. He only sees what he wants to see. What he assumes I did. Just like those bitches did. They didn't care about the truth. Neither does he.'

The thought stayed with me all day, growing like a seed deep inside me. When Tom came home from work our argument began again. I could feel it in the air as he came in through the door, hanging over us like a dark cloud.

We ate dinner. I watched how Tom reacted around Nan. Witnessed his look of disdain, the barely polite way he snapped at her when she tried to talk to him. Everything she had told me about him was true.

Nan went outside to sit in the late evening sunshine watching the sun set, her back turned, as always away from the ruined cottage.

Tom and I remained around the table, the air between us crackling with tension.

'How long will this go on for?' I asked, my words slicing through the silence like a knife. 'What go on for?' Tom asked, fingering his phone, turning it over and over in his hand.

'You. I can see how you feel about Nan. And so can she. You make your feelings blatantly obvious.' The words tumbled out of my mouth.

'I don't. I don't give a fuck about Nan.' He moved his dinner plate across the table in an angry gesture.

'And please stop holding onto your phone every second of the day. I won't touch it again.'

I met his eyes and saw absolute disdain.

'I'm sick of waking up night after night and seeing you sneaking off with my phone. Pretending I'm asleep. It's pathetic. You're pathetic.'

'Tom...' I twisted my fingers together, digging my nails into my palms to stop myself crying. 'I'm sorry. I shouldn't have said that. I just don't want to lose you. I want us to all be happy. Here. Together.'

Tom shrugged, shaking his head. The sound of the clock ticking was loud in the silence.

'This. Us. It just isn't working. I spoke to my dad today, told him I'm going home. Jack can't get anyone to replace me for a day or two so I'm staying until the weekend.' he said, his voice so quiet I had to strain to hear what he said.

'Tom. Please. Don't go.' I pushed myself away from the table and busied myself with washing the dinner plates.

He crossed the room to stand beside me. 'Mia,' his voice was barely audible.

I paused; my hands elbow deep in warm washing up water.

'About Poppy.'

'Poppy?'

'Did you hurt her?'

'What?' I spun around to face him, suds splattering over the kitchen floor.

'Even accidentally? Do you know more about what happened to her than you are saying?'

'Stop it. How can you say that? What are you accusing me of?'

Tom watched me.

We faced one another. I saw the emotions flicker over his face. His long eyelashes closing over his eyes, touching the freckles on his cheeks. He opened them again, regarding me solemnly, his mouth turned down at the edges as if he were curious about me.

He shook his head, as if ridding himself of a thought, clearing his head. A fly buzzed in the silence between us, whizzing across the kitchen, bashing itself against the window, the noise irritating, persistent. I longed to kill it.

'Wait there.' His words were a command. He shoved a chair out of the way in his haste, its legs scraping against the tiled floor.

I heard his feet pounding on the stairs, the sound of a drawer opening and closing and then him coming slowly back down, his tread heavy.

I stayed beside the sink, the water drying on my arms. My skin itched with the chemical of the washing-up liquid.

He came into the kitchen, a familiar shoebox in his hands. He tossed it onto the table in a gesture that made me start.

'You see I found this and it made me wonder...' His voice was cold, distant. I knew he had retreated from me to a place I could not reach him.

I watched as he sank into a chair, the legs scraped on the floor as he pulled it in towards the table.

'Open it,' he held out his hand in a gesture towards the box. It wasn't an invitation; it was a command.

The skin on my hands felt brittle, harsh with dryness from the washing-up liquid.

Leaning across the table, I eased the shoebox towards me. There was an image on one end of the shoes the box had once contained. Strappy high heels. The kind Mum loved to wear. I had no need to open it. I already knew what was inside. Holding the box to my chest I faced him, my jaw clenched with tension.

'Open it,' he repeated.

I met his eyes, forcing down the bile that grew in my throat, my breath loud in my nostrils. I was so hot, the flush seemed to grow from the depths of my stomach to the top of my head, prickling fingers of heat spreading over my body.

'Mia, do it.'

I did as he commanded, lifting the lid off the box.

He watched my every move, his eyes never leaving mine. 'Tell me how these escaped the fire. They weren't at my house. Why these weren't burnt along with everything else.'

He got up so abruptly the chair fell backwards, landing with a loud crash.

I picked up the box, running my fingers over Nan's letters.

'They must have been taken out of the house before the fire. You knew the fire was going to start. Did you kill them deliberately Mia? Please tell me you didn't. Mia, for god's sake.'

I watched him silently, the letters in my hand.

'And this,' he said, crossing the floor to fling open the kitchen cabinet. There was a moment while his fingers delved into the cupboard and then he drew back his hand holding my favourite china mug. Mum's mug. 'Tell me how this survived the fire.'

A line of snot trickled from his nose; he wiped at it with the back of his hand, angrily as if it were my fault he was upset. 'Did you kill Poppy?'

CHAPTER FORTY

'Stop it.' I sobbed, 'How can you even think that?'
I slid to the floor, my legs crumpling beneath me.
'Tell me then.' Tom's voice was harsh. He blew his nose on some kitchen roll.

'The letters were in my car. I was going to bring them to your house, the rest of my stuff was there. And the mug.' I shrugged helplessly. 'I don't know how it survived. I found it in the ruins of the house.'

He came to stand beside me, staring out of the window.

'I can't stand you doubting me. I don't want you to leave. I couldn't bear...'

'Oh, I think you'll manage.' His voice had a sarcastic edge I'd never heard before.

I shook my head, reaching my hand towards him. Tom took a step backwards away from me.

'I can't be here.' His voice was little more than a whisper. 'Not with all of this in my head. Mia you need to go to the police. Tell them what you've done. Get some help.'

'I haven't done anything.' My voice sounded shrill. My throat ached with the effort of speaking.

'So you say.' He shook his head slowly, his face a mask of pure hatred. 'Do you know how like Nan you sound. Denying everything. Making out you're the victim.' His repugnance filled the air.

I wanted things to go back to how they had been. For him to love me again. 'I need to check the yearlings in the top field.' I couldn't bear to feel his hatred. I needed to be away from his suspicion, out in the air where I could breathe.

'I'd better come with you. I suppose.' He pulled a pair of working gloves out of a drawer. 'Some of the wall up there has fallen, I'll put the stones back while you check the horses.'

'No need. I'll manage.'

'They're too heavy for you.'

'You're so considerate.

'You'll have to get one of the neighbours to help you when I'm gone.' He ignored my sarcastic jibe.

We sat in a tense silence, as I drove up the rutted track towards the top field, where Nan and I had scattered my father's ashes.

As I wrestled with the big steering wheel, Tom turned to me, 'What did Poppy ever do to hurt you?'

Below, as we climbed, I could see the farm, the house, the ruined cottage beside it. Solar and his buddies grazed beside the farmhouse. Nan was sitting on the bench outside in the sunshine, enjoying the last warmth of the day.

'Tell me what happened to Poppy. I need to know.' Tom continued; the pain etched on his face.

I owed him the truth. I shook my head as the words I'd held in for so long were finally spoken. 'I didn't kill her.'

'If you say so.' He looked at me his head on one side, as he let out a short snort of derision.

'She ruined my life.' As I spoke a wave of sadness hit me. 'She used me, took all of the horrible things that were happening to me, my mother's body being found, everyone knowing what my father had done to make herself seem more exciting to those fucking bimbos she was friends with.'

Tom glared at me as if he had never seen me before.

'So you killed her.'

'I loved her. I'd have done anything for her. I was always there for her… When she got done for shoplifting. When she was being bullied at school. But she didn't care about me,' I told him. My voice cold. 'She destroyed every chance I had of having a normal life. The hopes and dreams I had of having a career.'

'What really happened? I need to know what you did to her?' Tom asked his voice so quiet it was barely audible.

'I didn't mean to kill her.' And I hadn't.

Far below us the landscape blurred into a grey line where the sea met the sky.

'We were rowing. We crashed. We went off the road.'

I could picture the night as if it were just moments ago. The icy water, the noise, the headlights still shining, highlighting branches submerged in the water, air bubbles rising away from us.

'Then?' Tom's eyes bored into mine.

'She was trying to get free. She couldn't undo her seat belt. I helped her.'

I remembered Poppy clinging to me, her face in the pale light contorted with panic.

It had been easy. I'd used all my strength, pushed her back, deep into the water. Her sweater had got tangled on the branches of the submerged tree, she clawed at me, her fingers gripping at my legs. I kicked out, freeing myself, and in that movement forced myself up out of the water and into the fresh air.

'I managed to swim to the side. She'd been right behind me. But when I got to the bank there was no sign of her.'

I remembered emerging from the depths, my lungs burning, taking my first gasp of air, choking on the water, the icy cold of it. I'd been lucky, the force of the current carried me towards the bank. I remembered the fear, the speed as it swept me away. My hands found and clung to the grass on the edge of the river, my body filling with the relief and determination to survive. It had taken all my strength to haul myself out of the water. I could do nothing more than lie on the riverbank. The car lights had been extinguished.

'What then?'

'I managed to get to the road and flag down a car.'

My words had no way of relating the reality. The biting cold, the shivers that racked my body, the disbelief at what had happened. That while I hadn't actually killed Poppy, I had not saved her. I could have struggled with her and hauled us both to the surface. I had to get away from her she could have killed us both, in her panic.

She didn't deserve saving.

'The police came and I was taken to hospital.'

'Of course,' Tom spat the words as if they were distasteful to him. 'You lived and she died.

So now you've got that one off your chest tell me what really happened to your parents.' Tom continued. 'Did you kill them deliberately?'

'They wouldn't let me see Nan,' I said, my voice little more than a whisper. 'I couldn't bear not to see her. She looked after me. Stayed to keep me safe.'

'You are talking such bollocks!' Tom spat, 'Can't you see what she did? What your father did? She helped him catch those girls, helped him keep them prisoner. She knew what was going on. She turned her back on what was happening. She covered up for him when they died. When. He. Killed. Them. Mia.'

I shook my head. 'No. She told me she didn't.'

'Mia you are so fucked up,' Tom said. He leant towards the car door as if he wanted to put a big gap between the two of us. 'Nan's not the lovely innocent you think she is.' Tom's mouth twisted into a tight line.

'Don't say that.'

'What do you really remember about your childhood?'

I shook my head. 'Nan cared for me.'

'Really?' he rolled his eyes skywards. 'Do you really think that?'

'What are those then?' he said seizing my hand and pulled it towards him. 'These?'

He ran cool fingers over the faint lines.

'Only if I was naughty,' I snapped, snatching my hand back. I hadn't known he had noticed the scars, they were so faint. 'She didn't mean to hurt me. She was scared of what my dad would do. She had to keep me quiet.'

I shook my head, trying to rid myself of an impression of being shaken, lifted into the air, Nan's face, twisted with anger, then her arms around me, lifting me, kind words, her hands gentle on my hair. "If only you'd behave, do as you're told."

'Can't you see what she's capable of?' Tom let out a juddering breath. He stared out of the windscreen, at the patchwork of fields stretching to meet the sea.

Those memories were so vague, insignificant wisps that floated out of my reach.

'Go on then.' Tom's voice had a forbidding edge to it. 'You'd better tell me what happened to your parents. Get that off your chest too.'

'What difference does it make?'

He shook his head. 'I just need to know who you are. You're so damaged. You need help.'

'Dad was drinking a lot. The man who had easily downed a glass or two of wine in an evening had begun to drink a bottle, to fall asleep stretched out on the sofa. He wanted to escape who I was, the life I had wrecked. To mourn Patrick, the son he had lost and me, the daughter who had turned out to be more trouble than he could have ever contemplated.

I hated the thought of what I had done to them. Hated seeing the sorrow and disappointment in their eyes. I couldn't live with that pain.

'I didn't kill them,' I said quietly. 'The fire did that.'

Tom took a deep breath, his mouth twisting into a gesture of wry disbelief.

'Mia you let the fire happen.'

I shook my head. 'I didn't. I knew Dad was drinking. I know it was dangerous for him to be drunk and for him to be smoking, but I didn't make him do that. It was his choice.'

'Jesus, Mia,' I heard Tom's throat move as he struggled to swallow.

'You really believe you didn't cause this.'

I shook my head. 'I didn't.'

'I went to bed, I kissed him goodnight. It wasn't my fault he was drunk and that he had a cigar. He must have fallen asleep with the cigar burning and it rolled off and caught fire.'

'On the newspapers you laid out around the floor presumably.'

'He was an adult. He knew the risks.'

I remembered my parents, their pride in me. Then Grace had steamrolled into our lives with her news about my mother's body. I'd known then I would be forever tarnished by my past.

I knew in their eyes I was damaged goods, something they could no longer love.

'What are you going to do now?' I asked. I couldn't look at him and instead looked out at the land where we had scattered my father's ashes, the place he loved so much.

'Nothing.' Tom wouldn't meet my eyes and instead focused his gaze somewhere towards the end of the Land Rover bonnet. 'I'll go home, back to my Dad's house. You stay here. And that will be it. I won't go to the police. What would be the point? It won't bring Poppy back. Or your parents.'

He was lying. He would go to the police. He'd tell them about me, the reality of Poppy's death and that of my parents. Nan had no one. I had to be here to care for her.

'I'll walk over and check the yearlings.' I hunted in the glove compartment and found a tissue. I wiped my eyes, but it was no good, the tears would not stop falling. I waited for him to comfort me, to draw me to him, to hold me in the warmth of his body. He did not touch me; instead he remained, solid, stiff, immobile beside me.

After what seemed like an age, I managed to stop crying. I wound down the window and flipped the tissue out, watching the wind catch it and it flutter away on the breeze.

'Fucking hell Mia. You're fucking insane.'

I didn't recognise the man who sat beside me, anger and hatred surged from him.

'I can't stay here. I'm going.' He pushed open the door, scrambling from the seat as if he couldn't get away from me fast enough. The wind battered into the car

'Don't leave me.'

I watched him move around the back of the vehicle, stepping over the puddles, delicately trying not to get the soles of his boots muddy. I let out the clutch.

The bump was louder than I had expected. The massive vehicle stalled, jerking backwards. There was silence.

I got out, the wind whipping my hair around my face, pushing back the sides of my jacket. He lay, face up, behind the Land Rover. His head had hit one of the big rocks in the centre of the rutted tyre tracks.

Tom's blood was pooling rapidly from his head, mingling with the mud, the red soaking into the earth.

His eyes were open; he was blinking, slowly, his eyes were filled with resentment.

I stood over him, watching his chest rise, the faintest fluttering, like the breath of a wounded baby bird. His arms, outstretched, were in the mud, the dark red water soaking into the fabric, staining it, soaking into his jeans, the quilted gilet he wore.

The breathing became shallower, reaching his throat. His mouth opened as if he wanted to say something. I saw the redness of his tongue, his throat moving slowly, swallowing and then it stopped. He'd gone. Nothing remained. His eyes, still open were fixed on mine, still with that resentful glow of hatred in them.

I knelt beside him, feeling the mud soak through the fabric of my jeans. I ran my hand over his hair, feeling the silken strands beneath my fingers.

'Tom?' The wind whipped my words away.

Slowly, I got to my feet. Tom's arms were stretched out to the sides, the fingers curled, like he was asleep. My heart thundered against my rib cage.

I began to run towards the farm. Nan would know what to do. We'd have to call the police, tell them there had been an accident. My foot had slipped off the clutch. I hadn't meant to hurt Tom.

I scrambled down the steep hillside, my feet slipping and sliding on the damp grass. At the bottom I hauled open the yard gate and ran past the ruined cottage to the farmhouse.

She wasn't sitting on the bench outside.

'Nan!' I called, flinging open the front door. My voice was shrill with panic, my mind racing.

The kitchen was deserted. The remnants of the meal we'd eaten still on the side, cooling. The tea towel was still draped over the washing-up I'd done as we'd argued.

The lounge was empty too. I caught sight of my reflection on the blank television screen, my hair wild from running, my eyes wide in horror at what I had done.

I circled, confused.

'Nan!' I stood at the bottom of the stairs, yelling up into the silence of the empty house.

I ran outside, circling the yard. The garden was empty. A movement caught my eye. The door to my father's shed swung open in the wind.

'Nan?' There seemed to be no air in my lungs.

I stumbled across the yard, pushed the shed door open, flooding the building with light. It smelt of hay and old engine oil. The dirt floor was sticky with oil from years of leaking machinery.

She stood at the far end of the building. My father's toolbox was on the bench beside her. Nan had taken off the top compartment and put it on the bench.

'What have you got?' I asked, my voice little more than a whisper.

Nan held her hand out towards me. The sordid pile of necklaces and cheap jewellery glittered in the light from the doorway. 'I'd forgotten where I'd put these.'

THE END

WHERE IS MY DAUGHTER?

LOUISE BRODERICK

CHAPTER ONE
1989

She was used to pain. But not like this. He took pleasure in its creation, the anticipation of watching her endure the slow build-up of discomfort as he turned it unhurriedly to torment. She'd learned how to twist her body, to ease her muscles to gain some relief. She'd discovered how to deceive him, crying out, pleading before it was unbearable.

This, though, was relentless, bands of fire, agonising, gripped her body. 'Nan, help me.' Glanna shifted her position so she could see the older woman. Even she seemed to take no pleasure in watching Glanna's pain. Nan flung herself out of the wooden chair beside the bed and began to pace the room.

'Glanna. Do you want water?' Nan dabbed restlessly at Glanna's sweat drenched forehead with a damp cloth. The fabric was cool, giving momentary respite from the furnace which seemed to burn beneath her skin.

Glanna grunted a denial, the animal-like sound expelled through teeth that chattered against one another.

'Could be a long time yet.'

Glanna's head rocked from side to side against the stained cloth of the pillow.

Nan drew the cloth over Glanna's exposed skin. The chain, holding her wrist to the top of the bed rattled a rapid rhythm in time with the tremors that racked her limbs.

Glanna writhed again as another wave of torturous wave took hold of her. There seemed to be no beginning of it, nowhere she could ease to rid herself of it, and no end to it. There were, she was vaguely aware, brief respites when the pain seemed to retreat slightly before surging forwards in a tide which left her senseless.

When he was there, teasing at her body with the tools he laid out with such precision, she had learned to let her mind free. Her physical presence remained, the ties cutting into her wrists and ankles, while mentally she left the dank room, the soiled mattress, the creaking bedframe, and returned to the life she had once taken so much for granted. In her imagination she once more walked the rooms of her home, rested in the security of her family, laughed as she ran with her sisters along the golden stretch of beach near the house, she had grown up in. He could control everything she did, but not that. He could never reach her there.

But this pain was something she could not escape from, it held her captive. Had Nan removed the chain from her wrist, opened the door and told her to leave she could not. Glanna took a gasping breath, aware of the need to force air into her lungs. An image of home drifted ghostlike in front of her. She pictured herself curled with her sisters on the vast expanse of battered sofa which had dominated the lounge. A bowl, overflowing with popcorn moments before, spinning across the room, the yellow kernels spilling across the floor. Morwenna, the oldest of the three of them had caught it with a foot as they had pushed themselves back away from the television, in horror and disgust at the programme they were watching. On the screen a woman writhed and swore as, red and bawling, a wrinkled baby emerged. The girls had hidden their faces in their hands, feigned vomiting noises, before descending into fits of giggles.

The vision evaporated, frail strands Glanna could not keep hold of. She screamed; a noise she was only dimly conscious of as the pain ripped through her once more. She fought it pushing her heels into the damp sheets to try to straighten her body.

'Don't you try anything,' Nan's voice cut into the haze of pain. Glanna let her arm drop to her side, freed from the chain that had kept it bound to one end of the bed. The pins and needles that swept through from her elbow to her numb fingers were a minute distraction.

'Fuck off,' Glanna panted.

She was aware now of another sensation, a base instinct deep within herself. The need to push, to expel the child.

'Help me.'

Nan, beside her twined her fingers compulsively into one another, her fear palpable. She who had watched and taken pleasure in Glanna's torment, flailing now in the face of the younger woman's pain and terror.

He was there. She knew instinctively. Glanna had become vigilant of his presence, her senses tuned to his approach. The long months of captivity had made her aware of him, of his presence, his moods. She'd learned to sense his arrival, to brace herself for what he would do, to let the innermost part of her being go free where he could not touch it. In between the horror, it was almost easy to forget what a monster he was. His smile was disarming, charming even.'

Something now, a faint footfall, a shadow crossing the room had made her aware of him. He stood in the corner of the room, watching. His face, impassive as always beneath his dark hair. He had come to watch, to see the birth of the child he had planted in her unwilling body.

'How long will it be?' His voice, normally deceptively soft, had a tense edge.

'Eddie, how should I know? 'Nan snapped.

'Help me,' Glanna groaned. She moved her head and met his eyes. 'Take me to the hospital. Please.'

Eddie shook his head. 'It's just a baby. The animals give birth on their own all the time.'

Glanna screamed again, a shriek of pure anguish and panic.

'If she dies, you'll deal with it, Eddie.' Nan crossed the room towards him, hands on hips, her face contorted with rage. 'I'm sick of dealing with the mess you make. Stupid bastard.'

'Help her then.' His voice had a gentle note Glanna had never heard before.

'It's coming. Help me. Please.'

In the dim light of the cellar Glanna saw Eddie blink slowly as if to blank out the sight. His eyes when they opened again had a compassion she had never seen. Not for her, she knew, but for the child inside her. A small human they had created some time during the long months she had been his prisoner. Stuck in the dank, darkness of the cellar, he her only human contact.

'I don't know what to do,' Nan's voice filled with irritation.

'Haven't you brought enough calves and lambs into the world? What's the difference?'

Nan, for all her bulk, could move swiftly when she needed to. She crossed the dirt encrusted floor in two strides, fists raised she rained blows on Eddie. Glanna, despite her pain, watched him cower away from his mother. 'This is your fault. Stupid, filthy animal. You can't leave them alone can you?' Nan taunted.

Shoulders hunched to fend off her attack he backed out of the room.

'You like this don't you?' As the pain diminished momentarily Glanna met Nan's eyes, 'Watching me scream.' Glanna whispered, her voice weak with pain and exhaustion.

Nan met Glanna's eyes, the older woman dropped hers first.

Glanna gasped as another wave hit her. She couldn't remember how long she had endured the agony. Had it been this morning, when the first shafts of light began to illuminate the dingy cellar? Or yesterday? Time seemed to have lost all meaning.

At first, when she had come round, in the cellar, her face cut and bruised, she'd tried to keep count of the days. She'd used part of her hair clip to drag a mark through the yellowing, chipped whitewash that covered the walls. One mark for each time the light began to brighten the tangle of battered furniture in the damp room. She'd fought him so hard each time he opened the door and came into her, received so many punches that had knocked her unconscious that she wasn't sure if she missed days. Waking confused and only dimly aware of his presence.

Gradually she had stopped fighting. There was no point. He took enough pleasure in hurting her in other ways without giving him more reason. She'd tried pleading with him. Telling him about her family, her parents, sisters, her home, the life they had together. He listened impassively. She spoke about the course she was doing at the university in Exeter. She'd been walking home from writing an essay in the library, when he had picked her up. It had been quieter in there than the noisy house she'd shared with three other students.

In the days when she had first found herself in the cellar, she had cursed her stupidity, her naive trust of the man who had stopped his vehicle in front of her and asked for directions, struggling incompetently with the folds of a street map. She'd been engrossed in the map, tracing the streets with her finger to show him how to find the one he had asked for. She didn't remember much of his attack, a short, ferocious rain of blows which had left her reeling and unable to stop him bundling her into the back of his pick-up.

She had a vague memory of a journey, bumping and sliding in the back of the pick-up, her legs and hands bound, a strip of something across her mouth. It had been hard to breathe, let alone fight.

When the bumping finally stopped, he'd pulled her roughly out of the pick-up, shouldering her as if she were nothing more than a sack of animal feed. In the darkness she'd seen the silhouette of a house against the night sky, one single window illuminated, yellow glowing behind the curtains. She'd smelt the familiar tang of the sea and that of farm animals before he'd descended into the depths of a damp smelling building.

And that was where she had stayed. Sometimes tied, others not. The marks on the wall, painstakingly made with her hair clip became too many to count. It had been cold in the cellar, the only light and warmth coming from the sunlight when it penetrated the small oval window set high up the wall.

He'd thought of everything. There was a bed, a small table and chair, a litter of yellowing paperback books, their pages damp and curling. He'd even installed a small bathroom behind a bright, plastic shower curtain, adorned with frolicking dolphins. Food was brought regularly, along with mugs of coffee which were always cold by the time he had finished with her.

Months, she knew, had passed before she'd noticed changes to her body, there had been no choice but accept the awful truth that part of him was growing inside her. No matter how much she despised him and everything he stood for, it was hard not to feel compassion for the tiny form that moved and kicked inside her. His violence had stopped then and he had treated her with something which resembled reverence, resting a hand on the swell of her belly to wait for the inevitable kicks from within.

Glanna had cried, pleaded with him to let her go, promised not to tell anyone what had happened to her, what he had done. She longed for her mother, who she knew would be beside herself with grief for her missing daughter. She locked those thoughts away, knowing she would go mad with the heartache. She had to get through each day and wait, until one day she might get a chance to escape.

'The head's out.' Nan's voice contained a mixture of excitement and fascination. 'That's it. There's the baby.'

Glanna was aware of a slithering sensation, and the pain receding as if it had never existed. Glanna rested her head against the pillow, aware now of the chill of the room against her sweat dampened skin and of Nan, wrapping the baby in fabric. Within the folds of the cloth Glanna glimpsed a wrinkled, red face, the tiny button of a nose and small, rosebud lips.

'It's a little girl,' Nan tucked the baby into one arm, cradling her gently. The baby cried briefly and then was silent. She moved across the room, rocking the bundle.

'Nan,' Glanna, eased herself onto one arm, swung her legs to the side of the bed and levered herself upright. 'Nan. Is she okay?'

Nan, her head lowered towards the baby, raised her eyes to glare coldly in Glanna's direction before she took a step backwards.

Glanna held out her arms towards Nan. 'She's mine. Give her to me.'

Thank you for taking the time to read this book. I hope you enjoyed it, I certainly enjoyed writing it. Each time I sit down to write – and that is every day – I realise just how lucky I am this is my job. I can only keep this job because people like you enjoy my books and buy them. No words can express how grateful I am for that.

If you would like to find out more about my other books, please visit my web site, www.louisebroderick.com, or my Amazon Author page on Amazon.com.

I love to hear from readers so please feel free to contact me on via my Facebook page or by email. The details of these are all on my web site. If would like to hear about new releases, please join my mailing list which is on my website. I promise not to bombard you with emails.

If you have the time, I'd really appreciate it if you would leave me a book review on Amazon. It makes my day when I see someone has made the effort to do that. Reviews really do help other readers to find my books. Can I just say a huge thank you in advance to anyone who writes a review. I know very well how precious time is and am hugely grateful for anyone who helps me. Thank you!

Printed in Great Britain
by Amazon